REAL HAPPY FAMILY

REAL HAPPY FAMILY

Caeli Wolfson Widger

New Harvest
Houghton Mifflin Harcourt
BOSTON   NEW YORK
2014

www.hmhco.com

Library of Congress Cataloging-in-Publication Data
Widger, Caeli Wolfson.
Real happy family : a novel / Caeli Wolfson Widger.
pages cm
ISBN 978-0-544-26361-1 (hardback)
1. Actresses — Fiction. 2. Dysfunctional families — Fiction.
3. Reality television programs — Fiction. 4. Domestic fiction.
I. Title.
PS3623.I345R43 2014
813′.6 — dc23
2013033892

Printed in the United States of America
DOC 10 9 8 7 6 5 4 3 2 1

For Kris

You're so exotic!
You make me heartsick!
Like a rodent, rat, or raccoon
If I don't see you,
See you real soon
In the garbage
Or on the dance floor
And run my fingers
Through your short fur
I might go crazy, baby,
That's reality.
You see, I want you,
I don't want her
She's white as lilies,
You're brown as donkeys
You drive me crazy
That's reality.

— from *Exotic on the Dancefloor* by Skunkface
   featuring Colleen Branch

APRIL 2013

Prologue

NO ONE ELSE in Reno was running on the sidewalk connecting downtown to the Truckee River, but Lorelei had no choice. Something hideous was behind her.

She was still wearing her Lucky Bastard uniform, the tight black skirt and fitted white shirt unbuttoned too low. The plasticky high heels unsuited to waiting tables, much less running at top speed. Blisters blossomed on both feet and her ankles throbbed, but she pushed on.

The pain was nothing compared to the fear.

She was afraid to check over her shoulder, to see if the bartender was following. Up ahead, Reno glittered under a moonlit dome, the Sierra Nevada turned to black M's on the horizon. Something was different this time; something was wrong. The euphoria and the go-go-go were there, but they weren't pure. They were cut with panic. The stuff she'd smoked was letting in the feelings it normally stamped out. Not just letting them in, but amplifying them. And the perfect heat that usually suffused her whole body seconds after the drug hit her bloodstream was missing. In its place was a prickly fever in her face and icy sweat in her clenched fists. Her heart was slamming.

She veered onto Virginia Street, a wide, casino-flanked boulevard that cut down to the river, her heels pocking against the concrete. Her path was blocked by a throng of ponytailed girls in green-and-white jerseys and tall knee socks, some sort of sports team, their pace slow as cattle. Giggles fizzed from their mouths, and for a beat, she wanted nothing more than to be in the center of their pack, linking elbows and bandying gossip, being normal, the way she used to be, back in Fresno. Before L.A., before the show, before she'd cracked her mother's heart into pieces. Before *this*.

But then, when she was a dozen feet from the girls' numbered backs, the sound of their voices changed from happy chatter to piggish squeals, like the noise her mom's old cassette tapes made when Lorelei held down *play* and *fast-forward* at the same time on the boom box in the basement.

"Move!" Lorelei yelled to their backs, and when the girls offered no gap in their wall of meshed green polyester, she picked a spot between two of them and plowed through it, her palms shoving their shoulders in opposite directions as hard as she could.

She heard a smattering of screams, an "Oh my God!" and a "Cara, are you okay?" but she didn't look back. She barely even stumbled in her heels. She just kept running.

Whatever impurities were coursing through her system were causing her senses to work at peak performance, but she couldn't enjoy the heightened perception, because she'd gotten stuck somewhere terrible, on the border of a regular dream and a nightmare you woke from screaming.

If you woke at all.

Lorelei ran harder, fighting for breath. The huge white dome atop the Silver Legacy Casino lit up like a moon dropped from the sky, and she felt snow on her face. A digital billboard flashed smooth-chested Chippendales, drizzled with oil, and then sharp fingernails when it flipped to an ad for *Freak Illusion,* a live show featuring the goth magician Dave Devlin. The air was cluttered with synthetic light — lots of blue and purple, orange stars — and distant sounds like carnival music, voices sailing and clashing in the high desert air.

The river was getting closer. She could smell the water. She could smell the fish inside it.

Go, go, go, she commanded her body. Time was slipping, slipping, and something awful was coming — no — it was already here.

Pock-pock-pock. She needed to take off her three-inch heels, a half size too small, stolen off some discount rack during a binge with Don. She slowed down just enough to kick the shoes off and lost her balance, tumbling down to the sidewalk asphalt.

"Mommy," she cried out as she fell, the asphalt tearing into her knees. Lorelei had felt her mother's presence from the moment the bartender pulled her into the empty warehouse. Commanding her to survive. She tried to push up to her feet, but everything hurt too much. As she breathed against the ground, deep as she could to slow her heart, an old fact flashed to mind, something she'd heard at a party: it was the single most common word recorded on the black boxes of airplanes before they crashed. *Mommy.*

This was not the life she wanted. Lorelei swore that if she made it through this night, she was going to change.

LATE 2012

1

AFTER LORELEI VANISHED, what Colleen missed most was the driving.

It had been mostly a chore: covering the 250 miles from Fresno to Los Angeles and back again, week after week, the flat stretch of Highway 99 flanked by dairy cows milling in dirt pits and groves of frilly almond trees, the air musky with manure. "Corpse-y," Lorelei had called that smell. All they'd wanted to do was get there, into the Valley and out of the car, to whatever audition or casting call Robin had booked for Lorelei. To their fresh dose of hope.

Though too often it was hard to feel hopeful after they arrived at the studio and saw the "gazelle herd," as Lorelei named them, milling around with cans of Diet Coke and Red Bull, tank tops clinging to their long waists and curtains of shiny hair swinging behind their shoulders. Lorelei had neither their narrow torsos nor sheeny hair: like her mother, she was naturally petite — round bottomed and small chested — and she'd inherited her father's coarse auburn curls. Robin insisted Lorelei's *memorable* looks were what would land her a career-making commercial. Think of the Convo Wireless guy, she said, or the

1

Wreckless Insurance girl. Everyone in America knew them. They'd both earned fortunes, once they'd found the right roles. It just took time, Robin said. But Colleen found both those actors memorably unattractive: the Convo guy with his shlumpy posture and lamb-chop sideburns, and the Wreckless Insurance girl with her big nostrils and froggy eyes.

Week after week, some gazelle beat out Lorelei for a part. The rejections were disheartening, but sometimes Colleen was secretly relieved. She didn't particularly want her daughter to be the new face of Vajazzle!, "adhesive crystals to glamorize the bikini area." Or to have her red hair ironed straight and her dusting of freckles masked with makeup for a Brawny paper towels spot, in order to look more "every-girl," as the cold-tongued casting agents liked to say.

Lorelei, after all, was not an every-girl. Not by a long shot.

Marking the end of their long drive was the Grapevine, the mountain pass they had to clear before dropping down into the San Fernando Valley, the sun-bleached gateway to L.A. Where the cookie-cutter subdivisions alongside the freeway were separated from the continuous traffic by nothing more than a few feet of stucco wall. Places you didn't want to live: Valencia, Reseda, Van Nuys. Places like Fresno. If Colleen lived in L.A., she'd want to live farther west, close to the sea.

By the time they reached the Grapevine, they'd merged from Highway 99 onto I-5, and from there they picked up the 405 or the 101, depending on where the studio was. Burbank or North Hollywood, usually. Angelenos spoke of their freeways as if they were each a distinctive person with habits and temperaments and intentions. Colleen had begun speaking that way, too.

Up, up, up the Grapevine they'd drive, Colleen's Camry straining against the steep grade, the landscape turned from farmland to desert. Lorelei loved to blast a Minny Danvers album, the one she'd put out just after winning *PopStar!*, and Lorelei and Colleen screamed out the ridiculous, irresistible chorus to the number one smash hit, "Hotter": *"I am hot-hot-hot-hot-HOTTER / than your dot-dot-dot-dot-DAUGHTER!"*

Singing together, with both the Camry windows down and its A/C on, because that was how Lorelei liked it. Carl would combust if he knew Colleen was condoning this wastefulness, but so what? He wasn't there. He knew nothing of what it felt like to sing along with Lorelei in the car to Minny Danvers. Knew nothing of how, for a few giddy minutes, belting out those lyrics made Colleen feel not only close to Lorelei, but almost as if she *were* Lorelei. As if she were twenty-two and gorgeous, with her whole life in a big city sparkling ahead, instead of forty with sunspots and smile lines, increasing in number by the day from life in an overgrown cow town. Carl would never know how good it felt to have a Freon chill on your face while the hot desert wind sucked your ponytail behind you and the music blasted. Sometimes Lorelei would loose her mass of red-brown curls from their elastic band and let her hair fly wild.

I am hot-hot-hot-hot-HOTTER.

Threads of Lorelei's hair whipped against Colleen's arm.

This was what she missed most.

1987–1991

2

IF YOU GREW up in Hemet, California's worst town, you shouldn't have to end up in Fresno, California's worst city. But that's exactly what Colleen Branch, née Hassell, had done.

Ninety miles east of Los Angeles, Hemet was a dusty assembly of mobile homes and cheap subdivisions, popular among retirees and working-class families. The town's main street had once possessed a modicum of charm, with rows of palm trees stretching along both sides of Las Flores Avenue, shading the mom-and-pop storefronts. In the eighties, Walmart took hold of the ranchland on the outskirts of town, and many of the stores in the town's center shuttered. The temperatures got hotter and the rain scarcer every year, crisping the palm fronds of Las Flores Avenue to the color of potato chips. Later, after Colleen left, foreclosures left many neighborhoods with crabgrass and spineflower crawling up the foundations of abandoned houses, BANK OWNED signs staked into one parched lawn after the other, and gangs. But when she was growing up, in the seventies and eighties, Hemet was just hot and poor. She'd always wanted to get out.

Colleen lived with her parents, Jerry and JoEllen Hassell,

in a single-wide trailer flanked by a carport on one side and a covered yard — a square of gravel and dirt with a picnic table in the center — on the other. Her parents weren't bad people, just trampled by economics, occupations, and her mother's lousy health. Jerry managed a lube shop where he opened the work pit at seven A.M., six days a week; JoEllen cleaned Kmart from its close at nine until two in the morning. Their paychecks were steady but paltry; their health insurance catastrophic care only. It came up woefully short when JoEllen, devoid of willpower in the presence of any food product boasting hydrogenated oil and a long shelf life (especially when coupled with her 30 percent employee discount from Kmart), ate herself past the two-hundred-pound mark and into type 2 diabetes at age thirty-six. From the time Colleen entered junior high, there was no money for anything but survival items: food, beer, and insulin. Her clothes were from the Salvation Army, her shoes from a thrift store called Another Foot.

Her father was often absent from their single-wide trailer, with its shoddy A/C and faux wood paneling, while her mother was overly present on the couch, like some sort of land-dwelling whale. Since JoEllen worked the late shift, she was home during prime soap time and loved the shows with the skinniest, beachiest characters: *The Palisades. Sunset Point. Waves on the Sand.* Sometimes, after school, Colleen watched them with her mother, her eyes flicking between the size-two bikinied blondes and her mother's puffy hand dipping in and out of a Cool Ranch Doritos bag. Her mother formed deep, compassionate bonds with characters on her shows, women with names like Lorelei Goldenmoor and Natasha Cerulean who lived in balconied mansions wedged into the cliffs of Malibu and Pacific Palisades.

"She doesn't deserve this," JoEllen sniffed when Lorelei's husband, Samson Goldenmoor, paid off a vet to euthanize her beloved horse to avenge her having cheated on him with her trainer. "He travels three hundred days a year."

"Slim Jims have plastic in them," Colleen said, as she heard the gristly tear of her mother's first bite of jerky. "You should eat something more nutritious."

"Get off your high horse, Skinny Minny. Just be grateful that you've never gone hungry under my roof. That happens, right here in America, you know."

"I just want you to be healthy, Ma."

"That's what everyone says to fat people," her mother said, turning up the volume.

It was impossible to talk to JoEllen; everything Colleen said seemed to hurt her feelings or exhaust her. She was constantly sighing or shrugging or glaring at her daughter. She liked to begin sentences with phrases like "I know I'm always letting you down, Missy, but . . ." or "Even if I'm just a big fat embarrassment to you . . ."

Colleen frequently reminded JoEllen, "I've never said that," but her mother ignored her, behaving as if Colleen had branded her a permanent disgrace. Her mother's invented accusations felt like perplexing, unwarranted meanness. They took a toll on Colleen. She'd startled herself at a junior high sleepover when they'd gotten on the topic of their mothers, and she'd blurted out to a half dozen girls, "I hate mine! I really do!" Then she felt guilty and took it back.

At the end of eighth grade, Colleen made the cheerleading squad at San Jacinto High. Cheerleaders were pretty and popular, of course, but more important, they were busy: always either practicing or at a game. Being on the squad gave her a reason to be away from her undercooled, overly caloric household.

She was petite and flexible; she could drop into a backbend or split at a moment's notice without having to limber up. Although she was just a rising freshman, they wanted her on junior varsity as the flier, the girl who got tossed in the air and caught by a web of the other girls' slender forearms, or stood at the top of a five-girl pyramid. At 101 pounds, Colleen was plenty light enough for the role. But she'd need to watch her weight at all times, the JV captain, Aubrey, told her, eyeing Colleen's chest. It was easy to get too heavy once your boobs filled out.

Flying upside down beneath the lights of the school's scrappy stadium on Friday nights in the fall, balancing on another girl's shoulders as the splintering wood floor of the basketball court in the gym vibrated with pounding sneakers, switching boyfriends every few months — Colleen became one of the most admired girls at San Jacinto. Cheering changed her life

Her parents barely acknowledged it. "Cheerleaders always hated girls like me," her mother said. "But congratulations, honey. God knows my genes weren't any help." Her father said, "Proud of you, baby," but didn't ask when he might come to a game to see her cheer. He couldn't see past the end of the month, past the next payment on their trailer or her mother's next batch of sharps and insulin vials. Neither of them taught her to look ahead. Colleen's grades were mediocre, and higher education beyond Riverside Community College thirty-five miles away seemed unlikely.

Then her squad won a regional competition during her junior year. They traveled to Disneyland for state quarterfinals, and all over the park were large posters reading:

LOVE DISNEY? BECOME A DISNEY CHARACTER!

OPEN AUDITIONS FOR LIVE CHARACTER ROLES: MICKEY/ MINNIE MOUSE, SNOW WHITE, PINOCCHIO, CINDERELLA, AND MORE. MONTHLY STIPEND, ONSITE HOUSING, MEAL PLANS, AND UNLIMITED PARK ACCESS INCLUDED. MUST BE EIGHTEEN

OR OLDER. THEATER OR COMPARABLE PERFORMANCE EXPERI-
ENCE PREFERRED.

Cheerleading surely counted as performance experience. And while wearing a large rodent mask all day was out of the question, dressing as Cinderella or Snow White seemed okay. Disneyland's location in Anaheim didn't thrill her, but it was a ticket out of her trailer in Hemet. And it was only twenty-five miles from L.A., an easy drive to the bluffs over the Pacific Ocean that were home to her mother's friends Lorelei Gold-enmoor and Natasha Cerulean. And that part—being near the ocean, near the glamour and possibility of Los Angeles—well, Colleen would take it. She'd grabbed a flyer with all the Disney audition information and read it a dozen times on the bus ride home from the competition. She wouldn't turn eighteen for another year, but that gave her plenty of time to prepare for a princess audition.

During the summer between her junior and senior year, Colleen began to go to parties. Drinking made her bloated and sleepy. Marijuana tied her tongue and made her head feel disconnected from her body. Other drugs hadn't really infiltrated her crowd in Hemet yet; this was the eighties, before meth and painkillers began to ruin clusters of San Jacinto High kids every year. Raiding your parents' medicine cabinet for pill bottles wasn't uncommon, though, and occasionally one of the girls on her cheering squad might drop a Valium or Vicodin into her hand at a postgame party out near Thorn Hill Lake. JoEllen had a small army of pill containers in her bathroom, but they didn't tempt Colleen with their grim instructions: TAKE ONE CAPSULE AT MEALTIMES TO ALLEVIATE IRRITABLE BOWEL SYMPTOMS. CHEW TWO TABLETS TO PREVENT HEARTBURN; COMBINING WITH DAIRY MAY IMPEDE EFFECTIVENESS. The only bottle that interested Colleen contained yellow pellets

called Dexaphil and read TAKE ONE TABLET ONE HOUR BE-
FORE MEALTIMES TO CONTROL APPETITE; DO NOT EXCEED
THREE TABLETS PER DAY.

Colleen was thin, but the flier could always be thinner. She'd
put on a few pounds since freshman year — her boobs had gotten bigger, as Aubrey predicted — and Colleen worried about a
younger, lighter girl edging her out of the fly role senior year. So
occasionally, she took a Dexaphil. She didn't love the effects; it
gave her a clenched, antsy feeling for a few hours and made her
palms and armpits sweaty, but it did kill her appetite. She took
two, maybe three a week, depending on the level of the bottle's
supply. JoEllen took them, too, but clearly, they didn't work for
her. She maintained her snacks-and-soaps routine throughout
Colleen's high school career, increased it after she went on dis-
ability, and swelled up to about 225. While she'd never seen her
mom set foot on a scale, Colleen had developed a knack for esti-
mating other people's weight. Once, at a party, she'd drunkenly
tested her ability with several of the girls on her squad, pointing to each of them and calling out, "One-twelve! One-twenty-
eight!" until someone threw a beer can at her. Tall, big-boned
Marlene Jakes had stalked off crying after Colleen pegged
her at one-forty, but honestly, Marlene needed to shed a few
pounds. After Colleen's announcement, she had.

Colleen turned eighteen on a Friday in February. Monica
"Nica" Bangert, a cocaptain of the varsity squad, occasionally
waitressed at Sizzler on Las Flores on Friday nights, where she
had something going with one of the managers, a muscular guy
named Roy, who let her and a few select girlfriends eat at the
buffet and drink wine for free after the restaurant closed. Nica
declared Colleen's birthday a "V.I.P. Night" at Sizzler, and invited her and four other girls to meet there for a pre-party before heading to the trash-strewn, cracked-dirt shore of Thorn

Hill Lake, where half of the rest of San Jacinto High would be. The idea of spending her milestone birthday at Sizzler with five wasted cheerleaders was depressing to Colleen, but she was between boyfriends and had no better options. She consoled herself with the thought that, at this time next year, she'd be living a stone's throw from L.A., a princess in Disneyland.

On the morning of her birthday, her parents gave her a gold bracelet, and in the evening, a pizza dinner and birthday cake from Kroger. Colleen politely nibbled at one small sliver of the double-meat, extra-cheese pie her mother had chosen — "Thanks, but my friends are taking me out to eat." Her father gave her a disappointed look and said, "It's your birthday, suit yourself," which made Colleen feel guilty until her mother, helping herself to another sausage-heavy slice, added, "Well, I have no friends, and we didn't have the fifteen bucks to spend on pizza in the first place, so I'll eat Skinny Minny's share." A sit-down meal together, with cake, plus a gift, was a much bigger effort than her parents usually made on her birthday, Colleen told herself, trying to feel grateful as she sat between them in the vinyl-covered breakfast nook of their kitchen — the trailer's only dining area. But the bracelet was obviously a sale item from Kay Jewelers, probably the very cheapest thing in the store, and watching her mother scarf two large slices of cake left Colleen unable to eat more than a token sliver, the frosting gluey in her throat.

By 9 P.M. her parents were in bed, and Colleen popped a Dexaphil. Sizzler wasn't quite closed when she and Nica and four other girls arrived at 9:30. They passed around a bottle of Boone's Farm strawberry wine in the parking lot, which lifted them into high spirits.

Roy sat them at a round table, brought them each a water glass filled with vodka and ice, and told them to help themselves to the buffet. The other girls jumped up. They'd fasted most of the day for this occasion. Colleen hung back, moving slowly toward the steaming spread, debating. As she approached the food, her stomach roiled: the abundance was startling. The hunks of fat-slick rib eye and baked potatoes buried under piles of cheddar shreds and slops of runny sour cream; the fat yellow rolls pyramided next to vats of whipped butter. The mountains of spaghetti heaped with meat sauce; the salad bar rife with non-greenery like deep-fried onions and mayo-filled deviled eggs. The ice cream sundae bar leaking three flavors of soft-serve from its metal nozzles.

On the one hand, the buffet was revolting, and yet, Colleen never got to eat that way at home. Her mother was big on junk food but not on cooking, so virtually every meal Colleen ate at home, she defrosted herself in the microwave. A small but fierce part of her wanted to fill a big white plate with every warm, fatty, starchy, crispy, creamy, sweet item from the buffet at Sizzler and stuff her face. Fortunately, the Dexaphil kicked in before she caved to the urge, pushing her hunger away, so she returned to her place at the table with only a salad of iceberg lettuce, tomatoes, and shredded carrots. No cheese, no dressing but a splash of balsamic vinegar.

"Look at this bitch's discipline! On her birthday!" Nica called out, pointing to Colleen's plate, her cheeks bright with vodka, and the other girls chimed in, tipsily: "What are you, a rabbit?" and "Looks delicious, Ana!" (their nickname for "anorexic"). Colleen didn't mind their ribbing. They were just jealous. It made her happy.

By ten, Colleen and her friends were the only patrons left in the restaurant, aside from a loud group of middle-aged women eating sundaes, and a thirtysomething man sitting at one of the rotating, round-bottomed chairs at the counter near the kitchen. He nursed a beer and picked at french fries beside the half-eaten burger on his plate.

After another round of vodka, Nica dared Colleen to invite the man to come sit with them and she did.

Carl Branch did not live in Hemet; he was passing through on his way back from Phoenix to Fresno, where he lived with his eleven-year-old son, Darren. Carl had reddish-brown hair and was handsome in a blocky, chipped-from-a-granite-slab way. He also had a sadness about him that made Colleen feel she sparkled with life. It was a challenge to make him smile, but she could.

Colleen never graduated from San Jacinto High, or auditioned for a live-character role at Disneyland. Three months after her eighteenth birthday, she moved to Fresno to live with Carl and Darren. There was no sense in waiting another minute to get out of Hemet, and anyway, you couldn't parade over the moat of the Magic Kingdom in a corseted Snow White costume if you were pregnant, as Colleen was, with a baby girl she always knew she'd name Lorelei.

EARLY 2013

3

LORELEI HAD COMMITTED to leaving Los Angeles at precisely midnight on a Tuesday in January, but Don was delaying
their departure. At 11:50 P.M., his apartment in West Hollywood
was still a wreck. In a corner of the living room, Lorelei sat
cross-legged in his giant egg chair, on "loan" from one of Don's
father's furniture stores, white acrylic on the outside with orange fur on the inside. The chair was supposedly valuable, and
selling it was one of the many tasks on Don's to-do list that he
hadn't gotten around to. Lorelei was unimpressed with its comfort. The plastic was rock hard beneath the shaggy covering,
and its convex shape was awkward to lean against. But the way
it curved around her gave her a safe feeling, so she stayed inside it, chain-smoking American Spirits and drinking red wine
from a mug. One of Don's wine-snob friends had given him the
bottle, probably not intending for him to swill it from a mug on
a Tuesday night, but this was an occasion: they were getting out
of L.A. For a good long time.

"Hold on, hold on," Don repeated as he moved around the
room from one pile to the next, scrutinizing the detritus as if
he'd lost a diamond. He examined single sneakers, power cords

with no accompanying devices, empty cereal boxes, damaged PlayStation components.

"I'm holding on," Lorelei said, trying out smoking with unconventional fingers: her middle and her ring, her ring and her pinkie. "You can quit saying that."

From his knees in the middle of the dusty wood floor, Don looked up, holding a wide-toothed purple comb in one hand and a copy of *Harsh Reality: A Guide to Preserving your Sanity on TV* by Rita Cooper, PsyD.

"You want either of these?"

"If I did, I would've packed them." The book, which she'd only thumbed through once, had been a gift from her agent, Robin, who was always trying to smarten Lorelei up, to empower her.

Lorelei had learned to keep her cool when Don acted this way, not to snap at him. He always went through this OCD mood when he first got high on meth, until the drug settled into his system and he regained the ability to prioritize. They called it "Mote" — short for *motivation*, because that's what it provided, and Mote was less druggy sounding than crystal or speed or crank. Truthfully, though, it only motivated Lorelei. For Don, it mostly intensified his tendency to dither.

"What time is it?" he asked her.

"Eleven fifty-two."

"Shit!"

"Calm down, dude." She gazed at her flip-flopped foot, wondering if she was flexible enough to smoke with her toes. Probably not, but it might be worth a try. This was what happened to her when she first got high: methodical. More useful than Don's compulsive futzing.

"But we only have eight minutes and I still have this ocean of shit to sort through."

"Midnight is a made-up deadline," Lorelei reminded him. She'd conceived of it a week earlier at three in the morning, when she was full of fresh ideas after zipping up some of the top-grade crystal she'd scored in the parking lot of the new club WWHD?, which stood for What WoodHolly Do? — extra clever because the club was owned by the former-child-star-turned-professional-partier Holly Lohen.

"We will leave at the pulse of midnight!" Lorelei had declared, pleased that she'd come up with the word *pulse* instead of *stroke*, to indicate digital time over analog. That was one of the many benefits of Mote: it made the right words available, as if suspended in the air for her to pluck.

"Fuck yeah," Don had said, waving a fist in the air. "Suck it, Thompson."

Mitch Thompson owned the building where Don hadn't paid rent in three months on the apartment he'd recently begun sharing with Lorelei. Two weeks ago Thompson had given him the *final* final deadline of January 2. Every other day he slipped increasingly threatening notes under the door.

"Don't be crass," Lorelei had said. Don didn't seem to reap the same verbal acuity from Mote that she did. "Thompson has actually been really patient with you, so let's not fuck with karma."

"Sorry, you're right," Don had admitted.

Don held a watch to the ceiling, frowning at its face. He was always quick to defer to Lorelei, which alternately annoyed and pleased her. "Do you know where this came from?"

"Who cares? Let's go!"

"It's a Tag Heuer! It's worth a shitload. I think you stole it off one of those douches at Trapeze."

"Let's take it then."

They planned to sell as much as they could in San Francisco, to tide them over until they got jobs. Her mother's credit card would be only for emergency measures, a very last resort.

Don tossed the watch into his open duffel and went back to examining the floor.

The problem with his dallying was that it gave her time to think. To examine, yet again, her decision to leave. The irony of it, when she'd wanted to live in Los Angeles on her own for so long, instead of shuttling back and forth from Fresno with her mother, like a kid instead of a twenty-two-year-old woman. It had been embarrassing, that setup, but her mother would have been crushed if Lorelei proposed a change. Especially since Colleen had giddily suggested the two of them get a place together, in the Valley, to live in when Lorelei was working — a mortifying prospect. Fortunately, her father had quickly nixed the idea on financial grounds. Lorelei still hadn't earned enough money to come close to supporting herself, and Carl claimed he couldn't afford their mortgage in Fresno *and* a place in L.A. Her mother had whined, but Lorelei was secretly grateful to him.

And then, suddenly, just as Lorelei's career had been looking up, it nosedived, courtesy of her mother. Lorelei found herself exactly where she'd fantasized: living in L.A. on her own. Except that it had been all wrong. Instead of living with friends, she'd been stuck at her stepbrother's place. Instead of working in front of a camera all day, she was unemployed and dodging the most desperate paparazzi, the ones who hung on to her story long after *Access Hollywood* and *TMZ* lost interest, hocking unflattering photos of her to websites like Reality Graveyard and The D-List. The few friendships Lorelei had begun to develop with other girls in the business, Paige and Mindy in particular, faltered as they landed better jobs and she landed nothing. They were busy, yes, but they also seemed wary of Lorelei, after she and her mother became known around town as

minor train wrecks. In Hollywood, reality show castoffs occupied the lowest caste in the industry.

No, this was not the independent, exciting L.A. life she'd
imagined. She'd never thought she'd end up there broke and
audition-less, crashing with a semi-loser like Don. She'd also
never imagined herself doing hard drugs, especially not meth,
which she'd always perceived as a bottom-feeder substance,
produced in boarded-up trailers by crazed, emaciated guys in
the Midwest with rotting teeth and skin.

She'd dabbled with cocaine at the Hollywood clubs and
loved the high, but the euphoria was too brief and the crash
too brutal. After a night of sniffing it up through one nostril and
then the other, she'd lie wide-awake in Don's bed, watching the
sunrise bleed around the edges of the blinds, plagued by a bitter postnasal drip and racing dark thoughts. Several times she'd
considered taking Don's car keys and driving straight home to
Fresno, bolting into her childhood house, and climbing into bed
with her mother. By then, Lorelei hadn't communicated with
Colleen in more than two months and she missed her mother,
sometimes terribly. In many ways, Colleen was awesome, far
above and beyond the greatness of other mothers. She truly understood Lorelei. When Colleen was at her best, the two of them
were peas in a pod. At her worst, she was smothering and insa-
tiable, always needing more from Lorelei: more time together,
more details shared. More evidence of Lorelei's love.

But then Colleen had dipped to a low point. Gone out of control, violated boundaries, interfered with Lorelei's career. With
her whole life. So Lorelei had made a hard decision: no contact.
Just for now.

Shortly after making this decision, Lorelei discovered meth,
which she nicknamed Mote on the spot, short for Motivation,
at someone's after-after-party way up in the Hollywood Hills,

and said good-bye to cocaine. Mote was much longer lasting and useful. It made her extraordinarily productive. It enabled her to deflect unwanted thoughts and emotions. It strengthened her resolve to make a clean break from her mother.

Don was still dawdling over the piles of stuff on the floor. It was 12:15, time for Lorelei to get him moving, and there was one reliable way to do it. She hoisted herself out of the egg chair, stubbing her cigarette out in the wine-stained mug. She crossed the floor, her flip-flops making sticky sounds against the wood, and knelt behind him, slipping her arms around his shoulders.

"Donovan," she said, lowering her voice to a murmur. "It's time for us to blow out of town. Time to part with all this junk. Now." She touched her lips to the back of his neck, for extra emphasis.

He shuddered with pleasure. "Okay."

She tightened her arms around him. She felt his heart clipping away.

"Yes."

"Are you sure?"

"Yes. Can't you tell I'm radiating surety?"

"You're not worried that we're going to slink back into town in about a week? I mean, at least here, we have a roof over our heads, until Thompson finally cracks down, which could be a while still, and our friends, and —"

"That is a non-option. Why are you even thinking about that? You're funny. You have no problem with not paying rent, not returning the two-thousand-dollar chairs your dad loaned you, but as soon as we've got a plan of action, you freak on me."

"It's just we have hardly any money."

His voice practically squeaked. Maybe Mote wasn't his drug. Maybe he should've stayed a pothead, like he'd been before they met. He'd been so cute and mellow then, strumming his foot against the ground from the skateboard he rode all over the set of Lorelei's first big commercial, the HPV vaccine Preventus, where he'd worked as a PA, his butter-blond hair slanting across his forehead.

"We have to hang out," he'd told Lorelei, stepping on the back of his skateboard so it popped up into his hand. "If for no reason other than to tell people we met on the set of a genital wart ad." He was twenty-two but could pass for seventeen. Her gazelle friend Paige called him Peter Pan.

Now, he was a cranked-out mess.

"Don, stop it," Lorelei said. "You're with me. We're together. We can do this." Her confidence surged as she spoke, like a dimmer inside her had been pushed to its brightest setting. She massaged his shoulders.

"Lorelei—"

"Let's go," she said. She leaned over and kissed him.

Borrowing the credit card was easy—Lorelei had her house key and knew all her mom's hiding places, and exactly how much time she could be counted on to spend at the gym in the morning. Less than ten minutes, and they were back on the road.

That was the beginning and the end of their success.

Their bad luck began in the Bay Area, where Lorelei's childhood friend Jenna Conrad was in culinary school and had agreed to let them crash for a bit. But after just three nights, Jenna, who was full of tedious knowledge about mushroom foraging and béchamel sauce, told Lorelei and Don that she believed there was a miscommunication or a misunderstanding and that she couldn't host them any longer; they had to be out by the morning. Lorelei found this request awfully harsh and disloyal from a girl she'd known since third grade, so she'd had no qualms about skimming as much as she could from the bathroom. She'd foraged — Jenna could've appreciated that — without even glancing at labels, so she and Don left San Francisco with a backpack full of pill bottles, which turned out to be Benadryl, Midol, a couple of Advair inhalers for asthma, which did nothing, and a bunch of holistic shit like echinacea and zinc tablets. Nothing prescription but two expired capsules of something called clindamycin, which Lorelei was pretty sure was an antibiotic, but that Don had insisted on trying to snort anyway. It practically fried their nasal passages.

Don had friends with a supposedly empty Squaw Valley ski house they could crash in, but it turned out to be occupied by a bunch of fratty guys on a mountain biking trip who were even less welcoming than Jenna Conrad. At least they turned out to be careless with their cash; in the ten minutes they were in the ski house, Lorelei managed to lift $80 from a money clip on top of the refrigerator and $100 more from the wallet in a glove compartment of an unlocked car.

After two nights in a grimy hippieish hostel and one in Don's car, Lorelei decided they should try Reno. They had to pick a destination, and Don wasn't going to take charge of the logistics. Reno was cheap, she'd heard, and her dealer Reggie in L.A. had a Mote hookup for them there, some guy who ran a restaurant, who might be able to get them jobs. Their stash wouldn't last much longer, and she didn't want to deal with finding a new source. Plus, Reno had nightlife, even if it was the poor cousin to Las Vegas. Anything was better than L.A. After all, if Lorelei was going to take a hiatus from her old life, she might as well do it somewhere she never would've expected to find herself, and where no one would think to look for her. They still had Don's watch and a few other things to hock, but that cash wouldn't last forever. They needed money and somewhere to sleep, and jobs, and Mote, so Lorelei made the executive decision. Whenever she worried about becoming a junkie, she thought about how functional she was — about how much she valued having a plan.

"Brilliant, Lor," Don said, as he swung his handed-down Honda, an old green Accord, a sort of communal vehicle for employees at his dad's furniture store (it was not clear whether he was technically allowed to have borrowed it, but so far no problems), onto I-80 toward Reno at three in the morning, wired after celebrating the decision with some Mote and Coors Light, the moon a single wide-awake eye over the mountains. "You're so good at this."

4

HAVING NO IDEA where Lorelei was made the long days alone in Fresno miserable for Colleen. But what could she do? Lorelei was an adult. That she'd chosen to evaporate from Colleen's life — from the brand-new life they'd been making together — was Colleen's fault. And because Lorelei's absence was her fault, Colleen fought the urge to jump into her Camry and comb every inch of Los Angeles in search of her daughter. Being alone with Carl in Fresno was a punishment Colleen believed she deserved.

After Colleen's crucial mistake, more than four months ago, Lorelei left Fresno to live in L.A. with her half brother, Darren, and his wife, Robin, where they owned a large home on a palm tree–lined street in Santa Monica, blocks from the ocean. Robin was Lorelei's agent, and Colleen couldn't stand her. That Lorelei fled to Darren wasn't so bad — Colleen loved her sweet stepson, who'd been eleven when Colleen married his father, Carl — but picturing Lorelei eating a dinner of expensive, unpronounceable vegetables every night with Robin in her big house by the Pacific was too much.

After Lorelei moved into the "carriage house" in Darren and Robin's backyard, Darren gave Colleen brief updates tinged with Robin's phrasings: Lorelei was "processing her anger"; "working through her issues"; "establishing her own identity." Lorelei didn't pick up her cell when Colleen called, and refused to come to the landline in the main house when Colleen tried her there. Darren advised Colleen to "let it go." Lorelei would come around when she felt "healed enough to forgive." Definitely Robin's words, Colleen thought, kicking a barstool in her empty kitchen so hard it toppled over.

Colleen was heartened when Darren reported that Lorelei had moved out of the carriage house with no notice beyond a text message saying she'd be staying with friends in West Hollywood. Surely Lorelei had not been able to stand living with Robin and her hundred-dollar yoga mats. Surely Lorelei's anger at Colleen was waning, and she'd finally call home, and they would make fun of Robin together, like they used to, and Lorelei would come back to Fresno, and everything would start getting back to normal.

But Lorelei's call never came. Colleen checked in with Darren, but he barely heard from his little sister after she'd supposedly moved to West Hollywood. A few texts here and there; no details. Just that she was okay and figuring things out, Darren told Colleen. That she needed, for now, to be "family-free." That was the actual phrase Lorelei had written, Darren said. Colleen plucked a spatula from a metal cylinder on the kitchen counter and threw it at the wall, where it pinged and clattered to the ground, unharmed.

A week passed with no updates from Darren, and then three.

"Text her," Colleen said to him.

"I have," Darren said. "Several times. I ask if she's okay, and she just types back a *Y*. That's the best I can do. I've got to respect her boundaries."

Did Robin tell you to say that? Colleen wanted to ask, but held back. Darren always defended his wife. Always. Instead, Colleen said, "What if she means *Y*, as in *why do you want to know?*"

"Coll," Darren said gently, "Lorelei will be fine. In the meantime, you've got to live your life."

Now, Darren was gone, too, shooting a movie on location in Florida, with no time for keeping tabs on his sister, and Colleen was left in a void of uncertainty in Fresno. A total of four and a half months had passed since she'd seen Lorelei, and two of those had slogged by without any real updates. It was excruciating; in the past, she'd hardly gone four hours without talking to Lorelei.

Colleen tried to "live her life." She began her mornings with an intensive Pilates class, followed by a sugar-free protein bar and, if it was Tuesday, coffee with her old friend Marilyn Conrad at the Daily Grind. She'd enjoyed this weekly ritual with Marilyn for nearly a decade, ever since they'd met in a real estate licensing course at Fresno City College, but recently Colleen had begun to dread it. Dread it so much, in fact, that she'd begun swallowing a crumb of Zenzo in the parking lot outside the café. The lavender pill, a Pakistani-manufactured knockoff of Xanax she'd bought online, blunted the sting of any news Marilyn let slip about her daughter, Jenna, who was Lorelei's age and happily attending culinary school up in San Francisco. Marilyn was careful, but inevitably Jenna came up, and without the Zenzo, hearing snippets from the life of a normal twenty-two-year-old left Colleen in a clutch of anxiety. After coffee, she drove home to her silent house — trying not to wince at the dated look of the split-level gray ranch, at the hideous patch of rock siding between the garage and living room windows; trying not to start an argument with Carl in her head about how they needed to replace the damn rocks sooner than later — and went into her backyard for fifteen minutes of sunning, just long enough to soak up some vitamin D (caution with her skin was more crucial than ever, now that she'd crested forty).

All that and it was just noon. The rest of the day stretched in front of Colleen like a hallway in a dream: too wide, too bright, a harsh and sun-choked place when all she wanted was a cool, dim corner.

Before Lorelei disappeared, when her daughter's absence simply meant that she was at school, or at the mall with Jenna Conrad, or just back in her bedroom studying scripts Robin had sent, Colleen's afternoons weren't difficult at all. At the very worst, she'd rely on some daytime television to get her through until Lorelei got home. She'd make herself a Bloody Mary and flip through the half dozen reality shows she'd recorded on the Real & Documented network for research. R&D was clogged with programming ranging from *AstroNOTs*, which challenged eight strangers to test how long they could remain in a gravity-free chamber together, to *Monstresses,* which documented "real stories of mistresses who kill." Colleen was briefly fascinated by *Masticators,* which aired the lavish dinner parties thrown by a group of women who loved decadent food but hated getting fat, and so served each other rib eye and cheesecake and stuffed potatoes under the strict condition that no one was to swallow a single bite. They were to chew and spit their food into pewter tureens instead.

To optimize Lorelei's chances of landing a role, Colleen watched all shows that featured girls in their early twenties. She observed trends and took notes: *Tint lashes/brows. Earrings w/ feathers — trashy or fun? Tan lines = NO.* Robin was good at getting Lorelei auditions but lazy when it came to coaching her on her appearance. Colleen had taken on the responsibility herself.

She'd just taken it one step too far.

No nineteen-year-old on the planet needed her breasts done.

But Lorelei had worn Colleen down, piling on one new argument after the next: 38 percent of all actresses on television had some sort of cosmetic surgery; her friend Macy couldn't get a callback to save her life, but then she had a chin reduction and a "practically invisible" breast procedure, and now everyone recognized her on the street for starring in commercials for the new tablet computer for girls and women, the BFF. Everyone knew Jessalyn Fetters would've languished in obscurity were it not for the nose tweak and brow lift. Same went for Jennifer Aniston — had Colleen seen *Leprechaun,* back when Jen had that schnoz, those fullback thighs?

"Do you know how much money Macy's made from being the BFF girl?" Lorelei asked Colleen, as the Camry began to protest the steepening grade of the Grapevine.

"I can't say that I do," Colleen answered coldly.

"I'm sure it's a lot more than Dad makes."

"You're making me very angry," Colleen said.

"I hate fighting with you over this," Lorelei said, brushing tears away with the knuckle of her index finger. "I'm so sorry to keep needling you. It's just — " She hiccupped. It was very early on a weekday morning, but the traffic was already thickening on the pass.

"What, honey?"

"I just want this so badly, you know — "

"A boob job?"

"No, no." Lorelei sniffled. "For my career to happen. We're

31

both working so hard — you're like giving up your entire life, Mom. I just want to make sure I'm doing everything I possibly can. And sometimes I feel so stupid, going for the most impossible career in the world . . . I mean, what are the chances?"

"Oh, sweetheart, you are doing everything possible."

"I don't want to fight you anymore on this, Mom," Lorelei said. "We need to stay a team. You're the most important person in my life."

Colleen's heart sailed. What else could you want from your child but this?

She'd made the appointment for Lorelei.

Two hours in the office, Colleen pacing the waiting room and the parking lot and the Coffee Bean & Tea Leaf around the corner. Thirty-eight hundred dollars on the MasterCard. Afterward, Lorelei was a little tender and loopy on painkillers, but cheerful and surprisingly mobile. In just three days, she claimed to feel almost completely normal again, and the change was perceptible but difficult to pinpoint: she looked taller, trimmer in her waist, with a straighter back and longer legs — those were all the things you saw before you noticed, if you did at all, that her breasts were now a 34C instead of a 34B. Lorelei was thrilled. But Colleen never stopped feeling uneasy about it. She'd sent her baby under the knife.

Carl hadn't noticed. But Colleen felt that on some level, he knew.

5

THE FIRST PERFORMA had been lodged in the pocket of Lorelei's denim jacket, at the bottom of a mound of clothes on her closet floor that Colleen had finally forced herself to pick up.

A rectangular foil blister packet of thirty pills, PERFORMA 25 MG printed on the back of each of the push-out tabs. A Google search informed Colleen that Performa was a pharmaceutical amphetamine prescribed for attention deficit/hyperactivity disorder, ADHD, and used illicitly by college kids for its speedy and "smartening" effect. Lorelei most certainly did not have a prescription for it. Colleen would bet anything that Don was to blame. He was the lanky PA who'd just graduated from Cal State Northridge and rode a skateboard around the set of Lorelei's first big commercial (Preventus, a genital wart vaccine), bringing her Pellegrino and Twizzlers like a scrappy butler. He and Lorelei had become a tentative item; she'd begun to stay overnight with him in West Hollywood when her work schedule required several days in L.A., leaving Colleen alone at a motel. Colleen fumed but said nothing. What could she say? Lorelei was twenty-one then.

Surely Don had given her the Performa. Colleen was less upset at the pills than that Lorelei had been keeping secrets. Colleen stuffed the jacket into a laundry basket and dropped the pills into the back pocket of her own jeans. She almost threw them away, but at the last second changed her mind and put them in her sock drawer.

Several weeks ago, when she couldn't coax her mind or body into basic functionality, she pinched off the end of a football-shaped Performa and swallowed it.

A crumb, it turned out, was all it took to suffuse Colleen with a sense of purpose and push dark worries about Lorelei to the side. She'd taken to popping a crumb just before her morning shower, after which she'd be ready for action: scrubbing the residue of oatmeal glued to the pot from Carl's breakfast, ironing all of his shirts even though most of them were wrinkle-free cotton polos, making grocery and errand lists, organizing the drawers of the kitchen and office, folding laundry. She cooked sometimes, too: high-protein, low-carb lunches like chicken breast and steamed spinach, which she rarely got around to eating. There was too much to be done, plus the Performa zapped her appetite.

After she finished the housework, she surfed on her laptop in the office, then hit the elliptical for three miles. Another shower. A crumb and two ounces of Grey Goose on the rocks made dinner preparation festive. The vodka toned down her pep from the pills before Carl got home. They always sat down together for dinner, one of the leftover vestiges of Carl's attempt to instill old-fashioned family values. When Lorelei was old enough to talk, three or so, and Darren in high school, Carl began to require each family member to share one item from their day at the dinner table. Favorite Thing, Lorelei had named the ritual, bouncing in her booster seat, always volunteering to go first, always offering up a bit of minutiae that made them laugh: "Mommy got the hairbrush stuck in my hair and we had to use scissors but then I was extra pretty." "Me and Mommy went to the grocery store and I put four Twixes in the cart and she didn't notice till the checkout and then she let me buy one but not four."

Long after Darren left for college, Lorelei maintained Favorite Thing over dinner with Carl and Colleen, telling long, intricate stories about her day at school and its perpetual dramas, often much more than Carl cared to hear. Colleen could feel him wincing beside her as Lorelei reported news like "Melissa Young is pregnant, there's no other explanation." "Scott Ritter is dating this freshman who skipped a grade, and he got held back in kindergarten because of having pneumonia, so he's eighteen and she's thirteen." And "Mia's homecoming date wanted her to get naked about five minutes after they left the dance." Mia was Lorelei's friend, whom she was always careful to cast as the wild one in her anecdotes to Carl, portraying herself as the levelheaded adviser. Colleen knew half the time Lorelei was just substituting Mia's name for her own, to keep her father at ease. Even so, Colleen could feel Carl bristle at the table with Lorelei's ever-casual mention of the regular stuff kids did during high school, the parties and the couples who regularly slept at each other's house. Why was Carl such a puritan? Couldn't he see it was a roadblock to any sort of genuine connection with their daughter?

Now that Lorelei was gone, so was Favorite Thing. Over dinner, Carl would instead ask Colleen, "Have a good day?" as he cut his meat with precision. He was the sort of man who still required a 1950s-style triumvirate on his plate: protein, vegetable, starch.

Colleen would pause, pretending to consider, before answering, "Not bad."

"Anything worth telling me?"

He always used this phrase. She'd come to loathe it.

Well, let me see. Your daughter is still missing and I'm still miserable, but I'm not sure what those items are worth.

But she didn't say that. Usually, she lied; it was easiest.

"I dropped into Home3000 today," she might say. "Just to stay on their radar. For when they need a new agent."

Home3000 was the realty company where her friend Marilyn had worked as a residential properties agent for the past eight years. Lately, she'd been encouraging Colleen to renew her old real estate license and come work with her. Marilyn was ready for an assistant agent *now* — the housing slump was over and she had, as she phrased it, "inventory coming out of her ears" — but Colleen told Carl it was a proposition for some vague point in the future. He'd glommed on to the idea with such enthusiasm that she'd begun leading him to believe she was pursuing it. She'd never set foot into the Home3000 offices and, until Lorelei was back where she belonged, had no plans to.

"That's great." Carl's tone softened as he added butter to his mashed potatoes. Colleen looked away from the golden grease melting craters into the mounds of white starch. It turned her stomach. Carl hoisted a forkful up to his mouth. "Did you register for the licensing exam yet?"

"Yep," Colleen said, finishing her wine. Carl seldom drank alcohol anymore. "June twenty-eighth." She picked the date out of the blue, on the spot. Some random day several months away. Specificity, she'd learned, was the key to good lying.

After dinner, she'd flip channels while he read *Time* or *American Builder*, rewarding herself at 10:30 with half a Zenzo, and floating off into the padded sleep it delivered.

6

IN MARCH, TWO months after arriving in Reno, Lorelei committed to fixing the blinds in room 14 of the Sleep Inn. This was all temporary, Lorelei reminded herself, the yellow stains on the bedsheets, the grime in the sink, the bent frame of room 14's only window, which would not close or lock. The Sleep Inn was several long blocks off the city's main casino strip on an unfashionable street called Fashion Show Drive. There was a payday loan place, an adult video parlor, and a CVS. It was cheap, and the front desk staff hadn't yet noticed that her mother's credit card wasn't working.

"Is a little light coming in really such a big deal?" Don asked from his do-nothing post on the bed, where he was watching an old *Oprah* episode with the volume off, one where she was sort of skinny. Poor Oprah, with the yo-yoing weight. "Won't the shot look better if there's some natural light in the room?" Don asked.

"That's what we bought lights for, doofus," Lorelei said, "to create our own." They'd picked up some cheap lights on forked metal legs from Home Depot — a production trick she'd learned from her brother — but the truth was a little natural light wouldn't hurt. Lorelei was just feeling a teeny bit paranoid, and needed complete privacy in order to perform authentically for the camera. Reno speed wasn't as reliable as L.A. speed. She had a nice buzz going, from one fat line, but it wouldn't let her move on to filming until she'd banished sunshine from their motel room.

They were preparing to shoot a new segment of their web series, *The LAND Project*. (*LAND* for "Lorelei and Don," her idea.) The idea was to capture their current lives on camera with complete honesty — the complete opposite of all other reality shows, which were nothing but lies — and broadcast the series live online. The problem was, they didn't have the technical resources at the moment to stream their footage: they'd brought no laptop, and the Sleep Inn required an $8-per-day fee for wireless Internet access, a charge her mother's credit card had abruptly begun to reject.

No worries, Lorelei told herself. They had a video camera, thanks to her intrepid shoplifting skills. They had time. They had Mote for inspiration. What mattered now was the creative process: capturing the real, raw material. Later, they'd figure out how to show it to the world. It wouldn't be difficult. People ate this stuff up. Sure, maybe Lorelei had been a blip on the screen of *Flo's Studio,* but the show was still on the air, and its stars were still beloved. All she'd need to do was spin *The LAND Project* as the flip side to *Flo's Studio,* and audiences would eat it up. She was sure of it.

First, though, the blinds. She gave the chain a yank, and it snapped off its fixture.

"Easy on the hardware, m'lady," Don said.

The broken chain commanded her interest. She looped it around her neck and whirled around.

"Look what a cool necklace this makes!" The chain had plenty of length—she wrapped it around her neck a second time, one strand tight against her neck like a choker, the other hanging down at her belly. She moved over to the mirror to admire the doubling effect.

"Nice," Don said. "Except now what're we gonna do about the blinds? Want me to put a sheet over them or something?"

"No! They were meant to be broken," she said, her paranoia suddenly lifting. "It had to be done, for fashion. After all, we do reside on Fashion Show Drive."

She stared at herself in the mirror. The chemicals in the hair dye, combined with Reno's dry desert air, had relaxed her newly short locks to a nest of loose curls instead of their usual buoyant frizz. The result was a much sleeker appearance. Her parents wouldn't appreciate her diminished mane. Her father called her "Little Lioness" when her hair was especially bushy; her mother got defensive when a casting agent suggested Lorelei straighten it or go blond. Lorelei felt herself edge toward the brink of sadness, then shoved Carl and Colleen out of her mind. Mote gave you the freedom to steer the course of your feelings like a rowboat.

Lorelei jutted her hip out to the side. She looked excellent. The yellow microjumper—a strapless tank melded to shorts, which she'd stolen off the stylist's rack at some audition for a macadamia nut spot—fit perfectly, and the almost-new platform sandals, which she'd stolen from a Goodwill here in Reno, were only a half size too big. They were a little hooker-ish, maybe, but Lorelei always felt better in heels; she'd spent years being the shortest girl at every audition. Her summery ensemble was out of season, of course, but she wasn't planning on going outside.

Her necklace completed the outfit. That she'd broken the chain was a total stroke of luck. Good things were on the way. She loved how the concentric loops of rust-colored metal contrasted with the pale skin of her neckline and accentuated the delicate new shape of her clavicle. You could really see her bones. Her mother would die with jealousy. She wished she could have her mother try Mote. Lorelei had spent more than two decades sharing everything she loved with her mother. It was still hard to maintain the distance she'd imposed between them. The Mote helped. And, she told herself, it wasn't forever.

"Let me see this handcrafted necklace up close," Don said, crossing the room to stand behind her at the mirror. He rested his chin on her head. "I like it."

They were quiet, watching the reflection of their stacked faces. Don wasn't looking his best. He was a naturally pale-on-pale person: white-blond hair, hazel eyes, a fair complexion that had been boyishly sunburned at the cheeks, back in L.A., but that was now more along the lines of putty. He was prone to acne, which he normally controlled with prescription cream, but he'd recently run out of refills. Was this the same Don who, just six months ago, had taught her to skateboard and kissed her behind craft services and played guitar while they sang the Black Keys together until four A.M.? His sanguine charm that had attracted Lorelei was being overtaken by a junkyard-dog unease.

She made a mental note to get Don some Noxzema from CVS.

"Let's give you a shampoo later, okay?" she said.

"Including head massage?" He smiled at her in the mirror.

"Including," she said, meeting his eyes.

He was still cute when he smiled. Poor guy. In some ways, they were closer than ever now, but that was mostly the by-product of sharing a cramped room. In other ways — sexually, for instance — they'd become more distant. It was as if she had two boyfriends now, and Mote was handsomer and more fun than Don. The threat of sadness came again, but she booted it away. Sadness might interfere with the inspiration rising inside her, beginning to coalesce into words. She just needed to corral it, distill it, deliver it to the camera.

She shifted her gaze from Don to her own face.

"I look so human," she said. "People get so fat they obscure their humanity, you know what I'm saying?"

"Totally," Don said, bending to kiss her neck.

"Not now. We need lights and camera ready to go."

"Yes, madam." He pronounced it *muh-damm.*

"And no tripod today," said Lorelei. "I need to move around for this one. I need you to shoot me full-length, from lots of angles."

"Yes, muh-damm."

The topic was almost formed in her mind. It just needed one more kick of encouragement, so she returned to the vanity by the bathroom. She did not believe in sniffing through filthy dollar bills and instead crafted her own little powder-transmitting tubes with Post-it notes in different colors. She knew Darren would have approved her aesthetics, even if he'd disapprove of the drugs.

At the sink, she banded her hair at the nape of her neck and leaned over to zip up a line through her tidy bright pink paper straw. She felt Don watching, practically drooling, as she stood and savored the swift full-body tingle, the transition to her sharper, better self.

Lorelei was the self-appointed administer of their stash, a role she earned by procuring the goods. Don was too much of a chicken and she had a way with Chad, their boss at the Lucky Bastard All U Can Eat. Also, Don lacked discipline and would hoover up their supply way faster than Lorelei, if she didn't watch him.

Lucky for him, she was feeling generous.

"Get the lights done, then come have a bump," she said, dotting the air with her straw. "And then let's start."

"Okey dokey, smokey." He set up the lights in record time, throwing brightness into the space between the two beds — Lorelei's "stage" was a nightstand cleared of its lamp and Bible.

He bounded over to his line by the sink.

"Where're the cigarettes?" Lorelei asked.

"Over there," he said, pointing to the table with one finger as he leaned and brought the straw to his acne-raw nostril.

Lorelei scooped a crushed pack of Winstons off the floor, lit one, and seated herself on top of the nightstand, cross-legged and straight backed while she pulled on her cigarette — how delicious it was just after some Mote! — like a corrupt yogi. The nicotine swirled into the speed and distilled her spun thoughts into clean, muscular language.

Don was talking to himself in the mirror.

"Don!"

He bounced up in the air. "What?!"

"Get me the clapper and get yourself behind the camera."

She closed her eyes in final preparation.

"Check, check, check," said Don, jogging the ten feet to the dresser and pulling a notebook and extra-thick Sharpie from the top drawer. He handed them to her and hoisted the camera up on his shoulder.

Clamping her cigarette between her lips, Lorelei uncapped the marker, smelled it — she'd always liked the smell of Sharpies — and then scrawled on a fresh sheet of a spiral notebook (their makeshift clapperboard) *Ep. 3 / 1 / 1* on it and held it up in front of her chest.

"Marker!" she said.

"And action," said Don.

"Welcome to *The LAND Project*, episode three," she said, tossing the notebook to the floor. "Coming to you from Reno, Nevada, on the seventeenth of March, twenty-thirteen."

She pretended the camera was an old friend. Her awareness of Don evaporated.

"So," she said. "As you all can see, I've shed quite a bit of weight since my *Flo's Studio* days." She pinched the taut flesh of her upper arm. "And now that I'm not all covered with fat, I realize all that cellulite and padding was obscuring the real me. I had no idea who I was, so I didn't know what to do with myself, other than aspire to be like everyone else. Going to all those auditions and kissing ass and memorizing scripts about genital warts and tampons and basically whoring myself. The fat was keeping me down; it was making me a waddling lemming!" She paused, pleased by how the words *waddling lemming* felt peeling off her tongue.

"Now, I can hear people saying, 'Lorelei, you were never fat!' Well, maybe according to our warped American standards, I wasn't. But now that I've stripped away my excess, I realize I was fat, or at least obscured."

"Cut!" said Don.

"What?"

"You're talking a mile a minute."

"Okay, thanks." She had instructed Don not to interrupt except for a few very clear reasons, including talking too fast. It would be hard for people to love the show if they couldn't understand her.

"The fat was keeping me down! It was like trying to talk with a pillow over my face. Now that it's gone, I'm relieved of excess burdens, both physical and spiritual. And I've started to think that the reason so many Americans are dumb and depressed all comes down to how fucking fat they are. Even if they're not that fat, just moderately fat, which the average person most certainly is — I mean, have you been to Ohio lately?"

"Cut," said Don.

"What?"

"That'll offend viewers in Ohio, won't it?"

"We don't care, remember? The whole point of *The LAND Project* is to say shit that's too raw for so-called reality TV. And it's gonna be on the web, not TV, so people will be choosing to watch it, not just flipping channels."

"Okay, sorry."

"Don't apologize! It creates a bad power dynamic."

"What?" he asked, lowering the camera, looking confused. "With who?"

"With whom," she said.

"Okay, with whom does it create a bad power dynamic?"

"With anyone you apologize to in that automatic way! Back to rolling, please," she said.

He pointed the camera at her.

"I'm from Fresno," she said, deciding to nix Ohio after all. "Which is basically like the Midwest, except in Cow Country, California, and everyone's a total heifer. And they all drift around the malls with these lost, vacant expressions, like they're awaiting orders from God."

She'd hopped off the table and was pacing, from the room door, with its checkout-policies sticker half peeled off, to the bathroom and back. "Everyone's obsessed with how to make Americans less fat. Michelle Obama and the whole health care system and the media." She crouched at the vanity and worked a small clump under her pinkie nail and lifted it to her nostril. Drug use on camera was important to the show. Part of its realness.

"The fat police are going about it all wrong!" She skipped back to the beds and hopped up to stand on top of one of them.

"Doctors and magazines and the Lap-Band and Michelle Obama, all wrong! They use fear tactics — obesity will make you sick, it'll give you heart attacks, it'll give you diabetes, it'll make you enjoy life less and never have a mate, blah blah blah. Who wants to hear that shit? What if they said: Hey, fat people, how can you know who you really are when you're encased — or maybe ensconced? — yeah, ensconced in a layer of lard? What if your fatness is keeping you from knowing" — she paused for dramatic effect — "*who you really are?*"

She leaped from one bed onto the other, hoping Don was getting a good shot of her body, and then stepped onto the nightstand, easing back down into the Indian-style pose in which she'd begun. She made a slicing motion at her throat.

"Nice!" Don grinned, turning the camera off and setting it down on top of the TV. "Way to go, Lor! Best one so far."

"It was, wasn't it?! Let's go out." She skipped to the door. The night was just arriving, and teeming with opportunity. "We just worked hard. We've earned it."

"Can I kiss you?" he asked, placing a hand on either side of the wall beside her and leaning in.

"Yes," she said, closing her eyes.

The phone rang, the brash, outdated sound of a boxy landline. Don jerked like a marionette. Lorelei froze, and then, to prevent the jarring ring from happening again, she answered. "Yes?"

"Missus Branch?"

44

"Yes?"

"This is Keisha, at the front desk."

"Hi, Keisha."

"This is our last request, Missus Branch. You need to come by the office and bring us a different form of payment immediately. Your MasterCard was declined."

7

IN THE MIDDLE of a perfect March afternoon in Santa Monica, Robin Justus was still in bed, sprawled diagonally between her closed laptop and her cell phone. The white linen curtains covering the room's beach-facing windows arced with a light breeze off the ocean three blocks away.

She'd hardly moved all day, except once to the kitchen to eat, and another to the bathroom to give herself a hormone shot. In the stomach. Her third in three days. Her husband, Darren, was supposed to be administering them, but he was away, shooting a movie in Florida. Their house, a two-story Mediterranean with classic Spanish tile curving around the roof and the graceful archways between its unusually high-ceilinged rooms, felt conspicuously empty. Three thousand square feet was too big for two people, let alone one.

By now, there should have been three.

It had been a hard week: Darren was gone, hormones were smacking her moods around, and her parents' annual spring equinox party was tomorrow night, in Beverly Hills. She did not want to go, but then her mother would guilt-trip her for months. Darren's parents, down from Fresno, would expect her there, too, especially his stepmother, Colleen, who was barely older than he was and sure to be radiating

45

desperation over whether Robin had heard anything from Lorelei. Colleen's neediness turned Robin's empathy reflexes to stone.

Robin gathered herself into a sitting position. She stared straight ahead to the room's single wall decoration, a large abstract painting in soothing underwater colors — the art dealer had used descriptors like *seaweed* and *algae* and *midnight* — to block out the mess around her. Clothes strewn all over the white area rug and the dark hardwood floor, a week's worth of *Variety* and the *Hollywood Reporter,* scattered shoes, and plastic dry cleaning bags with paper-sheathed hangers. Several mugs with the cold dregs of red raspberry leaf tea — good for fertility, her acupuncturist claimed — cluttered her nightstand, and her dresser was covered with mail and makeup and a few wineglasses, though she only allowed herself an inch or two these days.

Darren was three thousand miles away and would never return unannounced, but the thought of his reaction to the mess still bothered her. It was one of their oldest arguments: he believed her messiness caused her stress; she believed it was his refusal to accept her messiness that stressed her out in the first place.

In an upright pose with her feet tucked under her butt — *something-asana* — Robin breathed, preparing to lower her back down on the bed, which would stretch her knees and upper thighs, and put some sort of positive pressure on her uterus. Slowly, slowly, she eased back, until her upper back rested against the comforter. *Breathe,* she told herself. *Visualize your body as a fecund garden.*

But all she could picture was the unwrapped ovulation stick on the bathroom counter, the smiley face on its tiny gray screen. The pose became too intense to bear. She jerked out of it, flipped over, fishlike, and burrowed her face into the duvet to blot her tears.

When she got ahold of herself, she turned her head to the side and noticed the light in the room had turned deep gold. The curtains had stopped billowing and she could hear gulls squawking in the distance, a sign that the sun was not far from setting. She had spent the entire day in bed, something she hadn't done since Jackie forced too much tequila on her in their twenties. At the thought of her oldest and closest friend, Robin picked up the phone to call Jackie, now a highly successful TV actress on the hit comedy *Three Mad Chicks,* then remembered that Jackie and her live-in French girlfriend, Naidre, were off in Palm Springs on a minivacation. Robin hesitated to calculate the rudeness of interrupting her trip and dialed anyway. Jackie never enjoyed vacations.

She picked up on the first ring. "Robs, thank God. I'm this close to ripping my hair out. It's like a hundred and twenty degrees here. And Naidre claims she *moost* have a new bikini," she said, imitating her young girlfriend's accent. "And it *moost* be a four-hundred-dollar Pucci. She won't stop pouting until I buy it."

"So buy it," Robin said. "Solved."

"But she'll only wear the bottoms!" Jackie said. "I refuse to squander my hard-earned cash on a single scrap of spandex. The girl's tits are undeterred by American social norms. Not to mention the goddamn desert sun. Everyone's staring. Including Robert Pattinson and Sofia Vergara." She sighed dramatically. "God, I wish I'd forced you to blow off your parents' thing and come with me to the desert. Your mom's a bitch whether you go to their parties or not. It wouldn't have mattered if you'd bailed on it."

"This is true."

"How are you, baby? I keep picturing you alone in your house, pacing around holding a syringe and crying, and it makes me want to twist Darren's balls."

"Jack!" Robin couldn't help laughing. "First of all, I'm just fertility challenged, not a heroin addict. We may cry a lot, but we don't pace around with syringes. And second, no one's allowed to mention my husband's balls except for me, even if that person *is* my best friend and a lesbian."

"Whatever. He should get his ass home. Now."

"Come on, Jack. You of all people know you can't just take a rain check on shooting a Toby King movie."

"Oh, please," Jackie snorted. "Darren's been futzing around for ten years with your full support. And now he just gets to blow you off, in your time of *extreme need,* for some pretentious indie film director he just met?"

"Don't be so dramatic. It's only been four years," Robin said. "And he's not blowing me off. He feels terrible about being away. It was a hard decision that we made together. But we decided the sacrifice was worth it, for his career. *We.*"

Even as she defended her husband, Robin was comforted to hear Jackie lambaste Darren for taking the job in Florida. It was the reason she'd called Jackie in the first place. Criticizing Darren herself made Robin feel worse, but when Jackie did it, she felt better.

"It's cute how much you love the guy, Robs," Jackie said. "Very old school. Some right-winger should hire you two to star in a pro-marriage campaign. But — oh wait, hang on. Naidre's asking me something." Robin could heard Naidre's melodic French accent through the phone, followed by Jackie's weighty sigh as she answered, "You know I don't *do* mud baths. But if you feel like paying three hundred bucks to have wet dirt seep

48

into every crevice of your body, by all means, you've got my blessing."

Robin pictured Jackie stretched on a cushioned chaise lounge beside a sparkling pool flanked with palm trees and desert flowers and beautiful people, attendants gliding by to spritz water on their faces. "Jack, go get the mud bath, okay? You're at a luxury resort with your French model girlfriend who currently has a ten-page spread in *Vogue*. Try to enjoy it. I'm fine."

"You are *not* fine," said Jackie, "but I guess I'd better follow that six-foot bare-titted brat to the spa before she charges the twelve-hundred-dollar package to our room. I'll call you as soon as I'm back in town, okay?"

"Okay."

"And, Robs, remember," Jackie said, "you will get your baby. Even if I have to fly to Africa and steal one from Madonna's personal orphanage. I *will* see to it that you have a child whom I can corrupt."

"Love you," said Robin, smiling as she hung up. She was lucky to have Jackie, who always made her laugh, and had a boundless well of sympathy for Robin's situation. This was especially generous, Robin thought, since Jackie swore she'd never have children ("Nothing to do with being a lesbian," she'd say cheerfully. "I've just always hated kids."), and lived the lifestyle to back it up, spending her troves of money on a revolving assortment of high-maintenance European girlfriends; an ultramodern house high in the Hollywood Hills with a glass-walled yoga studio and a sprawling deck offering jeweled views of the cityscape at night, where she hosted lavish parties; and a convertible Bentley. Robin had been horrified by that particular purchase, two hundred grand for a car, but Jackie had laughed her off: "Sorry, Robs, but I don't have any college tuitions to save for."

The sun had set and the light in Robin's bedroom paled to a pinkish gray. From the beach, gulls had begun squawking their good nights. She stretched out flat on her back again, noticing a rime of dust at the edges of the ceiling fan over the bed. She imagined calling Darren to report it: *Hey, honey, I actually noticed that something needed cleaning before you pointed it out to me!* The thought made her queasy with missing him all over again, undoing the little boost her call to Jackie had provided. That was the problem in relying on a friend like Jackie for support: well-intentioned as she was, Jackie couldn't truly understand Robin's situation. She'd always be a little off base. She was always mentioning adoption, for example, as if it were a direct substitute for carrying one's own child.

Robin considered adoption a very last resort. She was adopted herself. The story her parents, Mel and Linda Justus, told her was that Linda was unable to conceive, despite years of trying, but Robin didn't believe them. Her mother had been a minor soap star, playing a host of secondary characters on long-running shows like *The Palisades* and *Waves on the Sand,* and Robin suspected that Linda just hadn't wanted to trouble her bikini-perfect body or interrupt her acting career. She'd been in her early twenties when she'd adopted Robin. Too young, in Robin's opinion, to have known for sure that she was unable to conceive.

Robin's adoption had been strictly closed: all she knew was that her real mother had been a teenager when she'd gotten pregnant, and that she came from a deeply religious, poor family somewhere in the Inland Empire, the impoverished and dusty southeastern region of California. She'd given birth in the labor and delivery ward at Cedars; Robin's parents had covered all expenses. It was unlikely that Robin would ever know more.

They were good enough parents, Mel and Linda; they'd

provided Robin with every comfort and opportunity she could ever want, and were nice enough to her. But she sensed little urgency or depth in their love for her. Only fondness, like you'd have for a prized pet. Once, at the age of eight, a logistical mix-up had prevented both her nanny, May May, and her mother from picking her up from school. Robin had walked the two miles from Canyon Country Day to her home, switching her red backpack from one shoulder to the other when the muscles on one side began to ache, imagining how panic-stricken her mother would be when she realized the error and could not find her daughter.

When Linda found Robin at home eating Oreos straight from the bag, her feet blistered and her hair stiff with salt-sweat, she had said, "Oh my God, there you are." She'd gathered Robin into her arms without any mention of the Oreo crumbs all over her mouth, and stroked the back of her head, but Robin noticed her mother's mascara had been perfect. Robin's two-hour disappearance had not left her hysterical and weeping with worry, as Robin had hoped. Even as a third grader, Robin sensed it: she was not their blood.

Generally, her father was kinder and warmer than her mother, but Mel often looked at Robin with a confusion that said his daughter completely befuddled him. When he'd announced that she could pick out a car — *any car* — as a sixteenth birthday present, Robin had chosen a Ford Tempo, which was what May May drove. Instead of finding anything positive to say about his daughter's modest choice, Mel was enraged.

"Over my dead body will I buy American," he'd said.

"Then I'll ride my bike," Robin had said.

"This is Los Angeles!"

"If you get me a fancy car, I'll give it to May May and drive her Tempo."

Two months later, on Robin's sixteenth birthday, the white Volkswagen Cabriolet convertible turned up in the garage.

"I hope this is unfancy enough for you," Linda said, as Mel handed Robin a wrapped gift box with the key inside. That day, Robin rode her bike to Canyon Country Day and almost got herself killed in traffic several times. She drove the Cabriolet for the next twelve years, and promised herself that when she had children of her own, they'd be her own flesh and blood. That she'd be a mother with the sort of integrity neither of her parents possessed. She imagined living in a modest house somewhere near the ocean, comfortable but not ostentatious, bearing no resemblance to her parents' Beverly Hills taste. A husband who was down-to-earth and kind, maybe from the Midwest or Canada. And, most important of all, a baby, warm and chubby with a head smelling of sweet rolls, swaddled to Robin's chest, looking up at her with eyes that held nothing of Mel or Linda Justus inside them. She imagined the sort of primal connection she'd feel gazing down at a baby on her breast, and how that tiny person would offer her clues about her real mother. Perhaps, in the shape of her baby's mouth or the color of her eyes, Robin would feel the presence of the young woman from the Inland Empire who'd birthed her.

By thirty-four, Robin's "baby bug" was in full force, but she'd also been single at the time, and in the thick of running her agency, No Princess Talent, where she discovered and represented aspiring young female actors, models, and other entertainment-industry creatives. When she met Darren at a party, he'd been working sporadically as a freelance camera operator for commercials to support his own work making artistic short films. They'd fallen for each other hard and fast, but by the time they'd married, honeymooned in the Maldives, and settled into their life in Santa Monica together, Robin was thirty-seven.

They'd begun trying for a baby. And trying and trying. But month after month, Robin's period showed up. Her OB, Dr. Weiss, tested Robin's ovulation patterns, x-rayed her fallopian tubes, sonogrammed her uterus: all normal. She tested Darren's sperm for motility and count, and both were above average.

Weiss remained unconcerned. It often took a year, she said. Perfectly normal. Psychosomatic forces were likely at work. Only after twelve full months of trying the old-fashioned way should they consider other options.

Robin tried to stay positive, but it was difficult. Babies, it seemed, were everywhere: double strollers blocked the aisles at Gelson's; women brunched at restaurants while breastfeeding their infants, tiny feet protruding from beneath colorful nursing capes; actresses all over town took highly publicized maternity leaves documented in magazine sections with titles like "Celebrity Bump Watch!" Even one of Robin's own clients, a twenty-two-year-old plus-sized model named Molly Bench for whom Robin scored a contract with Lane Bryant, had already birthed a daughter and gotten back to work. The Facebook pages of Robin's friends from UC Berkeley, even the stauncher feminists from her women's studies program, were smattered with photos of their children, ranging from swaddled infants to middle schoolers with braces on their teeth.

Robin tried fertility yoga. She tried acupuncture. She dragged Darren way out to the desert, near Joshua Tree, to visit a hypnotist she'd read about in *Whole Parent* magazine, a woman who wore her gray-streaked hair in two long braids and supposedly "unblocked" couples trying unsuccessfully to conceive.

But Robin and Darren remained blocked. Her anxiety over it took permanent hold of her daily life. Darren, on the other hand, maintained an unflappable optimism. Month after month, when NOT PREGNANT flashed on the tiny oval screen of Robin's pregnancy test, he'd gather her into his arms, kiss the top of her head, and knead his fingers into the base of her scalp the way she liked. Then he'd drive them up the coast to Jupiter's, their favorite fish shack in Malibu, where they'd sit outside and listen to the ocean and eat fried clams washed down with cold beer, fingers linked across the splintered wooden tabletop. "Soon, Robs," Darren would say. "It's going to happen, I promise. It's only been nine months. I know it feels like a long time, but remember, anything under a year is normal."

At first, his reassurance comforted her. But eventually, she became suspicious of it. He was *too* calm. His lack of anxiety was too passive. While Robin tossed and turned in bed, thinking, *Baby, baby, baby,* Darren often spent entire nights in the home editing studio she'd installed for him, cutting new footage for an undefined new short film, emerging bleary-eyed but exuberant in the morning. He seemed perfectly . . . *fulfilled.* Without a baby.

"Do you really want this?" she finally asked him, on a gray March afternoon at Jupiter's, after her eleventh negative test.

"What?" He set down his beer mug and leaned forward onto his elbows.

She paused, feeling an amorphous anger rising inside her. "Month after month, you're just so calm. So accepting of Dr. Weiss's opinion. It's starting to feel like . . ." She paused, dropping a hush puppy back into its basket.

"Like what?"

"Like you might be secretly glad. Like you might not want to break from our cushy life to deal with the hassles of a baby. The sleep deprivation. Getting peed on. Not going to movies or restaurants or hiking or off on spontaneous road trips to Baja to shoot . . ." She cleared her throat, unable to stop herself. Later, she would blame it on hormones. "It's hard work, you know, having a baby. You won't be able to focus on your little projects so much, or — "

He cut her off, his voice hard. "My *little projects?*"

"Wait, I didn't mean 'little'!" She honestly hadn't — the word just slipped out. She hadn't been thinking clearly. Just emoting. "I'm not accusing you of anything. I'm just wondering if you simply feel satisfied with our lives the way they are now. You say all the right things every month when my test is negative, but you don't *seem* upset."

Darren stood up from the table as if he'd suddenly felt something sharp underneath him. "Unbelievable."

"What's unbelievable?"

"That because I'm not shedding tears and wringing my hands every month, I must not really want to start a family. That I'm secretly hoping to coast along in this luxurious life, not only unaccomplished, but childless, too, like some overgrown film school brat who — "

"Wait, wait!" Robin stood up, too, and tried to pull Darren back down to the table, but he wouldn't budge. Guilt closed in on her. "Why are you being so defensive?"

He twisted his arm from her hand. "All I've been doing is trying to support you. God knows you support *me* all the time, literally and otherwise. I'm just trying to be your ally."

"Okay! I believe you. I was just having a . . . moment of self-pity."

"Instead of accusing me of having too much self-restraint, why don't you work on cultivating some yourself? Do you know how much you just insulted me?"

"Darren — "

But he'd already turned and begun weaving swiftly around the tables dotting the weather-beaten dining deck toward the staircase exiting to the parking lot. She caught him at the top of the stairs and cupped his shoulder. "What are you doing?"

"Going home," he said, without turning around.

"Without me?"

"Without you."

"Darren, we're twenty miles up the coast. How am I supposed to get home?"

He cleared the six steps of the staircase in a fluid hop and landed in the packed sand of the parking lot. Then he turned around and looked up at her. "Figure it out," he said. "Call Jackie. Take a taxi. You can afford it."

She watched him swing the Prius from the parking lot onto Highway 1 and speed off. The day had turned chilly and raw, her hair tacky with salt and humidity against her cheeks, which were now streaming with tears.

It was the first fight of its kind they'd ever had — the first to broach the issue of their money, and how Darren had contributed none of it — and their last. That afternoon, from the windy deck of Jupiter's fish shack, Robin called her father for a favor. She generally hated utilizing Mel's connections, but the person she suddenly wanted to see, urgently, was Dr. Robert Amazo — nicknamed Dr. Amazing — a luminary in the fertility field whose office was way the hell out in Calabasas, who took no insurance, a man close enough to retirement to be literally booked for the rest of his career. Robin's father had helped the doctor find his thirteen-thousand-square-foot dream home — and pointed him in the direction of a few highly lucrative real estate investments.

Clearing her throat of tears, Robin asked her father to call in the favor. A coveted, impossible appointment with Dr. Amazing. Then she called a taxi to drive her home to her husband, to repair the damage she'd just done. She was ashamed of herself, of the accusations she'd made.

A week later, Robin and Darren sat in an examination room with pale blue walls, the air marble-cool against the midday heat of the Valley, listening to their new doctor explain the results of the various tests he'd run. Robin had expected a graying, avuncular type, but Dr. Amazo looked like a banker in scrubs.

"Robin, you've not been diagnosed with polycystitis before?" he asked.

She pressed her palm into the crunchy wax paper covering the exam table. "No. What is it?"

Dr. Amazing sighed and shook his head. "I'm very surprised it hasn't come up," he said, handing her a printed image of her ultrasound. "Very common. See the black spots on your ovaries here?"

Robin squinted at the photo, which looked like a whirlpool with, yes, faint black blobs on it.

"These are just eggs that aren't getting released when you menstruate, and cling to your ovaries as undeveloped follicles. This means that you don't actually ovulate when you get your period. That's why you haven't been getting pregnant. It's a common and correctable condition. We'll begin a mild hormone treatment immediately, which will trigger your eggs to drop, and I'm confident I can have you pregnant in several cycles, as long as you're willing to do your shots at home and attempt conception within a specific window afterward."

"Attempt conception?" Robin said, confused by what sounded like good news. "You mean sex?"

"Yes," said Dr. Amazo. "At this point, I see no reason to endure IVF. If you're still not pregnant in a few months, we'll revisit." He pulled a prescription pad from his breast pocket and began scribbling on it.

"How could Dr. Weiss have overlooked this?" Robin said as they emerged from the office into the dry heat of the San Fernando Valley. "Dr. Amazing made my issue sound so surmountable." She felt light and airy, unable to suppress her smile.

"Who knows?" Darren said, taking her hand and swinging their arms in unison. "Maybe she's a crappy doctor. Maybe she liked billing us over and over and over. It doesn't matter. This is a huge breakthrough!"

"It is, isn't it?" Robin said, skipping a few steps and pulling Darren forward. "Are you ready to stick needles in my tummy?"

"I can't think of anything more romantic." Darren led her to the passenger side of their Prius and opened her door.

Robin kissed him. "You sound like you actually mean that."

"I do," he said. "We're on a mission together. Syringes and all. It *is* romantic."

She'd felt so hopeful on the drive back to Santa Monica that day, unfazed by the ninety minutes it took them to cover the twenty or so miles back to the Westside, so connected to Darren, so certain that they'd finally, actually be pregnant soon. Her period was scheduled to show up in just over a week, and they could do the treatments and be back in Dr. Amazing's office in two weeks for the results.

And then Darren got the phone call that ruined everything.

8

DARREN GOT THE call while Robin was at her evening yoga class. He was in the office, tooling around on his Mac Pro with a new animation program, when his cell rang from a 212 area code. The perky yet all-business voice on the other end identified herself as Aspen Green, assistant to the filmmaker Toby King. She sounded very young, which in combination with her name caused Darren to picture a ponytailed girl standing on a golf course, head tipped to a cell phone.

"Darren, I'm calling because Toby's looking for a replacement DP for his latest film, *Equus Revisited*," Aspen said.

"Andy Patchell quit?" asked Darren. Toby King was a blazing directorial talent, just in his early thirties with two acclaimed independent features under his belt, both shot by the same cinematographer. Darren had met Patchell once, at a party, and found him pretentious.

"We'll just call it a difference in creative vision," Aspen said. "Andy left under positive circumstances. But now Toby needs a cinematographer with a super fresh eye who hasn't done a lot of narrative film in the past. Someone with a nonlinear vision."

"My work is definitely imagistic," Darren said, walking out of his office and down the hall to the bedroom. He'd produced so little that to call it "my work" made him cringe. That Toby King's assistant would be calling him on the basis of it was stunning.

"Toby's a huge fan of *Str8t Edge* and *Sayonara, Wacko.*"

"He is?" Darren stepped onto the balcony off the master bedroom, his hand sweaty around the phone despite the cool evening air.

Toby King was just the sort of director Darren had admired in film school in Austin: artful but unpretentious, avidly independent, opposed to the corrupting, repressive forces of big studios. The two movies Toby had already released, *Green Water* and *Magnanimous,* were huge hits on the festival circuit and critical darlings. Darren had loved them both. The director's upcoming picture, *Equus Revisited,* a modern riff on the seventies play *Equus,* was hotly anticipated.

"Absolutely," Aspen said. "He first saw *Str8t Edge* in Telluride and was blown away. So he looked you up, got his hands on *Sayonara, Wacko*, and put you on his short list of potential future DPs. Are you currently on a project?"

"I'm not, actually," Darren said. The last thing he'd done was *Str8t Edge,* the twenty-four-minute short film funded by his wife and screened at a few festivals. More than two years ago. He was proud of it, but suddenly embarrassed that it was his most recent work.

"Fantastic," said Aspen. "Toby will be out in L.A. this week, so I'll set up a meeting. Does Tuesday work for you?"

"Definitely," said Darren. He paced back inside the house and sat down in the soft leather reading chair in the corner of the bedroom.

"If things go well, we'll need you in Oaktree, Florida, on Friday. Production will start immediately, and Toby'll want you on location ASAP. He's got a unique methodology, really awesome."

"I've read about it," Darren said, remembering the profile of Toby the *New York Times* had run just after *Green Water* was released. Toby's approach to filmmaking was to have his cast and crew live in close quarters during shooting with very limited contact with the outside world. He enforced minimal phone and Internet usage, and permitted no visitors.

"Production's scheduled for a hundred days," said Aspen.

Darren stood up from the chair. "A hundred days?"

"Toby believes in shooting slow. He's meticulous. Do you have a scheduling conflict?"

He pressed his fingertips into the top of his head. Robin's treatment. Their plan. The syringes and vials of liquid hormone they'd picked up at Rite Aid that morning, stowed in a bathroom drawer. Ready for action as soon as Robin's body decreed it, which, according to the charts she kept of her cycle, would be in nine days. He'd need to be available for action, in person.

They'd laughed about it yesterday, after the visit to Dr. Amazo, how it'd be like a second honeymoon, and that they'd do everything possible to not make it feel like obligatory, goal-oriented sex. Even talked about picking up some toys, watching a porno — stuff they hadn't done in ages. They'd gotten tingly in the car, smack in the middle of standstill traffic on the 405, her hand kneading his inner thigh.

Robin had been patient — with his chronic lack of direction, and with her own body. Asking her to wait another three-plus months would not be simple. So much of her happiness — and thereby his own — was pinned upon this window of time.

But DP for Toby King. It would be a complete game change for his anemic career. Surely he and Robin could work something out.

"No scheduling conflict," he said to Aspen.

"Great. I'll text you the details for the meeting with Toby on Tuesday, okay? To this number?"

He cracked a beer and returned to the balcony, pulling on a fleece and grabbing his laptop. The March night was chilly and clear, and a fat yellow moon had risen. The shush of the ocean was soothing, but he couldn't get his fingers to stop trembling on the keyboard as he researched *Equus Revisited*. Aspen had been light on details, and he needed to know as much as possible before he hit Robin with the news when she got home from yoga, any minute now.

"Holy shit," he said as he scanned the film's IMDb page and learned that Marina Langley was one of its three stars. The other two, Heather di Notia and Ven Peebles, were both well-known actors in their late forties, past the peak of their popularity. Marina Langley, on the other hand, was in her early twenties and booming in Hollywood. Having her as a star meant that *Equus Revisited* might pull in a mainstream audience, beyond

Toby King's usual fan base of sophisticated urbanites. It meant that this movie might not only transform Darren's career, but set it on fire.

As his excitement rose, so did the messiness of his sudden opportunity to work for Toby King. He thought of Robin, so eager for him to administer her injections of hormones each night, joking in anticipation about her "follicles being stimulated" and feeling her "progesterone levels shoot up!" She was scheduled to ovulate next week, exactly when Aspen Green said he needed to be in Florida. Exactly when he needed to be at home, in bed with his wife.

He couldn't go to Florida. *But,* a louder voice in his head argued, *he* had *to go.* Robin's words at the fish shack last week had stuck with him. *Your little projects.* The suggestion that he wasn't game for hard work. Of course, she'd been speaking of the hard work associated with having a baby, but Darren couldn't shake off the larger implication that he was generally complacent. Until that afternoon at Jupiter's, it hadn't occurred to Darren that anyone, other than his money-worshiping, dismissible father-in-law, perceived him that way. The notion that his own wife, and possibly the rest of the world, might view him as lazy had rattled him.

True: he hadn't worked much in the way of a "day job" since he and Robin married. But, as she'd been the first to point out, why would he bother with the artless drudgery of making commercials if he didn't have to? Thanks to Robin's family, they certainly didn't need the money. Robin had encouraged him to do what he loved. She claimed not to care about money or traditional "accomplishment." And what Darren loved was playing with images, capturing motion and shape and color on camera, letting them emerge into a story. That was his process; he didn't believe in preconstructing a narrative and then plugging in the visuals to support it. He let the visuals guide him to a story. Which could take a long time, if it happened at all. This was why, in the four years since he'd met Robin, he'd completed only two short films, one of them, *Sayonara, Wacko*, just six minutes. It didn't mean he hadn't been working hard. He was constantly working: shooting, layering effects, experimenting with sound, cutting. The outside world just wasn't aware of it.

Since his fight with Robin at Jupiter's, he'd been thinking it was time for him to earn some conventional respect in the world. Women had a panoply of options for earning this: careers, beauty, happy marriages, babies. Any of those alone was an official signifier to society that she'd contributed something worthwhile to the world. Men's options were more limited: they needed power, prestige, or money to earn official approval. Darren had the latter, technically, but everyone knew he hadn't earned it. He'd simply married into the Justus family. Become an artist supported by his wealthy wife. This had never bothered him; he didn't subscribe to the warped value system of the larger culture. Neither did Robin. Or so he'd thought.

If not for the afternoon at the Malibu fish shack, Darren might have told Aspen Green no. That he had other priorities at the moment. But now, Darren viewed the sudden opportunity differently: if he let the Toby King job slip away, he'd continue to have accomplished nothing "real."

Yes, he would take the job. It was just a few months in Florida. Perhaps he could schedule some flights home according to Robin's ovulation cycle. Maybe Toby King was a more flexible guy than he'd been portrayed in the articles Darren had read.

As he felt the decision solidify in his mind, the reasonableness of it, he began to get truly exhilarated. He was a week away from working for Toby King. From shooting Marina Langley!

Marina Langley had been an indie darling in her early teens. She disappeared to go to college, and resurfaced a few years later to star in the Horizon trilogy about a society of doomed mermaids and mermen forced to enter the world of regular humans after ecological destruction of their remote portion of ocean made it uninhabitable. The films were huge hits, and Marina was now one of the most sought-after actresses in the industry. She was a solid actress, and also absurdly beautiful, a rare hybrid of willowy and lush, with dark eyes and pillow lips; recruited by Ford Models when she was a teenager, she squarely rebuffed them. "I had zero interest," she'd told *Vanity Fair*. "For me, acting is like that Rilke quote about writing. I don't live to act, I act to live."

"Straight from her publicist's mouth," Robin had said, rolling her eyes.

The press had dubbed Marina Langley a young Angelina Jolie. But she was more attractive than Angelina, Darren thought, because she projected an open, accessible quality, instead of the guarded aloofness of older female stars like Angelina, who were always pursing their lips and gazing off into the distance. In photos and interviews, Marina was earnest and expressive, bordering on awkward, despite her beauty.

She'd told Charlie Rose, "Hollywood is just a place to me. It's where I happen to work. Not some exclusive, glamorous club."

Her humility was appealing. Honest. Un-celebrity-like. Last year, at a dinner party Robin's friend Jackie threw, they'd all gotten drunk on mojitos — Robin and Darren; Jackie and her then girlfriend, Monique; Eva and her husband, Troy — and Jackie had forced them all to answer a host of inappropriate questions, including: Who would you sleep with if your S.O. gave you a pass?

Robin said Clive Owen.

Sober, Darren would have said Vivian Clark, the British actress in her fifties who still wore bathing suits on camera and looked amazing. Robin would have liked that answer. But he'd had three mojitos, and he said Marina Langley.

"You stole my answer!" Jackie had said, throwing a piece of bread at Darren.

"How original, you two," Robin had said. "I think I might throw up." It was unclear whether she'd been referring to Marina Langley or the amount of rum she'd consumed.

Darren hoped Robin wouldn't remember his answer. It was a stupid little thing, but a detail he didn't need in the mix when he broke the news of his new job offer to Robin.

As the night air cooled, he sat with his laptop on the balcony and reread the *New York Times* profile of Toby when he heard the front door opened and Robin call out, "Namaste, honey! You upstairs?"

"Up here!" he said, clicking his laptop shut and going inside, sliding the glass door closed behind him.

"Hel-*lo!*" Robin half skipped into the bedroom. She looked so happy, loose and relaxed in yoga pants and a stretchy tank top, cheeks pink from recent exertion.

"Baby," Darren said, pulling her to him and holding her. She felt soft — almost plush — against him. If a person could feel fertile to the touch, Robin did. He closed his eyes and breathed the mild tang of her sweat, trying to stave off his nerves, which were heightened by his wife's ignorance that he was about to topple her great mood.

She burrowed against him. "I just had the most amazing yoga class."

"I'm so glad."

"I'm starving. Let's go downstairs and eat. I got this insane Manchego from the cheesemonger this morning."

"Sure," he said. "But first, I have some news."

Robin pulled out of their embrace and studied his face at arm's length. "What?" she said, curious. But also suspicious. She was on to him already.

"Can we go downstairs and sit down?" He took her hand and pulled her toward the stairs. She didn't budge.

"Nobody wants to hear the suggestion of *sitting down* before a conversation."

He tried to lighten his tone. "Can we go downstairs and stand up then?"

She moved past him to the bed and plunked down on it. "Okay, hit me. What is it?"

He sat down beside her, both of them facing the large abstract painting on the opposite wall, its oceanic colors failing to calm him. "I got a job offer today, Robs. A *big* offer."

"Oh!" Robin gave a few bounces of relief. "Honey, that's great! Tell me everything."

He spoke quickly, wanting to get it all out. "Good news first: it's DPing a feature. Directed by, get this, *Toby King*."

"Toby King? Whoa."

"I know! Apparently, he's a big fan of my shorts."

"See!" Robin said, triumphant. "Have I not been saying for years how obviously talented you are? That's amazing, Dare. Tell me all the details."

"Well . . ." Darren forced himself to look her squarely in the eyes. "That's the thing. Primary location is some horse farm in Florida. Shooting starts this Friday. For about three months."

"*This* Friday?" The excitement drained from her voice. "In Florida? Why so fast?"

"The original DP just quit, a week before production was scheduled to start. Toby's assistant just called me out of the blue an hour ago. They need me right away. Three months is nothing. And I'm going to try to come home when it's time to —"

"It'll never happen," she cut him off. *"Never.* Toby King runs his sets like Alcatraz. He's famous for being inflexible — no visitors, no Internet — like some sort of fascist art camp. And for going way over production schedule. You'll be gone four months, minimum."

"Who knows? Even Toby King has to take a day off; it's SAG regulation. And even if I can't, you'll still be able to get good and fertile, and the second I get back, we'll pull the trigger. That's the worst-case scenario. We've waited this long. What's another three or four months?"

She burst into tears. "A lifetime, that's what!"

"Can't you agree it's an amazing opportunity?"

"Yes! Of course it is! But why right now, right this second? Why couldn't you have made this happen sooner? You've had years, Darren."

"This sort of break *takes* years to get."

"But it just fell into your lap!"

"Robin, you've been encouraging me to do more with my work forever. Remember our fight at Jupiter's? That wasn't lost on me, you know. I want you to respect me. I want to have a professional life beyond tooling around with my own stuff."

Robin threw up her hands. "Of course I respect you! God, Darren, I think the effing world of you. I was just pointing out, from an emotionally volatile state, I might add, that you seemed a little complacent. *About having a baby.* Not about your work!"

"Well, maybe I've been coasting on every front in my life. And now I have the opportunity to get serious about my career. To make myself professionally respectable."

"But I've been telling you for years that we can put money into a movie, if you wanted to make one! You've been sitting on the potential for this 'respectability' for ages! And now, just because Toby King snaps his fingers and says you're his runner-up choice for DP and need to hop on a plane tomorrow, you're all for it? Just when I need you here more than I ever have?"

"First of all, Robin, you know as well as I do that throwing money at some pet project of my own is completely different from working with an established director."

"Of course I do! But if you'd been a little more ambitious, and a little more willing to spend our money — that's *our* money, Darren, not mine — you might be in a totally different spot right now."

"Well, I'm not!" He stood up angrily and crossed the room to the sliding glass door. He opened it, needing air. "For whatever reason — let's pin it on my motivation problems — I'm nowhere right now, professionally, and an opportunity to get somewhere has presented itself."

"Opportunity is *always* present."

"Jesus, you sound just like your father! Maybe I should just start selling real estate!"

Robin covered her face with her hands and fell quiet. Then she spoke from behind her fingers.

"I'm sorry. I do sound like my dad. Really, Darren, I'm so happy for you. I really am. I just wish the timing wasn't so awful. That's all. I want you to take the job. Just not right this second. I — I —" Her voice cracked, and she took a ragged breath. "I just wish I could get pregnant first."

Instantly, Darren felt his resolve soften. When Robin was vulnerable and honest like this, he wanted nothing but to be in alignment with her. He went back to the bed, sat, and put his arms around her. She leaned in and continued to cry softly.

"I feel like a jerk," she said. "Even suggesting that you shouldn't go."

"No, no, no, you're not," said Darren. "You're completely right. I've had years to make something like this happen. I'll tell Toby no."

Robin wrested from her huddle against him. "No! You've got to go. I will not be the sort of wife who forbids her husband something he wants this much. I'll hate myself."

"You won't. It's okay, really. I'll call Toby's assistant now and tell her."

"You will not." Her voice was resigned but firm. "You're going to Florida, period."

He knew she was right.

9

ON THE NIGHT Darren broke the Toby King news, Robin hadn't been able to sleep. That Darren had dropped off minutes after his head hit the pillow felt like a minor insult; she knew it was a clichéd pattern of gender — the man snoring, the woman tossing and turning — but she couldn't help feeling incredulous that he was able to fall asleep so easily after the evening's turn of events.

Past eleven, she'd kicked the light down comforter off, feeling constricted, and cracked one of the west-facing windows open to hear the nighttime ocean. She concentrated on the distant whoosh of the waves and Darren's slow, steady breathing, hoping the two rhythms would lull her to sleep, but she remained wide-awake. She reached over and touched his head lightly, his thick hair soft and dense under her fingers. She loved her husband. Unquestionably. He was sweet, thoughtful, attentive, always noticing details that other husbands wouldn't, remembering when they were out of soy milk or toilet paper, built shelves in her office, kept her bike tires filled with air and her Prius gleaming.

Up close, Darren was practically perfect. In the big picture, less so. He wasn't much of a long-term planner. He'd gone to film school at the University of Texas for cinematography, and had built a distinctive reel of projects that got him plenty of freelance work in his twenties; but by the time Robin had met him, he'd never really pushed past the small-scale gigs that fell into his lap. Shorts, unsold promos, sizzle reels for television shows that would never air. He had amazing instincts behind a camera and in the editing bay. He'd been teaching himself some animation programs, too, which he could lose himself in for hours. Darren was talented, but not ambitious. He preferred staying up late working on his own projects, arty little segments that Robin didn't really understand. Trippy-looking waves crashing on the beach. Boulders rolling down the street. "Visual art." Cool to look at, but what could he do with it?

Robin didn't understand why he didn't funnel part of his energy for pet projects into shopping his reel around town, making contacts, all the stuff you needed to do to be successful in the film world. It had nothing to do with making money; it was about honoring his obvious potential. Robin had told him a million times that she'd support funding a serious film project of his. If only he'd come up with an idea, lend some real focus to his passion, he'd have every resource at his fingertips.

After all, why had she worked so hard to access her trust fund, if not to use the money however she pleased? Mel Justus had built one fortune in commercial real estate and a second in venture capital, and as his only child, Robin had always been set for life. The technicality was Mel's stipulation that she could not access her trust unless she'd proven capable of earning her own money. Not by working for someone else, as Mel did not believe in working for other people, but by starting a business of her own.

And so he'd made a deal: Robin could go to college anywhere she pleased, on Mel's dime, with his Visa tucked into her wallet, so that she could focus exclusively on her studies and on the college experience. She hadn't chosen Berkeley to intentionally rankle her mother, but it had. A state school! Even if it was the best in California, Linda was disappointed.

(Once, when she was a senior in high school, she'd overheard her mother say to someone on the phone, "Well, at least your daughter isn't a communist," because she was going to Berkeley instead of to Yale.)

Mel was less bothered: if Berkeley was what she wanted, fine. The second part of his deal was that Robin had to start her own business if she ever wanted to receive another dime from him.

"This country has changed," he'd announced in the hunter-green-walled expanse of his office, leaning back against a hefty leather desk chair. "You don't get rich from putting one foot in front of the other in some career and socking part of your paycheck away. That's a recipe for living by the skin of your teeth."

Robin sat across from him, cross-legged on a gold-and-maroon-upholstered armchair with some vague tie to Louis XIV that her mother had triumphantly won at a Christie's auction.

"Doesn't it depend on how you want to live?" she had asked. "Like maybe if you're one of the few people who doesn't live in Beverly Hills?"

But Mel was impervious to sarcasm. Wry challenges bounced off him like rubber bands.

"No, it doesn't!" he'd said. "That's the attitude that's got every other thirty-year-old in their parents' basement right now! If you want to live decently—and, no, not just Beverly Hills, Robin—this applies to goddamn Tulsa, too—if you want any sort of security, you have to think entrepreneurially."

"But what about thinking idealistically, Dad? Is that only for foolish people?"

"Of course not," Mel said. "Idealism and savvy capitalism aren't at odds. Why don't you think up a business that embraces them both? You don't have to make a million bucks off the bat, but I need to see a sound business plan, I need to see a path to growth, I need to see profit potential, I need to see an ROI."

"Dad, do you hear yourself? You just told your daughter she needs to deliver an ROI to you. That's not normal!"

"I sure as hell did say that!" Mel said. "I'm not going to sentimentalize a quarter million bucks, Robin. That's what I'm prepared to invest for you. I worked down to the bone for that money."

"In a manner of speaking."

"What?"

"It's not like you were doing any sort of manual labor, Dad. There's this strawberry farm in Watsonville I just heard about on the radio, where the workers' hands are completely flayed and they have skin cancer from strawberry-picking their whole lives. That's what I'd call working down to the bone."

"Don't bring NPR into this!" Mel pounded the air with both fists.

So many times, Robin had wanted to say, *You can keep your fucking money.* Mel wasn't the type to humor a bluff: if she was going to refuse his offer, she needed to really, really mean it. And in her heart, she meant it. Seventy percent. It was the other fraction of her conviction that kept her from not only saying

Keep your money, but also *Fuck you and your power play.* Because that's essentially what Mel was doing,

Robin imagined herself presiding over an office with muted colors and comfortable furniture, a wall of books with academic titles, a pitcher of water with floating orange slices next to the Kleenex box, a teenage girl with jutting collarbones trembling on her couch. Growing up in weight-obsessed Los Angeles had inspired her to specialize in food issues. After two semesters at Berkeley, she'd cautiously lobbed the idea at Mel: her entrepreneurial venture would be a clinical psychology practice, after she'd gotten her PhD.

"I'm not saying it isn't respectable — noble, even," he told her, spreading his arms like an eagle. "But I don't see how you'll truly monetize it, beyond having a successful practice, which could be lucrative, but will also plateau. As I've said over and over, Robin, I must see the potential not just for growth, but for *wealth-building.*" He snapped his fingers. "If you can show me that, then you will have earned the security I've built for you, and you can do whatever you want. You can hang out a shingle, you can buy a whole building and fill it up with shrinks, anything you want."

"That's a nice way to talk about a profession that requires a doctorate, Dad," Robin had said, tears constricting her throat.

Mel softened his voice. "I'm sorry, honey. I've got the utmost respect for psychology. Look at what it's done for your mother."

Robin squeezed her nails into her palm to keep from picking up the crystal Lalique horse head on the sideboard and hurling it through the window. Her mother's experience with psychology consisted of a monthly hour-long pilgrimage to Claremont to see a therapist named Rita Cooper who had authored a line of self-help books, including a few niche titles specifically devoted to the psychology of show business, making her a Hollywood darling. Dr. Cooper made the rounds of morning talk shows, and had a highly secretive client list known to include a host of A-list celebrities. When you told people in Beverly Hills that you were unavailable on a particular day because you "had to drive up to Claremont," it only meant one thing: you were going to see Dr. Cooper.

Her father kept talking. "Oversensitivity will bankrupt you, Robin. You've got to toughen up."

He did not want to hurt her, Robin believed, but he was so single-minded, he didn't know how to speak respectfully outside the parameters of his interests. Which revolved around making money. She remembered something she'd heard on the radio recently. An interview with a woman, Trixie Ozman, who'd pulled herself out of the depths of poverty — she'd been down to her last three hundred bucks, sleeping in her car — and somehow made herself a millionaire and inspirational dispenser of homespun financial wisdom to the common people. Robin couldn't remember the details of the story — how she'd gotten out of her car or made her millions from nothing — but she remembered one line she'd repeated several times over the course of the interview, with several different phrasings: "Money is freedom." "Money will set you free." "Money is not about buying things, but about liberation."

She shifted in the Louis XIV chair, feeling its velvety bristles dig patterns into the backs of her legs. Perhaps she *should* be a little tougher. It was an enormous privilege, after all, an absurd, offensive privilege, for someone, not even of legal drinking age, to have a seven-figure trust fund in her foreseeable future. There were all sorts of good things a person could do with money, Robin reminded herself. She could still become a psychologist. She could travel to Africa or India and work to empower girls there. She could help eradicate a disease.

"Okay, Dad, let's say I actually do come up with an idea you think is . . . wealth-building-y?"

"Scalable," Mel corrected.

"Okay, scalable. How long do I have to do it, before I get the trust?"

"Assuming your business gets off the ground, assuming you're a thirty-percenter?"

"Assuming what?"

"Roughly thirty percent of small businesses succeed. If you achieve that category, which is a requirement of accessing your trust, then the terms of your involvement with your company will be up to me. Your job will be to do the job you've created for yourself, and forget about the carrot I've dangled. When you get to eat it is entirely up to me." Robin heard the pleasure in his voice. He knew.

She'd spent a large part of 1997, her senior year at Berkeley, trying to come up with an idea that would satisfy her father without crippling her with self-disgust. She was determined to turn his "exercise in entrepreneurship" into something with integrity. Once she had access to her trust fund, she would make a positive contribution to the world. Robin's roommate Eva, a sweet communications major from Alabama who'd never said anything particularly enlightening to Robin before, gave her the idea.

They'd been watching TV together in their off-campus apartment, procrastinating writing papers, when they landed on an episode of *Famous at Three*, a reality show documenting the world of child beauty pageants. The tiny girls wore full faces of makeup and slinky gowns. Robin couldn't turn away.

"That's what you should do!" Eva said, sitting straight up on the chair and setting her wineglass down on the end table with a clang. She knew the pressure Robin was under to come up with an idea.

"Get pregnant and enter my kid in beauty pageants and ruin her life?"

"No! You should do something in TV."

"Oh please. How would getting on TV count as starting a business?"

"I mean *produce* a show. Or become a scout. I just read this article about reality TV scouts and how it's going to be this whole new profession, because reality TV's taking over. You could totally do it; you have the best instincts about people. Robs, I'm serious!"

The idea of starting a talent agency lodged in Robin's mind. She liked the idea of spending her days looking for potential in strangers. And because it offered the possibility of having people working under her, it just might fly with her father.

For three months Robin watched copious amounts of both regular and reality TV, and took notes. She learned how to write a business plan and wrote one. She pitched it to Mel. An hour later, his face locked in a grin; he said he would be pleased to provide the capital Robin needed to start No Princess Talent.

Her mother hated the name, said it sounded holier-than-thou, which only motivated Robin. Fortified her faith in her own instincts. Made her confident she could pull this off.

And she had.

Twelve years later, No Princess Talent had become successful, partially due to Mel's connections, but also because of the niche Robin chose. She represented young women only: girls with obnoxious stage mothers, willowy teenagers looking to model underwear (Robin steered them away from this if at all possible), starchy all-American midwestern-looking types hoping for a Tide commercial. No Princess had a small but solid client list, ranging from actresses to stand-up comediennes, and Robin had four employees: two junior agents and one senior, and an administrative assistant. Originally, she'd meant to imbue a feminist angle to her business, but her intentions had been too vague and the business too cutthroat for her to attend to her ideals. Who had time to transcend the value system of the appearance-obsessed entertainment world when there was so much work to be done, all the time, just to stay afloat?

No Princess became successful because Robin worked her ass off. She combed high school performances—dance, theater, open mike nights, dressing room areas of hip stores, and hangouts around high schools—looking for unique talent and beauty to sign. Eva did the publicity, so well that she was recruited by the Dwyer Group and moved to New York to work for them. Robin kept her on the board.

L.A. was full of generic good looks and ambitions of fame. So Robin's challenge was finding who stood apart from the herds of threaded eyebrows and blown-out hair and straight white teeth. When she couldn't stand approaching one more trio of girls who already looked famous, she realized she was looking in all the wrong places.

She switched her scouting territories to less moneyed and less white parts of L.A. Places she had only been vaguely aware of when she was growing up: Mount Washington, Boyle Heights, Pico Rivera. She'd spotted Yolanda Ruiz in East L.A. playing basketball in a city park; a few months later, going by "Yola Roo," she landed a recurring role on a popular Nickelodeon tween sitcom. Robin found girls who didn't receive her interest with entitlement, but with embarrassed and flattered surprise. Robin found she had not only an eye for talent, which wasn't so unique, but one for charisma. She became an expert eavesdropper, listening in on the conversations of interesting-looking girls at malls and burger joints and eight-dollar-mani-cure nail salons. She looked for unusual facial structures, brash accents, gapped teeth. And then, heart accelerating with nerves and possibility, she handed the girl her card.

Most of the time, nothing came of it. But when it did, well. There was the initial rush, when she met with the girl in her office, face-to-face, and knew that she'd been right: the girl had something special, something that made it hard to turn away from her. And later, when the girl landed a job, Robin's gratifi-cation was even bigger: not only were her instincts correct, but her business sense wasn't bad, either.

The work wasn't entirely pleasurable. After the excitement of the early stages of landing a client, the hunt and the court-ship and the makeovers and coaching, there was the grind of cattle call auditions and often a pummel of rejections. There were the endless pep talks Robin had to deliver to her new clients, the constant reestablishment of faith. And then, for the few girls who did become truly successful, there was the constant upkeep, even after they'd gone on to have managers and publicists: they'd whine to Robin for more work, for more money, make outrageous requests for her to sign their friends or sisters. Not to mention all the other issues that fell to Robin: several girls gained or lost dramatic amounts of weight. Oth-ers pleaded for plastic surgeries and orthodontics that would change their look and ruin their careers. Some of the girls couldn't handle even the first tastes of money and success; they'd blow their paychecks at clubs and ask Robin for grocery money. They'd stay out all night and sleep through auditions. And some had unbearable family members who called Robin at three A.M., ranting about one injustice or another.

And then, of course, there had been Lorelei. The only client Robin hadn't discovered for herself. The only one she'd signed as favor to another person: Darren. And the only one who'd been a total disaster."

"It's good to have one train wreck on your list," Gregory, the excellent senior agent she'd hired, had told Robin cheerfully, attempting to console her. Gregory had worked for a seriously high-powered, asshole-of-a-big-shot agent at CAA for ten years before Robin had lured him to No Princess, and Gregory's insider knowledge of show business and deep network of connections had proved invaluable. "Because then you can be responsible for her comeback. I had lunch with Delia Gray last week, and she said her career peaked after Bo got out of rehab and landed *The Goatman*."

"Bo Briggs is a major movie star," Robin reminded him. "Lorelei did a few commercials, then made one appearance on a cable network reality TV show. One."

"But what an appearance it was!" Gregory chucked Robin's shoulder. "That episode was the highest rated *Flo's Studio* ever. She's got nowhere to go but up. Salvage her, Robs."

Thankfully, Lorelei hadn't wanted to be salvaged, and Robin was relieved. She hadn't wanted to put forth the effort, nor had she wanted to divert time from her other clients who were already much more successful than Lorelei and who warranted more of her attention. Yola Roo, for example, who now hosted her own show on NickTeen. And Jonice White — black and gorgeous, from Pico Rivera, spotted reading a magazine in the waiting area of a Jiffy Lube — had won first place on the reality competition *U.S. Supermodel*, then went on to sign with Victoria's Secret. Robin flushed with pride when she passed a billboard featuring Jonice's ten-mile legs and signature bushy hair. And Monica Mookjai, the boisterous Thai

American comedienne, whom Robin had overheard ribbing her friends at a Dodger game, and DeeDee Sims, whom she'd seen play Frankie in a high school version of *Grease* in Compton, and who'd just costarred with the Wilson brothers in a Wes Anderson movie.

As her clients flourished, so did Robin's press coverage. The *Hollywood Reporter* ran a flattering profile on No Princess, followed by mentions in *People* and *O, The Oprah Magazine*, and a page in the *Los Angeles Times Magazine* "Women to Watch" issue. Phones at the agency rang off the hook, jamming the voice mail system with oily-sounding messages from managers. Her e-mail flooded with headshots and clips and links to portfolios. Her little endeavor had officially made a name for itself. She was able to hire a few fresh-from-college, bright-eyed junior agents and some administrative support. Last year, Robin awarded her receptionist a bonus large enough to buy a car in cash.

Now, twelve years after Eva's brainstorm on their couch in Berkeley, Robin was perfectly poised to hand the operations of No Princess Talent over to Gregory. She'd put her twenties and almost half her thirties into the business, and, at thirty-four, had almost forgotten why she'd started it in the first place. She'd become so involved in the work that she'd stopped thinking about the huge pot of money on the other side of it. Maybe she wasn't saving the world, but she was changing the lives of a few young women in Los Angeles, women who hadn't grown up in houses with "staff" in Beverly Hills, as Robin had, but in cramped, hot apartments where gunshots sometimes peppered the night. In her own little way, Robin thought, in the small hours of the morning, she was paying respects to her own roots, to the grim little life she might have led if Mel and Linda hadn't rescued her from the Inland Empire.

Yolanda Ruiz won an Emmy. DeeDee Sims was nominated

for a Best Supporting Actress Oscar. Monica Mookjai landed a permanent role on an HBO comedy.

And then Mel's secretary called Robin to say her father would like to meet with her.

Robin sat in a hard acrylic chair that had replaced the Louis XIV piece. Since their original conversation about the business, Robin's mother had supervised a complete remodel of Mel's office, replacing the wood panels with alabaster and the dark furniture in maroons and hunter greens with white leather and glass, a hushed spaceship aesthetic that bore zero resemblance to Mel's fist-pounding personality.

"Robin," he said, "you know why you're here."

"Do I?" she asked, her heart rate kicking up.

Mel rose from his chair and strode around his desk. He took her hand and guided her over to the long bench Linda's designer had installed beneath the picture window. It was hard to imagine a less cozy piece of furniture, Robin thought, as Mel eased her down beside him. Nonetheless, this physical affection from her father felt wonderful. He kept one of his arms around her as they sat. She burrowed against his sturdy yet very soft shirt, like a little girl, something she hadn't done in a very long time.

"Look," Mel said. "I'm beyond impressed by what you've accomplished. You've knocked it out of the park. In fact, you've bought the park and turned it into a superdome."

Robin started to cry. Her father had never complimented her so directly. She'd never heard him sound so proud of her.

"What's wrong, honey?" He produced a tissue from somewhere and handed it to her. "Are those happy tears?"

"Um," Robin croaked. "Yes."

"I know you thought business wasn't in your heart," Mel said. "But you've proven that you have a real gift for it, whether you want it or not. The only reason I've held back with praise is I didn't want you to get complacent. I wanted you to see No Princess through, soup to nuts." He released her from his embrace and gripped both her forearms with his large hands.

Robin's throat was too constricted with tears to say anything.

"You're done now, if you want to be. I'll give you all your access codes today and make you exclusive on all your accounts. My name will be gone from them. You're welcome to keep using my financial adviser, but it's up to you. I hope you won't let No Princess go entirely, but it's your decision."

She pulled her arms from his grasp to cover her face with her hands.

"I know this is a lot to process. You don't need to make any changes right away. Or any at all. Just because you have your money doesn't mean you should stop working. I know a business is like a baby. There's no reason you need to give it up. The agency can still thrive, whether you want to make it the center of your life or not."

"Thank you," she said.

"You'll need to be cautious, going forward," Mel said, draping his arm around her again. "People treat you differently, if they know you have a lot of money. You'll be surprised at how many people want to be your friend when you have money."

"I guess I won't get *million* tattooed on one butt cheek and *aire* on the other then."

Mel kept pontificating on the ramifications of wealth.

Later that day, Robin's mother called. "Your father told me the big news. I started to cry. Honey, I'm just so proud of you. There aren't the words for me to explain it, but—" And Linda Justus's voice actually caught in her throat. In her entire life, Robin had never witnessed this much emotion from her mother. Not when Robin had broken her arm after falling off a pony in sixth grade. Not when she'd graduated from high school, salutatorian in a class full of high achievers. Not when she'd packed up her childhood bedroom and gone off to college.

No, in the end, what made her parents weepy with pride for their daughter was when she'd proved her ability to become a wealth-building entrepreneur. When she'd proved her ability to be just like them. At first, their praise had felt good, but the more she thought about it, the more it began to upset her. They'd never gotten worked up with love for her until now. In some way, she thought, in her darkest moments, she'd had to buy their love.

10

ON THE DAY before the Justuses' annual spring equinox party, Colleen got ready to pick up her Missoni dress from Once 'n' Again, a classy tailor and consignment shop downtown, improbably run by a pair of Orthodox Jews. It had been a huge find, the one-shoulder, floor-length dress that fit her like a second skin, V-patterns jutting in metallic hues all over it, unmistakably real Missoni, not the cheap version you could find at Target. Not only was the brand practically unheard of to find on consignment, especially in Fresno, but the dress was only two seasons old and $650, a total steal considering it had retailed at around $1,800. Carl would have been aghast at the price, because he did not understand fashion at all, much less the true artistry of the piece, which Colleen knew had been knit and hand-painted in Italy, so she planned to put the $750 plus tax on her secret MasterCard that day, for the cost of the dress and alterations. She was proud of herself for using the card sparingly of late, and felt the dress was a worthy investment for the party, considering she'd be in Beverly Hills surrounded by gazillionaires who never shopped on consignment.

Her receipt said the dress would be ready after 4:00, so at 3:55 she was showered, dressed, keys to her Camry in hand.

The only problem was she couldn't find her MasterCard. Anywhere. She'd put the required $100 deposit for the dress alteration on Carl's AmEx, but charging the whole amount to the card whose statement he scrutinized each month would raise questions. Would cause a fight. She needed the MasterCard.

That she couldn't recall having seen it in weeks wasn't unusual. She hid the card from herself, sometimes, when she'd been using it frequently, swearing she'd buy nothing that wasn't Carl-friendly. She imagined he sensed it, when she was racking up the bill, even though he didn't know it existed. She'd acquired the card a half dozen years ago, when the tanking national economy had ground Carl's cabinetry business to a halt, and he'd imposed an "austerity period," requesting that Colleen spend as little money as was reasonably possible. Which, to him, meant cutting out pretty much everything but food. So Colleen had gone to the Capital One website and signed up, plucking her handsome silver card out of the mail a week later. She'd been surprised by the high credit limit they'd awarded her — $34,000 — as she'd never applied for her own card before; she'd always been just an authorized user on Carl's accounts. He'd assured her that having her name on their mortgage and car loans would build her credit, and evidently it had.

Of course, it was probably just her own paranoia that made Carl seem extra edgy about their finances right when she happened to be secretly overspending. Wasn't it? The coincidences were unsettling, though, like the time he'd grumbled, "Stopped by Whole Paycheck, I see?" when she'd come home holding a brown Whole Foods bag in each hand, even though she always shopped at Whole Foods, and he'd never said a thing. But that day, she'd picked up some dinner items right after an amazing complimentary workout — she'd never even known it was possible to target your outer glutes — with a new personal trainer named Patrick at her gym. She'd put $1,250 for twelve additional training sessions on her MasterCard, and the $58 worth of groceries on the debit card she shared with Carl.

Or the time he had joked, "Sure, if you can lend me the cash," after she'd reminded him that they really ought to upgrade the sofa — a puffy eighties-style humiliation — in their den. His comment came several hours after she'd gotten a full hard wax and electrolysis treatment at the new spa-salon over in the Old Town part of Clovis that Marilyn had recommended. The aesthetician had convinced her to try a new kelp-based body-slimming wrap that her other clients raved about. The wrap had felt nice, though it hadn't delivered the noticeable toning of her butt or waist or upper arms the aesthetician had promised. Colleen was two pounds lighter when she stepped on the scale afterward, though, and felt invigorated by the treatment. That she'd paid an additional $225 for it, on top of the $300 in waxing and electrolysis (bikini area only), was another matter, but she didn't regret it.

Carl would've blown a fuse. He could never understand why women needed these indulgences. Colleen could never adequately convey the feeling to him, the itch for a minor upgrade, and how a little wax or wrinkle freeze or teeth whitening made you feel not only prettier, but somehow a little more hopeful, as if the world had a bit more to offer. And anyway, Carl *did* appreciate the extra mile she went to keep her skin youthful and her smile gleaming, even if he wasn't aware of his appreciation. He was a man, and men were visual. Therefore, her extra expenditures were little gifts to their marriage, Colleen reasoned, viewable pleasures he enjoyed on a daily basis and should not be denied. If all it required for the upkeep of these pleasures was a minor omission on Colleen's part — the ongoing concealment of a stupid piece of plastic — well, so be it. She was hardly extravagant, anyway — she'd never even had her boobs done! Plus, wasn't Trixie Ozman, the financial guru whose talk show, *Money Girl!*, had replaced Oprah's spot on NBC, always saying how important it was for women to have their own accounts?

The MasterCard had become extremely important when Lorelei entered her senior year of high school and auditioned frequently in L.A. The competition was fierce, even for bit parts in regional television, commercial spots, and catalog modeling for butch athletic wear, and certain expenditures were imperative. In Colleen's opinion, Robin was far too conservative in her recommendations for Lorelei's professional appearance: "stay fit," "eat healthy," "take care of your skin," "be yourself." In fact, Robin's advice seemed so off the mark that Colleen sometimes wondered if Robin cared about making Lorelei successful, or whether she was just going through the motions of representing Lorelei because she was married to Lorelei's brother (half brother, though Carl opposed *half*), Colleen's son (stepson; Carl disliked *step*). Robin and Darren were so loopy for each other that Robin couldn't be trusted to focus on the talent agency she'd righteously named No Princess. Robin's moral superiority was one of many qualities Colleen disliked about her.

Robin had the connections needed to book Lorelei on closed casting calls, but Colleen was the one who knew Lorelei should have a weekly mani-pedi, regular waxing and facials, laser-based teeth whitening, cosmetic and skin care products of the highest quality, a strict workout regimen that included Pilates because it elongated your appearance, and gold-blond highlights to dissuade casting agents from simply labeling her a redhead.

Lorelei had to be well dressed and on trend. And she needed a headshot for each of a range of different looks, taken by a top photographer. Plus, there was the cost of gas for the frequent five-hundred-plus-mile trips from Fresno to L.A. and back again.

Colleen's MasterCard funded all of this. Lorelei knew about the account and that it was not to be mentioned to Carl: *Of course I'll keep it on the DL, you don't need to keep reminding me.*

Last Colleen had checked, her balance was $28,000. After that she'd stopped checking. She received a minimum payment alert, which simply texted her the lowest dollar amount she needed to pay each month. Carl would've exploded if he knew about the twenty-eight grand, but that was the thing about Carl: he didn't notice details associated with topics that didn't interest him, or to which he was opposed. And he'd been staunchly opposed to Lorelei delaying college to try to break into acting or modeling — furious, actually — so his brain declined to absorb the associated details.

The MasterCard statements were sent to Colleen electronically, with no paper trail in the mail, easy as clicking the *Go Green!* button on the Capital One website. She paid tiny portions of the balance each month with a money order, which she went to the post office to get with the cash she'd withdrawn in unsuspicious increments from the ATM. She enjoyed the whole ritual. It felt old-fashioned. Almost virtuous.

Not that she wasn't conflicted. Yes, Trixie Ozman championed wives having their own accounts, but she also said, "All financial dishonesty stems from emotional dishonesty." Once Colleen had cut the card up, but she'd ordered a replacement the next week. Since then, she'd just taken to hiding it from herself. She had so many different hiding spots for it: wrapped in a pair of tights at the back of a drawer, at the bottom of a sleeve of Q-tips under the bathroom sink, in a boxed deck of cards at the bottom of a file cabinet in the office. Sometimes, when she managed not to use it for a stretch, she forgot where she'd put it, and had to ransack the house while Carl was at work.

On the day her Missoni dress was ready, though, she simply couldn't find it. She'd spent the better part of two days looking, utilizing crumbs of Performa to keep up her commitment to locating it. After she'd checked every possible hiding place, down to the inside of a cowboy boot deep in the back of her closet, it was almost six o' clock. The store closed at seven, she remembered, so she'd just have to use Carl's AmEx to cover the balance she owed Once 'n' Again for the Missoni plus alterations. Otherwise, she'd have nothing to wear to the party. She'd figure out how to deal with the consequences later, when Carl's bill showed up.

At 6:20, she pulled the Camry into the store's empty parking lot. The orange-and-brown sign was clearly visible from the driver's seat, but she got out of the car anyway, pressed her face against the glass storefront, and knocked and knocked.

The store's unlit interior stayed silent. Colleen's memory had been correct: Once 'n' Again closed at seven. Except on Fridays, when it closed at six and didn't open again until Sunday. Back in the car, Colleen punched the steering wheel hard with her fist, chewing her lip to fight the tears. The horn let out a short, weak honk.

11

"PROMISE YOU WON'T disappear," Robin's mother said, when they were getting dressed for the equinox party in Linda's over-mirrored bathroom, which had more seating than the average person's living room. "It's rude. You're a partial hostess."

"I'm not," Robin said, tugging on the dress she'd bought for the party after spotting it in the window of a boutique on Montana Avenue. She almost never tried clothes on before buying them, and was usually good at it; but this dress already felt too tight around her midsection without having been zipped. Perhaps she'd willfully overlooked the consequences of the comfort snacking she'd been doing since Darren left town.

"I don't live here, Mom," Robin said. "I didn't lift a finger for this party. If I'm a hostess, then May May is, too." Her parents' housekeeper — also her childhood nanny — had been preparing for the event for weeks and had probably been working from the crack of dawn that morning, making sure the caterer and florist and equipment crew left no trace.

"Don't start with me on May May," Linda huffed as she examined herself in one of the half dozen *pieces* that she was considering wearing that evening. This one was a sleeveless lavender dress that bared her slim shoulders and cascaded down her body in layered tiers of silky fabric, landing mid-calf. "What do you think?"

"Reminds me of a flapper."

"Exactly. The twenties were Joliet's inspiration."

Joliet LaBouche had been designing custom pieces for her mother for as long as Robin could remember. Linda turned a 360 in the mirror, unnecessarily, as the bathroom was designed to enable a viewer to see herself from all angles without moving her head. Just stepping inside it made Robin queasy, both the unapologetic devotion to vanity, and the way it forced her to confront every one of her physical imperfections. To Darren, she referred to the bathroom as her mother's Chamber of Worship.

Standing next to her mother among multiple reflections was a glaring reminder to Robin that they were not related by blood. The mirrors revealed every discrepancy: Linda's olive skin and green eyes, her statuesque frame that was remarkably fit and trim for sixty, thanks to a lifetime of exercise and pampering. Versus Robin's dark hair and dark eyes behind glasses, her ample curves and milky complexion. As she looked at her mother, the former actress, in her lavender Daisy Buchanan dress, the familiar, depressing thought entered Robin's mind: *Who is this woman?*

"I don't think it's age appropriate, Mom," Robin said. "No offense."

"Hmm . . ." Linda stuck out her arms and swiveled her torso from left to right and back so that the purple layers of fabric flared out, making the dress look as if she'd woken it up. "Joliet is usually very sensitive to my age. What's appropriate does change from season to season."

"I disagree," Robin said. "But who am I to challenge Joliet?"

"Right," Linda said, stepping into a pair of green open-toed heels, also too youngish. "I would never have chosen this color of shoe myself. Did you know Louboutin even worked in green? But Joliet always says you should be right on the border of your comfort zone for a party."

"Profound," said Robin.

"Please don't be grouchy," Linda said. "I know you're having a hard couple of weeks, but there's no need to take it out on me." Her eyes roved over Robin's black dress. "What other options did you bring?"

A hard couple of weeks. The limit of her mother's perspective never failed to amaze her. Her ability to ignore the parallels between her own history of alleged infertility and Robin's. Her refusal to commiserate and offer wisdom.

"Zilch," said Robin, the anger rising like hot vapor to her face. She turned her back to her mother. "Can you zip me up?"

"Seriously?" Linda said, tugging at the zipper. "You didn't bring any plan Bs?"

"No." Robin felt the fabric of her dress constrict her stomach and breasts as her mother closed up the back. The hormone shots were probably making her bloat. It had only been a little more than a week, but Darren's absence had been even harder than she'd expected. Without him, her parents were unbearable. He was her ally. He was her family.

"I can call Joliet," her mother said. "I'm sure she could bring you over some pieces."

"What's wrong with this one?" Robin asked. "It's a little too tight, sure, but the fabric is good, and I like the three-quarter-length sleeves. They make my arms looks smaller. You know I don't like my arms."

"I wish you'd just let me get you some sessions with Trey," said Linda, unzipping her own dress down the length of her side. Trey was her personal trainer and an essential source of local gossip. "He could take care of your arms in a month."

"My arms are taken care of, thanks," Robin said, stretching her hands over her head to make sure the tight dress allowed enough range of motion

"Look, your dress is fine," Linda said. "It's just that it's business-y, not festive. This is a celebration of springtime we're going to, not a board meeting."

"I like it. I'm going to wear it."

"I don't have time to argue. But at least wear Spanx underneath. I'll lend you some."

Linda stepped out of her heels and walked out of the bathroom into her attached closet, big as a studio apartment, to select one of the many pairs of flesh-colored, modern-day corsets. She knew better than to ask whether Robin had brought her own.

12

TRAFFIC CRAWLED THROUGH the San Fernando Valley. Colleen and Carl had left Fresno late and the Justuses liked to start early; the party would be in full swing by the time Carl and Colleen arrived. But Colleen was grateful for the congested freeway. She wasn't ready for the Justuses yet. She'd been up half the night, trying on the many dresses Marilyn lent her in place of the Missoni, all of them expensive but dowdy and too big, and finally rooting through Lorelei's closet until she'd found the silk-twill Marc Jacobs one of the gazelles—a girl named Paige with horsey teeth and cankles—had loaned Lorelei. The dress was a deep Chinese red patterned with white curlicues and bibbed with white floral embroidery around the neckline. It was pretty, but a touch too girlish; Colleen worried people would think she was trying too hard to look young. But it was the best she could do.

"So I'll bid next week," Carl said, as he steered the Camry through the sludgy traffic, punching the horn as a red Audi cut in front of them. "And keep our fingers crossed. This job would be huge." He'd been telling her about a large new cabinetry project he was trying to land, in the new house of a Silicon Valley multimillionaire, a vacation mansion on a ranch, right outside Sequoia National Park.

"I hope you get it," Colleen said, staring out at the familiar freeway scenery: In-N-Out Burger. Car dealerships. A franchise technical college. The sun was beginning to drop, the sky hazing to the color of a dingy pearl.

It was hard to pay attention to what Carl was saying. She'd gotten excited about his *huge* jobs in the past, only to be disappointed when construction delays, unreliable workers, and fickle clients interfered with Carl's net profit, leading him to grant Colleen only the most necessary of her desired lifestyle upgrades: yes to new tile on the bathroom floor, which was cracked and damaged in sections; yes to a stainless steel refrigerator because the old one hummed and leaked; yes to the new eco-friendly washer/dryer combo. No to a new car, to new furniture, to new bedroom and living room carpet. He claimed they couldn't afford such extras.

"If I win the bid, you could come with me. We haven't been up to the Sequoias forever," Carl said. "I'll need to stay up there for the first week of the job. Maybe ten days. Owner's paying for the motel. After that I'll commute."

Motel. Not hotel. Colleen knew this was probably Carl's preference; he wouldn't ask an employer to put him up somewhere too nice.

"What would I do by myself all week?" She'd traveled with Carl to job sites before and hadn't enjoyed herself. He was always too stressed and tired, working under tight construction deadlines. He seemed to only want her there for his own comfort, the way a child carried a special blanket, and this made Colleen resentful.

"Hike. Rent a mountain bike. Curl up by the fire in the lodge."

"But we wouldn't be staying in a lodge. Also . . ." She almost added, *What if Lorelei needed me, and I was stuck up in the mountains?*

"Also what?"

"You'd be working long hours the whole time, and I wouldn't get to see you, and I'm just not an outdoorsy person. You know that."

"I know, I know," he said. But he didn't sound completely okay with it.

She reached over to rub his knee. "I really appreciate the invitation."

They'd crossed the Sepulveda Pass, which lifted them out of the Valley suburbs and down into real Los Angeles. Traffic picked up. Colleen stared up at the Getty Museum, hulking in the hills like a massive khaki crown, a sign that they were almost at the Wilshire exit, which would lead them to Beverly Hills.

Colleen's stomach turned sour and knotty. She pulled out her makeup travel case and lowered the visor mirror to check herself. Even if the dress wasn't perfect, she looked good. The laser resurfacing she'd had a few weeks ago had worked: hardly a trace of the shadows of sleeplessness that had begun to frame her eyes, the spider wrinkles around her mouth and eyes barely perceptible, her cheeks rosy and poreless. Her skin tone was excellent, with just a touch of gold from the BronzeLite treatment her aesthetician had talked her into getting. Completely natural looking, superior to the new pigmentation treatment everyone was getting lately that left their skin looking like Peking duck.

Carl thought Colleen spent too much time and money on her appearance, and that it was absurd she occasionally missed dinners to attend Intensive Pilates. But he didn't understand. It wasn't mere vanity. Pulling down the mirror and seeing her face lineless and glowing, or feeling her trim, fatless frame move beneath the Marc Jacobs designed for a twenty-year-old, got her through events like the party ahead, in cavernous rooms with impossibly rich people whose children were entertainment lawyers and movie producers, people who would nod slowly with faux interest and swirl their wine when Colleen told them, "My daughter works in television, but she's taking a little time off," assuming she meant that Lorelei either couldn't get a part or was in rehab. They never asked, "Oh? Time off doing what?" — Colleen's vagueness suggested the unpalatable topic of failure — but flitted their eyes past her, planning their exit.

She was thinner and fitter than nearly everyone she came into contact with, even many of the gazelles, so gifted with youth and good genes they didn't bother with exercise. Colleen could already detect the consequences in their skinny-soft arms and the slight wobble of their upper thighs when they wore string bikinis. Colleen's own taut arms and thighs helped her through nights like last Wednesday, when she'd been up at three A.M. picturing Lorelei dead in a Dumpster, the Zenzo feckless against her imagination. Finally, she'd gone into the bathroom, stepped out of her nightgown, and stood staring at herself in nothing but panties in the full-length mirror, amazed at how good her body looked. Even at forty.

She could never explain this to Carl. While he regularly complimented her on *looking great*, he could never understand the time and effort she put forth to achieve her appearance, or the layers of gratification she experienced from maintaining her strict diet and exercise routines, and her lineup of monthly appointments.

"Colleen?"

They'd exited the freeway now and were clipping through

tidy neighborhoods lined with Mediterranean-style homes, the blocks getting nicer as they drove north toward the hills, the lawns wider, the houses larger and set farther back from the street. The richer you were, the more privacy you got.

"Colleen!"

"What?" She snapped the visor shut and pushed it up.

"I'm sorry. We're here."

In the circular driveway of the Justuses' house — Mediterranean revival, Darren had explained to Colleen, while Lorelei called it "Spanish tacky" — Carl handed the valet the keys to their Camry. That was a great thing about a valet: they made your car, the crappiest one at the party, disappear. As an attendant helped Colleen from the passenger side, the lightest sprinkle of mist from the nearby lit-up fountain grazed her face, and the new evening air felt soft and fresh on her bare skin. Carl offered his arm to her and she took it, appreciating how handsome he looked in the outfit she'd chosen for him: gray light wool pants and a blue dress shirt in gorgeous Italian cotton, both by Bonobos, a few hundred dollars each, charged to her MasterCard and worth every penny. At six-foot-two with his curly, reddish-gold hair still plentiful and only a hint of thickness around his midsection, Carl looked good for fifty-five. If only he'd take better care of his fair Irish complexion, which had weathered and ruddied from so many years in the California sun. Still, for the moment, Colleen was proud to be on his arm.

"This will be fun," she said, smiling up at him, as they stepped along a walkway lined with dense, curly bushes tamed into uniform shapes.

"Sure," he said.

At the oversized double front doors, recessed beneath a cream-colored archway, a willowy girl welcomed them with a tray of champagne. Colleen accepted; Carl declined.

In the great room, forty or so guests drank from slim flutes or enormous wine baubles, happy and relaxed, planning to stay a long while. The light was bright enough to make out faces from a distance, and low enough to flatter. Colleen took quick inventory of the designer dresses, and was pleased to find no dress resembling hers, and no one thinner than her. She pulled Carl over to a long buffet table to examine a cornucopia of decadent party snacks, each labeled with little silver-framed placards: NOVA SCOTIA + CRÈME FRAÎCHE & DILL, DUCK CONFIT + FONTINA ON PUFF PASTRY, MATZO BALL SOUP. The soup glistened in individual tureens, each with a miniature, starchy orb in the center, swimming in broth. Reflexively, the calculations began in Colleen's mind: probably a good 500 calories in the mini-soup, a whopping 800 in the puff pastry concoction. And these were just the snacks; never mind the entrées that would appear later . . . She felt a threat of fatness, just looking at the spread.

"No one's eating yet," Carl said. "Should I break the seal?"

"No!" Colleen said. "Wait a while. We just walked in."

"I'm hitting the head, then."

She found an inconspicuous spot by the wall, and plucked a Zenzo from the liner pocket of her clutch, a metallic gold Hermès borrowed from Marilyn. She made sure it was purple and round and not white and oblong, like the Performas she'd also stashed there. Those were for later, when she needed energy. Right now, she needed to relax. She pinched it in half between the tips of her acrylic nails — subtle French manicure acrylics — dropped half back in the pocket and swallowed the other.

Then she heard Linda Justus trill, "Favorite!" Colleen turned to see the party's hostess trotting toward her on the balls of her Louboutin heels, arms spread wide. Linda called everyone "favorite" — friends, acquaintances, members of her staff — which had perplexed Colleen enough to ask Darren if he knew why his mother-in-law used such an insincere term of endearment. He had, in fact, known why: during one of her breaks from Berkeley, Robin had come home and demanded her mother stop calling everyone "honey" or "baby."

"It's about time!" Linda sang, pulling Colleen into a fragrant embrace. "I just ran into Carl and had to come find you."

"Sorry we're so late!" Colleen said, cheek kissing her. "Getting through the Valley was brutal."

"You look gorgeous," Linda said, touching the embroidered white flowers at Colleen's collarbone. "This piece is made for you. It's Marc, isn't it? And how are you so thin?"

"I'm not, but thank you," Colleen said, feeling a current of satisfaction. It was comments like these that made her vigilant diet and brutal workouts worth it. "You look amazing yourself, honey," she said, an overstatement. Linda looked very good for sixty, toned and trim, but her lavender flapper-esque dress was too playful, so evocative of youth that it actually made her appear older. Colleen reached out and touched the silky material. "This dress is gorgeous. What a stunning party."

"Thank you! It's so much fun for us. Oh, you need a fresh drink, don't you? The Kassels brought a petite sirah from their vineyard that just feels so alive in your mouth, but not too brazen, so interesting for such a young wine. Ask the bartender for the Kassel 2008 Reserve." She lifted her glass in the direction of the bar.

"I'll do that," Colleen said.

"And then come find me." Colleen was always having to come find Linda, give Linda a call, let Linda know when Colleen's calendar was free. At first, Colleen had fallen for it, thinking Linda actually wanted to be chummy. But after Linda's umpteenth vague invitation failed to materialize, Colleen realized that Linda simply wanted a fan club.

"Mwah," said Linda, kissing Colleen's cheek, then turning to walk away. But before she could move, a middle-aged couple and a thirtysomething guy materialized, trapping her in place.

"Neighbor!" said the older man to Linda. He had the well-kempt athleticism of a tennis coach.

"Favorite neighbors!" Linda said back, and the four of them group-hugged. Colleen took the opportunity to move on, but Linda untangled and caught her by the wrist.

"Wait, Colleen, you must meet the Hesslers! This is Valerie and Tom, from across the street. And their son, Ben." Linda reached out and gave the younger man a faux pinch on the cheek. "I've known Ben since he and Robin were *this big.*" She opened her right palm and lowered it toward the ground. "And Colleen," Linda said, grabbing Colleen's hand like a schoolgirl, "is Robin's mother-in-law."

Colleen always cringed when she watched people trying to do the math, to figure out how she might be the mother of someone Robin's age. She could tell the older two Hesslers, Valerie and Tom, with parallel preppy good looks and perfect smiles, were doing exactly that, while Ben's expression didn't change at all — he just kept smiling kindly, his teeth straight and white, not breaking eye contact with her.

"*Step*mother-in-law," Colleen said, though she could hear Carl's voice: *Don't explain yourself. It devalues our family.* "Nice to meet all of you."

"I've heard your name." Ben extended his hand. "So it's nice to encounter the real thing."

Ben was tall and loose limbed, with tousled hair, extremely handsome. He reminded Colleen of a more refined, slightly feminized version of her stepson: dark-haired and light-eyed, but thin where Darren was solid and curved and tapered where Darren was straight: Ben's nose was delicate, his cheekbones high. His hair was much longer (Darren's was always cropped short) and curly, and Ben wore glasses with severe hipster frames. If he was an old friend of Robin's, he'd probably heard all kinds of terrible things about her.

"Ben goes by Bundy now!" Valerie said.

"Whichever," Ben said, shrugging.

"Bundy's his stage persona," Tom said, air quoting *stage persona*. "He's a musician."

"How cool," Colleen said.

"Change of topic, please," Ben said.

"Where *is* my darling Robin, anyway?" Tom asked.

"Oh, she's here somewhere," Linda said. "Either that, or still primping up in her room."

"How'd the reno go on that room?" Valerie asked.

"Reno is a city in Nevada, Ma," Ben said.

Colleen tapped the shoulder of a waiter whooshing by with a tray of champagne and swapped her empty flute for a full one.

"Excuse me," said Valerie, "I meant reh-no-vay-shun."

"It went beautifully!" Linda said. "I'd love to show it to you later."

"Yes, please," Valerie said.

"I was just off to get some food," Colleen lied. "Can I bring anyone anything?"

"We're on our annual cleanse," Valerie said. "Always coincides with Linda's party."

"So inconsiderate of her!" Tom said, checking Linda with his khakied hip. The three of them burst into laughter.

"You could bring them two Cloroxes on ice," Ben said to Colleen, smiling in a way that said, *Sorry my parents are assholes.*

"Very funny, honey," said Valerie.

"I'll get myself some in a bit, but thanks, favorite," Linda said to Colleen. "Please come find me later."

"Of course." Colleen waved at the four of them as she walked away, draining her champagne.

The party had gathered into a singular thrum beneath the soaring ceiling of the great room. A woman in a tuxedo played the grand piano. The lights had dimmed, softening faces. Patches of illumination splayed up to accentuate the large, gold-framed landscape paintings on the walls, the ones made fun of by Darren and Robin. At the bar Colleen ordered the wine Linda had recommended. It tasted like liquid bacon, but after a few sips, on top of the Zenzo and the champagne, Colleen finally relaxed. She looked for Carl — he could have gone from the bathroom straight to the game room, where a group of men clustered during this party each year to watch the opening games of baseball season.

She scanned the room again: no sign of him. The guests were all arranged in sparkly huddles, diamond-heavy fingers swatting the air as the women talked and laughed. Colleen felt conspicuously alone and a wave of anger at Carl passed through her: he was doing this on purpose. He hadn't wanted to come to the party, but she'd insisted, so he was punishing her by leaving her to fend for herself. She pulled out her phone and started to text him *WHERE R U*, but then thought better of it. Why should she chase him down? So she could stand next to him in the background while he sulked and stared at some game on a giant TV? So she could smell the resentment rising off him like cologne?

Carl never wanted anything to do with L.A., and he blamed Colleen for inviting the city and its warped values into their lives. Blamed her for what happened to Lorelei. He just wouldn't come out and say it. Instead, he'd just abandon her at a party in

Beverly Hills, in a room with a chandelier that cost more than he made in a year, having to overhear phrases from other guests like "It kills me to put the Vail house on the market, but Jackson Hole is really much more us" and "James Cameron's a client, so we're headed to New Zealand for the premiere . . ." Carl's wordless way of telling her: *You want L.A.? Here you go!*

Still, despite his disdain for L.A. and its conspicuous wealth, she knew Carl wasn't impervious to envy. He was a man, after all, with an old-fashioned sense of what men were supposed to do with their lives: work hard, provide for their families, succeed and prosper. And he was probably miserable, watching sports with the sort of men who owned sports teams, men who probably reminded Carl that he was a carpenter from Fresno with a filmmaker son who'd made no real films, and a daughter who'd flickered briefly on trashy television before disappearing.

Part of Colleen wished she could go to Carl, rescue him from the sea of Armani in the den, make them have fun together. But it was far too late for that. Lorelei had created an unclosable rift between them. Parenting decisions, Colleen had learned, could be harder in a child's absence than when she was under the same roof. She and Carl had always diverged as parents — he'd been the sort of father who wanted his kids to call him "sir," who conducted inspections of chore completion before allowances were issued, whereas Colleen was more of a "companion parent," a phrase she'd read in a magazine, the sort of mother whose kids told her their secrets, who truly didn't mind doing their laundry.

When Lorelei was still in high school, she'd head straight to Colleen's bedroom on Saturday mornings to fill her in on the news of the night before — the game and the after-party she'd been to, the boy with whom she'd made out — lying on Colleen's bed, red curls splaying out from her head, ankles propped on the headboard. If she was hungover she'd admit it, always re-assuring Colleen that Jenna Conrad had driven her home, and Jenna didn't drink or have sex. As for sex, well, Lorelei in-formed Colleen that tenth grade was considered *the year,* but Lorelei had waited until eleventh, when she and Jeremy, who played goalie for varsity soccer, had been dating six months. Although it made her slightly nauseated, Colleen took Lorelei to her gynecologist for an exam and birth control pills, paying out-of-pocket with the MasterCard instead of using Carl's in-surance. It was the right thing to do.

This was the sort of parent Colleen wanted to be. She knew she hadn't been perfect. That she shouldn't have routinely tossed two six-packs into her grocery cart, Mike's Hard Lem-onade and Mike's Hard Fruit Punch, as Lorelei requested. But it was hardly even booze, Colleen told herself. It wasn't as if she was buying her a bottle of vodka. "It's okay if you don't want to, Ma, we'll get it either way," Lorelei had said. "Tess has a fake ID and Mia's parents have this giant liquor cabinet."

Of course this was true. Teenagers had been drinking since the beginning of time. Better that she control the situation, Col-leen reasoned, instead of Lorelei driving with Tess out to the shady convenience store on Old Archer Road to use a fake ID, or stealing from Mia's parents.

This was where she and Carl diverged: she wanted to be in the trenches with Lorelei, elbows linked, and he wanted to stay on a perch high above, looking down. Colleen learned, after Carl had become certain Lorelei was doing drugs, that his phi-losophy was the basic idea of Al-Anon: *Stay away. Leave your child alone to figure things out.*

It was bullshit, Colleen thought, after Carl dragged her to a meeting. Al-Anon was an excuse to be a lazy, distant parent.

Colleen swallowed the last of her bacon-wine, the tannins

103

leaving her mouth dry, and decided she was ready to talk to someone. She couldn't spend the whole party on the sidelines, waiting for Carl to emerge from hiding. She surveyed the crowd, denser and louder now, the syrupy glow from the chandelier picking up the highlights from the women's hair, and saw only one other person not immersed in conversation: Robin. Her daughter-in-law stood across the room by the buffet in an ill-fitting black dress with a shiny belt, her hair (thick, dark, and lustrous — her best feature) gathered into the world's most boring ponytail, at the base of her head as if hair were nothing but a nuisance.

Colleen would have to talk to Robin sooner or later, so she might as well take the initiative, "establish authority," as Trixie Ozman said on her show. Plus, Robin undoubtedly knew some details about Lorelei. Even though Lorelei generally shared her mother's low opinion of Robin, she worshipped her brother (half brother), older by twelve years, and Darren and Robin were spouses who told each other everything, like gossipy girlfriends. It was highly likely, and infuriating, that Robin possessed information about Lorelei that Colleen didn't.

Colleen watched Robin fill her plate, overeating as usual, and strike up a conversation with the beautiful girl who'd handed out champagne at the front door. The girl said something into Robin's ear, and Robin threw back her head in laughter. This girl looked precisely like the type of girl Robin represented at No Princess Talent; Robin had never acted that warmly toward Lorelei, had never bothered treating her as though she were more than a favor.

A conversation was in order. After a little Performa. Colleen was feeling awfully mellow from the wine and Zenzo; she needed a sharpening. Making her way to an inconspicuous spot in the shadow of the curved staircase, she extracted the Performa tablet with her right hand from her purse — no chance to break it in half — felt that it was indeed the oblong one, and got it to her mouth without even glancing down at it.

She wove her way through the crowd to the buffet to speak with her stepdaughter-in-law.

Be kind but strong. Kind but strong, kindbutstrong. A Trixie Ozman mantra.

13

BY NINE, ROBIN had endured all she could of the party. First, she'd gotten stuck listening to Jody Kassel, her mother's best friend of four decades, wax on about the vineyard she and her husband bought in Sonoma as "a retirement present to himself." Then Robin had run into her cousins from Granada Hills who still smoked cigarettes and stocked their fridge with processed deli meat. Then Tom and Valerie Hessler, her parents' jaunty across-the-street neighbors, practically mauled her with hugs, made her deliver a synopsis of the current state of her life, and told her to keep an eye out for their son, Ben.

That Ben Hessler, the boy who'd grown up across the street from her, was allegedly in attendance piqued her curiosity. Since he was four years younger, she hadn't given him much thought when she'd lived at home with her parents, cute as he was, with his thick, messy curls and guitar-strumming right on the front porch, not something people did much in Beverly Hills. From the time he was in middle school, he acknowledged her only with a single protracted nod of his head and a two-syllable "Heh-aaay," clearly on the path to greater coolness than she'd achieved.

Robin, heh-aaay.

He'd gone to Canyon Country Day from first grade through high school, like she had, but he was practically a little kid, and in an entirely different world of guitars and skateboards and video games. Until Robin left for college, her interaction with him involved little more than "heys" issued from opposite driveways across the distance of their parents' ample, landscaped front yards.

But then, when she was twenty, something happened between them. Something juvenile and stupid, but still. She was already a sophomore at Berkeley, and while she was home on winter break, Ben threw a party. He was just a sophomore in high school, all of sixteen, and had stayed home while Val and Tom were off skiing in Colorado, supposedly under the eye of their housekeeper, who lived in a cottage out back and took a sleeping pill every night at eight o'clock.

Jackie had insisted on dragging Robin across the street to the party. This was during Jackie's brief cocaine phase, before she came out — "My flaming idiot phase," as she referred to it now — and had hopes of finding some over at Ben's, where many Canyon Country older alums were going to be. Robin didn't approve, but she went along to keep Jackie out of trouble.

But she didn't stand a chance: there had been coke, plus a vast wide-open liquor cabinet and a buffet of other recreational substances. Robin had taken half a tab of ecstasy, her first and last experimentation with drugs, after Ben had convinced Jackie and her to do shots of tequila with him. Somehow, Robin had ended up alone with Ben in the Hesslers' vast backyard, in an urgent, confessional conversation, during which she'd spoken at length about having been adopted, and her lack of deep love from her parents, despite wanting to love them, et cetera, et cetera. They had kissed, and kissed, Ben murmuring about how *real* she was, and how amazing both she and the grass they were rolling in felt, and Robin saying over and over, "I feel so free, I feel so free," until Ben's girlfriend at the time, a rangy redhead who sang in his band, literally tackled them both, screaming about what a drugged-out piece of shit Ben was.

After Robin escaped the girlfriend's attack, she found Jackie half-naked in the pool and marched both of them back to her parents' house. The next day she felt worse than she ever had in her life, embarrassed to have hooked up with a sixteen-year-old, and couldn't get on the plane back to the Bay Area fast enough. She hadn't spoken to Ben since.

She'd told Darren the party story once, and they'd had a good laugh. Almost two decades had passed. Every once in a while, he'd even toss out an "I feel so free" and she'd throw a pillow at him.

From the sidelines of her parents' party, watching the gem-encrusted crowd air-kiss and chatter under the soft glow of the great room's lights, manicured hands pressed to wineglasses, lipsticked mouths pecking at puff pastry, gossip about real estate and undiscovered vacation spots flying, Robin missed Darren more than ever. Nothing made her feel more alone than her parents' crowd. No matter how privileged a life they'd given her, no matter how lovely her house in Santa Monica was, no matter how padded her bank account would remain for the rest of her life, one raw fact remained: she was not one of them.

"Champagne?" A striking girl in the all-black uniform her parents required of staff appeared with a tray of flutes, the bubbles effervescing gaily at the rims. Robin had been avoiding alcohol for the sake of fertility, but really, what was the point? Darren had promised to ask Toby King for a few travel days, but now that he was on location, he'd confessed to Robin, in a hushed, apologetic tone, that the time had not yet been "right" to broach the issue with his director.

"Soon, soon," he'd said.

"Bullshit," Robin had said, unable to restrain herself. "The time will never be right."

Toby King was not the sort of director who casually granted his cinematographer a quick vacation. She would have to accept that Darren would not be around to get her pregnant until the film wrapped in three months. But she was finding it difficult to maintain the generosity she'd felt back when she'd insisted he take the job. Especially not when her ovulation stick flashed a smiley face. Her phone conversations with Darren — only a few per week, because of the bicoastal time difference and his hectic shooting schedule — were strained and unsatisfying, nothing like their usual easy, close rapport. The unfamiliar distance between them made Robin sad, and yet she found herself unable to soften toward him, unable to stave off thoughts like *Oh, so now you finally want to work hard. Because Toby King wants you to.*

She took a glass of champagne.

"Enjoy. You look like you could use it," the server said in a heavy accent, maybe Russian or eastern European. "No offense, of course."

Robin registered the girl's dramatic, unique beauty: wide, high-planed cheeks, full brows and lips, a squarish chin with a faint cleft — features casting agents would call masculine. And then there was her body, maybe five-eleven and slim as a ribbon, and her lustrous cap of bobbed dark hair, short but girlish.

"Thanks," Robin said, taking a sip of champagne, her professional reflexes kick-started by the girl's appearance. "Are you a model?"

The girl laughed. "Oh, no. I am a student. Here from Iran for one year to study at UCLA."

As quickly as Robin's wheels had begun turning, they ground to a halt. She no longer needed to recruit unknown girls and try to make them famous. She was done with No Princess Talent if she wanted to be.

And she wanted to be.

"Enjoy California," Robin said, and walked away with her champagne, over to a table of cured meats, olives, canapés heaped with caviar, and salmon flecked with dill and capers. Her bad mood had induced a surge of hunger — she was not a woman who couldn't eat a thing when upset — and she decided to have a snack before beelining upstairs for the rest of the night. Let her mother be pissed. Robin just wanted to sleep.

She'd only eaten a few bites when Colleen pounced, in a bright red dress designed for someone half her age, silky with a neckline cut too low for Colleen's small chest. The dress's Asian style couldn't be less suited to Colleen's chemically blond hair and too-tan skin, and its whimsical, curlicue patterns contrasted harshly with the severity of Colleen's form: the sinewy arms and blade-thin torso. She was a human pair of scissors. That she had actually been pregnant once, nourished and birthed another human life, was hard to believe.

"Robin!" Colleen greeted her. "Hello, baby!"

Poor Colleen, her speech too breezy, her hair too long and blown out too straight, her cheeks and lips injected with something that gave them a clownish exaggeration against her elfin features, unnatural as a peacock's plume grafted onto the back of a sparrow.

Robin knew she should have only sympathy for Colleen, but Colleen made it impossible. She was too desperate, her energy sucking oxygen from the room. Her singular conversation topic was whether anyone had heard from her daughter, Lorelei. Which Robin hadn't, beyond Darren's report that she kept texting to ask for money. Sure, Robin had been involved with the disaster that preceded Lorelei's disappearance, but only from the periphery. What had happened was no one's fault but Colleen's.

Colleen's cherry-red lipsticked mouth was moving fast.

Robin looked past her to the stairway, just two dozen feet away. Colleen was blocking her route like a defiant cheerleader.

"This conversation doesn't feel appropriate, Colleen," Robin said.

Darren would want her to be kinder, Robin knew. "She's got nothing," he'd remind her. "Nothing."

But Robin was in no mood to do him any favors. She'd done enough.

14

COLLEEN NEEDED TO get away from the party. Desperately.

She'd spoken to Robin for only a few minutes, but the news her daughter-in-law had casually delivered smashed Colleen like a high-tide wave: *Lorelei's been texting Darren here and there.*

Lorelei was alive and intact enough to communicate with Darren. As much as this relieved Colleen, it stabbed at her, too. She'd sent Lorelei at least a dozen texts and gotten no response. Her daughter was still mad at her.

Still.

Of course, Robin would divulge nothing further. Colleen watched her recede through the crowd, kissing cheeks and side-hugging every few paces. A few hot tears leaked down Colleen's cheeks and she slapped them away.

She washed down a Zenzo crumb with two big glasses of water, and got another bauble of Kassel 2008 Reserve from a buffed, probably gay bartender and downed it in three gulps.

She crossed the great room, checking for Carl and not seeing him, to the long, wide hallway that led to the rest of the house.

There was a den, she remembered, a little pocket of a room, somewhere this way where she could rest.

With a little trial and error, opening first the door to a bathroom and then to a utility closet, Colleen found the den. The door a third open, a dim light on. She pushed the door wider and peered into the room. Someone was already there.

It was the son of the neighbors. What was his name again? Benji? Benny? He was reclined on the center of a large couch, eyes closed and head against the cushion, his loose dark curls and stubble of beard contrasting with the sleek perfection of the caramel-colored leather sectional. Headphones engulfed his ears like giant clamshells. Maybe early thirties. He resembled Darren, but handsomer, like a painter's idealized version of her stepson: the delicate cheekbones and almost feminine mouth, the broad shoulders and strong forearms, the muscled upper body rising from his narrow waist. He wore a white T-shirt, good jeans, and black-and-white-checkered Vans. Glasses with dark green plastic frames that perfectly suited his olive complexion and curly dark hair.

He sensed her gaze and opened his eyes.

"Hey," he said easily. "It's Colleen, right?"

"Sorry to disturb you."

"Bundy," he said.

"Sorry. I know. We met before."

"Want to have a seat, or you just cruising the hallways?"

"I was just trying to get a little break from the party."

"Have a seat. Twenty-six baby cows died to give this couch its buttery smoothness, so you ought to pay your respects."

"Baby cows" reminded her how Darren used to call Lorelei

111

"Baby Chipmunk." If she moved, she might start to cry, so she stood still and said nothing.

"Hey," Bundy said, sensing something. "I'm kidding. Was that offensive? Are you vegan?"

"What?"

"You look upset."

"I'm not." She sat down on the couch, a little unsteadily, but careful to leave a full cushion between them.

"What are you doing back here?" she asked.

"Just avoiding conversations about cars and the disappointment of domestic help."

"You don't like cars?"

"I don't hate them. I just hate the people who love them. Do you know Mel converted the guest house out back to a residence for his Ferrari?"

"What?"

"He made it into this luxury garage that doubles as a man-cave. Climate controlled. Big couch, big flat screen, wine cabinet, glassed-in parking space for the car with track lighting for a sexier effect. He doesn't even drive it. Just cozies up and gazes upon it. Brings all his friends back there to ogle it."

"Seriously?" Colleen hadn't known Mel owned a Ferrari. He and Linda drove various Mercedes-Benzes. She and Carl had never been invited to view the Ferrari.

"Don't look so surprised. It's Beverly Hills. Do you live around here? I got the feeling you don't. I mean that in a good way."

"Fresno." She was unnerved by his having a "feeling" about her, a minute into conversation. But pleased.

"Ah, Fresno," he said, draining the last of his drink and clinking the ice. "The Midwest of the West Coast."

"I like that," she said. "It's true." She forced herself to sit up straighter. She'd popped another Zenzo crumb in the hallway, and it was giving her the liquid, tongue-slowing feeling.

"It's a line from a song."

"Who sings it?"

Just loud enough for her to make out the words, he sang: "*I got stuck in the Midwest / Of the West Coast / Burned by the sun / When I needed it most.*" His voice was wobbly but melodic.

"Um, you do? You sing it." Musicians made her uncomfortable. Several of Lorelei's friends who used to hang around their garage, all boys, played music, spoke in coded mumbles, seemed to exist in a state of perpetual disdain. "What type of music do you play?"

"Pop-ish indie-ish rock-ish stuff," he said, leaning back and crossing an ankle at his knee. "What do you listen to?"

"Talking about music makes me nervous. I always feel like I'm saying the wrong thing."

"Fuck, I know," Bundy said, tipping his head to the right to look at her without sitting up. "'What do you listen to?' is such an obnoxious question. And anyone who judges the effect music has on another person is a flaming asshole. But I am a non-judgmental non-asshole. So tell me. What was the last song that made you really happy?"

"You'd probably hate the music I listen to. Very upbeat stuff you hear on the radio. I mostly listen to music when I exercise, so it's got to motivate me."

"Quit stalling. Name a song."

"Probably one by Minny Danvers? I never know the names. See? Bad music, right?"

"Not at all. 'More Woman Than You' is a fucking great song."

"Seriously?"

"Absolutely."

His approval of the song felt like an affirmation of her overall taste. She relaxed a little, leaning back into the couch with her legs still crossed, the peep toe of one Charlemagne pointing up to the ceiling. She'd scored the shoes off eBay last year for just $500, unworn, incredible since new Charlemagnes were always four figures. People always complimented her on them. They were gorgeous, two tones of gold, one soft and the other brash, made of delicate hagfish, a rare sort of eel, she'd learned from the seller's description, with three-inch heels. Bundy was staring at them.

"Just looking at high heels makes me tired," he said. "I know they're sexy, but man, they're like *arduous,* too."

It was nice to hear someone acknowledge this. Carl liked her high heels the way he liked her cooking—in passing, with no attention to the effort she'd put into it.

"Fucking arduous!" she said, and Bundy laughed. She felt herself lighten, the weight of Lorelei's absence and the sting of Robin's brush-off rising off her chest.

"So, Colleen, the Fresnoian. The Fresno-ite," Bundy said. "Give me the scoop on your hometown. Doesn't all the most surprising shit happen in places like Fresno?"

"Are you joking?" She needed more Performa; her head was fuzzy.

"No, no. Everyone I know lives in L.A. or New York, where so much stuff is happening all the time, it's not interesting anymore. You get numb to it. But when something happens in Fresno, it packs a punch."

"But nothing ever happens."

"Oh, come on. Isn't Fresno where that guy raised his kids exactly like farm animals, and when they were finally discovered they only knew how to moo and crawl on all fours?"

"That's not 'interesting,'" Colleen said. "That's just twisted and disgusting."

"Shit, you're right," Bundy said, waving his glass. "Clearly, I should not pontificate under the influence of absinthe." She realized he might be drunker than she was. His phone beeped and he pulled it out of his pocket. "Sorry, hang on a second." He smiled at her before turning his attention to his phone. His teeth were very white.

Like coconut meat, Colleen thought. That was the phrase the cosmetic dentist who'd bleached her and Lorelei's teeth had used to describe the results he produced. It was accurate. But she was certain Bundy's teeth had not been chemically whitened.

He finished texting and returned the phone to his pocket. "Sorry, that was my mom."

"Seriously?"

"Wondering where I am. I come home for a week, and I'm fourteen again, to her."

"How old are you?" she asked.

"Thirty-four. How about you?"

She hesitated. "Forty."

"No shit!"

"Excuse me?"

"I just can't believe you're in your forties. I thought you were closer to my age. You can slap me if you want."

"It's okay," she said, smiling to herself. She'd have to tell Patrick, her trainer, about this.

"May I interest you in some absinthe?" He leaned over and picked up a squat liquor bottle off the floor, two-thirds filled with a greenish-gold liquid.

"How come it's that color?"

"Because that's the color of absinthe."

"It looks like pee."

"Totally," he said, flashing the coconut smile. "Have some."

He handed his glass to her.

"What will you drink from?" Colleen asked.

"This," he said, raising the bottle and tipping it directly to his lips. "Burns a little, but in a good way."

She took a cautious sip. It did burn in a good way: like licorice with jalapeño. "Yum," she said.

"Cheers." He clinked the bottle to her glass. "Seriously, what's your deal? Your party-escape story?"

The topic of Lorelei rose in her like a fever.

"Basically . . ." She hesitated, but the wine and pills and absinthe had banished her inhibitions. "My daughter and I are in a fight. And I don't get along well with my daughter-in-law. That sort of stuff."

"And they're both out at the party?" He raised the absinthe bottle toward the door of the den.

"No, only Robin."

"And she's your daughter-in-law?"

"Step. Married to my husband's son, Darren."

"Where's your husband?"

She paused. "I don't know."

He set the absinthe bottle on the floor and raked his fingers through his hair. Colleen could feel his dark curls as she watched, knowing they'd be coarse but soft, like the coat of her friend Marilyn's standard poodle. Bundy's eyes were on her — all over her — and he was smiling like she'd just divulged a good secret.

"So I'm talking to Robin Justus's, let me see . . ." He touched his finger to his chin in mock concentration. " . . . stepmother-in-law! Crazy. You know, I haven't talked to Robin in a hundred years. I had a huge crush on her when we were young, like maybe eleven or twelve, and she was like sixteen with huge boobs. She was never very friendly to me."

"She was never very friendly to me, either!" said Colleen.

"Tell me more. I like hearing about family dynamics."

Colleen wanted to talk to Bundy. She really did. It wasn't only that she was attracted to him, but it was how he made her feel: like what she said was interesting and important. The opposite of how Carl made her feel, which was that she was superficial and difficult to understand.

The problem was the room was underwater. She'd finished the whole glass of absinthe, and on top of the wine and the Zenzo and without food, she'd gotten shitfaced. She just needed a Performa, to clear her head, so that she could talk to Bundy without making a fool of herself.

"Hang on a second, okay?" she said. Despite being drunk, she was able to open her purse and find the right pill without a fumble.

"What's that?" he asked. "Ecstasy?"

"What? God, no!" she said. "I'm forty, remember?"

"I was joking — relax."

"It's Performa," she said. "I have ADD. I mean HDHD."

He laughed. "HDHD? You mean ADHD?"

Embarrassment sliced through her drunkenness. "It's the absinthe."

"I'm going to venture, my new friend Colleen," he said, and she loved how it sounded, "that you do not have *HDHD*."

"Why would you say that?"

"I can just tell you were lying. It's all over your face, my dear."

She felt as if he were shining a light inside her chest. "My dear." A strange phrase — old-fashioned, husbandly — like he was already fond of her. "You're right. I just take one every once in a great while to like wake up."

"Dude, don't apologize! Who doesn't love Performa?"

"What?"

"How about this?" He moved closer to her, so only a quarter cushion separated them, leaning into his palm, his hand just inches from her leg. "You share your Performa with me, and I'll corroborate your HDHD story to anyone who asks, for the rest of my life."

She smiled back. "Okay."

He extended his hand.

"Deal," she said, and let his large, warm hand envelope hers. Then she located another Performa in her bag and handed him both pills. "Here. Have two."

"Thanks! Do you have a credit card or anything on you?" he asked. "I just walked over from my parents' house, so I didn't bring my wallet or anything."

"Why?" she said. Could he possibly know something about her MasterCard?

"Whoa," Bundy said. "Easy. I'm not going to rob you or anything. It's just that Performa is kind of a special occasion, so I prefer to ingest it nasally. If that wouldn't bother you. So I need a credit card to crush it with."

"Oh," she said. "Okay." She reached to the floor where she'd put her clutch, and pulled a Chevron gas card from the liner pocket.

"Perfect, thank you." He expertly crushed two Performas on the onyx-topped coffee table, and arranged it into three tidy lines of powder.

"Sheesh, that looks like cocaine," Colleen said. "Not that I've ever done it."

Bundy laughed. "You're awesome, Colleen." He sounded

like he really meant it. He pulled a dollar bill out of his pocket, rolled it into a tube, and handed it to Colleen. "Here you go, Colleeny."

"Oh, no, no thanks."

"Oh, come on," he said. "It's way more fun this way."

"I wouldn't even know how. I'm too old."

"Don't be insane! You're in your prime. I mean, come on. Have you looked in the mirror lately?"

"Oh, cut it out," she said, fully awake now. "Fine. Show me."

"Gladly," he said.

He held her hair back, his fist resting on the back of her neck. The Performa granules burned her nose, made her eyes water, and shot an instant fizzy feeling to her head. It hurt a little, in a strangely pleasant way.

"Good job!" Bundy said, and kneeled to zip up the remaining two lines, one into each nostril. He used his index finger to wipe the residue off the table, then deftly rubbed the last of the granules on his lower gums.

"Gross," Colleen said, feeling light-headed but vibrant.

"Nah," he said. "Just making sure we leave no trace."

"My brain feels ... carbonated." A memory surfaced from the fizz, clean and bright: "We used to stick pins in our forearms," she said, leaning back on the couch, noticing the sudden warmth of her skin against its cool surface, the kicked-up pace of her heart. "Me and my girlfriends in high school. To see who could stand the most. I always won. Because I liked how it hurt. I could make whole constellations on my arm. The Big Dipper, the Little Dipper, Orion, the Seven Sisters — or is it the Six Sisters? Sometimes I'd connect my little scabs with pen ink when I was bored in class at school." The words were coming on fast-forward, with a will of their own.

"Fucks you up fast, doesn't it?" Beside her, just a few inches of couch between them, Bundy was smiling his coconut smile, looking amused. He was gorgeous, what a young Rob Lowe might've looked like if he'd surfed and played in a band.

"I don't think pinpricks in my arm fucked me up, no," Colleen said. "But lots of people in Hemet, where I grew up, were very fucked up. Now *there's* a town you could write some songs about."

"Maybe I will," he said. "But I was talking about the Performa. Goes straight to the brain. Nice job on the snort, by the way. You're a natural, Colleeny."

She was seized by the urge to confide in him. The Performa had removed her filters. It wound her up, but also freed her. She felt she could say anything to Bundy, and it would be okay.

"Look at me," she said, facing him squarely. "Do you recognize me at all?"

He paused, considering, his eyes traveling over her body and then latching to hers. "I don't think so," he said. "Should I?"

"Let's try a musical hint," she said. "Name this tune." She took a deep breath and began to sing: *"You're so exotic, you make me heartsick. Like a rodent, rat, or raccoon. If I don't see you, see you —"*

"Sure, sure," Bundy interrupted her. "That Skunkface song. Great tune. For that sort of thing."

"That's me." There. She'd said it.

"Skunkface?"

"No. He based the song on stuff I said. On TV like six months ago. That's my voice, dubbed in over the music toward the end."

"No shit! That track was everywhere for a while. It must've been awesome for you."

"You're not understanding, Bundy. I had nothing to do with the song. The guy's making fun of me. I made a fool of myself on *Flo's Studio* — do you know that show?"

"Of course. Never watched it, though. Girly fashion stuff, right?"

"Right. Good. Then you wouldn't have seen me on it."

"Making a fool of yourself is what you're supposed to do on reality TV, Colleeny. Who cares? It's the best entertainment. You were serving your audience to the best of your ability. And then on top of it, you inspired a kickass song. You should be proud of yourself."

He held up his hand, and when she high-fived him, he laced his fingers with hers and held on. She couldn't remember the last time she felt so happy. His reaction to her confession was liberating. As if he'd freed her permanently from the humiliation of *Flo's Studio*.

"I feel perfect right now," she said.

"Me too," Bundy said, lowering his hand to his lap without letting go of hers. She wished the Performa weren't making her palms sweat. The room was warm, too warm, and she imagined what it might feel like to peel off her red dress and let it wilt to the floor, and then he was kissing her, his hands running along the side of her body, fingers kneading her, then to her lower back, pulling her into him. His lips were gentle at first, then insistent, his breath booze sweet, his tongue soft but urgent in her mouth. He lowered to kiss her neck, pushing her head back against the cushion, his hand roaming down the front of her dress. The blast of clarity the Performa had given her melted, and her head swam. His lips migrated lower. He kissed the base of her neck. Each collarbone. Then the border of her low neckline, an inch from her nipples.

She heard herself moan. Then she heard a tinkling sound.

Her phone, from inside her clutch, signifying that a text had just arrived from Carl. Panic punctured the spell of Bundy's kisses. She pushed him away and bolted upright. Carl could be right outside the door.

"Hey," said Bundy.

"Sorry," said Colleen, reaching to the floor for her clutch and pulling her phone out.

WHERE ARE YOU? Carl had typed.

"Where were *you?*" she said too loudly.

"Where's who?" asked Bundy.

"Nothing," Colleen said. "Just my stupid husband. He can't fend for himself at a party." As soon as the words flew out she wanted to take them back.

"Oh," he said, eyes steady on her. "I thought you said you didn't know where he was."

"I don't. I mean, he's somewhere in this house, but" — she tried to laugh — "it's a really big house."

"We should probably head back out there." Bundy's voice was drained of festivity.

"No," Colleen said. She refused to abandon the moment she'd just had in her grasp, literally. She wanted him to kiss her again — just for a minute. She needed him. "Not yet. Please."

"Yeah," he said, standing up from the couch. "I think we should." He swung his hand toward the door. "You go ahead, first."

"I thought we were having a nice time?"

"We were."

His tone was final. What an idiot she was. *My husband, blah blah.* Now Bundy was basically demanding to usher her out of the den. He'd crossed his arms and leaned against the wall, clearly waiting for her to leave.

"Um," she said, "how can I listen to your music?"

"My band's called the Double Negatives. Google us, Bundy Hesse and the Double Negatives."

"Actually, what I meant was how do I see you again?"

He shifted from one foot to the other, impatient. "We're playing here in L.A. in a few weeks, at Moonrock, over in Silver Lake. Sweet venue. Not that you'd want to come all the way down from Fresno or anything."

"But I might."

"Might you?" he said with a trace of teasing. Was it working? Was he warming again?

"I'll try."

"And *might you* be a little clearer on your husband's whereabouts next time?"

She detected the hint of a smile playing at the corners of his lips. "Bundy, look. I'm sorry if I was misleading. My husband and I are barely even speak—"

"Colleen," he cut her off. "Not now. Back to the party. Separately."

She picked up her purse and walked toward the door.

As she passed him, she stopped and kissed him on the lips.

He pulled his head back, thwacking it hard on the wall behind him.

"Ow," he said. "Jesus Christ!"

She bolted out of the room, slamming the door.

Alone in the hallway, the sounds of the party rolled again from the next wing of the house.

She ducked into a bathroom—there were so many!—and sat on the toilet lid for a minute, hands on her temples, eyes closed, trying to blot out what had just happened. She took deep breaths to slow her galloping heart.

She'd never cheated on Carl before, not officially. There had been a few kisses here and there. And the thing on New Year's Eve a while back, when she'd stayed up drinking and talking to Carl's tennis buddy, Alan, in the kitchen after Carl had gone to bed. They'd polished off another bottle of champagne, and then he'd smothered her against the island, his tongue reptilian, his hands grabby, and she'd regretted it instantly. Alan was in his fifties, balding with a paunch. Nothing like Bundy.

Now Bundy was gone. And she was alone in a bathroom, at a party she'd been invited to out of pure obligation, where no one had an ounce of true interest in her. The Justuses merely tolerated her. To keep their fan club numbers up. To keep their fat daughter happy. Colleen had never admitted this fact so squarely to herself, but it was time to face the truth. Their friendship was bullshit. She'd never come to another of their parties again.

She stood from the toilet and looked in the mirror, startled by her dishevelment. Her hair looked slept on, poofed up on one side, her face tired and wan beneath it. Her bright lipstick had smeared above her lip. Bundy had done this. He was also responsible for the faint red mark on her neck, where the skin was ever so slightly thinned and crinkled, the one place on her body where her age stubbornly revealed itself. She ran the faucet over a hand towel and pressed cold water to the red mark. With her other hand, she smoothed her hair, blinking at herself in the mirror.

"You will not cry," she said.

Then the ache of missing Lorelei bloomed violently inside Colleen; she wanted nothing more in that moment than to talk to her daughter.

"Baby, where are you?" she said, her voice sounding hollow in the empty bathroom. She pulled out her phone and speed-dialed Lorelei, whose photo flashed on the little screen: big sunglasses and green bucket hat, mid-laugh. The hat was stolen, Colleen remembered, a Kate Spade from Nordstrom, where Lorelei's friend Mia worked on weekends, and Mia had removed the alarm tag so Lorelei could walk right out of the store with the green hat on her head. She remembered the moment Lorelei had confessed this to her, one of those Saturdays with the noonday light streaming into Colleen's bedroom and her hungover daughter giggling next to her on the bed.

"I know we're bad," Lorelei had said. "We won't make a habit out of it."

"You'd better not," Colleen had said, trying to sound stern.

"Wait until I show you the hat. I guarantee you'll be stealing it from me." They'd both dissolved into laughter. The moment had been one of perfect happiness. Not one of "abysmal parenting," as Carl had called it, after Colleen tearfully recounted the scene at an Al-Anon meeting, the first and last time she'd let herself open up.

Lorelei's phone didn't even ring, not even a few staccato trills of false hope, no clues to help Colleen through the rest of the night. Just straight to a recorded messages: *The person you are trying to reach cannot receive calls at this time . . .*

15

ROBIN KICKED OFF her heels, peeled off her mother's Spanx, unbelted and unzipped her dress halfway down her back, and flopped down on the bed. A cranberry-colored duvet covered the Tempur-Pedic mattress her mother had installed on a queen-sized frame that had replaced Robin's canopy bed. Linda had also replaced her NOW! poster with a characterless painting of the ocean, and her white sticker-bedecked bureau with a walnut armoire. A matching nightstand displayed *Architectural Digest, Golf, Sunset,* and *Luxury Car Magazine.*

Her childhood bedroom or a hotel/dentist's office?

The room faced the street from the second floor. A window was open a few inches, and Robin could hear the guests' heels clicking on the stone walkway. It was only 9:30 but she was already exhausted. Darren hadn't called. He'd warned her that they were shooting at night, so he might not be able to sneak in a phone call without getting shit from Toby King. She switched off the lamp on the nightstand and lay down on the bed, cradling a throw pillow, and closed her eyes.

She was submerged in a hard sleep when the trill of her phone woke her. HUSBAND, read the caller ID. She jolted upright.

"Dare?"

"Robs?" His voice was low and rushed.

"You called!"

"I keep thinking of you at the party. How awful is it this time? Is your dad forcing people to view the Ferrari yet? Is my mom wasted?"

Robin laughed. "Probably and probably. I already escaped. I was sleeping. These shots are making me — "

"Darren!" She heard a voice in the background.

"I'm so sorry, Robs, I have to go. We're on a break and Toby just left the barn for a second. I just wanted to hear your voice."

"You're in a barn right now?"

"We're shooting this scene where the horse trainer character catches the jockey sleeping in the stall with his favorite horse, and there's this unbelievable tension between them, which is mostly silent, so it's hard for the actors to capture it exactly the way Tob — "

"Darren! Need you in the village right now!"

"The village?" Robin asked.

"Sorry. I have to go. Miss you, love you."

And he was gone.

She tossed her phone, and it bounced from the edge of the bed onto the floor, landing on the cream-colored area rug with a soft thud. She rolled onto her side and drew her legs up into her stomach. It would have been better if he hadn't called at all. It had been a tease, to hear just a snippet of his voice like that, a reminder of just how far away he was from her, and how inaccessible. That, for now and for months, all that mattered was *Equus Revisited*.

He hadn't even asked about her treatment. Just the stupid party. She closed her eyes and pressed lightly on the lids, taking in the orange blobs and yellow streaks, trying not to cry. She wanted him with her, right now, to make her laugh, to end her misery and resentment. It would make everything so easy. That was how everything had been with Darren, from the time they'd first met, four years ago, until they'd begun the pregnancy quest: effortless, natural. Their rightness for each other was clear. Jackie had dragged Robin to an art opening in Los Feliz. Jackie had gotten very drunk and hooked up with the artist, an aggressive, beautiful abstract sculptor named Louise. Jackie had little memory of the tryst, and wanted to assess Louise sober, but didn't want to go alone.

The sculptor had turned out to be a pretentious bitch, Robin and Jackie agreed, but her friend, Darren Branch, was over six feet with short dark hair, a few days of stubble, and bright blue eyes. His features were clean and even — straight nose, square jaw, white teeth — a reassuring face. His laugh was kind and easy and Robin immediately felt safe in his presence. They'd gotten into a lively argument about Lars von Trier, whom Darren loved and she detested, and at the end of the night, he'd handed her his phone.

"Put your number in," he'd said. "I'll call you and we can watch *Dogville* together."

"Over my dead body," Robin had said, grinning and tapping her number into the phone and handing it back to him. "Number's under *Overrated Danish Misogynist*." She'd had a few glasses of wine, but it wasn't the booze that made her feel so loose and easy around Darren. It was just him.

"Watch it," he'd said, smiling back. "Or else I won't call you."

The next day, he'd called. They met at a restaurant in Culver City on a Friday night, and he didn't leave her house in Santa Monica until Monday morning.

"Can't you just not go to work?" Darren had asked her, at ten, the light in Robin's bedroom misty gray. "Isn't that the beauty of being your own boss?"

He was naked on his stomach across her bed, while she was fumbling through the ever-present piles of stuff on her floor, searching for a stray black patent leather Mary Jane to match the one already on her foot, the shoes she always wore with the green skirt she'd chosen. It was hard making clothing decisions with Darren right there on her bed. The long slope of his back was a distraction. She chucked a braided black belt from the floor of the bedroom into the open walk-in closet and stole a glance at him. His body was lean and tan, smooth and spare, a tidy contrast to shaggy brown hair and three-day stubble.

As much as she wanted to scrap work and climb back into bed with him, she had to get over to the No Princess offices in Westwood to have a sit-down with DeeDee Sims, who'd heard that Gregory was taking over and was furious with Robin for "abandoning" her.

"I'd love to not go," she said, toppling a hill of shirts and jeans. "But I have to, for about six more weeks."

"Right, your hiatus."

She'd told him that she'd been running her own talent agency for twelve years and had gotten burned out. She said she was taking a breather, to figure out what to do next—no mention of the inheritance. That wasn't the sort of information you dropped on a first date, even a sixty-hour one. Plus, they'd been busy tangling naked in bed and eating delivered Thai food. Darren had told her he was a shooting-and-editing guy, freelance, working on various film and video projects.

"Some of my own stuff, some of other people's stuff," he'd said, tipping a beer bottle to his lips with his right hand and giving a dismissive wave with his left. "Nothing too mind-blowing right now."

"Well, when you have something mind-blowing to show me, I'm ready to watch," Robin had said.

"You'll get a free pass to the advance screening, for sure," he'd said, and reached for her leg.

"What's the day got in store for you?" she asked.

"I thought I'd clean up your room, for starters," said Darren, settling on his back with his head propped on a fat down pillow.

"Shut up!" Robin laughed, her face flushing warm. "I didn't expect you to come home with me! It was our first date."

"Didn't the possibility even enter your mind? At least enough to do a tiny little bit of preemptive straightening up?"

"I thought you'd want to see the real me," she said.

"I'd like to see the real you right now. It's too obscured by all those clothes. Get over here."

She smelled a pair of socks to make sure they were clean and threw them at him. "Quit tempting me. I have to work. Don't you have somewhere to be?"

"At some point."

She was sorry to find her missing shoe, under a dry cleaning sheath on the floor.

"What's this meeting that's skewed your priorities so drastically?"

"I have to defuse a high-maintenance actress who thinks she's the center of the universe."

"Oh, you're meeting with my sister?"

"Your sister's an actress?"

"Actress-*ish*, as she'd put it." He sat up and rested his back against the headboard. "Is it just me, or is the parlance of kids getting lazier with each generation?"

"Absolutely," Robin said. "They can't speak a direct sentence. It's all -*ish* and *like* and *sort of.*"

"And let's not forget *literally*. Lorelei has trouble communicating without that one."

"I know!" Robin laughed. "My girls love *literally.*"

"Your girls?"

"The girls I represent. My clients. At the agency."

"Oh, okay, Jesus, you scared me for a second," he said. "I thought you were about to complicate this situation. Not that I don't love kids. I'd just prefer if you didn't already have them."

"So what sort of acting does your sister do? Plays? She's in high school, right?" Was she crazy, or did she detect an implication of a long-term future together in how he'd said *already*? She fastened her second shoe and glanced at herself in the full-length mirror. Her hair was still wet from a hasty shower, but overall she looked pretty good: heather-gray top, green skirt, shiny shoes.

"You look great," Darren said. "I like that skirt. My sister, Lorelei, graduates from high school this June. She's done some plays, but she's got the more noble aspiration of working in TV. Her dream job involves talking to celebrities on camera while wearing something extremely fashionable."

"Like Yola Roo?"

"I'm ashamed that I even know who that is. But I do. She's basically Lorelei's hero."

"Where's Lorelei going to college?" Robin asked, not ready to disclose that Yola Roo was a client.

"College?" Darren's tone was mock incredulous. "Why would a rising television star go to college? Lorelei plans to move straight to L.A."

"Is that so terrible?"

"I feel sorry for her, thinking she'll just show up and make some kind of glamorous career happen. Hit some auditions, and bam, her face'll be everywhere. Somehow the whole California-dreamin' cliché just passed right over her head. She's like some modern version of a gold rusher, pointing her wagon toward the Pacific and thinking she'll strike it rich if she just starts shoveling." He sighed and reached to the floor to pick up his T-shirt. "My stepmom doesn't help. She's Lorelei's biggest cheerleader. I wouldn't be surprised if the two of them ended up being roommates in some grim apartment complex in the Valley. The whole thing is embarrassing — but she's actually a really good kid, Lorelei. Just devoid of positive influences. Unless you count my father, who she never listens to."

"What about you?"

"We don't talk enough to make much of a dent," he said. "I wish we did. But she's almost twelve years younger than me, so we weren't close growing up. And I resented her mom, Colleen, when I was young, for barging in and brainwashing my dad. She was your typical hot-young-girl mess, I think, wanting someone to solve all her problems, and my dad was Mr. Stable and pretty lonely so, presto" — Darren snapped his fingers — "it was love."

"What about your real mom?" Robin was surprised and delighted by Darren's openness. Too often, in talking to men, she'd felt like an interviewer, but Darren invited her right into his life.

She sat down on the edge of the bed, resisting the urge to kick off her Mary Janes and stretch out beside him.

"My real mom died when I was nine. After that it was always just me and my dad, and I liked it that way. We were sort of stoic bachelors together. Shared a bedroom for a while, until he could afford to upgrade us to a bigger place. He was old-fashioned, had me call him 'sir' and check off a long chore list every week, but he was a great dad. When he complimented me, it really meant something. When he bought me something, it was a big deal. I was a happy kid. And then Colleen came along, all needy and high maintenance, and my dad went right along with it, spending all his money on her, which we didn't really have, and reassuring her all the time. He didn't seem like himself anymore."

"And then they went and had a baby together, right?" said Robin. "Which must have made it even harder."

"In some ways," Darren said thoughtfully. "But I fell for Lorelei right away. She was so damn cute. And Colleen had this crazy bond with her. It actually freed my dad up a little, I think."

"Was he strict with Lorelei, too?"

"Not really. She had the same brainwashing effect on him. And Colleen had this special gift for positioning every little luxury as a life-sustaining *necessity* for Lorelei. Dollhouses, new clothes, bikes, you name it." He laughed, a little bitterly. "The sort of stuff I'd have to mow a million lawns to get, Lorelei got at the drop of a hat."

"Sounds like a recipe for serious resentment."

"For a while I did resent Lorelei. But there was always something a little trashy and desperate about Colleen that made me feel . . ." He paused. " . . . a little sorry for them, but also superior. Does that sound bad?"

"Not at all," said Robin. "That's exactly how I feel about my parents, actually."

"No wonder we get along." He put his hand on her thigh, smiling up at her.

"So you said Lorelei's an aspiring mactress? Do you think she has talent?"

"An aspiring what?"

"Model/actress/hostess, whatever. Industry slang for people who just want to be on camera."

Darren laughed. "That's Lorelei for sure. She could probably be an okay actress, with some training. And she's very pretty, though I know that's a bare minimum qualification. But she definitely has a spark. Charisma, I guess, would be her most notable quality."

"Which is more important than anything," Robin said.

"Oh yeah?"

"I've built a whole career out of spotting charisma."

"Is that what got me here?" He smiled. He pushed himself up and maneuvered his body around to hold her. She sighed and pressed her cheek against his chest, the clean, bleachy smell of his detergent still detectable. Beneath the electric novelty of his embrace was another feeling; below the anticipation of the long kiss that would begin in seconds, something both more stirring and steadying at the same time: the sense that this — that Darren and she — were exactly right together.

Robin wanted to be with him. She wanted to give him everything. She knew it then, after one weekend.

"Introduce me to Lorelei," she said. "I can help."

After Darren had woken her with his call from Florida, only to hang up on her sixty seconds later, Robin curled on her side and drifted back to sleep. The fatiguing side effects of her hormone shots must be taking hold. And when she was woken for the second time, by a knock on the bedroom door, she was so sodden with exhaustion that she thought it must be Darren, coming to rescue her. But then she remembered: he was three thousand miles away.

It was Colleen, she bet, drunk enough to hunt her for another round of interrogation. Or her mother, demanding that she stop being antisocial and rejoin the party.

Robin dunked her fingers in the glass of water on her nightstand and dabbed her eyes. With the edge of her mother's million-thread-count pillowcase she blotted her nose.

The knock came again.

"Just a second!" she said, and pushed off the bed to fling open the door, ready to stave off whichever pushy woman had come to stalk her.

For a moment, she thought the man standing in the hall was Darren.

"Robin Justus," he said. "Surprise."

"Ben Hessler?"

He pulled her into a full-body embrace, his fingers pressing over the bare triangle of skin on her back where she'd partially unzipped her ill-fitting dress.

16

COLLEEN STARED OUT the passenger window of the Camry, hands folded in her lap atop the velour of her True Religion sweatpants. She rested her head on a sweatshirt of Carl's and tried to sleep. But it was impossible; the misery of her hangover trumped her exhaustion. Traffic on the 405 was usually light on Sundays, but today — the morning after the Justuses' party — they'd barely made it past the Getty when the northbound lanes slowed to a crawl.

"You've got to be kidding me," Carl said to the traffic. He reached over to open the glove compartment and pulled out a CD he'd borrowed from the library, something about World War II that bored Colleen to tears.

The dour voice of a British narrator filled the car. Colleen knew she was probably stuck with the sound of it for the next three or four hours, all the way back to Fresno. Carl had been stone-cold all morning, from the time he woke her at the hotel this morning with a rough nudge to her shoulder and four words: "It's ten. Get up." She hadn't slept so late in a decade.

Last night she'd tossed and turned from the time they got in bed, around midnight, until nearly four in the morning, queasy and dehydrated from alcohol, wired from Performa, the tarry taste of the two cigarettes she'd bummed from a waiter lingering beneath the mint from her toothpaste. Her mind had lurched in all directions, from Lorelei to Bundy and back again, her memories ping-ponging through time — Lorelei as a baby, toddling in a blue gingham pinafore, then grown-up in the slinky silver dress they'd bought for her final reality audition. The images came to Colleen in no particular order, like photos drawn from a hat, and were interspersed with flash memories from her time with Bundy at the party. How his fingers had looked rolling the dollar bill into a cylinder, large but nimble. His white teeth, white as the Performa he'd crushed into powder. The thudding sound his head made hitting the wall as he dodged her kiss.

She'd groaned under the crisp hotel sheets as Carl snored beside her, and she'd gotten up three times to check her Hermès clutch for a stray crumb of Zenzo, emptying the contents and shaking out the lining, but she'd taken the last of it at the party. Eventually, she'd gone downstairs to the hotel's twenty-four-hour gift shop to buy Benadryl and the only booze they stocked — an unrefrigerated six-pack of local beer called Celebrewty. On her way upstairs, she removed one bottle from the cardboard carrier and shoved the rest in a garbage bin. Back in the room, sitting on the edge of the tub, she swallowed three Benadryl and downed the bottle of warm, bitter beer as fast as she could, hid the empty under the sink, and finally, she slept.

The morning, after Carl woke her, was murder. Her hangover was vicious and Carl wasn't speaking to her. Her memory of leaving the party was spotty, other than the vise-tight grip of his hand on her shoulder when he'd found her pacing on a terrace, the few words sputtered between them —

Robin was mean to me. I had to get away from the party.

Mean to you? How old are you, Colleen? His voice hard and sober. *For an hour?*

I lost track of time.

How much have you had to drink?

He'd lectured her all the way back to the hotel. This morning, she couldn't remember the details of what he'd said, only that he'd using plenty of Al-Anon phrasing: "Choose to let go." "In control of no one but yourself." And a few condescending questions: "Do you really feel better when you're sloshed like this?" et cetera. She couldn't recall exactly how she'd answered, just how miserable she'd felt. How, for a wasted moment, she'd considered coming clean with him completely. Telling him about Bundy. About Lorelei's pills. About her credit card. About the utter misery of her days in Fresno. Her mind had been teetering, pinballing, and for a woozy beat, she'd imagined what a clean slate would feel like, what laying herself bare before Carl and inviting his judgment of the Real Colleen would bring. She could sense the relief on the other side, beckoning, but she couldn't cross over. She was too afraid.

Traffic eased after they passed the junction with the 101, always a clogged mess of intersecting highways. As Carl accelerated, Colleen was hit with a wave of nausea and uttered an involuntary "Ohhhh," her hand flying to cover her mouth.

"Here," Carl said, and pulled out a bottle of cold water wedged between his seat and the car door. "If you're going to throw up, try to give me some warning." He spoke as if to a child. Her head throbbed.

"Thanks," Colleen said weakly, taking the bottle.

Carl cracked her window open, letting the warm spring air swirl into the car. Its freshness made her feel a tiny bit better. She didn't want him to be mad at her anymore. It was too exhausting. She couldn't take it, on top of everything else. But it could be days until he treated her normally again.

"Chapter twenty-six," said the British narrator, "Guadalcanal."

Just past Santa Clarita they hit a stretch of freeway lined with a spate of cheaply designed billboards for the Lap-Band, an alternative to gastric bypass surgery, flashing at Colleen every hundred yards: NEED TO LOSE 50 LBS OR MORE? THE LAP-BAND WORKS! Under the caption were two photos of the same blond woman, very fat and frowning in one, medium fat and beaming in the other. Colleen stared over her at the flat blue canvas of midday sky.

Carl's cell rang, and he ignored it, but when it stopped and started again seconds later, he tapped his phone on to speaker and warily answered, "Yes?"

"Daddy?" Lorelei's voice jumped into the air around them.

"Oh my God!" said Colleen, a physical reflex. The uncapped plastic bottle dropped from her hands onto the floor, still half full, and water splashed over her flip-flopped feet. "Lorelei!"

"But the Imperial Japanese navy had occupied Tulagi," said the narrator.

Colleen smacked the stereo off. "Honey! Where are—"

"Hi, Lorelei," Carl cut Colleen off, stabbing the air with his finger in her direction: *Stay out of this.* She narrowed her eyes at him and poked her finger right back at him, mocking his gesture, knowing he'd call her juvenile later, not caring.

"Am I on speaker?" said Lorelei.

"You are," Carl said. "We're driving. It's California law." His tone was matter-of-fact, as if he spoke to his daughter all the time. Colleen threw his balled-up sweatshirt, which she'd been using as a pillow, onto the floor, and stepped on it to blot the spilled water.

"I need to talk to you in private, Dad," Lorelei said. "Take me off speaker."

Colleen stifled a moan. She wanted to grab Carl's phone and jump out of the car and talk to Lorelei alone, crouched on the side of the freeway, just long enough to tell her she was sorry, so unbelievably sorry, for what she'd done; that they could, now that the hype had subsided, start over again, if Lorelei would just come home. They could fire Robin and get a new agent. The damage to Lorelei's reputation was definitely reparable. Five months had passed! Nobody cared anymore! Five months was a lifetime to reality television. There were a million other shows for Lorelei.

If only she'd come back.

But Colleen couldn't say any of this, because she was trapped on the 405 beside Carl, who was already unhappy with her and would only become furious if Colleen spoke in a manner that "blurred boundaries," as the Al-Anon meetings had taught him to say. There was nothing she could do but stamp on his sweatshirt and dig the white tips of her acrylic nails into her palm.

"There's no one here but your mother and me," Carl said. "You've got privacy. What's going on, Lorelei?"

Colleen heard her take a breath and knew Lorelei was nervous. And when her daughter got too nervous, she withdrew. If Carl wasn't careful, she'd hang up before he'd gotten any information out of her. Colleen jostled Carl's arm from its perch on the center console and opened the compartment to whip out the pen and Post-it pad she always kept inside. Using the dashboard as a desk, her handwriting shaky from the motion of the car and her addled nerves, she scribbled, *Find out where she is. Ask for landmarks.*

Carl's eyes flicked to the hot pink square, then back up at the road. "Are you in L.A., Lorelei?"

"No."

"Are you in California?"

"No."

"I will not play twenty questions, Lorelei."

"Take me off speakerphone!" she said. "Or I'm hanging up."

Colleen slapped another Post-it on the dashboard and wrote, *Do it!*

Carl looked at the cell phone's screen.

"Seven-seven-five area code," he said. "Are you in Nevada, Lorelei?"

"I have nowhere to sleep," Lorelei said, starting to wail. "I need you to pay for one night in a hotel, Dad. I mean motel!" She was crying — Colleen could hear some theatrics at the bottom of her daughter's voice, but there was real desperation there, too.

"Honey, it's Mom. Come home. We'll take care of everything if you'll just say yes."

Carl reached over and snapped his fingers near Colleen's mouth — *shut up* — a sign he was officially losing his temper. She had a flashing impulse to bite his hand.

"I don't want to come home," Lorelei said, quavering. "And I can't! I'm at work. In the back of a restaurant. Working my ass off."

"Does this restaurant job issue you a paycheck?" said Carl.

"Y-y-yes."

"Why can't you pay for your own motel with your paycheck?"

"Because I get paid minimum wage. And I don't get paid until tomorrow. I'm using my last quarters to call you right now. My cell's cut off."

The instant Lorelei said it — "My cell's cut off" — Colleen realized something. All the emotions that had been swirling inside her went quiet, eclipsed by a single new fact, flashing like a knife in the sun: Lorelei had taken her MasterCard.

Of course. She'd been paying Lorelei's cell phone bill for years with the card via auto-pay. Lorelei had gotten her hands on the card somehow, maxed it out, and the last charges must not have gone through. Colleen knew this with total certainty — motherly instinct, whatever you wanted to call it — the way she'd known Lorelei had started with drugs before having any proof.

Lorelei's voice filled the car again, cracking and tinny through the speaker. "Daddy, I just need money for one night. Come on."

"You know we can't do that, Lorelei," Carl said.

Colleen couldn't hold back. "How much do you need?"

Carl reached into the breast pocket of his shirt and pulled out his cell phone's wireless earpiece, hooked it onto his right ear, and took Lorelei off speaker.

"Let me talk to her, Carl!" Colleen cried, kicking her foot against the underside of the glove compartment. She already missed Lorelei's voice in the air.

"You're welcome to come home," Carl was saying. "Your mother and I would welcome you home right this minute, and we will buy you a plane ticket to Fresno."

"Tonight!" Colleen said.

"And that's all we will offer," Carl said.

Faintly, Colleen heard Lorelei's voice coming from Carl's earpiece. She couldn't make out the words. It was like a terrible dream, having her daughter's voice in the car with her, and then not having it, and now almost being able to hear her words, but not quite. Colleen took long breaths, focusing on the exhales, like in Pilates. She looked out the window at the reddening hills, running her finger up and down the edge of her seat belt. Traffic was finally easing up, but they hadn't escaped the parade of Lap-Band billboards yet.

"Dammit, Lorelei, hello? Lorelei?"

Carl pulled off his earpiece and threw it onto the floor in disgust.

"She hung up," Colleen said. She had been right on the edge of rage toward him, but now that he'd lost his cool twice in a span of minutes — highly unusual — she felt a small commiseration between them. Carl was struggling, too.

"Yeah." He laughed. "By all means, Lorelei, just check right into the Bellagio."

"You made her hang up, Carl. Before I had a chance to begin to maybe fix things with her. If you'd have just let me apologize, she might be on her way home right now."

"Colleen. Stop it. I did not make her hang up. I simply stated what we were willing to do without any enabling language. You're the one who completely violated our policy by offering her money! I was shocked by that, frankly."

"Yeah," Colleen said. "A few months in Al-Anon and suddenly you're their disciple. Suddenly you're an involved parent. You've got a *strategy*." Her anger reared, and she added, "After five years of barely paying attention to her."

"That," Carl said, his voice suddenly sharp, warning her, "is a different conversation. And as for my 'strategy,' you agreed with it, Colleen." It was never a good sign when he started using her name. A low-key battle cry. "You agreed that helping her" — he made air quotes around *helping* with one hand — "wasn't actually helping her at all. We set a policy, together, and you agreed to it."

"That was right after the meetings, when I was brainwashed!" Colleen regretted ever setting foot in Al-Anon's meetings, with their shitty coffee and phony camaraderie. "You know what my policy is, Carl?" She spoke his name as if it tasted bitter in her mouth, knowing it was a mistake to let the argument escalate when they still had another three hours in the car ahead. "My policy is to keep our daughter alive."

"Colleen, stop. Let's just stop right now." He was better than her, in this way. He knew when it was time to step away from an argument and could retreat in an instant. "Lorelei *is* alive. You know she's bullshitting about needing money for a motel tonight, and we can't fall for it. She'll never get better if we keep playing into these games."

The tears surged behind her eyes. If she spoke they'd fall. She cracked the knuckles of her right index and middle fingers against the side of her jaw, a nasty habit she'd developed in high school.

"Please," Carl said, a peace offering left dangling in the air. She heard the sadness in his voice.

"Okay," Colleen said, closing her eyes. They'd reached the beginning of the Grapevine, having switched from the 405 to the 5, officially exiting greater Los Angeles. The road began to narrow and steepen, the scenery turning browner and starker as the Camry pushed up the pass. Normally she liked catching sight of Pyramid Lake on the ascent, the swath of blue water glittering from the center of a parched valley, but now she didn't want to look at the scenery. No stretch of road reminded her more of Lorelei than this one.

Carl was no comfort. She wanted a Zenzo, and couldn't stop picturing the little purple pill, like a tiny amethyst with the power to banish her worries and ease her to sleep.

Her head continued to pound, in sync with her heart.

Just three more hours, Colleen thought, reclining her seat. Three hours until they got home to Fresno and she could swallow a pill, open her laptop, check her Capital One statement. Three hours until the statement would reveal Lorelei's whereabouts.

Carl switched on his audiobook again, and the narrator droned on.

They pulled into the driveway at four, and Carl went straight to the shower. Colleen went to the kitchen, poured two inches of Grey Goose into a large glass and filled the rest of it with ice water. In one swallow, she washed down two ibuprofen, her multivitamin, and a whole Zenzo. Then she drained the rest of the drink and went upstairs to the office, where the sound of Carl's shower assured her a few more minutes of privacy. She opened her laptop. The Capital One website took forever to load, and then she mistyped her password. Finally, her account summary appeared:

> Credit limit: $34,000
>
> Current balance: $34,657.98
>
> Available credit: $0.00
>
> *Your account is over limit. Please remit payment immediately or contact customer service.*

And then the itemized recent charges:

Relapse Libations & Night Lounge, Reno, NV: $324.76

The Sleep Inn, Reno, NV: $592.83

CVS Arroyo St., Reno, NV: $87.51

Jackpot Buffet at the Circus Circus, an MGM Resort, Reno, NV: $38.59

Sole Search, Reno, NV: $19.99

Reno.

17

CARL STAYED IN the shower until the bathroom mirrors ghosted over and the hot water ran out, something he'd asked Lorelei not to do a thousand times. But he needed to scald the weekend off him. The Justuses' party and Lorelei's call on the drive home had left him with so many layers of unease that he wasn't sure where he'd start when it was his turn to speak at Al-Anon that night.

Maybe he wouldn't even share. He just needed to be there, in the presence of the group. Especially in the presence of Wendy, who'd been going to meetings for a long time and suffused the room with a sense of normalcy, as if the group was there to discuss a church fund-raiser instead of a spouse's recent bender or a son's fresh track marks. Colleen had mocked Wendy for her feathery, frosted hair and pleated jeans, but Carl liked her instantly.

After Colleen had decided Al-Anon wasn't for her, Carl had begun talking to Wendy after the meetings, over weak coffee and packaged cookies, chitchat at first, and eventually more. By now, she knew all about Lorelei, plus a little bit about his wobbly marriage. He knew her husband had consumed mas-sive quantities of whiskey before driving headlong into a tree four years ago. Yet Wendy still came to meetings every Sunday night. She believed it was not pure chance that she'd married a man who'd functioned as a serious alcoholic for a decade. She believed substance abuse was a "family systems" issue, never simply the fault of a single, out-of-control individual. When her husband was alive, she'd kept their cupboards stocked with Jameson (that she'd bought for him, reasoning he'd be driving drunk to the store if she didn't) and slept with her cell phone beside her pillow, so she could drive him home from wherever he'd ended up: *I thought I was helping him do what he'd be doing no matter what, but more safely.*

Al-Anon helped her understand herself, she'd explained to Carl and Colleen when they'd first met, scraping the filling of an Oreo off the cookie with her teeth, unselfconscious, while Colleen invisibly rolled her eyes. "Sad, sad woman," Colleen had commented on the drive home. Carl disagreed. Wendy was the opposite of pathetic. She was confident and generous. She always had sound advice for him. In the past months, Carl had come to consider Wendy a friend.

He shaved in the shower, until his face was free of the fast-growing reddish stubble Colleen disliked. Then he swiped fog from the round mirror suctioned to the wall, and studied the crags around his eyes. Was it his imagination, or was he aging on fast-forward? Fifty-five was supposed to be his prime, wasn't it? So why did he already feel on the brink of decline?

Carl had brought his clothes into the bathroom, and he dressed in a white polo and jeans while the fan slowly sucked the steam from the air, its blank whir pleasantly numbing. He'd started dressing in the bathroom because it prolonged his time alone with a closed door between himself and Colleen. She confused him these days; the air around her was both distracted and fraught, a force field not meant for him. It radiated from her: she did not *want* to be understood by her own husband. Of course, he should demand that she communicate with him, or ... what? That was where he fumbled. He wasn't prepared to issue an ultimatum. To risk being alone. Not yet. Not after he'd tried so hard, all these years.

The beginning of his relationship with Colleen had been a classic recipe for failure — their fifteen-year age gap, the accidental pregnancy, her refusal to finish high school — but he'd refused to let it fail. His first marriage had hurt too much: he and Jody had been wildly in love, their future wide and welcoming, and then she'd died from a cancer so aggressive and swift he was bewildered for weeks before the sadness crashed down. Colleen, angel-bright against the grimness of a Sizzler in the godforsaken town of Hemet, had been the first thing to make him feel alive again, two full years after Jody died. And then, so quickly, there was Lorelei, too, beaming at him with her tiny gapped teeth, her scalp smelling of sugar. He'd promised himself he'd never let either of them go.

But he hadn't considered that Lorelei might discard *him*. First, for her fame-craving life in Los Angeles, and then for whatever she was doing now, somewhere in Nevada. If he allowed himself to picture the worst-case scenarios — seedy clubs, men in cheap leather coats, track marks, his daughter chain-smoking and hollow eyed — his grief would surge and become unbearable. This was how Al-Anon had saved him: it taught him how to prevent these thoughts from defeating him. It forced him to view Lorelei as a person completely separate from himself, with desires and volitions upon which he could have no effect. Whether he pictured her dead or alive bore no influence on reality. Sending her money in a panic was of no use. Nor was jumping in the car, as Colleen wanted to do, and driving to Nevada to find her. Lorelei's will would always trump his own. What she wanted to be would be. All he could do was love her from a distance, and have faith that all his years of loving her, of gazing down at her in wonder while she slept in her crib, or dabbing tears from his eyes when she sang onstage in high school, had provided the solid foundation she needed to change herself. According to Al-Anon, the only way Carl could help her now was if she alone decided to change, and reached out to him to help. If she asked to come home, or for help kicking whatever habits she'd picked up, well then, he'd be there in a heartbeat. But his meetings had convinced him that he could not influence her decision to change. Until she made it herself, he would have to stay put. He knew Colleen saw the Al-Anon approach as cold and uncaring, but he had not only come to believe it: he needed it to get through the day.

If only he and Colleen could be in the Lorelei situation together. Even if she rejected Al-Anon, there must be a way, something better than this semi-estrangement. But he could not bring himself to initiate the shift. A part of him was still too angry with her for contributing to Lorelei's situation. For all those years of shuttling her back and forth to L.A., for encouraging her to delay college to pursue some nebulous career in Hollywood, for supporting a value system that championed appearances and vanity. For the surgery he was pretty sure she'd let Lorelei have. Colleen thought he hadn't noticed, but it was obvious: Lorelei's breasts had grown overnight. At first he thought his eyes were deceiving him — he didn't spend time looking at his daughter's chest, after all — but after months of watching her parade around in tight clothes, he was almost certain she'd had something done, and that Colleen was behind it. He'd come close, but hadn't been able to bring himself to ask.

If the answer was officially yes, he might not be able to forgive her.

Dressed, he unpacked his weekend bag, separating laundry from dry cleaning, tucking unworn items back into the dresser and hanging two shirts back in the closet. Colleen would leave her bag packed for days, he knew, picking items from it and stuffing the dirty clothes back down, like a spoiled teenager waiting for the maid to take care of it. Not bothering to unpack, a woman of forty, with nothing but time on her hands. Carl sighed, opening the closet for his brown belt and wincing at the look of the little square walk-in space, which was packed with her things, hanging wall-to-wall on all four corners— *clothes*, he supposed, though he could hardly even identify half the stuff, all the wisps and colors and asymmetrical cuts, stuff so complicated he'd never be able to figure out how to put it on. And then there were all the replicas, like seemingly identical jeans hanging in one corner, eight or ten pairs, probably, at what? Eighty bucks each? A hundred? Two? Every time he guessed a price on an item of her clothing, he underestimated by at least half. Of course, she meticulously removed price tags and hid receipts, as if that might fool him into thinking she'd gotten them for a bargain, but occasionally, he fact-checked through their AmEx statement or, twice, had asked Wendy after a meeting, as casually as possible: "How much would you say that guy Marc Jacobs charges for a purse these days?" She hadn't known either time — "I'm a Tarjay woman," she'd said and smiled — but she'd asked another woman at the meeting, and Carl had been stricken by the number.

He turned off the closet light and shut the door. He didn't want to think about it. Colleen hadn't always been this way, and perhaps she wouldn't be forever. Yes, she had always been girlish and loved pretty things — and what man didn't like a woman who knew how to put herself together? — but there had once been a lightheartedness about her attention to her appearance, a sense that she had priorities. That she knew stuff was nothing more than *stuff*. That being attractive was an added bonus in life, but who you were on the inside was what counted. *That* was the Colleen he'd known and loved. Sure, her smooth brown legs flashing beneath a white miniskirt and her bright blond hair framing her dollish face had attracted him to her in the first place, but what kept him was the potential he'd sensed underneath. He used to believe that being petite and beautiful was the crutch that Colleen would rely less and less upon as she grew up, as she cultivated the more substantial parts of herself: her sharp mind, her way of seeing right to the core of things, her ability to understand people long before Carl did. He'd thought he'd be able to help coax those wonderful parts of her to the surface. What inspired him was the possibility that he, a carpenter's apprentice from Arizona, a single dad, could transform another human being for the better. If not for him, he'd told himself, Colleen might have actually tried to become a princess at Disneyland — a choice one step up from pole dancing, Carl had thought, in terms of a job that would build a woman's self-respect. Or maybe she would have gone the way of many of her classmates at San Jacinto High: to the checkout register at Walmart, to drugs, to another couple of decades in a dingy trailer with a bunch of grimy kids, to nowhere. He hadn't exactly whisked her away to a grand life, but he'd given her the opportunity to become a complete person, a complex person, who was beautiful inside and out.

And had she seized the opportunity? Well, he thought, pulling on a pair of clean socks, that was debatable. At times, yes. She'd once had a promising career in real estate. For a time she'd volunteered at the Humane Society twice a month. She'd gardened and read food books and cooked comforting meals with ingredients like pasta and cheese, foods she now would not touch. For a stretch of years, she'd been a normal young mother. Her devotion to Lorelei was always fierce, but didn't strike Carl as unusual. After all, he and Darren were also a unit, sharing a history and closeness that seemed to intimidate Colleen. It made sense that she and Lorelei would form a similar bond. The difference was Carl understood that Darren was his own person. He understood how to let him go. Yes, he'd wished Darren had chosen a path that Carl could relate to — the arty camerawork his son had made into a career (*semi*-career, really) had created a rift between them that had only widened over the years. But Carl had let Darren do what he'd needed to do, while carrying on with his own life.

Colleen had not done the same for Lorelei. As their daughter grew up, Colleen shifted harder toward her. It had begun around the time Lorelei turned sixteen and was allowed to drive herself to school and stay out until eleven on weekends. Colleen's late-night pacing (Lorelei never observed curfew), the long mornings she spent talking to Lorelei behind a closed bedroom door, the hours and hours at the mall together on Sundays, when Carl went to church alone and returned to an empty house. The whispering and giggling together. Their exclusivity. How solitary it made Carl feel. Darren by then had graduated from college in Texas and become involved with film and the brainy, irreverent people who devoted themselves to it. A few had visited Darren in Fresno, the rare times he came home during holidays — a girl with purplish-black hair and a nose ring, a guy who carried a banjo and said "Right on" all the time. As the years passed, Carl knew his son less and less, but he accepted it. This was healthy parenting, wasn't it? Grow your children, then set them free?

Not to Colleen, he thought glumly, sitting down on the bed. She'd practically become an appendage of Lorelei, right under his nose. And look where they'd all ended up: unknown to each other, separately miserable. Lorelei possibly in serious danger. Should he have done something to stop it earlier? *Could* he have? Absolutely not, Al-Anon promised him. He hoped they were right.

He was stubble-free and fully dressed now, with no good reason to procrastinate leaving the bedroom. The house was completely quiet. Too quiet to distract him from the memory of Lorelei's voice on the phone that afternoon. He was terrible at reading people over the phone — Colleen liked to point this out: *Couldn't you hear that I was upset? Are you already losing your hearing?* He hated talking on the phone, period, the way he hated texting and e-mail, because he was bad at it, terrible at interpreting tone and words without the help of facial cues. Clearly, though, Lorelei had not been herself. He no longer had to fight too hard to resist all his old urges: to call her back somehow, to trace the number she'd called from. His meetings had given him the strength. Wendy had reinforced it. Colleen could mock Al-Anon all she wanted, but it had saved him.

The faintest squeaking sound emerged from downstairs, recurring every five seconds or so like a trained mouse. The treadmill. Colleen was already on it, not an hour after they'd walked through the door. Carl believed in physical fitness, for sure — sound body, sound mind — but there was a grimness in the way Colleen exercised, as if it were a punishment.

He descended one flight of stairs and then another into the basement. Colleen was running on a steep incline, her head-phones so loud Carl could hear the music from across the room. Her ponytail spasmed as her feet pounded the belt, and she stared straight ahead at the wall, eyes locked on an invisible spot. She did not sense his presence but went on running with intensity, as if finishing out a sentence. A few swaths of spandex clung to her body, a sports bra and shorts, tight as sealskin, and Carl was again struck by the starkness of her body, somewhere between a little boy's and a half-starved actress's. She'd always been petite, but at some point she'd lost her soft, girlish edges. Suppleness had given way to plain tightness. He vacillated between wanting to support all her vanity efforts — *whatever makes you happy* — and wanting to load the treadmill, the weights, and the cardboard flats of protein bars into his truck and dump them at the Salvation Army.

In the cool dimness of the basement, he watched her reach out to the console and jab a button with her index finger, and the belt spun faster. *Thomp-thomp-thomp.* She still hadn't sensed his presence. If he'd just been angry, it would've been easier; he'd have just turned and walked up the stairs and out the door to his meeting without saying a word. But anger was just the scrim. Below it was the bewildering sting of her having abandoned him when they should have needed each other most. The bewilderment of looking at her and thinking, *This is not the woman I married.*

The power cord for the treadmill lay thick and coiled between the machine and the wall — it was a gym-grade machine, heavy duty, devouring both electricity and the credit on his AmEx. Three freaking grand. He crossed the room, and yanked the cord's prong from the wall.

"Hey!" Colleen yelled, as the belt slowed, more abruptly than Carl had anticipated. She stumbled slightly, and he reached out to steady her. "What was that for?" She spread her arms and widened her eyes with incredulity.

"I didn't know how else to get your attention."

"How about just showing your face? You scared me!" She

picked up the towel draped over the bar of the console and mopped her brow.

"Sorry," he said. "I just wanted to let you know I'm going to a meeting. Do you want to come?"

"I can't."

"You can. All you have to do is get in the car."

"Carl." She stepped off the treadmill and pushed off one sneaker with the toe of the other. "Everything I'll hear at that meeting will be the exact opposite of what I believe in. I'll just want to get up and start throwing coffee cups."

"The exact opposite, how?"

"Oh, you know! You'll *share* that Lorelei called you." She said *share* as if it tasted sour. "And then six people will tell you how great it was that you pushed her away, and then I'll have to hear a strategy session about how to keep her away."

"It has nothing to do with pushing her away." He felt the exasperation rising in him. "It has to do with preventing her from falling back into destructive patterns that could get her killed."

"Did you memorize that from your Al-Anon handbook?"

"Don't mock me."

"I'm not mocking. It's just . . ." She paused, and pulled the elastic from her ponytail so her hair fell around her face. "Going to those meetings feels like taking a stand against Lorelei. It feels anti-motherly. It goes against all my instincts."

"Then come for me." His voice, to his dismay, was almost pleading. "Isn't that enough of a reason? Because you love me?"

She paused for what felt like a long time.

"I do love you," she answered finally, "but I also love Lorelei. And I thought you did, too."

"Stop. Don't stoop to saying things like that." He'd begun clenching both his thumbs between his index and middle fingers, as if restraining his fists.

Colleen appeared not to have heard. "If you loved her," she continued calmly, "you'd be driving me to Nevada right now."

"Are you out of your mind? You want me to just point the car in the general direction of an entire state and start driving? Maybe get some white shoe polish and write *Lorelei* on the windows? Would that prove my love, Colleen?"

"You'd find a way. You'd figure it out. That's what men do." She inhaled, as if summoning her strength, and stepped closer to him, close enough that he could smell the musk of her sweat and something sharper underneath, like alcohol. God, she must still be sweating it out from last night. "That's what a good father would do."

That did it; any remaining softness he'd felt toward her snapped. "You can't handle your liquor," he said, turning away. "You still smell like booze, twenty-four hours later. Do you have any clue how much you drank last night? You're an embarrassment. Go take a shower." And he walked up the basement stairs and out of the house, into the dwindling afternoon.

18

EQUUS REVISITED WAS filming on a horse farm just north and inland of Miami, an easy drive to the Atlantic, but Darren had no sense of being anywhere near Miami or the coast. The cast and crew were staying on the property in tiny mobile homes, to parallel the situation of the main characters, a down-and-out horse trainer and a jockey, who were scripted to live in a trailer park next to the bottom-tier track where they worked. Toby was old friends with the owner of the farm, so could afford to shoot for a full hundred days, practically an eternity for a mid-budget indie.

The farm — or, more accurately, "Thoroughbred training fa- cility," complete with six fancy barns and a half-mile racetrack — was blanketed with turgid grass that gave up shoe-soaking amounts of dew in the morning. Massive oak trees hung with coarse moss canopied the land, providing natural respite from the sun; there were several ponds full of bullfrogs, turtles, and water moccasins. It was beautiful, but too humid and swampy for Darren's comfort; even in March, it felt fecund, teeming with unseen critters and smelling of loamy manure. The loca- tion intern had given him a detailed tour shortly after he'd ar- rived, pointing out the hair and makeup trailers and where craft services set up before casually warning that Darren should ex- pect to encounter roaches and wolf spiders ("gigantic but to- tally harmless"), and that alligators showed up "once in a great while" near the ponds.

Darren had just settled into a rare moment of solitude, watching yesterday's dailies, when Toby stepped into the edit- ing trailer. Toby wore flip-flops, and his burly frame was furred by a black fleece bathrobe much too thick for the mild morning. Darren couldn't get ahead of the guy. Toby was practically glued to his shoulder, sitting beside him in the editing bay and cri- tiquing the footage Darren and his team had just shot, tugging at his bushy orange beard and turning the hat he always wore over his bald head backward and forward and back again. Even now, at the crack of dawn, he was wearing the stupid thing, a gray cap resembling one worn by a Depression-era newsboy, though Toby insisted on calling it a "tam o'shanter." Both the hat and Toby's name for it bugged the crap out of Darren.

"Morning, Toby," Darren said. "Aren't you hot in that robe?"

Toby looked down at his outfit. "Yeah. I wasn't thinking when I put it on. Too much on my mind." He opened a folding chair and eased into it. "How's yesterday looking?"

"I was just getting started," Darren said, biting the inner side of one cheek. He wasn't confident in what he'd shot the day before. Heather di Notia exuded a bitter-edged impatience, as if she couldn't wait to wrap and get on to more important things. She didn't like playing the mother of Marina Langley, whose youth and golden-girl status surely reminded Heather of what she used to be.

In addition to her bad attitude, Heather was hard to shoot. Once naturally beautiful, her face was now plumped in the cheeks and lips by collagen injections; self-conscious of her so-called cosmetic upgrades, she faltered in her scenes that required close shots. And, thanks to Toby's rigid opposition to "shielding" actors through creative camerawork or flattering light, bare close-ups of Heather amounted to a considerable chunk of the movie. All day yesterday, she'd been balking on camera, and they'd had to do a million takes of the same scene.

In fairness, Toby had warned Darren before the shoot started that Heather would be tough to shoot the way he needed to shoot Delilah, Heather's character, a horse trainer with a vodka and anger problem. He'd said, "I'm counting on you to help me make it happen. You've got a gentle, emo sort of vibe about you that I think she'll respond to."

"Um," Darren had said. "Thanks?"

Now, in the half-darkness of his editing station, as he cued his favorite take of the scene, Toby leaned forward. It began as a conversation and ended in a wild, saddle-hurling argument between Delilah and her love interest and nemesis, a talented but troubled jockey named Willie Bass. Willie had many strikes against him, including being five-ten — outrageously tall for a jockey — and prone to forming obsessions with the horses he rode. Toby's decision to cast the actor Vendler Peebles in the role of Willie had raised eyebrows in industry circles; Peebles had faded into near obscurity over the past decade. But Toby prided himself on his knack for coaxing jaw-dropping performances out of unlikely actors.

"God, the light's exquisite," Toby said.

Darren's work glowed on a giant monitor and Heather's throaty voice entered the trailer — "What the fuck's going on here?" — as Delilah discovers Willie sleeping in the stall of her prize racehorse. Shot at the peak of a clear morning, the frame was suffused with honey-and-lemon sunlight. It was a perfect juxtaposition with the characters' haggard faces — Willie exhausted from sleeping in the stall, too devoted to the horse to leave it overnight, and Delilah ragged from a night of Stoli and Virginia Slims. Hair and makeup had done a great job.

"Let's see more takes," Toby said. Darren checked his timeline, meticulously compiled by Sy, the intern who'd been up all night logging the footage, and picked out a half dozen alternate versions of the argument scene. He stole glances at Toby as they watched, hoping for a positive reaction, but he couldn't get a read: Toby looked like an entranced, plus-sized teddy bear, left thumb and forefinger pressing opposite sides of his face in concentration.

"Nope, nope, nope," Toby mumbled into his hand, eyes locked on the screen. After watching the takes, he said, "We need to reshoot it. I'll have Aspen change the call sheet."

"Seriously? We spent fifteen hours on it yesterday."

"Seriously. Every take is too controlled. I want the audience to feel unstable while they're watching Delilah throw the saddles around. You're making her meltdown look too tidy. You're protecting her with the camera. I thought we talked about this."

"Are you thinking we should switch to handheld?" Darren asked.

"God, no. Subtler than that. More angles. More cuts. Slicier and dicier. Not that shaky faux documentary style everyone's so into. Here, have another look." He took over Darren's track pad to replay a few seconds of footage. "Can you see what I mean?"

"Maybe," Darren said. "But I think eighteen and twenty-seven are close to perfect. And the score will really make a difference in getting the audience to that uncomfortable place. Don't you think?"

Toby shook his head. "Relying on music for emotional effect is lazy. I want a deaf person to be able to feel this movie just as much as anyone else, if not more."

"Umm. Yeah."

"Look, I know you haven't shot a feature before. Working with the same actors for weeks is way different from doing a commercial, and way, way different from catching gnarly shots of birds flying and rain bouncing off a roof."

Darren blanched. He'd worked his ass off to nail those bird and rain shots on his reel, sitting on top of Robin's roof in the middle of a downpour, his camera swaddled in tarp. *Catching gnarly shots,* as if Darren had just happened to leave a camera on while he was out surfing or something. It reminded him of what his father-in-law had said after he'd seen the work Darren had done on Robin's house: the new landscape design for the front yard, the tomato and herb garden in the back, the slate-blue paint job on the carriage house, built-in shelves in the office, the ascending pictures opposite the staircase, which he'd made with amazing old frames he'd scoured from junk shops and revitalized. "Solid upgrades" was all Mel said about Darren's many, many weekends of work.

Darren tapped his finger on the desk, staring at the pink-and-green *Bottle Rocket* poster Sy had tacked on the wall, a just-out-of-film-school kid trying to prove he knew hip references from Darren's generation.

As much as he wanted to tell Toby to go fuck himself, Darren couldn't.

Toby said, "Not that I didn't think *Str8t Edge* was cool. Don't take this the wrong way. I'm just trying to help."

"I know," Darren said. "I'm just thinking about your suggestions. Taking them in."

"Awesome. I think your core tactical issue is a hesitation in shooting Heather. Like you're trying to make sure the shots are flattering so she won't get mad at you. Very common reaction to divas like her."

Darren wanted to pluck the trackball from its socket and throw it at Toby's head. Even if he was largely right, he didn't have to be so condescending. Darren inhaled and counted slowly to three before letting it out. He teased Robin about her "yoga breathing," but it actually worked.

Toby leaned in toward Darren, one elbow on each of his knees, making purposeful eye contact. "Prettiness fucks with the integrity of a story. Your shots are too pretty. So what I need you to do is this—"

Darren's cell phone chimed with the arrival of a new text message.

Toby tilted his head and squinted at Darren. "Come on, man. Don't you know how much I hate fucking cell phones? Have I not stated my policy ad fucking nauseam?"

"You have. I didn't know it was on. And it's not official call-sheet hours."

"Have some common sense. If we're watching dailies, your volume's off. Period."

"You know, Toby," Darren said. "I respect your policies, but you just showed up in here at the crack of dawn, and—"

"It's not policy. It's ideology. The infrastructure of our culture is anti-art. The arrival of one text message might seem harmless, but look how it's pushed us right out of our zone, out of a moment of creative communion." Toby snapped his fingers.

Darren summoned all his power to remain diplomatic, reminding himself how Robin always complimented him on his ability to talk to "assholes of any caliber." She'd been referring to her parents' phony friends, but still. "Toby, you're a purist, and I admire that. It's one of the reasons I wanted to work with you. Going forward, you can count on my phone being silent, okay? I was just waiting to hear from my wife. Sometimes when she's up in the middle of the night in California that's the only chance we have to talk."

"I get that." Toby reached out and touched Darren's shoulder in a half rub, half chuck. "I totally get that. I don't mean to diminish your personal relationships. That's why I've got Aspen checking the barn landline all day. Your wife can call there any time."

"Got it."

"Anyway, what I'd been about to say is this: I need you to confront Heather with the camera, not comfort. Can you do that for me? Confront, not comfort."

"Definitely."

"Say it for me."

"Are you kidding?"

"Do I sound like I'm kidding?"

"Confront, not comfort."

"Awesome. I know you'll kill it today. God, I need coffee. And to get the hell out of this bathrobe. It shouldn't be this hot in March. I'll see you at the barn, dude. Great talking with you."

After the door of the trailer clicked shut Darren said, "Fuck you, Toby," and grabbed his phone to read the text from Robin. God, he missed her.

But the text was from Lorelei, the first in three weeks: *DARE!*

I'm low on $ but full o' love 4 U so can you please send me a few hundo to Cash Now on Fashion Show Dr in Reno and I SWEAR I will pay you back ASAP? Xo Lor.

Darren knew Lorelei was on a detour from regular life — an extended temper tantrum to punish her whole family, especially Colleen — and that she'd get ahold of herself and come back to L.A. eventually. But still, he was worried about her. What was she doing flat broke in Reno of all places? She'd once been exuberant and goofy, full of life. "Baby Chipmunk," he'd called her when she was little; her cheeks had been chubby back then.

He hovered his thumbs over the keypad of his phone. With a few taps, he could wire money to any depressing Cash Now storefront, and alleviate the guilt that would undoubtedly distract him from the long day ahead, navigating Toby's bulbous ego and Heather's fragile one. It wasn't as though Robin ever logged in to their checking account; he was the one to eyeball it each month, confirming that their monthly $12,000 had auto-transferred in from various investment accounts. She'd never notice.

LATE 2012

19

FLO'S STUDIO **WAS** the R&D network's biggest hit. When Robin said the show was searching for a fourth girl to join its stars, and that she'd landed Lorelei a spot in the first casting call, Lorelei was ecstatic.

Colleen knew she should have been thrilled, too — the show averaged almost a million viewers a week. Landing it would change Lorelei's life. But Colleen hated *Flo's Studio*. Set in downtown L.A., it followed three twentysomething gorgeous girls obviously from rich families (though this was never mentioned) who'd gone to a fancy design school in Rhode Island — and were now trying to launch an apparel company called Flo's Fauxes. The show focused on the risks and stressors that accompanied their brave ideas, such as producing jeans and handbags made from 100 percent recyclable, nontoxic materials recovered from landfills. The Faux Girls — Flo Flanders, Hillary Overstreet, and Zoey Chandler — planned to employ underprivileged inner-city youth across the country (their "materials managers") to scour dump sites for trash suitable for transmogrifying into pants and handbags that would sell in upscale boutiques. Part of the profits would be kicked back to these materials managers, supplementing their hourly wages.

"It's a huge win for everyone involved," Flo had explained to Zo and Hill in the first episode, her eyes shiny with self-satisfaction. "We're minimizing the profit gap between the manufacturing team and retail. Nobody else in the industry is doing this. Nobody."

The three girls inhabited a live/work space in an old Los Angeles factory, once a sweatshop that made socks, before all socks were made in China. It was a forbidding place, a decrepit airplane hangar with small, grimed-over windows, weak light, and dust coating all surfaces. In the footage aired at the end of the pilot episode, you could see junk everywhere: half-fallen stacks of long, narrow tables, dozens of chairs upside down or on their sides, metal scraps, broken industrial fans, coffeemakers, food wrappers.

"See, this is the sort of reality I'd like to do," Lorelei had said, when she and Colleen were settled on the couch, watching together. "Something that isn't totally superficial, like *The Canyon* or *Purse in Boots*."

"Mmm-hmm," Colleen had said, thinking that *Flo's Studio* was worse than either of those shows. At least they didn't pretend to be anything more than they were: just thirty minutes of beautiful girls shopping, catfighting, and complaining about their boyfriends.

On the TV screen, Zo said, "I can't work here, Flo. It's a massive dump."

"It's like a crack house crossed with a haunted house," Hill agreed.

"Don't be so unimaginative, girls!" Flo said. "This place has amazing potential. It could totally be transformed into state-of-the-art. And it's all we can afford. It's a great deal, actually, considering we can live here, too."

Zo gasped.

Colleen wanted to throw up.

Next to her on the couch, Lorelei was smiling ear to ear. "I can land this show, Ma," she said, "I have a feeling."

Attached to Faux Girls' workspace was a smaller enclosed area, like an attached two-car garage, that the girls would turn into their living area, the *Studio* part of the show's title. Hill and Zo shared a bunk bed with Flo's twin just a few feet from the lower bunk, orphanage style. The girls were often shot curled up on their beds, dishing about their love lives and brainstorming about their business.

"She's right, Zo," Hill had said. "We've got to fake it until we make it. We have no other choice." Flo had linked an elbow through each of her friend's arms and the Minny Danvers song "Even Tuff Girls Fake It Sometimes" blared over the scene. The camera pulled up toward the ceiling, slowly panning into a wide aerial shot of the factory with the girls at the center, trying to envision the future.

What irked Colleen the most about the show in the first season was how the girls were always pretending to struggle. Because they didn't have day jobs but were instead "risking everything" to launch Flo's Fauxes, they lived on the cheap, denying themselves meals at regular restaurants in favor of food trucks (and even then, bitching about burritos costing eight bucks), scouring thrift shops for their clothes or making their own. They were constantly poring over their "budget" and nervously preparing for meetings in which they were asking people for funding and getting rejected.

Colleen's IMDb and Wikipedia queries revealed that Hill and

Zo were from Newport Beach, and Flo was from Santa Barbara. They'd gone to private schools all their lives. They'd originally met at a famous creative arts camp on an island off Washington State. Their quest to make it in the world via their own creativity and innovation was the central story of *Flo's Studio* and also the reason it was praised for being more substantial than all the other shows featuring pretty girls and the fashion industry. But Colleen knew those girls had already made it, before they were born.

Flo Flanders, the show's star, annoyed Colleen most of all. The media loved to portray her as an inspiring role model for girls everywhere, and constantly drooled over her originality and substance. In Colleen's opinion, the most substantial and original thing about Flo were her looks: half Filipina and half Swedish, her combination of Pacific Island and Nordic genes turned out just right, landing her height, caramel-hued skin, delicate features, and big brown eyes. She kept her hair boyishly short, a look that had not only become her trademark, but was now so well-known that you could walk into salons in New York or L.A. and ask to "go Flo."

In addition to English, Flo also spoke Tagalog and Swedish. The network subtitled the Tagalog she burst into when she became angry, which had earned Flo accolades as "a truly postracial role model for tweens and teens." This drove Colleen crazy. What, could Flo really not express her anger in English?

Lorelei shared none of Colleen's feelings toward Flo or her show. Her excitement over the possibility of becoming the fourth Faux Girl was insuppressible.

"This is what we came to L.A. for!" she said to Colleen. "Finally, Robin's coming through."

"It's just an audition, honey," Colleen reminded her.

"Yeah, but it's not *open*. Robin bent over backward to get me into the first call. She thinks I've got a real chance."

"Of course you do," Colleen had said, thinking Robin hadn't exactly bent over backward as much as she'd simply made a phone call or two. Flo's off-screen best friend was Robin's client Yola Roo, and through Yola, Robin had become friendly enough with Flo to bump Lorelei to the front of the very long audition line.

It was the least Robin could do. For years, it had seemed to Colleen that she'd been setting Lorelei up for failure: the shampoo commercial, the teen savings account, the leg-toning sneakers. The Preventus ad. Colleen had been opposed to Lorelei being the face of the newest genital wart vaccine for teenagers. But she'd landed the part, and Robin lobbied hard for the upside: widespread network exposure, as the ad routinely ran during prime time, and residuals, and the legitimizing presence of a Big Pharma commercial on her reel.

The ad had run for a month, and then gotten pulled when the FDA suddenly reversed its approval of the drug. A few girls who'd taken it had sprouted facial hair. This was what Robin had wanted for Lorelei! Association with a product that grew beards on women! Colleen had been on the brink of firing her and finding Lorelei a new agent when the *Flo's Studio* possibility arose.

"Can't you just see me as the fourth girl?" Lorelei had said, returning to the couch with a bowl of Greek yogurt and starting another episode of *Flo's Studio*. "Doesn't it seem meant to be?"

"Absolutely," Colleen said, forcing cheer into her voice.

20

LORELEI MADE THE first cut, and the second. The word *audition* seemed implicitly banned from the *Flo's Studio* selection process, Colleen noticed, with irritation. Instead, there were acronyms: CFT (Casting Face Time), an event with two dozen finalists, and CSD (Casting Sit-Down), to which only twelve were invited, the others having been eliminated. The sugarcoating of what was really going on — the scrutiny of her daughter — made Colleen more and more anxious. There were no lines to help her learn. Lorelei's assignment for all stages of the *Flo's Studio* audition was to simply hang out with Flo, Hill, and Zo and be herself.

"Unlike casting procedures for other shows, we're not interested in judging you," Flo had said to the twenty-four girls at the CFT event, which was held in the new showroom, a gleaming industrial space with long racks of clothes slicing across the polished concrete floors. The stars, along with some unidentified female producers, disguised to blend in with the candidates, met with the Faux Girl hopefuls in small batches at various "fun, uncontrived environments where they could all just get to know one another."

Colleen always accompanied Lorelei to auditions, careful to keep in the background. She'd been hoping *Flo's Studio* would bring them to some interesting L.A. spots for the more intimate Casting Sit-Downs. But Lorelei's first CSD took place at a bowling alley/nightclub hybrid that leaned more toward bowling alley, and the second more intimate sit-down was at a restaurant in Venice called KinderGarden, featuring dishes like Buckwheat Groat Risotto and All Hale Kale!, which Lorelei had ordered because Flo declared it "transcendent."

"Honestly, it was just super-chewy," Lorelei later told Colleen, laughing.

The R&D network announced it would reveal the identity of the new Faux Girl on live television. It had been Flo's idea, and the show's producers had gone around and around with it, finally agreeing to the format.

"Other shows wouldn't dream of doing this kind of reveal," Robin said. "It's way too edgy. *The Canyon* and *Purse in Boots* are so afraid of keeping their stars' images perfectly intact that they'd never do a live segment. Reality's too scary for them."

"I love it!" Lorelei had said. "Flo's awesome."

The two-minute segment was slated to be broadcast "live and unedited" at the end of a half-hour recap of the season. It would be shot at Drain, in Silver Lake, where the girls would arrive for a cocktail after their day of thrift-shopping and lunching. For authenticity, the bar would be open during the shoot, though management would limit the number of patrons. Colleen had left the decision of her attendance up to Lorelei — Robin had quickly bowed out, and had urged Colleen to do the same, reasoning they'd make Lorelei more nervous. She was half right, Colleen thought — Robin would make her more nervous, but Colleen's presence would only fortify Lorelei, make her more relaxed, more herself.

"Of course it's up to you," Colleen had said. "But I think it would feel good for you to have me there, don't you think?"

"Um." Lorelei examined a cuticle. "I think so. I'm just not sure if the other girls' families are coming."

"It's just me," Colleen had said, surprised by Lorelei's hesitation. "Wouldn't it be strange to know I was back at the hotel, watching you on TV?"

Lorelei didn't answer. She continued inspecting her hands, using one thumbnail to scrape beneath the other.

"If you don't want me there — " Colleen began.

"No! I do." Lorelei looked up, her green eyes wide. "I'm just . . . nervous about the segment, Ma. I mean, it's *live*. I can't think clearly when I'm nervous."

"I'll just be in the background, honey. You won't even know I'm there."

"Okay," said Lorelei, too flatly. Colleen let the subject drop. It was incomprehensible that Lorelei wouldn't want her at the bar to witness the biggest moment of her career. Not after all Colleen had done to help her get here.

The details surrounding the announcement of the fourth Faux Girl were secret. Robin could only tell them that Lorelei was to arrive at Drain at noon on a Tuesday.

Lorelei and Colleen drove down from Fresno the day before and spent the night at a Marriott in downtown L.A., an easy drive from the shoot.

"How're you doing, honey?" Colleen had asked Lorelei over breakfast in the hotel lobby — two black coffees, one order of steel-cut oats split between them, and shots of apple cider brought along from Fresno for its energizing and fat-cutting properties. After doing a cleanse, even a spare breakfast seemed extravagant. "You're being so quiet."

"I'm great," Lorelei said. "I'm just trying to do what Robin said and just stay in the moment. It's amazing; if you do it, you can't get anxious."

This was happening more and more: Lorelei parroting Robin's advice. Colleen didn't like it, but she had to keep her eye on the ball, which was to keep Lorelei in an optimal frame of mind.

"That's very wise of you," Colleen said. She herself had been thinking about this day with an intensity bordering on obsession. But she wasn't the one who would be evaluated, so it was okay. Mothers were supposed to fret.

"Are you still excited about your outfit?"

"Totally."

"You're going to look bananas."

"Ma! Don't say bananas, just because that one judge used it as a compliment on *Sew What*."

"Sorry."

"But thanks. I think the dress is perfect."

"I love that we went with the long tank. It shows off your body just enough. And the steel metallic makes your eyes pop." Colleen took a bite of her oatmeal and washed it down with ice water.

Lorelei had been doing a cleanse all week, to look her absolute best for the camera, and Colleen had joined her in solidarity, despite Carl's incredulousness ("Explain to me what's dirty inside you?"), and both of them had shed a few pounds — Lorelei three and Colleen five — so that Lorelei looked particularly glorious in the outfit she and Colleen had chosen, under Robin's supervision: a clingy steel-gray tank dress by Traci Tong and open-toed platform ankle boots. The dress was perfectly fitted, just tight enough to display Lorelei's amazing body without looking slutty, and the shimmery stuff embedded in the material provided just the right touch of glamour in certain light. The boots added the assertive but sexy edginess that Robin had said was the embodiment of *Flo's Studio*'s core values. As much as she disliked agreeing with Robin over clothes, especially since Robin could barely dress herself, Colleen had experienced her first sense of solidarity with Robin as they'd watched Lorelei model the outfit in the corridor of a dressing room at Nordstrom. As Lorelei shifted and turned in the three-way mirror, twisting her neck to assess herself from every angle under the harsh fluorescent lighting, Colleen noticed Robin watching Lorelei with appreciation, admiration, and a touch of envy.

Colleen realized the one thing that could make you like your enemies in a heartbeat: seeing that person love someone you love.

As a salesgirl carefully packed the Traci Tong dress in tissue at the register, Colleen had no qualms about handing over her MasterCard to cover the $1,298.52. Shoes included.

21

COLLEEN WAITED IN the car for ten long minutes while Lorelei was inside Drain learning the day's logistics, and she was so relieved to see her jogging back to the car, grinning, curls bouncing in the sun.

"Ma, this is fun!" Lorelei said, leaning through the driver's-side window to kiss Colleen's cheek. "Me and the Fauxes, and the two others finalists, basically just get to hang out in the neighborhood all day! Have some lunch, hit some thrift stores, brainstorm ideas for the Faux line."

"On camera?"

"Of course on camera!"

"Okay, that's great. What should I do all day?"

Lorelei shrugged. "There's an actual lake around here, somewhere. You could check it out. Take a hike. Just make sure you're back before four, in time to watch the final segment of shooting in the bar. First the girls and I will have cocktails and reflection time, and then Flo announces the winner. By five o'clock I'll know if I'm on the show!"

"Wow."

"I love you, Mom." Lorelei gripped Colleen's arm, flashing her sky-blue nails. Somehow, it was the perfect color, so unlikely, and yet Lorelei had chosen it without an ounce of hesitation, and wore it as if her nails were always meant to be bright blue, as if they were natural that way. Colleen felt a wave of pride. Lorelei would be the next Faux Girl.

"Love you, baby," Colleen said. "Break your legs."

"Bye, Ma. Try to relax and enjoy yourself."

"Aren't I supposed to say that to you?"

"I already am," Lorelei said.

"You're going to get this part, Lorelei."

"No jinxing," Lorelei said, and jogged gracefully back into the bar.

Colleen had tried to relax and enjoy herself. She drove to the lake, which looked like dull aluminum, and got out of the car; but the harsh glare of the sun muscling past her dark glasses only made her edgier. She browsed magazines at a bookstore, visited a vintage boutique, and got a latte from a surly, pierced barista. Around two, Carl called, from a job site in Visalia, to wish them luck. He wouldn't be able to watch live, but promised to view the recorded version as soon as he got home that evening. His words were kind enough — *You've both worked so hard for this* — but vague, and his voice lacked feeling. The call was short. Wandering the neighborhood again, Colleen worried she might run into the Faux Girls and their prospects, and perhaps embarrass Lorelei and throw off her focus, so at two o'clock she went back to Drain — to simply wait.

The bar was open and there were no signs of a camera crew, just a sprinkling of midday patrons, all resembling the too-cool barista Colleen had encountered earlier, drinking beer and eating burgers. She was already jittery from too much coffee, but she felt lame ordering seltzer from the scruffy, handsome bartender, so she ordered a Bloody Mary.

He measured and poured liquids and spices, finally setting down a glass of rich tomatoey liquid flecked with pepper and speared with two long points of asparagus. It smelled delicious and tasted even better. Probably — she did a quick calculation — 170 calories. Colleen didn't care. She liked the way it burned her throat.

22

THE FIRST BLOODY Mary went down so easily, Colleen ordered another. She figured two were the caloric equivalent of a big bowl of gazpacho, and she hadn't eaten anything since the oatmeal she'd shared with Lorelei. This would be a late lunch, and the bartender didn't seem to be judging her for drinking in the middle of the day on a Tuesday.

"My Bloodys are kind of epic, huh?" He stopped polishing pint glasses and started mixing her drink.

"Yes. Spicy," she said, wincing at his ears, which were pierced with the wide black disks that gradually stretched the lobes.

"Gotta be careful with them. Hard to tell how strong they are, but they'll kick your ass." He held the vodka bottle up high, letting it stream into the glass.

"How do you do that without splashing it everywhere?" she asked.

"It's all in the amount of ice," he said, performing the same trick with a pitcher of doctored tomato juice. "That, and a lot of practice." He ground a pepper mill over her drink, his wrist moving fluidly. Colleen noticed the muscles of his arms. She'd been distracted by his earlobes, floppy hair, and bizarre tattoo along the ridge of his left jawline, some word in a serpentine script she couldn't decipher, all features that didn't match his gym-toned body. He was maybe early thirties? An actor?

He slid the drink across the wide bar.

"Thanks." She bristled with self-consciousness, realizing she was the only person seated at the bar. Drain was dark and cavernous, and not as much a dive on the inside as it appeared from the exterior. In fact, it was quite nice, its spotless wood floor dotted with sleek round tables and low black booths hugging the periphery, low light seeping from what looked like upside-down lollypops, and slim rectangular windows high along the edge of the room, giving the illusion of being subterranean, letting in just enough sunlight to keep your dopamine flowing and gently remind you it was daytime.

"I'll join you," he said, pouring an inch of coppery liquor into a shot glass. "If you don't mind."

"Of course."

"Cheers." He clinked his shot to her and tossed his back. She sucked at hers through the black stirring straw, then remembered Lorelei making fun of her for that — "You don't drink through that, Ma, unless it's like your first drink ever." She set the straw on the cocktail napkin.

"This is the best Bloody Mary I've ever had."

"Thanks," he said, polishing.

"Are you an actor?"

"Yeah." His eyes flicked up. "Are you?"

"Me? No. I'm here for the shoot later on."

"You work on *Flo's Studio?*"

"My daughter might."

"She's one of the girls on the chopping block today?"

"Chopping block?" She chewed a pickled onion. Her jaw tightened from the brininess. "It's not a cooking show."

He chuckled. "I should keep my reality show jargon accurate. Is your daughter part of the talent?"

"She's one of the finalists."

"I'll root for her."

Colleen's second drink went down easier than her first, and she had no qualms about asking Lance — the bartender/actor — for a third.

"You want some smoked almonds to go with that?" he asked. "Or should I bring you a menu?"

"Almonds would be great," she said, light-headed and happy, trying to remember the number of almonds that equaled one serving. Lance clattered some into a bowl that looked like it was made from a church window. She ate two. They were delicious, crunchy and salty.

A production crew had shown up, six or eight kids in their twenties with the R&D slogan — YOU LIVE IT, WE MAKE IT — in red print on the back of their black T-shirts. They'd cordoned off the back of the bar, a semicircular space surrounding a big round booth, with a retractable elastic railing, the kind that kept people in line at airports. They set up lights and fit cameras onto tripods and taped blackout paper over windows with a feverish intensity. Overseeing them was a pretty Indian woman with lustrous hair swept back in a yellow headband, maybe in her late twenties. She moved with military confidence around the set, directing her crew in a tidy British accent. Colleen admired how she'd covered her black T-shirt with a pair of camouflage overall shorts with the signature Dolce & Gabbana logo on the back pocket. The overalls were girlish and fun, but the camouflage was tough, ready for work.

Colleen checked the clock over the bank of liquor bottles behind the bar: 3:20.

"Listen," she said to Lance, who was pulling an amber beer from a tap into a tipped pint glass. "Lorelei's the one with the curly red hair. Reddish hair. Goldish auburn."

"TV needs more redheads," Lance said. "I'm rooting for her." She heard his interest in the conversation waning. People under thirty were crowding the bar, all good-looking in the sloppy way Colleen hated, as if they were half joking about their outfits, the boys in cardigans and skinny jeans and canvas gardening shoes, the girls in dresses inspired by men's bowling shirts. She had the best body in the room, even if she was the oldest.

What she wanted now was to smoke, something she only did when she'd had several drinks.

"Hey, Lance!" she yelled over the rising din in the room.

"Whatcha need?"

"Do you have a cigarette I could borrow?"

He pulled a slender silver case from the front pocket of his snap-up western shirt and handed her a cigarette. "Keep it," he said. Yes, he was definitely finished with her. Had she come off as overeager, a Mrs. Robinson daytime drinker in a hipster bar? He was probably a loser, anyway. Otherwise he'd be acting, not polishing pint glasses. She weaved her way to the exit.

The afternoon was sparkling and cloudless. R&D people were running all over the place, setting up lights and yellow barricades on the sidewalk, yelling instructions. She found a spot off to the side of the bar's entrance, out of the way, beneath a tree blooming with purple flowers. Ducking her face behind the trunk, Colleen lit Lance's cigarette with a matchbook she'd plucked from a bowl at the hostess station, DRAIN printed in typewriter font on the cover. The sun felt good on her bare arms, and she closed her eyes for a moment to savor her first drag, but it hit her much harder than she'd expected, making her dizzy and faintly nauseated. She opened her eyes to the Indian girl in the camouflage overalls frowning in front of her.

"First off, there's no smoking within twenty feet of the entrance," she said. "And secondly, we're trying to shoot a TV show here. Please relocate."

"Oh," Colleen said, trying to anchor herself in the wooziness that had descended. "I . . ."

"Are you all right, then? You look a bit ill."

Colleen took a deep breath, her cigarette pointed at the ground.

"I'm fine," she managed. "I'm . . . I'm with the show. I'm Lorelei Branch's mom." She pulled out the ID card somebody had given her earlier. "She's one of the finalists."

"Oh! Mrs. Branch! I'm Sashi Sabaratnam! Supervising producer for *Flo's Studio*. Fantastic to meet you. You must be so excited." She stuck out her right hand, but Colleen's was occupied with her cigarette, so she offered up her left and Sashi gave it a squeeze. "Sorry to reprimand. It's just the girls are two blocks away and we're about to roll cameras. I'd recommend going inside the bar and getting a good seat, but if you must stay outside, please step over there." She pointed to a grassy patch across the sidewalk.

"I will."

"And the cigarette, please?"

"Sorry!" She dropped it to the sidewalk and stubbed it out hard beneath the signature red sole of the Louboutin heels she'd borrowed from Marilyn.

"No big deal," said Sashi. She cupped her hand toward Colleen's ear and whispered, "I'm absolutely pulling for Lorelei," before striding away, calling out, "Fifteen seconds, people!"

Colleen felt the presence of her daughter nearby, like a caught scent. She wanted to see her before the crowd did, to transmit good luck somehow, even if it was just with eye contact. She crossed the sidewalk, trying not to wobble. She felt the crushed cigarette stuck to the sole and worried she might have caused a burn mark on the $1,200 shoes borrowed from Marilyn.

She tried lifting up her leg to look, but she was much too drunk to stand on one leg. She plucked the shoe off, and as she was examining it with one foot bare, Sashi yelled, "Approaching!" and Colleen looked up to see the girls swinging around a corner toward the bar. They walked in two groups of three girls across, and Lorelei was in between Hill and Zo, in a green microdress — the wardrobe designer must have nixed the Traci Tong — and fringed brown open-toe boots with three-inch heels, her big curls flying. Colleen felt a thrill seeing her daughter there between two stars, outshining them with her superior hair and face, and petite but curvy body. She was by far the most captivating girl in the pack.

As six pairs of lean legs scissored down the block toward Colleen, certainty of Lorelei's victory took hold of her. She needed to make contact, just for a second. Just so Lorelei knew, in that moment, how proud she was.

Of course, there were cameras, in front of the girls and behind them. The street was closed to allow the crew to shoot from golf carts that rolled along the sidewalk. Some guys shouldered big, boxy cameras and others extended microphones toward the girls on contraptions that looked like fishing poles.

When the girls were within earshot, Colleen called out, "Hello, hello!," poking her high heel up to the sky in a greeting. She'd forgotten she was holding it.

Lorelei looked up and her face tightened and froze.

A dozen feet away, Lorelei mouthed, *No,* to Colleen and shook her head. *No, no, no.*

Okay, thought Colleen, *okay, I get it!* The other five girls were still chattering away. They hadn't even noticed her. Nia, one of the finalists, a sinewy black girl with a shaved head, said, "But now you can get local anesthesia for Brazilians. I swear, there's a place in Larchmont!" And Flo Flanders, taller and more exotic at close range — a sleek jungle cat — said, "That is absolutely brilliant."

Colleen was a statue as the girls passed, and Lorelei widened her eyes and locked them on Colleen: *Do not say a word.*

She waited until the girls disappeared inside the bar, feeling as if she'd just been slapped. Was Lorelei ashamed of her? Would it really have been so humiliating for her to say hi to her mother?

Colleen crunched an Altoid, checked her face in the mirror of a compact, and freshened her lipstick. She flashed her guest badge to the PA at the door and went back inside the bar.

Drain had gotten very crowded; her spot near Lance was now occupied by girls drinking beer. Kids in their twenties filled the round booths, spectators clogged the periphery of the room, and young guys barking into their headsets crisscrossed the hardwood of the bar's main floor. In the largest booth, in a far corner of the room, with ten feet of space cleared around them to accommodate cameras, Lorelei and the rest of the girls sat with their heads together like a flock of rare birds. Hair and makeup had done a touch-up on them, and Lorelei's hair was pulled back into a tight ponytail at the back of her neck, her curls smoothed into a dense bunch trailing down her back. She was smiling, showing off the expensive teeth whitening Colleen had paid for, two days after she swore she'd stop spending behind Carl's back.

Colleen wended her way up to the bar, using her elbows and the politest "Excuse me"s she could muster. She ordered a shot of vodka from the bartender, a girl with bracelets tattooed right onto her wrists, Kate Moss skinny. Colleen thought she detected a smirk, so she didn't tip, and quickly knocked back the shot to quell her nerves.

PAs began to shush everyone in the bar.

It was time.

Colleen made her way back toward the middle wall, to have a better view and be closer to the girls' table.

They sat in a horseshoe, their colored drinks in martini glasses looking like liquid candy. They lifted their glasses in a toast, and then Flo, Hill, and Zo wriggled out of the booth and went outside, sunlight folding in and out of the door.

"Where're they going?" Colleen asked the guy standing next to her.

"To confer on the final decish," he said. "We're down to the wire."

"Oh," said Colleen, her throat constricting with an anxiety no amount of vodka could blunt.

"Everybody, quiet down please," he called out, and stepped forward. "Take it down just a notch. We're about to find out who the next Faux Girl will be!"

Colleen was dying for one moment of eye contact, just to get a feel for how Lorelei was really doing, and to let her daughter know she was there for her. She stared as hard as she could until Lorelei finally felt it and looked up. And smiled. Colleen mouthed, *I love you*, and Lorelei mouthed it back, and Colleen could tell, even from thirty feet away, that Lorelei wasn't unhappy with her, and that the Faux Girls were going to choose her. This knowledge passed between them, and Colleen tingled with excitement.

Flo and her sidekicks reappeared and squeezed back into the booth. They would deliver the news in the guise of a private conversation, though they were miked and projected up onto monitors.

"This has been one of the hardest decisions I've ever made," Flo began, and Hill and Zo nodded. "You're all so unique with so much to offer."

"Honestly," Zo said. "We just wish we could keep all three of you."

"God, we really do," said Hill. "This is actually torturous."

"The suspense is killing me!" said Piper. She was the antithesis of Nia: Icelandic, all shades of cream, with alpine eyes and French vanilla hair.

"Right, we totally can't postpone this one second longer, you guys," Flo said. "After much deliberation, our new Faux Girl is . . ." She paused, and then she and Hill and Zo sang the name in unison: "Nia!"

The girls hugged one another, all six of them crying. Even Lorelei was crying, and as Colleen pushed toward the booth, she could tell they were real tears. Colleen's heeled foot caught a slippery patch on the floor and she tripped, had to reach out and grab the shoulder of some fat guy to steady herself. Then she kept moving. People were grabbing at her, girls with ponytails, interns or PAs, saying, "Excuse me, we're still shooting." "Excuse me, you can't go over there." But Colleen pushed them off.

"Mom!" said Lorelei when Colleen arrived at her table, and Colleen read the urgency of her tone as relief: the arrival of her one true ally, *get me out of here*. But then Lorelei hissed, "Get away! We're still shooting!" And it felt like a second pummeling.

"I'll get away in just a second." Colleen looked down at Nia's beautiful coffee-bean-colored hands, resting next to her martini glass, nails painted white, her oversized watch bright gold, the bone of her wrist pushing up beneath her skin in a high peak. Even her wristbone was unique. Nia was like the subject of a Gauguin painting. Lorelei had never stood a chance.

A PA pulled at Colleen's wrist. She shook her off. "One second," she said, raising her hand, and the PA backed off.

"I just want to tell it like it is," she said.

"Mom!" Lorelei cried, helpless from her position in the center of the ring of girls.

The words rose from inside Colleen. She didn't have to search her mind; they just emerged.

"Lorelei, honey, it's okay. I just think someone ought to say what complete bullshit this audition is — oh, sorry, I'm not supposed to say *audition,* because you bitches are too good for that! I mean, what complete bullshit this *evaluation* is, and you Flo Girls are acting all holier-than-thou with your homemade Dumpster clothes and your *charity mind-sets*" — that particular phrase, which had felt so accurate on Colleen's lips as she said it, had been widely mocked later; even Jon Stewart had made some joke about it, "charity mind-sets" — "and your scalped heads, like your ancestors would just choke on their peace pipes if you grew some hair!"

Someone in the background said, "Call security!" and someone else said, "Yes, but stay back. Still rolling."

Colleen saw that Lorelei, pinned in the booth, was covering her face with her hair. Cowering into the shoulder of the blond girl beside her. Well, maybe Lorelei was content to avoid the reality of the situation: that *Flo's Studio,* like every other reality show on television, was rigged, but Colleen refused to sit there and let these self-righteous rich girls pretend it was anything else.

"You're all fucking phonies! Pretending like you're more real than everyone else. This whole audition is a total *crotch*" — she'd meant *crock!* Of course she had! — "You obviously had your minds made up from the start. You didn't care about picking the best person. It's just a rigged crock of PC bullshit. Obviously you were always going to vote for the exotic one. You needed some dark skin and some more dykey hair to round out your clique.

"And Flo just wanted some exotic company, because she has a few Asian genes in her, and so you all just said, 'Fuck it,' and ignored the talent factor. Totally fucking ignored the talent factor, even though my daughter is fucking irradiating talent" — yes, for some reason, the word came out as *irradiate* — more fodder for national joking, ha ha ha — "You just picked this anorexic Somalian bitch" — famine in Somalia had been on the news that week — "because she fits the fake image of your fake show, and —"

Two security men took Colleen by her elbows and pulled her away from the table.

"Wait, wait!" She'd begun to sob. Things had gone horribly wrong, but maybe she could still salvage them. "Where's Lorelei? I need my daughter." She'd begun to cry, tears burning her face.

"Just come with us, ma'am." Hands gripped her on either side, guiding her through the crowd. She had no choice but to comply. Her gait was wobbly, her mind thickly hazed and twitchy.

She was wasted.

Everything that came next was a dark blot. She remembered only that she'd vomited, several times, and that she'd been driven back to the Marriott where she and Lorelei had stayed the night before. She could recall the motion of the car, from where she laid flat in the backseat, and the sound of murmuring female voices. That she'd tried to call out Lorelei's name, but her mouth was so terribly dry.

She'd awoken in bed fully clothed to a bright morning sun, her head hammering. Someone had left a bottle of water on the nightstand and neatly placed Marilyn's shoes beside the bed. Colleen's handbag was on the floor, its contents intact. Her suitcase was on the stand where she'd left it. The Camry was in guest parking. But Lorelei and all her things were gone. Her cell phone was turned off.

Panicked, Colleen had called Carl.

"She called yesterday evening, when I was driving home from Visalia," he said, sounding perplexed. "And made me promise that I wouldn't watch her audition. She said she'd bombed, and it would be too humiliating for her if I saw it. She made me swear I'd delete it without watching. So I did."

"Oh. Okay." Temporary relief suffused Colleen. Carl didn't yet know what had happened. In that moment, she loved her husband fiercely. Only *he* would have the self-control to honor Lorelei's request. Anyone else on the planet would have let their curiosity get the better of them.

"I love you," Colleen blurted out.

"I love you, too," Carl said. But he sounded uncertain.

"Do you really?" She suddenly needed to be sure.

"Yes, of course. Can you just tell me what's going on? You sound miserable. Lorelei said the two of you had a fight, and that she'd be staying at Darren's for a few days."

"Can I just come home first? And we'll talk?"

She hung up the phone and began to sob.

Colleen's entire monologue at Drain had been captured on camera. On many cameras, including numerous ones held by phone-wielding spectators. The video, in its raw entirety, was promptly posted on YouTube, where it captured more than a hundred thousand views in twenty-four hours. It was titled "The Exotic Rant." Colleen learned this from Marilyn, who'd heard about it from her daughter, Jenna.

"Don't watch," Marilyn instructed her firmly, but with compassion. "Spare yourself."

Colleen didn't watch. But she couldn't help reading a little.

"We hope this incident inspires open dialogue about issues of race that still exist in Hollywood," Flo Flanders had said to the *Los Angeles Times*. "Although we stand behind the color blindness of *Flo's Studio,* and our commitment to creating socially responsible reality television."

An edited version appeared on *Flo's Studio*. Colleen didn't watch that, either, but Marilyn slipped to her that the episode Colleen appeared on was the highest-rated *Flo's Studio* ever. That the show had since been renewed for two more seasons.

Marilyn's intention was to cheer her. "The *Flo's Studio* people love you, honey," she said, in the weeks after the so-called Exotic Rant, when Colleen was inconsolable. "Lorelei will come around. Give yourself a break. Shake it off. Everyone's forgotten about it already."

Perhaps Colleen could have shaken off being nationally humiliated. But she could not shake off her daughter's silence. Lorelei moved into Robin and Darren's carriage house, not "for a few days," as she'd told her father, but indefinitely. She would not answer Colleen's calls. When Colleen showed up in Santa Monica, Lorelei refused to see her. Robin and Darren stood in the front doorway, speaking in diplomatic tones but physically blocking the entryway, saying that Lorelei needed more time to process and regroup. Two and a half months after the disaster at Drain, Lorelei disappeared from L.A.

POSSE RAP WITH FLO FLANDERS
By Justina Stroh
November 22, 2012

Posse *sat down with the 22-year-old fashionista to talk cruelty-free lingerie, Japanese rice balls, and the recent disruption to her hit reality show,* Flo's Studio.

Posse: Your new line of vegan bras, underwear, and other sexy little items has just been picked up by Victoria's Secret. What makes your lingerie different?

FF: Romantic lingerie is often made from silk because it feels great to touch. What people don't realize is that hundreds of millions of silkworms are killed every year just to produce bras and underwear. Flo's Fauxes lingerie is made from 100% no-kill silk. We patented a blend of cellulose fiber, cornhusks, and seaweed that feels virtually identical to the worm-based version. In fact, many women swear it feels even better!

Posse: Next to fashion, food plays a central role on your show. You and the Faux Girls are always sampling the more adventurous foods of Los Angeles. What's your latest food obsession?

FF: Well, I follow a plant-based diet, so my adventurousness is somewhat limited. But right now I'm completely addicted to omusubi. They're Japanese rice balls with different fillings inside. Pickled plum and seitan is my favorite. I literally can't get through the day without them! Luckily, there's an omusubi truck that parks right near the Flo's Fauxes headquarters.

Posse: *Flo's Studio* is one of the most popular reality shows on television, and last week's episode, in which your core cast selected a new member during a live broadcast, was hugely anticipated. What was your first reaction when you realized an out-of-control drunk woman was about to sabotage the key moment of the show?

FF: I totally froze. We'd worked so hard all season, and decided to take this huge risk by doing a live broadcast, and then all of a sudden this random woman is charging the cameras and screaming at us. It was pretty terrifying.

Posse: But she wasn't a random woman, was she? Her name was Colleen Branch, and she's the mother of Lorelei Branch, one of the girls you were considering to join your cast.

FF: That's true. But I personally had no idea who she was at the time.

Posse: Colleen Branch's meltdown was ostensibly a reaction to your choice of Nia Bauman as the new Faux Girl, instead of her own daughter, Lorelei. It was not only angry but highly racist, and was partially seen by millions of viewers watching the show, before your crew cut to a commercial. Many thousands of other people saw a longer version, captured on video with a smartphone and posted to YouTube, where it became known as the Exotic Rant, due to the hateful disdain Colleen expressed for multiracial individuals like yourself. How did this incident—and the large audience it reached virally—impact you?

FF: What the woman said was very offensive, of course, but honestly, I just feel sorry for her. The video became popular largely as fodder for humor. This country has come a long way. If you're going to be outwardly racist, you're likely to become a laughingstock.

Posse: Do you resent the recognition the video got? Even as a source of humor? Couldn't you say Colleen Branch's racism has made her a little bit famous?

FF: Fame only counts if it lasts more than two weeks. I'm afraid Colleen's doesn't qualify.

Posse: What about Lorelei Branch? She had dreams of being where you are today—a reality TV star, admired by millions of Americans. Any words of advice for her?

FF: Follow your passion, and the recognition will follow. I promise.

EARLY 2013

23

AT THREE A.M., Darren was wide-awake on his flimsy cot, on his back under a single sheet. Unlike L.A., Florida didn't cool off much at night. Every time he shifted, the lattice wire frame groaned beneath him, too loud in the quiet of the early morning. Even the crickets had signed off.

He'd decided not to send Lorelei the money. Which, by daylight, was the right decision. He'd even ignored her pathetic secondary requests, also issued via text: *Pleeeeeese?!?!?! This will be the last favor EVER*, et cetera.

But now, in the humid darkness, he was questioning his decision. Scenes flipped through his mind: Lorelei crumpled in the bathroom of a nightclub, her delicate limbs jumbled in unnatural angles. Huddled on the stained carpet of a bottom-budget motel where sweaty tweakers with mustaches and rodent eyes paced in filthy jeans, and saddle-skinned strippers rapped at the door. Careening through the pinball-machine belly of a casino, high out of her mind, scanning for untended handbags to steal.

If he'd sent her money, he might have kept her safe.

But he also would have broken the promise he'd made to Robin: no more cash for Lorelei. After she'd moved into their carriage house, Darren had given his sister a few twenties here and there, and Robin had held her tongue. But then Lorelei started getting home at four in the morning and blasting music, coked up with a bunch of clubby friends, waking Darren and Robin up with screams of laughter and top-volume, off-key singing. Once, their neighbors had called the cops. Lorelei also stole from them: a jug of coins, hundreds of dollars' worth of wine, a couple of Robin's designer handbags, and one of his video cameras.

One afternoon in January, Lorelei moved out, notifying Robin and Darren with the same message: *Thanks 4 the hospitality, moving in w/ friends to West Hollywood, let's keep in touch xo.* She'd left the carriage house a wreck, ashtrays and liquor bottles everywhere, and she'd taken a lamp and all the towels. Darren was shocked, but Robin was furious and insisted they keep their contact with Lorelei to a minimum going forward. They would only communicate with Lorelei if she truly wanted to clean up her act. Their marriage therapist had agreed that Lorelei had problems, and chasing her down and trying to fix them would only postpone Lorelei's healing.

Darren disagreed — what was family for if not helping each other? He and Lorelei had grown distant over the years, but he was still attached to the cuddly little girl she'd once been. The one who'd followed him around when she was three, sucking her thumb and twirling her corkscrew curls, begging him to "play movie," meaning film her with the bulky VHS camcorder Darren had received from his father on his fifteenth birthday.

Yes, Lorelei behaved badly while living in the carriage house. Yes, she'd pushed Darren's marriage closer to the edge, where it had already been inching, thanks to the baby issue. Robin had every right to be angry. So he'd had to block out the image of the redheaded toddler and promise his wife: no contact with Lorelei, unless she was seeking real help. As in therapy or rehab. Asking for money did not qualify.

Darren was sorry Robin had ever taken on Lorelei as a client.

From bed, he ran his hand over the trailer's cheap carpet in search of his water glass and took a long drink. Then he checked the time on his phone: 3:30. Call time was at 6:15. He needed to sleep. He could not afford to fuck this job up by letting his personal life distract him. It wasn't just his career and his marriage that he'd put on the line to be in Florida; his dignity was at stake, too. It wasn't easy to be Mel Justus's son-in-law. His voice steamrolled through Darren's mind.

You looking for steady work these days, or do the art projects keep you too busy?

So interesting, your generation's definition of work.

Remind me what you did for work, before you and Robin met?

On the morning of their wedding, days after Robin's trust had been released to her: *You sure timed this one right.*

Nothing's more important, to my mind, than that my grandchildren learn the importance of good old-fashioned work ethic.

As soon as Robin's back was turned, Mel let Darren know that, until Darren provided evidence to the contrary, Mel would believe he spent his days drifting in some sort of arty cloud. Never mind the sixteen-hour days Darren had spent on the set of commercial shoots (okay, there'd only been a few of those), or the months and months he'd devoted to his shorts. All Mel saw was a man who'd never had "steady work," who'd married his wealthy daughter.

The implication that Darren had married Robin for her money made him want to smash Mel's tan, doughy face against the nearest wall.

Of course, he never rose to Mel's bait. He said as little as possible, a tactic he'd learned from his own father.

The best revenge was to get his name attached to a high-profile project, and now here he was, on location for *Equus Revisited*, after Toby King had contacted him out of the blue on the merit of the very projects Mel had dismissed. As much as he disliked Toby's arrogance and criticism, Darren knew that *Equus Revisited* would prove to Mel that his career was alive and kicking. It might not be a film Mel would appreciate — *Iron Man* was more his speed — but with a star as big as Marina Langley on its marquee, it would be enough to shut him up. Darren and Robin might even end up at the Oscars.

Darren did not disclose to Robin the extent of Mel's goading, which Mel was careful to deliver only after his daughter left the room. She was already too disappointed in and embarrassed by her parents, too anxious that they didn't fully love her. Darren worried she'd crack if she knew that Mel harassed him with mocking snippets every chance he got.

Occasionally, Mel and Linda dropped by their house in Santa Monica unannounced. "We were on our way to the Levines' in Malibu and practically drove right by your house — we couldn't not say hi!" "We got last-minute tickets to a play at the Broad and drove over early to beat traffic, so we had to come say hi!"

Once, they'd dropped by at two in the afternoon on a Wednesday. Darren had been sound asleep on the living room couch. He'd been up the whole night before, cutting *Str8t Edge*. Robin was out at the No Princess offices, still mired in the seemingly endless process of transitioning the helm to Gregory.

"Sorry to wake you," Linda had said. "We didn't mean to spy, but I could see you right through the lookout window in the front door. You should cover that up. I know the greatest custom drapery place on Pico." She set a cluster of hyacinth in a slim vase on the foyer table. "Aren't these gorgeous? So delicate, yet sturdy."

"The man needs his rest," Mel had said. "We'd better let him get back to it, or his art will suffer. Give Robin our regards when she gets home, okay, my man?" He'd stuck his hairy-knuckled hand out for Darren to shake, his finger bulging around his wedding ring like a fat kid squeezed into an inner tube.

"Your parents stopped by," he'd told Robin later. "Your dad was raving about how No Princess stole Ashlyn Lewis from Spangle Talent. He was so proud. And your mom left these for you — something about hyacinth being the symbol of delicate power, like you."

Robin had snorted. "Really? What a couple of cheese balls."

But he could tell she was pleased.

He'd come to excel at creatively interpreting Mel and Linda in such a way that proved their love for Robin, a small tweaking of the truth to serve the greater good and keep her from joining weepy adopted-child support groups or devoting her life to tracking down her birth parents.

Thinking about how he'd constructed a livable bridge between his wife and her parents calmed him, and finally, Darren fell asleep.

24

BY MIDMORNING, DARREN'S throat was raw from the dust, hay, and woodchips that permeated the air of the barn, where they'd been shooting for hours and still, no sign of wrapping the scene.

"Heather, you're getting flat on me," Toby yelled, pulling off his tam o'shanter and flapping it at her. "We were close, but now you're withdrawing again. Remember, think raw. Inside and out. That's where Delilah's at right now. I want you to picture what the skin of your chest would look like if you scrubbed it with a fucking Chore Boy. Speak from that place. Can you do that?"

Heather tore off Delilah's wide-brimmed hat and hurled it to the raked-dirt floor of the barn. "It's him!" She pointed at Ven. "He's the one holding back."

"Bullshit," the normally unflappable Ven yelled, smacking the air with the back of his palm. "Don't point the finger at me, Heather."

"Toby, he's sabotaging," Heather said. "He's completely walled off."

"Has she even read the whole script?" Ven asked Toby. "It's called being in character. Willie *is* walled off."

Heather balled both fists. Darren braced himself for another of her tantrums.

"As a matter of fact, asshole, I've read the script many times, although I know you think I'm illiterate." She stamped her boot and swatted at a fly. "That's how I happen to know that your character is actually trying to connect with my character in this scene, but you're refusing to let it happen." She glared at her assistant, a hyperefficient girl in cat-eye glasses named Cassie. "Can someone bring me some goddamn bug spray?"

Darren knew it was just a matter of moments before Toby yanked her away for a private conversation. Which would prolong the workday by still more hours.

"It's called subtlety, Heather," Ven said. "Which I realize you know nothing about."

"Shut the fuck up!" Heather screamed, and charged him.

Cassie and an intern intercepted and restrained the outraged actress.

"Break for twenty!" Toby said with a sharp clap. "Heather, Ven, come with me." He ducked under the outer railing of the shed row and jerked his thumb at the actors. Darren watched them walk off toward one of the shady pastures, Toby a buffer between them, Heather hysterically crying.

Darren went to sit under his oak tree. No way would Toby's powwow take less than an hour. They never did.

The tree he'd grown fond of was a football field away from the barn, over a little hill and on the other side of a fence, in the pasture where they turned the horses out to graze. The area was secluded, out of sight, but still close enough to the barn to hear the producer summon everyone back to set with her bullhorn. Near the massive trunk, he found a sloped patch of grass and stared up at a thicket of Spanish moss. It felt so good to lie down after his insomnia last night, the relentless thoughts of Lorelei and Mel.

He stretched his legs out and stared at the darkening sky through the hand-shaped oak leaves and the tendrils of moss, and, for the first time in days, truly relaxed. He pulled his No Princess baseball hat over his eyes and closed them. The air was damp, a sign that a brief afternoon thunderstorm was coming. Maybe Toby wouldn't finish his conference with Heather and Ven before the rain started. Maybe he'd get a double break. His fatigue tugged him downward into sleep.

"Darren?"

He lurched upright.

Marina Langley was a vision in cutoffs and a yellow tank top, her hair glossy and dark.

Waking from his nap in the grass and seeing her there, Darren's mind flashed to Jackie's dinner party, how when he'd said Marina's name to the group, she'd been nothing but a concept of desirability, a face on a screen.

Now she was standing over him, so close he could see the mosquito bites on her legs, and the amusement in her jewel-green eyes. "Callback to set was ten minutes ago."

"Shit. I fell asleep. I'm coming." He sprang into a jog. Her hand shot out and caught his wrist.

He pulled it away. He very much did not want her to touch him. She was way too tall and too pretty and too young.

"Let's clean you up. Toby's already pissed; another five seconds won't matter. Best if you don't look like you just woke up." She handed him his No Princess baseball cap, and brushed the dirt and leaves from his clothes.

"I got it. But thanks." He took a step back.

"Warning, Stephanie has a search party going for you." She swatted at the back of his T-shirt. "I was in my trailer prepping for my big scene with Ven tomorrow and I hear her on the bullhorn yelling, 'Attention all hands, send DP to set immediately, stat. Darren Branch to set, stat.'" She giggled. "Like she works in the ER. I saw you sitting up here last week, so I thought I'd come check." She whipped out a tiny bottle of hair spray from her pocket and took aim at Darren's face.

"Hey!" He shielded himself.

"It's just Evian mist," she said. "It'll make you look less nappy. Move your hands."

He dropped his hands from his face, and she spritzed him with cool mist.

"There. No sign of nappiness. Let's go." She began to walk languidly toward the barn, a football field away.

"I'm gonna jog," he said. "I'll see you later."

"Bad idea. You should walk with me. I'll tell Toby I asked you to take a walk to talk about my scene for tomorrow. That we were on a roll and missed the callback. It'll take your ass off the line."

"Why would you do that?"

"I'm a nice person. And I worship *Str8t Edge*. And I sense a lot of imbalance between you and Toby on the set. He pushes you around, and it's throwing off the whole chi of production." She lifted her hair off her neck, then let it drop. "Goddamn, it's hot."

He touched his wedding ring, trying to think of a way to tell her not to be this close to him or this nice, that it just made him feel guilty and too far away from his wife. Had he imagined — fuck, was he hopeful? — that'd there was a suggestiveness in the way she'd just lifted her hair? He wouldn't be a red-blooded male if he denied the attention from her was exciting, but . . . no.

"Let me handle Toby," he said, as they swung around the front of the barn toward the throng of cast and crew milling near the hot-walker, a machine that resembled a small carousel, used to mechanically walk horses in a circle after their workouts.

"Not to be arrogant," she said. "But I can handle him better."

"Darren Branch, last call to set before you force a wrap!" Stephanie yelled through the bullhorn.

"Here we are!" Marina said.

"Darren, what the fuck?" Toby said. "Do you know how much every minute of this production costs me? Don't answer, because I'll tell you: a whole fucking fuck of a lot. Where the hell were —"

"It was my fault," Marina said. "I kidnapped him. I was in my trailer reading for tomorrow, the part when Bess and Willie reunite, and I had these thoughts about the angles for their conversation scene, and I was dying to talk to Darren about it. I made him take a walk and hear me out."

"And you managed to not hear Stephanie's pterodactyl screeches?"

201

"I made him stop by the cutting trailer to look at a scene from *The Wrestler*," Marina said. "You can't hear anything in there. We thought we had a little more time. You know your conferences tend to go long, Toby."

"*The Wrestler?*"

"The father-daughter scene. It gave me some ideas I needed to talk over with Darren."

"First of all, Marina," Toby said, "do not compare me to Aronofsky, that pretentious Ivy League fuck, or draw parallels between his movies and mine. Secondly, I'm the director of this picture, not Darren Branch. Thirdly, a ten-minute break in the middle of a critical scene is not the time to steal my DP."

"You're right. I'm sorry. I was just excited about how to kill my scene tomorrow. I'm all OCD about this movie, Toby."

"Yeah, just don't do it again, Langley," Toby said. "And, Darren, next time, take your cues from me, not from talent."

"Got it," Darren said, back at his camera, which waited for him on its tripod like a loyal horse. He felt like he'd fallen asleep and woken up in an alternate universe, where a five-foot-eleven twenty-year-old movie star was vehemently defending him to their boss, a renowned film director. He busied himself with the camera, checking the lens and his cables, not wanting to look at Marina again until he absolutely had to.

"Back to work, people," Toby yelled.

"Places!" said Vince, the second AD, and the group began to reorganize themselves for the scene.

"Thanks again, Darren!" Marina said.

He looked up. She winked and shrugged her shoulder, then twirled back toward her trailer, yellow top flaring.

"Okay!" Vince said, opening the see-through acrylic clapper. "Resume! Scene seventeen, take twelve."

"Wait!" Toby said. "Heather, Ven, one last reminder: we will not wrap until each of you divides your desires. You've each got to convince me that Delilah and Willie want two things at the same time. Your horses and each other. Come at me from the dead center of these two desires. Dead fucking center. Come out of the emotional corners you've been keeping your characters in. Move to the center, or we'll do takes until my kids are in college!"

"We got it!" Ven yelled.

Heather nodded.

Normally, this type of mumbo jumbo from Toby would have gotten Darren's blood simmering. But Marina's wink had buoyed him. Even if he needed to keep her at a distance, having her as an ally was empowering. And exciting. And he really needed someone on his side.

Vince snapped the clapper. "And action!"

Darren fixed the opening shot on Heather, jogging toward the barn.

They nailed the scene.

25

DARREN KNOCKED ON the door of Marina's trailer. The first fat drops of rain had begun to fall. The air smelled like a pond. It was not customary for a crew member — even the DP — to knock on the door of the lead actress's trailer, but he needed to thank her, and to explain himself. She hadn't asked why he'd been sleeping in the grass in the middle of a shoot. But he needed her to know.

"Come forth!"

Clothes, shoes, and sheaves of script were slung around the

room, but the bed was neatly covered with a sun-and-moon blanket, and a burst of tropical flowers in a vase cheered from the metal desk. Marina stood barefoot and ponytailed on a yoga mat in the middle of the room, dressed in loose white pants and a tight white tank top that bared a band of her toned brown stomach. Darren had never seen her without the heavy makeup applied for filming, but now that her heart-shaped face was bare and her lush lips pale, he noticed a little acne sprinkling her jawline, the slight thickness of her upturned nose. She almost looked like a regular person. Almost.

Beside her was an exercise contraption resembling a complicated hammock. She seemed taller standing still. He remembered reading somewhere: "The talented stunner is a former high school basketball player."

"Sorry to interrupt," he said, as coolly as possible. But his nerves were flaring.

"No, no, not at all! I was starting my cooldown. I'm so addicted to my Persona Non Gravitas. Have you tried one?" She pointed to the hammock thing, a curved wooden structure with netting and streamers hanging off it

"'Non gravitas'? You mean 'non grata'?"

Raindrops beat a tinny patter on the outside of the trailer.

"Would you mind shutting the door? No, Persona Non Gravitas. It's a suspension device, so you can do strength training elevated."

"Looks like you could catch a bunch of fish with it, too." He closed the door and felt a wave of claustrophobia.

"Right?!" She laughed. "Some people use it for yoga, but personally I think that's bullshit, like very disrespectful to an ancient practice. Aerotonics is a modern exercise series designed specifically to be done off the ground. Like I said, so addictive. Anyway, how are you? Did you guys wrap already?"

"In one take. That's why I came by. To thank you for intervening."

"No problem! Toby's brilliant, but he can really let his temper usurp him."

She said *usurp* like she'd just learned the word. It was sort of cute, but he didn't want to think about her cuteness. He forced himself to think of Robin, how she'd feel if she saw him right now, this close to a sweaty Marina Langley.

"For what it's worth," he said, "I wanted to explain that I'd been up editing the whole night before and just zonked out in the grass while Toby was having a conference with Heather and Ven."

"I'd never judge you for sleeping," she said, dropping to sit on the mat with one leg straight in front of her and the other pulled up against her body in a tight V. "Mind if I stretch?"

"Go ahead."

"I don't subscribe to our culture's disdain for sleep," she said, tucking her chin into her chest, then slowly tilting her face up toward the ceiling. "Sleep is one of the four supreme acts of physical self-respect."

"What are the other three?"

"Swimming, sustenance, sex," she said, switching one bent leg for the other.

He looked at the little square window near the top of the trailer door, which Marina had covered with frilly white fabric. "Anyway, thanks for covering me today. You didn't have to."

"I know I didn't," she said. From the edge of his vision he saw her ease down onto her stomach and grab an ankle in each hand so her body formed a U shape. "I don't respond to what I think I *ought* to do. It took me a long time to figure out how to live that way, and it's so totally worth it."

"Hmm," Darren said. A decade in Los Angeles had made Darren weary of young women who carried rolled yoga mats everywhere and spewed aphorisms with conviction: "It is what it is." "It's all good." "We're not in control." Robin loved yoga, too, but made fun of these "Vanity Buddhists," as she'd named them.

Marina smiled at him from her curlicue stretch. "Do you want to sit down? The bed's clear."

He hesitated. He didn't want to get comfortable. She was acting way too comfortable already. The casual touching, the chummy way of speaking, the stretching. It wasn't flirtatious, exactly, but there was an intimacy she hadn't earned. It made him feel on the verge of transgression, when he hadn't even done anything. He resented this feeling. He resented himself for finding Marina attractive.

"Does stretching gross you out?" she asked. She lowered her legs to the ground. "You have a weird look on your face. A good friend of mine actually barfed during Cirque du Soleil."

"No, no," Darren said. "My wife does yoga at home all the time."

"So sit down," she said cheerfully. "Just kick over anything in your way."

The bed was the same cheap twin as his, and squeaked under his weight. He leaned back on his hands and concentrated on looking at anything but Marina. The door seemed far away, even though the entire trailer was only thirty feet long and half as wide, and the air felt clammy. He focused on a half dozen sticky notes on the wall beside the bed, each crossed with loopy handwriting: *Inhabit your character's interior. Rawness = Realness. CONFRONT, NOT COMFORT.*

Toby's filmmaking mantras. He clenched his back teeth together, irritated by Marina's little shrine of Post-it notes.

The sound of the rain intensified.

"Almost done," said Marina, singsongy, pressing the sole of one foot to the opposite thigh and lifting her arms over her head. There was simply no way not to notice her breasts flaring against her skintight top. It was impossible not to think of what they might feel like. Darren made himself think of the most disgusting thing he possibly could: goji berries. They made him gag.

It worked for a minute. Then his brow began to sweat.

Marina seemed perfectly at ease, as if she writhed around half-naked in front of people she barely knew all the time. And she probably did.

"Ommmm," said Marina softly, eyes closed, hands peaked in prayer position.

She had the luxury of doing whatever the fuck she wanted at all times, Darren thought, with increasing irritation. Never mind her impact on other people. Having *this* freedom was why people lusted after celebrity. Craving that freedom was what had ruined his sister.

He stood up and waited for her *om* to end.

"I'm out," he said. "Thanks again."

"Wait!" She dropped her hands to her sides. "Am I seeming obnoxious to you?"

"Um," he said. "No."

"Liar!" she said. "I can tell you think I'm obnoxious. Ugh, I'm sorry. It's just that *Str8t Edge* blew my mind, so I'm a little nervous, being around the person who made it, and when I'm nervous I start doing physical things. Basically I stretch instead of pacing."

There was a boom of thunder and the rainfall turned to a downpour, smacking the aluminum panels of the trailer like spoons banging pots.

26

LORELEI HAD A feeling about Keisha, who worked the front desk most weekdays. She couldn't put her finger on it, but she was beginning to recognize a certain quality in strangers, a sense of kinship via shared hobby. Like overhearing someone order the exact same peculiar thing on the menu that you always ordered: mustard with french fries, bacon not crispy.

Lorelei liked Keisha. She hadn't heard much from her, except for the expressive way Keisha chewed gum and used a don't-fuck-with-me tone on the phone. Keisha had big white teeth and one prominent gold one, and plaits in her hair ending at her shoulders in silver beads that clacked against one another when she shook her head. She had a tiny waist, a bubble butt, the singed-looking remains of a tattoo she'd had removed on her left forearm, and a fresh one on her right that read *An-Drae*. Lorelei liked her. Before heading to her ten-to-seven shift at the Lucky, she did a pinch of Mote in her room for bravery and headed straight for the desk.

"Girl, your ass is getting booted before checkout time tomorrow," Keisha said. "Just warning you."

"I get paid on Friday," Lorelei said, which was theoretically true. Except that since she'd taken advantage of her boss's offer to purchase his product via deductions from upcoming paychecks — his payday loan program, she and Don called it — their wages would bounce right back to him.

"Today's Wednesday," said Keisha. "You owe . . ." She tapped at her computer with fuchsia-painted nails. "Four hundred and twenty three dollars and" — she snapped her gum — "forty-eight cents. Friday ain't gonna fly."

Lorelei checked the glass door of the office to make sure no one was in sight. "What if I gave you another form of payment?"

"By all means, girl. We even take freaking Discover card."

"I meant more like a recreational supplement I could give you, and you could keep me in good standing with Duncan, just until I get paid."

"What the fuck's a recreational supplement? You want me to go jogging with you or some shit?"

"Can I come around to your side of the desk?"

Keisha paused. "I don't smoke weed."

"Neither do I."

"Come on back, then."

With a slip of a plastic baggie into Keisha's hand, Lorelei and Don were granted a few more nights at the Sleep Inn.

Elated by her accomplishment, she ran the whole way to work. Sure, the deal she'd struck with Keisha was a short-term solution, but she wasn't worried: Darren would come through. He always did.

She arrived at her restaurant job ten minutes early. The Lucky Bastard All U Can Eat ($10.99, including prime cuts of USDA-certified beef, plus a back room full of slot machines) was situated on a trash-strewn side street between a shoe repair shop and a Bob's Big Boy, a full mile from any casino. Hardly a primo gig, but she needed the cash, and it was better than stripping, which had been her other option. The owner, Chad, was a certified douche bag, but he'd given both her and Don janitor/busser/server jobs on the spot, and reliably paid them minimum wage plus tips.

Today, there was plenty of work to be done at the Bastard, and Lorelei was in the mood to work. She slipped in the back of the restaurant, said hey to the line cook, and wondered if Don was around. She couldn't keep track of his schedule, and they'd been passing like ships in the night. He usually worked grave-yard, and there was a fair chance he was still futzing around the front of the house, folding napkins and sweeping away imagi-nary dirt and finding other means of passing the time before he came down enough to go back to the motel to try to sleep. Thanks to her, his key would work. She headed to the supply room for another quick pinch of Mote — doing it in tiny incre-ments meant there was always something to look forward to.

"Top Sheen, Top Sheen!" she chanted under her breath, while searching for the polish to brighten the stainless steel of the salad bar. For a slimy dude, Chad insisted on surprisingly high standards of hygiene inside his restaurant. It was probably Mote that kept him meticulous. At the moment, he was likely holed up in his office, revving up for the day with coffee, a pipe of speed, and a round of Internet porn.

Ah, there it was! A white plastic spray bottle with TOP SHEEN in red letters. Way up on a high shelf, hiding behind a giant con-tainer of Pine-Sol.

It was ten, lull time in between the departure of the late-late-night crowd and the early lunch crowd, who began trickling in around eleven for the $5.00 rib eye sandwiches and $1.00 beers Chad offered when they played the slots in a cavelike room at the back of the restaurant.

She opened a step stool and stretched her arm up over her head to reach the Top Sheen, and noticed her right armpit was so sweaty that it'd created a wet patch that crept around the front of her maroon staff shirt toward her khaki apron, and down her left side as well. She sniffed at it and smelled nothing. "Only water, only water!" she said. Weren't humans 80 percent water, or was it 90 percent? Never mind. She disliked the look of her sweat stain, as would Chad, but he couldn't be too pissed, could he, when he'd sold her the sweat-causing speed in the first place?

She still couldn't reach the fucking Top Sheen.

"Donovan!" she called out, though she had no idea if he was even at work, let alone within earshot. But she sort of sensed that he was. Was Mote making her psychic? Possibly, because in about thirty seconds, he appeared in the doorway.

"Well, well, well," he said. "Top of the morning."

She hopped off the stool, spreading her arms out. "I cannot reach the Top Sheen, Sir Donovan," she said, affecting a British accent. "Can you do me the honor?"

"Don't call me Donovan," he said. "And I'll consider it."

"Apologies, my prince." She batted her eyes at him, although he looked like shit.

"What're you Top Sheening?" He handed her the spray bottle and leaned against the wall.

"The buffet, Donov . . . I mean, Don, the buffet. How will customers judge us against other top establishments in Reno, if not for the sheen of our buffet?" She hopped back onto the stool, liking the height.

"You don't need to sheen it, Lorelei. It's like a mirror out there. Maybe you could help me polish the flatware."

Don's eyes drooped shut as he leaned on the wall. He looked very sweet all of a sudden, the skinny, six-foot-three frame of him trying to snatch a micronap standing up. She felt a rush of tenderness. This how it worked: he annoyed her for hours on end, so much that she couldn't help being a bit mean, and then she caught a glimpse of him looking so boyish and vulnerable that she was compelled to touch him.

She hopped off the step stool and put her arms around Don. He smelled like meat, onions, cleaning chemicals, and BO. He put his arms weakly around her — conditioned not to trust her affection — and she squeezed him tighter. The crystal was working beautifully in her system now, making her ultraclear and full of goodwill.

"You stink, Donovan." She giggled. She pulled the tie of the apron above his butt. "Take this thing off."

He pulled it over his head and dropped it to the floor. "Lorelei," he said with a sigh. "I've been working for the past seven hours in this meat pit. What do you expect?"

"Get thee home to our castle then, and let down your hair. And take a shower."

"That's Rapunzel," he muttered. Clearly he was coming down in a big way. Just as she was ascending like a freshly filled helium balloon.

"I know it's Rapunzel." She giggled again. "I know Rapunzel! DeeDee Sims is gonna play her." Mostly, she kept her old life in L.A. out of her mind, but every once in a while, it came up.

"You hate DeeDee."

"I don't hate anyone," Lorelei said.

"Except your mom," said Don.

"Don't be a downer. I was stressed when I said that."

"Do you think they cut off our keys yet?"

"They have not. Guess who bribed Keisha with some product?"

"Wow." He blinked down at her. "Nice work. I'm going there to sleep now."

But Lorelei was in too good a mood to be alone, so she kissed him.

"Cut it out," he murmured, turning his head, but Lorelei could tell he didn't mean it, so she slipped one hand under his shirt and moved his head with her other so that she could return her mouth to his and keep on kissing.

"Hey," he went on. "You know if Chad catches us we're shitcanned. And he's like right next door." His words were slurred and hard to decipher, with her mouth covering his. She closed the door and pushed him against it.

"Grrrmph," he said.

"Shh." In her arms, he felt like a windup doll that had wound down, but he wasn't pushing her away; so she kept at it, untying her apron and tossing it, and then his shirt, and leaning over to run her tongue over his belly and chest. She stopped for a minute to pull her hair on top of her head, securing it with a rubber band that had appeared around her wrist, like magic, as she had zero recollection of putting it there. She took this as a sign to keep on going. Tying her hair up on top of her head made her feel instantly sexier, her movements suddenly liquefied, and she pulled off her shirt and bra, until she wore only her black miniskirt and the sky-high heels Chad said were part of her uniform. She did a little dance, shimmying in to rub up against Don and then back toward the far wall, dancing in reverse until her back brushed up against a tall metal shelving unit laden with cleaning supplies, scrub brushes, buckets, and rags.

"Do you like it, do you like it, do you like it?" she sang, some song she heard approximately one million times per day at the Lucky Bastard. Don was leaning against the wall, but his eyes were fully open. She couldn't believe how good and effortless it felt to dance. Maybe she should audition at one of the clubs after all, and make beaucoup money instead of the minimum wage plus shitty tips she made here at the Bastard.

She swiveled her hips and flipped her skirt up at Don, flashing the ratty drugstore underwear she kept having to wash in the sink. She'd left all her nice underwear back in L.A.

Through Don's cheap khakis, she noticed his boner. She wiggled close to him and grabbed his hands and moved them onto her butt to force him to dance. He groaned in protest but began to sway in sync with her.

"If you like it, if you like it," she sang in his ear. When she felt her back brush the metal shelves, she knelt down and unzipped his fly.

"No — wait — Chad," Don said.

"Don't worry," Lorelei whispered. "He's always in his office until eleven." She didn't know this for sure, but she rarely saw Chad until they convened at the front of the house at eleven for the daily "staff meeting," which usually consisted of nothing but his petty complaints about their "performance." Don went quiet as Lorelei worked his pants down to his ankles. He was underwear-less.

Funny, before she'd hooked up with Don in L.A., she'd never even given a blow job. She'd had a fair amount of sex, but blow jobs had always seemed dirtier. But since she and Don had become a couple, her initial perception of them seemed hilarious and juvenile, because they were the easiest things in the world. It was a joke, how easy they were. And being able to give them as well as she did now was like having a replenishing amount of money in the bank to spend however you liked. Like in the past week, she'd felt hints of Don's puppylike loyalty straying. She couldn't put her finger on it, but she thought it couldn't hurt to resolidify his commitment.

As she went to work, he had trouble standing still. He kept rocking back and forth, bonking her back against the metal shelves. She tried to ignore the discomfort and focus on her task, which she was sort of enjoying. It had been a while since she'd been in control like this.

Just as Don was about to lose it, she decided to torture him a little and pulled back.

"Hey," he protested.

"Hey," she echoed, looking up and smiling.

"Why the intermission?"

"Because," she said, feeling her momentum wane. "Hold on for half a sec."

"Damn, Lorelei," Don said, looking ridiculous among the brooms and buckets, pants at his ankles, dick jutting straight out.

She located her purse, and whipped out her baggie and scooped a tiny bit onto her pinkie nail, then up to her right nostril. It burned, and she loved it. *The fire of life.*

"What?" Don said.

"What what?"

"Did you just say *fire of life?*"

"Oh!" She floated on top of her own laughter. "Guess I did! Want some?"

"Man," Don said. "I was thinking I should get some sleep."

"Sleep's for suckers," Lorelei said. "But you'll have to find your own straw."

"I'll use this," Don said, bending to pull a glass pipe from his pants pocket.

"When did you start smoking?" Lorelei handed him the baggie. She knew smoking Mote was the widely preferred method, but it scared her. She'd heard when you smoked it you got wild and tweaky right away and that it lasted forever.

"A while back," he said, lighting the bowl.

She liked the way Mote smelled when it burned, acrid and gorgeous. How could something smell so harsh and so delicious at the same time? Don's eyes closed, and Lorelei recognized the little half-smile on his face. Savoring the zoom of a fresh hit.

She looked down at herself, still naked from the waist up. She liked what she saw. Finally, she had the concave belly she'd never been able to get pre-Mote, no matter how many Pilates classes she went to with her mom, or how strictly she stuck to eating greens and lean proteins and avoiding bad carbs, all the shit she used to do. Now, she didn't exercise and ate whatever she pleased (though she didn't desire a lot), and the fat just melted off her, leaving her with what she felt was her real body. Too bad she'd decided to tell her career to fuck off now that she had the body she needed to really succeed; but it was still satisfying to be way skinnier than Flo or Hill or Zo had ever been. If she'd looked like this back during the selection process for Flo, would she have gotten the part over Nia? Who cared? Her body was bananas now. She ran her hands all over her torso, then dipped into her underwear. Her Brazilian wax had grown out, and she liked the sensation her fingers created moving over the long stubble. She pushed into herself, moaned a little, and then pressed her wet fingers to Don's lips.

"Ohhhh." He opened his mouth and sucked on them.

Now that he was sky-high again, he sounded confident, alert. He looked better, too, sort of rock star in his haggardness, and she pulled her hand away and slipped her arms around his waist. His skin felt very, very nice.

"You're hot," she said.

"God, you, too," he said, gently pushing her head downward.

As she lowered back to her knees, she heard the footsteps.

There was no time to cover her breasts, or pull up Don's pants, or move the glass pipe from where she'd left it on the shelf. No time to flick off the light switch and dim all the evidence of their crimes. Lorelei froze, her knees on the concrete.

"Jesus fucking Christ," Chad said as he swung the door open. Lorelei pictured the scene through his eyes: Don's bare ass, her half-naked, the pipe on the shelf, and the little baggie of powder.

"You two are a class act," he said. "Why am I not surprised?"

Don was having trouble rebuckling his belt.

Lorelei scanned frantically for her shirt, a dishrag, anything to cover herself, but there was nothing in reach. The clean rags she'd folded into a tidy tower taunted her from across the room.

Chad hulked beside them, and blocked the door. "I should've known better than to hire a couple of cranked-out little shits."

Lorelei heard real anger gathering in his voice and realized Chad was high. Dangerously high. Her heart rammed in her chest as he grabbed a large rag, wrapped it around his right fist, strode over to the pipe, and smashed it. "Mazel tov!" he said, pounding the shattered glass. "Too bad your mothers couldn't be here. They'd be so proud!"

Lorelei's fear turned to rage.

"Shut up!" She leaped to her feet. "You washed-up limp-dick loser junkie pedophile! You're forty-five years old and running the shittiest restaurant in Reno and fucking strippers and holing up with drugs and porn. How dare you bring my mother into this?"

Chad lunged at her.

"Don!" she cried. His T-shirt was half over his head, covering his eyes, so he didn't see Chad shove Lorelei with all his might, sending her flying into the shelves behind her, scrub brushes and scouring pads and bottles of bleach and Ajax raining down on her as she crumpled on the floor.

27

A LITTLE MORE than a week after the Justuses' party, Colleen reached a decision: she needed to see Bundy again. Something special had passed between them in that back room, and then she'd gone and ruined it. One minute she'd felt so connected to him, and the next, completely dismissed. What had turned him off so abruptly? Was it the notion that she'd intended to seduce him, with her husband just a few rooms away? Had he suddenly seen her as trashy and desperate? As a drunken, sex-starved "cougar"?

But Bundy had kissed *her*, for God's sake. He'd initiated everything!

She just needed to talk to him. To clear the air. To know that he respected her. She would not touch him; she was married. She would behave honorably. But if she didn't see him just one more time, she'd go crazy. She already *was* going crazy, in fact, sitting in her den in Fresno all afternoon, watching old episodes of *Soft Hogs*. Bundy's band, the Double Negatives, played during the opening and closing credits, and in listening to his songs over and over, she'd gotten hooked on the show.

The Double Negatives were playing in L.A. on Wednesday night at a club in Silver Lake called Moonrock. A perfect opportunity to see him. After all, hadn't he invited her to the show? She could hear him clearly in her mind, the teasing note in his voice after she said she might come: *Might you?*

Much as she hated Silver Lake and its painful memory, she needed to go.

First, there was Carl to deal with: she'd have to figure out how to explain the need to be gone overnight. Without Lorelei, she had no justification for driving to L.A. She'd have to come up with an airtight lie. The thought of doing this made her feel ill. She and Carl were on such rocky ground right now. One more slipup on her part, and who knew what he'd do. She couldn't imagine them splitting up — they'd been together twenty-two years — but they couldn't go on like this either, could they? She wanted to be a better wife, but it was so hard, when Carl disapproved of her all the time. Before she even opened her mouth, he pushed her away. It was in the way he looked at her, with a sort of pitying judgment. *Why are you the way you are?*

And yet she still loved him. Over their years together, she'd grown up, from a lost teenager into a mature woman, a mother. Without Carl, she wouldn't have Lorelei. Without him, she'd have never known true happiness.

You couldn't have that much history together and end up apart, could you?

She was going to try harder. Very soon. As soon as she purged Bundy from her system. The lie she'd tell Carl to get to the Double Negatives show would be her last. Then she'd get serious about improving her marriage. She couldn't allow it to fail. She'd already failed as a mother, after all. Lorelei hated her. Darren liked her well enough, but she only saw him twice a year, and Robin always got in the way. Carl was all the family she had.

Midafternoon on Monday, she poured herself a glass of wine. She'd DVRed a *Soft Hogs* episode she hadn't seen, so she took her Chardonnay down to the den and curled up on the paisley-patterned couch Carl refused to replace. She swallowed a third of a Performa with her first sip of wine, and smiled at the show's familiar opening sequence: a montage that cut between the bearded dads bouncing toddlers on their legs and racing motorcycles fast and helmetless on a highway. She loved hearing Bundy's reedy voice arch over the jangly music with a desert sky in the background. She'd been listening to the songs the Double Negatives streamed on their website, and was now obsessed with their music. There was a certain feeling that ran through it. At first a song sounded jumbled and discordant and basically ugly, but then a reassuring, catchy melody rose from it, often with soaring strings, as if Bundy were elegantly defeating the chaos. Colleen bought both full-length albums plus an EP online and listened to them over and over, in the car and at the gym.

Having gotten her fill of the opening credits, she watched an episode of *Soft Hogs* involving one dad's clash with his son's preschool teacher over whether a studded leather jacket was appropriate attire for a four-year-old. Then Colleen switched to live TV, which landed on the R&D network. As she watched the end of an episode of *Choosing Love*, the very boring show about women who'd adopted Namibian babies, a banner at the bottom of the screen read, "Next up: *Real Happy Family*."

Colleen turned up the volume.

Real Happy Family began with white text on a black screen:

> "Every unhappy family is unhappy in its own way."
> — Tolstoy

> *Real Happy Family* follows real-life formerly happy
> families facing serious troubles, and documents their
> quest to regain their happiness.

The episode featured a family named the Rawlinsons in Montana who'd been raising cattle for generations but had fallen into bankruptcy, sold their farm, and moved in with the wife's parents in Nebraska. It was oddly compelling: the camera caught the family in seemingly authentic moments of raw emotion. The final scene left Colleen in tears: the Montana Rawlinsons sat around a crowded dinner table in the Nebraska grandparents' kitchen, squeezing hands and saying how grateful they were to have what truly mattered — each other. Plaintive country music ran over the credits. Colleen was about to click the television off and wash her face when she read the third credit from the top: Sashi Sabaratnam.

Colleen remembered: the gorgeous Indian girl in camouflage overalls at the *Flo's Studio* finale. The last person she'd spoken to before her televised meltdown. The producer who'd been kind to her. The one who'd been rooting for Lorelei.

Colleen's throat clenched. How had she managed to screw up so much in a single night? Why had she even gotten so angry? Was it such a big deal, that Lorelei hadn't been chosen for some stupid TV show? Wasn't there always another?

Her mind had begun moving fast. Sometimes, Performa brought on rapid-fire insights. It was a truth serum. And now, it was paralyzing Colleen with a thought: Would she have done what she did if Lorelei hadn't given her *that look?* With that *please-please-please-don't-talk-to-me* look of shame? Had she been, on some level, trying to punish Lorelei for that, when she attacked Nia and the rest of the girls?

No wonder she had failed as a mother.

The credits ended and a final message from the show appeared on the screen.

Colleen drained her wine, set the glass down hard on the coffee table, and picked up her phone to dial the number.

28

COLLEEN'S CALL WAS answered by a prepubescent-sounding guy identifying himself as Joel, reality development associate. She left a message with him explaining she had a story to share, but only if she could speak with Sashi Sabaratnam about it.

Joel said he'd see what he could do.

Colleen swallowed half a pinch of Performa and brought her phone into the bathroom while she took a very hot shower. Before she'd finished drying her hair, Sashi called back.

"Of course I remember you, Colleen." Her voice bordered on merry, and the British accent gave it substance, like a smart foreign exchange student who'd joined the cheerleading squad.

Because you were briefly the laughingstock of the reality TV world, not to mention the entire country. But no, Colleen could tell right away that Sashi wouldn't bring up the Exotic Rant.

"Tell me about your situation," she was saying. "This phone call is a confidential, judgment-free zone."

"Lorelei stopped talking to me after . . . after what I did during the *Flo* finale," Colleen said. "I haven't seen her since. I want to change the situation; it's torture."

"It must be, Colleen. I'm so sorry you've had to endure it. Let me start by saying that calling me was a brave choice."

"I didn't want to talk to a random person."

"Of course you didn't. And I understand how you might feel conflicted about approaching another television show. Because your experience with *Flo's Studio* ended up being so awful and exploitative. But *Flo's Studio* has an entirely different mission from what we do here at *Real Happy Family*. That's one of the reasons I made the switch. Flo is a crowd-pleaser. She wants the coolness factor, she wants the ratings. The fashionista-with-a-social-conscience thing. I do respect her work, but the show is one big promo for her projects."

"Yes! It's good to hear you say that." Colleen wrapped herself in a bathrobe and paced over the wall-to-wall carpet in her bedroom — who had wall-to-wall anymore? — her headset dangling from one ear. Her slippers left imprints in the old navy fibers as she paced, listening to Sashi, hating not only the carpet but the mirrored sliding glass doors on the closet and the floral print on the curtains. How could Carl stand it? *We'll do it when we have the money. It's carpet, Colleen. Something you step on.*

"At *RHF,* our mission is to help people tell their stories authentically," Sashi was saying. "And to make the medium of reality serve a positive function in their lives. I know it sounds corny, but we really do strive to help our subjects."

"Seriously?" said Colleen. "That's so great."

"I'm glad you think so. My job is to listen to your story, and to assess whether we can have a positive influence on the outcome by bringing it to television."

"And how do you assess it?"

"Great question. My colleagues and I evaluate the key relationships at work in your story, and whether they're portrayable on-screen, and whether those relationships might benefit from a staged Convergence."

"An intervention?"

"It is similar to an intervention, but we call it a Convergence, because it's a coming together. The show simply facilitates a crossing of paths between people who love each other very much, but who've become estranged by misunderstanding."

"But how can you gauge that? I mean, whether or not a, um, Convergence is a good idea?"

"Well," said Sashi. "Essentially, I talk to you, and then my colleagues will conduct a number of conversations with Lorelei, both on screen and off. And with anyone else who's relevant and wants to participate in the healing. Then we make a decision. We would never stage the Convergence if we felt it could be a detriment to either party involved, or if the relationship stood to suffer even more than it already has."

"And how will you even get Lorelei to agree to an interview? She's hell-bent on staying separate from her old life. And from me."

"Leave that to us. We might ask you for some guidance, but we'll completely handle the outreach. It's what we do."

"Okay," said Colleen, suddenly uneasy. Was she going to go through with this?

"Listen, Colleen, I hear the trepidation in your voice," said Sashi, reading her mind. "And after what you've been through, I don't blame you one bit. How are you making it through the day?"

She sounded like she truly wanted to know, which no one had in a while, so Colleen blurted out, "It hasn't been easy." And then, to keep her rising tears at bay, she began to talk and talk.

"I only wanted to give Lorelei the best possible life. But I went too far. I got too involved. You . . . you saw what happened with her show." Still in her bathrobe and slippers, her wet hair wrapped in a towel, she padded downstairs to the kitchen for a little more wine.

"That was just a mistake," Sashi said gently. "Everyone makes mistakes."

"Not like I have!" Colleen removed the cork from the wine bottle very slowly, to avoid making a pop that Sashi might hear through the phone. "I don't know any other mother whose daughter went from being her best friend to hating her."

"I know quite a few, actually. And Lorelei doesn't hate you."

"How can you know that?" Moving her mouth away from the phone's speaker, Colleen took a small sip of wine and sat down on a stool at the island. Afternoon sun streamed into the kitchen. Carl wouldn't be home for a few hours yet. She could talk and drink her wine freely.

"I watched the two of you together during the whole *Flo* screening process," said Sashi. "Obviously, you have a deep and loving bond with each other. Lorelei might be angry, but she'll never hate you."

This information, coming from an objective third party like Sashi, was such an unexpected kindness that Colleen began to cry freely. She knew Sashi wouldn't mind.

"Don't hold back, Colleen," she said. "No one but me is listening. I want you to remove your filter and keep talking to me. I don't care how long it takes."

The call lasted one hour and fifteen minutes, according to the timer on Colleen's phone, and spanned another Performa crumb and second glass of wine. She'd told Sashi everything: how inferior Robin's rich family made her feel; how she'd experienced a strange and unexpected connection with a semifamous musician at a party hosted by that family just a weeks ago; how he'd made the Lorelei-sized hole in her heart feel more bearable.

She'd even told Sashi his name. That's how unfiltered she'd gotten.

"Oh, I'm familiar with Bundy," Sashi said, matter-of-fact. No surprise, no judgment. Colleen loved talking to her; her perpetual cheer was not superficial but all-accepting.

Finally, Colleen said, "And I think that's it."

"That was just awesome," Sashi had said. "Your openness and honesty are inspiring. It's premature to say anything for certain, but between you and me, I'm thinking your situation might be perfect for a Convergence."

"But what if it makes Lorelei hate me more?"

"If after talking to Lorelei, we feel there's any risk of that, we won't do the show."

"So now what do you need me to do?"

"You can provide us with any useful information on Lorelei's whereabouts. We don't want to make her feel tracked down when we contact her; we prefer to approach her in a very mutual, natural way."

"Like how?"

"For example, if we identify certain spots she's been frequenting—coffee shops, bars, whatever—we'll situate ourselves in proximity to her there and simply strike up conversation when the time is right."

"That sounds creepy, kind of." Colleen poured herself another quarter glass of wine—that was *it,* she told herself, stuffing the cork back into the bottle as far as it would go. Then, because she couldn't remember when she'd last eaten, she opened a jar of olives with pimentos to suck the little red pepper strips from their holes.

"Trust me, it won't be. We know what we're doing. Our approach will be totally gentle and organic."

The brine of the olive tasted fishy, a little nauseating. Colleen's pulse accelerated in her neck. "I—I—Lorelei uses a credit card of mine sometimes."

"Oh?" said Sashi.

"I've checked the statement online. It lists some places in Reno."

"If you'd be comfortable sharing that information"—Sashi's voice was coaxing, firm—"it could definitely speed the process up, but we'd never pressure you to utilize a resource if it makes you uncomfortable."

"Yes," said Colleen. "I'm comfortable."

"I'm listening, whenever you're ready."

"Hang on, I'll need to get my computer."

She muted the phone until she'd pulled up the latest Capital One statement on her laptop. She took the deepest breath she could manage and switched Sashi off mute.

"I've got it for you," she said, and recited the list of places Lorelei had used her card, starting with Relapse Libations and ending with the shoe store.

"I'm proud of you, Colleen Don't worry; you've done the right thing."

"Thank you."

"I'll pass this information along to the team of scouts who'll be interfacing with Lorelei in Reno. After they've established a rapport with Lorelei and secured her agreement to work with us, I'd like to meet with you in L.A."

"How will they get her to agree?"

"They'll be completely honest about their *intentions,* without specifying with which show they're affiliated with. Probably, they'll invite her to be in a documentary about life in Reno."

"Okay; that seems good."

"Assuming all goes according to plan, which I'm confident it will, when are you available to meet me at the R&D studios in Hollywood? Maybe we could schedule something in a week or two?"

Colleen's heart thumped. Bundy's show was the following week. "How about next Wednesday? It just so happens I'll be in L.A. that day anyway."

"Brilliant," Sashi said. "That'll still give us plenty of time to interact with Lorelei. Let's plan to meet at one at R&D. I'll e-mail you all the logistics."

The week ahead brightened as if Colleen had parted the curtains and opened the windows of a dark, stale room. She would meet with Sashi and go to Bundy's show. No matter what. She'd figure out something to tell Carl. In the meantime, she'd be as nice as possible to him, so that he'd be less likely to question her absence.

She went upstairs to get dressed, scrub the wine off her breath, blow-dry her hair. She wasn't in the mood to make dinner; maybe they'd go out. By the time she heard Carl's key in the front door at six, she was sober and calm, a good wife reading a magazine at the kitchen table while she waited for her husband to get home from work. She'd even put on clothes that felt clean and honest: jeans and a fitted white V-neck. Simple silver hoop earrings. Minimal makeup. A Carl outfit.

"Col-leen!" Carl called from the foyer. He sounded oddly cheerful.

"In here!"

"Happy Monday," Carl said, stepping into the kitchen, holding a bottle of champagne in one hand and a check in the other.

Colleen closed her magazine.

"What's up?"

"I got the Sequoia job," he said. "Owner signed the contract this afternoon. Paid me fifty percent on the spot."

She'd completely forgotten he'd bid on the job. "Oh my God," she said, standing up from the table.

He handed a check to her.

"Take a look," he said. "This job actually puts us ahead for once. We can do some of those upgrades you wanted. The couch in the den. The bedroom carpet."

She looked; it was for $25,000, made out to Branch Cabinetry. Sweat beaded down the back of her neck. "Wow," she said. "Congratulations."

"I'm doing custom installations in three rooms. The owner is made of money. I need to head up to Kings Canyon on Friday to meet the architect and get started." He pulled her into a hug, the champagne bottle cold on her back. "I'll have to be up there for a week. I know you don't want to come with me, but can we at least celebrate tonight?"

"Of course," she said, tightening her arms around him, hardly believing what she'd just heard. *I'll have to be up there for a week*. Just like that, her problem was solved. She wouldn't have to make up an excuse for her trip to L.A. after all. She could just go, and Carl would never know. "I'm so happy for you."

"For us," said Carl. "Let's uncork this sham-pahn-yay."

They clinked glasses, and then he chopped onions and garlic for pasta sauce while she made a salad.

Carl had put on music in the kitchen, the Chicago blues he loved, either Muddy Waters or someone who sounded like him. Colleen hated blues; she could never latch on to the meandering guitars and screaming horns. It took her nowhere. She needed a chorus, melodies. She watched him hum under his breath as he tossed garlic into the pan, the aromatics infusing the air with fragrance and humidity. Carl swayed his hips very subtly as he cooked. For him, this was dancing. It meant he was happy, happier than he'd been in a long time, maybe since Lorelei was in high school.

Guilt rose inside Colleen as she dumped bagged lettuce into a bowl. His news was almost *too* good. It freed her to go to L.A. It allowed her to worry less about the huge MasterCard bill she and Lorelei had racked up; he'd be netting fifty grand from this job alone. Now, they could probably afford all the spending she'd done behind his back. Two of her problems had been magically solved in the course of two minutes.

So why didn't she feel better? Why did seeing him light-hearted and moving to the music make her feel empty inside?

He deserved to be happy more often, she thought. Deserved to be happy *with* her. After all he'd done for her. But she didn't know how to make him happy anymore. At some point, they'd stopped wanting the same things. She couldn't help it; she'd begun to desire a bigger, more interesting life than they had together. She didn't know exactly what that meant to her anymore, post-Lorelei, but she knew it didn't match Carl's goals of a slow, predictable fade-out in Fresno.

He'd come to resent her spirit, Colleen thought, cutting into a cucumber. Begun judging her for thinking differently than he did. She'd begun lying to him only to avoid his judgment. She hadn't meant to make such a habit of it, honestly. Perhaps she was a terrible person. But what else was she supposed to do, after twenty-two years together? Leave him? At times, the idea glimmered with allure, but mostly, it terrified her.

She watched him add a large can of diced tomatoes to the pan and sprinkle salt over them. Then he turned around from the stove to face her. His cheeks were flushed with cooking heat. He wore his work uniform of denim and khaki. Colleen still found him handsome, in his rough-hewn, Irish-bred way, but his age was showing: crow's feet fanned from his eyes and gray hair had begun to invade his natural red. His complexion was ruddier, his midsection thicker. He needed to exercise more, she thought, to stop relying on his natural fitness and weekly tennis game to keep trim.

"Would you like to go jogging with me in the morning?" she asked.

"Sure."

"Really?" She was surprised. And pleased. He never wanted to exercise with her.

"Really. You look beautiful right now, you know."

"No, I don't," she said, suppressing a smile. Her sadness began to lift.

"You do," he said, pulling her to him, still swaying his hips to the meandering, horn-heavy song. He'd had half the bottle of champagne already, more than he usually drank. She'd barely had any. A switch-up. She closed her eyes, her cheek against his sturdy work shirt. It felt nice to be pressed against him, for a change. To feel he actually wanted her.

"Oh, Carl," she murmured breathily.

"Everything's going to be okay," he whispered. "Including Lorelei. I'll make sure of it." He ran his hands down her sides.

"Okay," she whispered back. "Okay."

29

"MISS ROBIN JUSTUS," said Jerome, the cheerful parking attendant at the glass building in Westwood that housed No Princess Talent. Jerome was sixty and had worked in the building for three decades. His maroon uniform shirt was always pressed, his smile toothy and bright. "What a nice surprise, on this beautiful spring morning! I thought you didn't work here anymore."

"I don't. I'm just visiting." She got out of the car, balancing a platter of bagels and fruit she'd picked up on the way over. "So nice to see you, Jerome." The familiar sight of him gave her a pang of missing her old life. She hadn't been to her office in six months. She dropped her car keys into his outstretched hand, keeping her sunglasses on despite the dimness of the underground lot. She didn't want him to notice her eyes, bloodshot with sleeplessness.

"Gregory's upstairs," said Jerome. "Rosie, too. They'll be happy to see you."

"Great," Robin said, thinking, *Dammit*. It was barely 8:30; she'd been hoping none of the No Princess staff would be in yet. She'd never known Rosie, the receptionist, to show up less than a minute before nine, and Gregory, who now ran the agency, was usually on the midmorning-to-midnight shift. Robin had planned to pick up her mail and other miscellany she'd been allowing to accumulate at the office, drop the breakfast platter in the break room, and be on her way without seeing any of her former staff. She loved them all, but was feeling too fragile, too transparent. As if they'd be able to see right away how much she'd devolved since she'd stopped being their boss.

"Robin lives!" said Gregory the second Robin opened the door to the airy office, sleekly decorated, blue hydrangeas greeting her from the center of the Eames table in the waiting area. Gregory was standing at the reception station, hovering over Rosie's computer monitor as she typed. Robin set the bagels down on the front desk.

"Sweetie!" said Rosie, fashionable as ever in a fitted marigold dress, nails lacquered dark red, hair piled in a loose bun. She clacked across the hardwood floor in her three-inch heels to give Robin a fierce hug. "We miss you. You look awesome!"

"And by 'awesome,' she means 'like death,'" Gregory said, jostling Rosie out of the way to issue his own hug to Robin. He looked crisp in a button-down shirt and Helmut Lang khakis, full of caffeinated morning energy. "What's with the red eyes, Justus? You look like you haven't slept in a month. I thought retirement was supposed to be restful."

"Insomnia." Robin shrugged.

"I've got a stash of Ambien," Rosie said. "You want one?"

"That's okay, thanks. I was just stopping by to pick up my mail and bring you guys breakfast."

"Oh, not bagels," Gregory said, craning his neck toward the platter. "Have you ever seen Rosie eat a bagel? She scoops out the inside and only eats the hollow crust in these teeny little nibbles. Then I have to look at the innards sitting on her desk all day."

Rosie gave his shoulder a playful shove. "At least I don't put mayonnaise on my pizza."

"Veganese! So I add a small amount of fake mayo to my cheeseless pizza. What's the big deal?"

Rosie turned to Robin. "Can you please tell Greggers it's time to ditch this vegan phase?"

"*Phase?*" Gregory said, dropping his jaw. "Try 'deeply held conviction.'"

"Please!" said Rosie. "It's been like three months! Ever since DeeDee Sims got into animal rights. Anything for DeeDee!"

"Enough, you two," Robin said, smiling for the first time in days. She didn't miss her work, but she did miss this: the office camaraderie, the ribbing, the easy banter. "Where's all the mail and packages you guys keep nagging me to pick up?"

Rosie pointed to the corner office Robin used to share with Gregory, now all his. "Waiting for you in there."

"Now if you'll excuse us, we have to get this contract out in the next" — Gregory looked at his watch — "twenty-four minutes. Ahem, Rosie. Robs, you go sort through your crap in there and we'll talk after, okay?"

"If I have time," Robin said.

"Hello, it's *us!*" said Rosie. "You have to have time!"

It was strange to be inside her old office. Gregory had left her desk perfectly intact and Rosie had arranged Robin's mail neatly, by size. Her computer was still set up, the flat-screen monitor dust-free. Robin quickly sorted through the envelopes for anything important looking, and tossed the stack of industry publications straight into the recycling. There were a few packages — the networks frequently sent her swag, and managers tried to bribe her into taking meetings by mailing little gifts. She scanned return addresses — Nickelodeon, Blitz Media, Hamilton-Clarke Talent Management — and tossed the majority into a box for Rosie.

Then she saw it: a small padded manila envelope addressed to her in unfamiliar handwriting, tidy all-caps, green ink, no return address, a heart hand-drawn over the seam of the seal.

Inside was a CD in a clear plastic case. Taped to the case was an index card with a message in green ink: *If you like what you hear, we're live at Moonrock on 4/6. Nice seeing you, etc., the other night. — BH.*

Robin dropped the CD and it clattered onto the desk.

What was he thinking?

The memory of it had already taken on a smoky quality in her mind, like something that happened a decade ago, instead of a little more than a week. She'd been so sleepy and upset the night of her parents' party, hormonal from the injections, not in her right mind, and Bundy had appeared from nowhere at her door, an apparition in Vans and a clean white T-shirt. Wanting her, out of nowhere. Like Darren's understudy.

She turned on her computer and pushed the CD into the disk drive and clicked the mouse a few times, bracing herself.

She'd never heard the song — punchy guitar, some keyboard, distant strings — but she recognized the voice, even though he'd stylized it with a plaintive wobbliness and some reverb.

The chorus soared to two lines of vocals, repeating over and over: *"I'm so sorry that / I'm not sorry."*

The song was good.

She quickly ejected the disc and threw it in the trash. She rested her forearms on the desk's polished teak surface and put her head down, wanting to cry but unable to. She just sat there, face to the wood, paralyzed.

"Um, Robs?" asked Gregory.

She shivered. "Yeah?"

"Are you okay? Sorry, stupid question. Clearly, you're not okay. What the hell's going on? You know you can tell me." He rolled his desk chair over beside her and sat down.

"I've made a serious mistake," she said, keeping her eyes on the wall behind him.

Gregory slung his arm around her. "Welcome to the club of everyone-who's-ever-lived."

"No," Robin said, choking on the word.

"Yes," Gregory said.

He kept his arm around her and let her cry. She burrowed her face into his shirt. The spicy, rum-like smell of his expensive cologne filled her nostrils. She longed for Darren, to be breathing the simple, soap-clean scent of *his* shirt. She needed her husband.

Gregory handed her a Kleenex.

She blotted her eyes.

"Whatever it is," he said. "I know you can fix it. You're Robin Justus. You're the only woman in Los Angeles who can make Mel Justus quake in his boots. If you can do that, you can do anything."

"I'm scared that I might be pregnant. Like barely. Too early to even take a test."

Gregory lifted his arm off Robin's shoulder, straightened his back. "And Darren's been gone awhile, right?" he said. "On location for the Toby King movie?"

She nodded, staring at her knees. "I'm an idiot," she whispered.

"Robin," Gregory said.

Robin knew that Gregory liked Darren very much; at one point they'd even played a weekly racquetball game. She couldn't think of what to say.

When Gregory spoke again, his voice was different, all business. This is what made him a good agent — better than her, Robin thought: his intuition, discretion, ability to pull away and not to let his emotional investment affect his behavior.

"So deal with it," he said. "Go get one of those tests. The beta-whatever."

"I don't know what that is."

"A super-early pregnancy test. Expensive, but whatever. Let me grab a card from my desk . . . Here, this has the address of a medical clinic in Pasadena."

"How do you happen to have this on hand?" she asked.

"I represent six female artists under the age of thirty," Gregory said. "I'm prepared."

"Thank you," said Robin.

"Go."

By early afternoon, she was in Pasadena with her answer.

She was eight days pregnant.

Too early for a heartbeat.

How many hundreds of time had she imagined getting this news? Imagined how her heart would soar, how all her anxiety would vanish and be replaced with wild excitement and giddy relief? How she and Darren might actually dance around together, goofily, laughing and teary, the way people did in movies?

Now it had happened, and she felt none of those things. Nothing but numbness and heat.

30

"RUN IT AGAIN," Lorelei said.

"I ran it a hundred times," said Keisha. "I need another card, or some cash, or you and Mr. String Bean have to get gone."

"Let me go call Capital One."

"I know that trick, girl. Call from right here." Keisha waved a cordless phone at her.

"Would you accept any other *form of payment?*" Lorelei raised an eyebrow. She didn't have any Mote to spare, but it would be easier to procure than cash or a working credit card.

"Nope." Keisha clacked her nails on the counter. "I ain't risking my ass for you again. I need this job. Plus, that shit is nasty. I was twitching for days. You should give it up."

"I'll get the money," Lorelei said, "just give me a little time."

"Twenty-four hours!" Keisha yelled after her.

She woke Don up, and dragged his ass over to Circus Circus, because he'd gotten lucky on their slots twice before. When they'd first gotten to Reno, they used to eat at one of the buffets there, because a "greeter" named Ally, who also danced at the Kitten Club, would let them in sans the $22 admission in exchange for a pinch of their Mote. Lorelei had found it fun to experience the needless extravagance of the buffet when it opened for lunch at eleven: hand-sized steaks, poached salmon, towers of bread, entire salad crops, cheesecake slabs, eggs Benedict — all perfectly untouched, like a wedding called off at the last second.

Now, the thought of that fluorescently lit orgy of calories was unappealing. It was so much more than anyone could possibly eat. Excess was most disturbing when you were down to your last few bucks and final crumbs. Lorelei kept the baggie with the last of the Mote jammed in the corner of her jeans pocket, the plastic soft from her constant fiddling with it.

If she didn't come up with a solution, they were going to be homeless and drugless very soon. Lorelei sat at a small round table, nursing a watery gin and tonic. She wished she'd ordered coffee, but she'd forgotten it was morning. Residual jitters were firing weakly in her system, but they were waning fast, and the waning scared her. She felt like she was floating in a steadily draining pool. The image of her mother's face kept veering into her brain, like a loose horse. Without enough Mote, Lorelei found it difficult to stay in the present. She missed the way her mother smiled at her, with all that adoration. The way she always smoothed Lorelei's hair with her hands one last time just before her name was called at an audition. How they rolled their eyes at the same things, loved the same clothes, the same songs. It had been so long since Lorelei had heard any music beyond the ancient classic rock Chad played on loop at the Bastard, or the grating electronica at Relapse, the one club in Reno she'd been to. She missed listening to Minny Danvers. Missed singing that stupid song "Hotter." At the moment, she'd give anything to be driving somewhere with her mother, blasting it and singing along.

Every time Lorelei began to sober up, she considered calling her mom. But she hadn't. Couldn't. She had gone too far. The one time she'd called her father, knowing her mother was right there beside him — that conversation had left her feeling so god-awful she'd sworn she wouldn't do it again. Then she got so glassed she didn't sleep for three days. No, she couldn't call her mom, not when she was living like this. Her mom couldn't handle it. She'd beg Lorelei to come home, or up and drive to Reno and get her. It wasn't just that she'd be worried. She'd also feel left out. This was a realization Lorelei had come to in Reno: she and her mother had been a two-person clique. She hadn't been able to see this until she'd broken free. Distance had given Lorelei clear, unnerving insight about Colleen. Well, distance, plus Mote.

But instead she was stuck here under the brownish lights of the Circus Circus. Don was on the slot machine that had granted him victory clangs and a $58 voucher two weeks ago.

He tensed forward toward his machine in pure concentration, as though he were playing high-stakes poker.

She was tired of being the stable arm of their operation. Lately Don had been even flakier than usual, disinterested in *The LAND Project*. Two nights this week he hadn't come back to the Sleep Inn at all. Could he be seeing someone else? Ally? Lorelei didn't ask. She wanted to convince herself she didn't care.

Currently Don was pissed because she was holding on to their quarters and only letting him play nickels and dimes.

"You have to spend money to make money," he'd whined in protest as she'd zipped them into her purse. "No risk, no reward."

"Tell that to our stash, Warren Buffett."

"Who?"

"You know, the investor!"

"Is he related to Jimmy Buffett?" He sang the chorus of "Margaritaville," severely off-key.

"Don! Cut it out!"

"Okay, grouch." He went back to the nickel slot.

She had no patience left. She was too weary. But she needed his loyalty; she'd grown reliant upon it. Especially when coming down. Suffering through sobriety alone was too hard.

She moved from her table to a penny slot a few stations down from Don's and rested her head against the console, the ping-ping-pings of machines all around her like erratic heartbeats. She could hear Don's grunts going from hopeful to bitter, as he pulled the lever over and over, feeding the machine like a bad parent giving a kid unlimited candy. Despite the elaborate air purifiers and ventilation system, the stale scent of cigarettes and spilled booze could never be purged from this room. Lorelei stared at the row of images on the slot console — a cherry, a cowboy on a horse, another cherry, a diamond, a black X — and shut her eyes again. She saw blackbirds darting against a gray sky.

Speed completely dissociated closing your eyes with the slowing of your mind, because your mind never switched off; you just got a darker canvas to think against. Usually she loved this perpetual on-ness; but now, down to their very last lines, which they were cutting with garbage like NoDoz (Don had actually suggested coffee grinds this morning), she could feel the natural tendencies of her body take over. Sleep deprivation was a piece of cake when you weren't aware of it. But as soon as the thought of it slipped into your mind, you got miserable fast. It wasn't that she even felt tired, exactly, but that her mind was telling her that she was tired — profoundly, outrageously tired — and yet she could do nothing about it. Sleep seemed as far away as her old life in L.A.

God, she missed that life.

Focus! she told herself, and straightened up in her chair. She had problems to solve. She hadn't set foot near the Lucky Bastard in three days, and she'd made an interim score from some fratty guys out by the pool of the Silver Legacy. Their stuff had been low-grade shake-and-bake, but she and Don had burned right through it.

They needed a replenishment of Chad's good stuff, ASAP. But after he'd walked in on her and Don in the supply room, Chad wouldn't be doing her any favors.

Unless, perhaps, she was willing to go to certain measures.

Which she was.

She could do it. She'd just close her eyes and think about other things.

Too bad all her clothes were filthy and she couldn't afford

to part with the quarters necessary to do laundry. She'd just have to do the best she could at tidying herself up before she went over to the Lucky. Maybe lift a cheap tank top from a shop inside Circus Circus, just something to trick Chad's eye into thinking she looked fresh and appealing.

Lorelei pushed up from her seat and walked over to Don's machine. His gaze was locked on the blur of moving pictures, his fist clenched around the lever. She wondered if he'd somehow gotten his hands on some Mote. She just didn't trust him lately. If she blurred her eyes, he still looked okay, tall and scruffy-cute, but in focus, he resembled a homeless person. He'd really dropped weight since they'd rolled into town. So had she, of course, but she only looked better for it.

Poor Don.

She touched his shoulder. "Hey, Donovan."

His slots spun and landed heart/crown/sea horse/black X.

"Goddammit," he said, eyes glued to the machine.

"Take it easy," she said.

"Yeah, yeah," he said, unclenching his fist from the lever and turning on his stool to face her. "What's up?"

"I'm going grocery shopping." One of their euphemisms for a Mote hookup.

"Really?" He brightened. "With what funds?"

"Just leave it to me."

Don blinked rapidly at her, as if trying to coax her into focus. "Okay. Cool."

"I mean, unless you have another solution, other than—" She opened her hand toward his slot machine.

"I've only been here like five minutes," he said.

"Will you be okay if I leave for an hour or two?"

"Of course I'll be okay." He was trying to sound blasé, but the fear was plain in his voice: he was coming down.

Panic stuck her to the spot. Sobriety had arrived, a bruise-colored cloud.

Neither of them could handle it.

She touched the baggie in her pocket. She'd been planning to finish it herself.

She tiptoed up to his ear. "We've got maybe two decent rails left. Let's go."

"Seriously?"

"Bathroom on the mezzanine's usually empty."

He offered his elbow to her, a habit she'd found charming when high.

Now it just made her sad. If he'd been with Ally those two nights, Lorelei deserved it. She didn't treat him with enough respect. He was just a nice guy from Glendale. Just the friendly PA on a skateboard who'd happened to be working on her Preventus commercial and brought her Pellegrino and Twizzlers without being asked. She'd met him just when things were starting to happen for her, when she was starting to feel real possibility in L.A. She was getting paid twenty grand to be on TV, even if it was a spot for the genital wart vaccine, and she'd gotten friendly with two of the girls from auditions, Mindy and Paige, who lived together in Studio City in a courtyard building with a pool. They'd given Lorelei her first bump of Mote and knew bouncers at all the good clubs; the velvet ropes lifted like railroad arms all over Hollywood for them. They'd wanted Lorelei to move in with them. *Commuting from Fresno's insane!* But her mother couldn't have dealt with it. She couldn't handle Lorelei being friends with the gazelle girls, let alone roommates. She'd warp with jealousy, like a plastic spoon near a flame.

Which was not a normal reaction in a mother, really.

Guys like Don — not rich, not square-jawed, driving a Honda — didn't bother her mom nearly as much as a bunch of pretty girls. He didn't threaten to loosen her bond with Lorelei like Mindy and Paige did, in their bandeau bikinis by the pool, their twenty-year-old skin smoother than Colleen's no matter how much La Mer she slathered, their bodies effortlessly trim, not whittled into submission.

Her mother had made her choose Don. And then he'd sort of fallen in love with her, even though Lorelei was never very nice to him.

She thought she might throw up on the maroon-and-gold carpet of Circus Circus.

"Hello?" Don was still crooking his arm at her.

"Sorry." She squeezed her eyes shut and jiggled her head. "Let's go." She linked her arm through his and they went to the mezzanine bathroom. They each did one line through a mealy dollar bill, licked the final dust off the plastic, and flushed the empty baggie inside a wad of toilet paper.

In fifteen seconds, her internal weather changed and her mind began to hum and whir. She couldn't wait to get outside.

"Let's go, let's go!" she said to Don. Back among the slots she kissed and kissed him on the lips. It felt good — kissing always did, in this condition — but even through her fresh buzz, she could feel something was off in Don's response.

"Are you cheating on me?" she murmured into his ear.

"No," he said, too quickly.

"I need you," she said. It came out like a threat.

"I need you, too," he said, breathing into her hair. His reciprocity sounded rote. But then he added, "You're so beautiful," and pulled her more tightly against him.

That was all she needed, for now.

She stepped away from him, smiled, ruffled his hair, which was clean and soft today. The Noxzema she'd gotten him had diminished his acne, somewhat. But his face was gaunt.

"Get back to work!" she said, pointing at a machine. She opened her purse, dug out all the quarters, and filled his hands with them. "Win us a fortune."

"Will do, will do!" Don pumped a fist in the air.

"See you back at the Sleep a little later?"

"For sure!"

Outside, Topsy, the giant clown statue beside the Circus Circus, grinned at her, his orange lollipop jutting up to the sky.

"Cheers," she called to him, and set off for the Lucky Bastard, the sun sweet on her face.

31

FROM UNDER THE covers Robin surveyed the state of her bedroom and felt worse than ever. She was not only a terrible wife, but a slob. Darren's absence had unleashed it in her. He usually kept their house so spotless and orderly that May May's weekly cleaning day was rarely necessary. Alone, Robin had made a wreck of the place: clothes all over the floor, mugs and juice glasses on top of the dresser, an empty cereal bowl on the ottoman at the foot of the bed. She'd knocked over one of the potted plants Darren had lined on the mantel of the fireplace in their bedroom. She'd hastily cleaned up the soil but hadn't gotten around to vacuuming, and the dirt had ground into the beige area rug. There was a greasy blotch on the mirror over her vanity from leaning in too close to inspect a blemish, and bumping it with her just-moisturized cheek. All evidence of her laziness, of her lack of respect for stuff.

"I don't get it," Darren had said many times, as he ran his finger over the top of the fan, the stove of the kitchen, or the bookshelves, and showed her the grime on his index finger. "Don't you ever feel the desire to clean up? Don't you ever look around and feel the itch to make it tidy? Or do you just not see the mess?"

"Of course I see it," Robin had said. "Of course I want it tidy."

"And by make it tidy, I don't mean call May May to make it tidy," he'd said, teasing her, but also not.

"Don't get all righteous on me," she'd replied. Teasing but also not.

He'd once said she had the habits of a frat boy. She'd thrown a shoe at him. Now, she saw that he'd been right.

Robin kicked off the covers and got out of bed.

She pulled on an old orange Texas Longhorns T-shirt out of Darren's undisturbed side of their dressers, cringing at how hers was choked with stupidly expensive clothes bulging from half-opened drawers. She wanted to be close to him, and this was the best she could do at the moment. She put on some old yoga pants and got to work.

She swept armfuls of clothes from the floor to the hamper, shelved books, dusted the mantel and windowsills, even the ridge of the headboard. She carted dishes to the kitchen and laundry to the washing machine, tossed stacks of the *Hollywood Reporter* and *Variety* into the recycling, stripped the bed, vacuumed, righted plants and straightened photos. In the bathroom, she pulled on a pair of May May's pink rubber cleaning gloves to clean the shower with bleach and scrub the tiles with, yes, a toothbrush! She Windexed windows and the sliding shower door, Ajaxed the sink and Lysoled the toilet, making a note to switch to all-natural products going forward.

There was a rhythm in the work she found a little bit pleasant. *Look at me,* she said to Darren in her mind. *The spoiled brat herself.* He'd never called her that, but he should have.

When the bathroom sparkled, Robin moved downstairs. She got down on her hands and knees to wipe the baseboards and where the kitchen floor met the bottom of the island. She climbed on a step stool to sponge the top of the exhaust fan over the range. She oiled cutting boards, switched the oven to its "clean" setting and hoped for the best. She used a Swiffer for the first time.

She started to make coffee but remembered caffeine was off-limits, and heated the kettle to make rooibos tea instead. She put on music, but everything reminded her of Darren, of their life together, so she switched to NPR.

Robin cleaned and she cleaned. She cleaned the way Darren cleaned.

When she finished, it was ten o'clock, and her living room was awash in sunlight. She turned off the radio and flopped down onto the pale blue cushions of the Danish sofa Darren had reupholstered. She'd vacuumed it with the hose attachment.

The house was quiet except for the soft clatter of the open wood blinds against the windows. Fresh air swirled in, tanged with salt off the ocean. She pulled the Longhorns shirt up over her nose, breathing in her own sweat and a trace of cleaning chemicals, and underneath those, the smell of her husband. The astringent peppermint soap he'd used for two decades. And something else, something uniquely Darren. Warm but fresh, like mown grass.

He was the one person in the world who loved her the way she wanted to be loved.

Her baby would be the second.

Keeping his shirt over the lower half of her face, she stared up at the pretty arches of the Spanish-style ceiling. Finally she knew the true reward of cleaning, beyond the restoration of hygiene and order and calm: deep cleaning delivered a state of pure avoidance.

Now she had to figure out what to do.

32

DARREN TRIED TO call Robin whenever he possibly could: during meals, after they'd wrapped at night; twice he'd even called her from inside a porta-potty on a five-minute break. In his first week in Florida, he'd assumed the blame for their lack of communication, but lately, he realized, she was the elusive one. And unlike his, her hours were her own. If she wanted to speak to him, it would be happening. Instead she returned phone calls hours later with texts: *Fell asleep, try you later, xo. @ lunch w/ Jackie, can't talk, love you. Walking into movie; will call after if not too tired.*

He understood she was at home in Santa Monica with too much time on her hands, wallowing. She'd earmarked this time for getting pregnant and being pregnant, and he'd ruined it. Mel and Linda had both overindulged and under-attended Robin, so she was hypersensitive to anything resembling abandonment. He and Robin had talked about this for years. She had plenty of self-awareness and self-disgust. But it didn't keep her from punishing him with the silent treatment from three thousand miles away.

He knew her resolve would weaken. It always did, and then she'd be all affection and remorse, repeatedly saying how guilty she felt. In most instances, Darren did not believe in feeling guilty and rarely experienced it. He believed it was mostly a way to secure reassurance from others. If you made good choices up-front, you didn't need guilt. But Robin's inaccessibility was making him feel guilty, and he was losing patience. Hadn't she demanded he take the job? She was usually not the type of woman to say one thing and mean another.

If he'd been at home, he could have softened her by now. But with only his phone, he was powerless.

And speaking of guilt: Lorelei was still begging him for money in her texting lingo that tried hard to sound breezy but reeked of desperation. Most recently: *roses R red, violets R blue, I AM BROKE BUT I LOVE U! How about just $150, what a bargain?!*

Each message made his stomach tense up. He felt himself starting to cave. It would be so easy to send her a few hundred bucks. She'd spend at least a part of it on food, wouldn't she?

On top of the stress his wife and sister were causing him, there was Toby. They'd resumed an uneasy peace, but Toby still viewed him primarily as a technician. Darren refused to step back and let Toby make the key aesthetic decisions he'd hired him to make as DP. Yesterday Darren had brainstormed with one of the animal handlers to shoot from between a horse's ears. They'd figured out how to affix an ultralightweight camera to the top of the horse's bridle.

But Toby had said, "Ix-nay. Too film school."

"Nobody in film school shoots with trained horses," Darren said. "Think of interspersing the footage with Ven's dream sequence. The contrast of the herky-jerky horse cam with the soft, fluid dreamscape. It's a great idea. I'm really excited about it."

"Save it for David Lynch. No horse cam."

Darren didn't get it. The horse cam was exactly the kind of edgy choice he'd made in *Str8t Edge* and *Sayonara, Wacko*. If

Toby had been such a fan, why was he shooting down all these innovative ideas? But fighting with Toby just wasn't worth it.

Darren's only friend was Marina Langley, a fact that he might have found hilarious if he wasn't so exhausted.

He'd gotten used to her touchiness, her New Agey–ness, her forwardness — as much as that was possible. He tried to think of her as a sister. And mostly, he could. That she'd begun making references to a boyfriend helped. Darren peppered his sentences with *my wife* and *we*, but kept the details of his married life vague, out of respect to Robin. He wished he could tell Marina about their baby problems, because he knew she'd respond with unflappable optimism, and he needed some optimism about the situation. And then *he* would feel confident that it would. He initially found Marina's upbeat nature a little corny, but it could also be contagious, in a good way.

Robin would hate Marina.

He and Marina had taken to hanging out under the oak tree in the afternoons when Toby reluctantly issued their SAG-mandated break. She simply followed Darren there, with a jaunty "I'd better come along, to keep you awake." Now it had become ritual, often the single bright spot in his long days of shooting and reshooting, sweating under the tropical sun, enduring Toby. From the outside, he knew it must look outrageous: a regular guy like him, hanging out with an A-list movie star. There probably wasn't a man on the planet who would believe that what he wanted most from Marina was friendship. They'd say he was lying to himself. That his goal *had* to be the narrow twin bed in her trailer.

Except for his dad. Carl would believe him. Darren usually didn't think of Carl very often, but lately he'd been missing his father's clear moral code, his simple way of moving through the world, impervious to its superficial temptations. Darren did not believe his connection with Marina was superficial, but he wasn't entirely comfortable with it, either. Was it okay for a married man to spend hot afternoons alone with a beautiful young woman who was not his wife? Who maybe — *maybe* (the notion still bewildered him) — had a crush on him?

Carl would know the answer.

Darren was fairly sure what it would be.

33

"WHAT WILL IT take, Heather," Toby shouted, "to get a semblance of real feeling out of you? I need you raw as steak fucking tartare and I'm getting beef jerky!"

It was day twenty of shooting, Darren's most miserable workday yet. For hours, he'd been shooting Heather in a solo scene, the part of *Equus Revisited* in which an angry Delilah compulsively grooms her favorite horse, detangling his mane and polishing his hooves over and over with frenetic rage. Marina and Ven observed the shoot from the sidelines, their characters scripted to enter the scene after Heather finished.

If she ever finished.

"It's my fucking allergies!" Heather shouted back to Toby. "I'm so fucking itchy I can't focus!" Her assistant, Cassie, rushed over with a tube of topical Benadryl, ducking fluidly under the barn railing. Heather waved it away. "That shit is useless. I asked for calamine lotion, Cassie!"

Darren looked at Marina, who was over by the hot-walker. She was leaning against a post in her costume of skintight jodhpurs and tall black boots, hair in two braids, arms crossed over her white shirt. She tipped her head in Heather's direction and rolled her eyes, smiling with closed lips, as if containing laughter. Darren smiled back with his eyes, knowing Heather would progress to full-scale meltdown if she noticed anyone finding humor in her situation.

"Sorry, Heather," Cassie said, "Benadryl's pink, too. I got confused. Be right back."

"I thought you went to Columbia!" Heather yelled after Cassie, who was jogging back toward the medic's trailer.

"Give in to your itch, Heather," Toby said in the soothing tone Darren had come to know as capable of hypnotizing temperamental actors. "Give in to it completely. Let it take over. *Become the itch.*"

"Okay, okay, Toby," Heather said, closing her eyes. "Just give me a minute." She stepped closer to her horse and rested her head against his chestnut neck.

The horse, whose name was Fargo, stamped lightly with impatience. Tethered loosely between two shanks on the raked-dirt shed row of the barn, he was now overdue for the ten-minute break the Humane Society of the United States guaranteed him after each hour of work.

"Take your time, Heather," said Toby. He handed his headset to a PA and ducked under the rail into the shed row to Heather. Darren hoisted his camera from his shoulder down to the tripod, his jaw tightening with the prospect of yet more delay.

Toby stroked the side of Fargo's head with one hand and put the other on Heather's shoulder. He whispered in her ear. Fargo pushed his nose toward Toby's face, as if he wanted to hear, too. Darren watched the multispecies huddle and fought the urge to turn his camera on them and document the ridiculousness.

Slowly, Heather began to nod.

What is Toby saying? Darren wondered for what felt like the millionth time. *How do the actors keep falling for his motivational gibberish?*

Fargo stomped again and his handler, Anton, said, "Shh, boy," but didn't move toward the horse, afraid to interrupt Toby's moment with Heather. Everyone on set — the PAs, interns, grips, a couple of producers, Marina and Ven — had fallen silent. Spontaneous conferences with actors were sacred.

"Could I get more sunscreen?" Darren said at regular volume to Sy the intern, who brought him the bottle with an anxious look toward Toby, as if Sy expected to be reprimanded for merely associating with someone speaking in a nonwhisper.

Fargo whinnied, a high-pitched squeal cascading down into a throaty bray. He threw his head up toward the ceiling of the barn, slamming the bony plane of his nose into Toby's mouth.

Toby howled in pain and Heather screamed. Anton rushed to Fargo, unsnapped the shanks, and led him down the shed row, talking to the horse in rapid Spanish.

"My fucking tooth!" yelled Toby; it sounded like *toof.* His mouth was bleeding. Profusely.

Darren and Marina exchanged small smiles.

"Medic!" yelled Aspen Green, materializing by Toby's side and leading him briskly out of the barn.

"Peeth-of-shit horth!" Toby screamed over his shoulder, punching his fist in the air. "You're fired, Anton!"

"Break!" yelled Stephanie through her bullhorn. The crew scattered. Darren zipped a sun cover over his camera, humming under his breath. His exhaustion and bad mood had lifted.

Marina weaved her way through the crew to him. "Yikes. That looked painful. Tree time?"

"Sure," Darren said. "Toby's oral surgery ought to take a while, right?" He grinned at her.

"Poor Toby," she said, but her eyes were sparkling. "Poor

Fargo, too. Clearly, he was hungry and thirsty. Anton should've swapped him out for Honeybear an hour ago."

"How could you tell?"

"I just could. I love horses. We have a thing." She waggled her fingers around her head.

They fell into step together down a woodchip path leading away from the barn toward the open pasture. When they were settled under the oak tree's broad canopy of shade, Marina said, "Heather's a total diva, but I can understand why she has such a short fuse. I mean, acting's the least interesting job in film, and she's been at it forever."

"But you're an actor."

"For now," she said. "Eventually I want to direct. Like really nonmainstream stuff. All my favorite films are art-positive ones that value images over the story line. Old stuff, like *Baraka* and *Waking Life. Tree of Life,* minus the religious stuff. Everything that Sofia Coppola has done. *Requiem for a Dream,* of course. And *Silver Face,* that one P. T. Anderson only released virally — did you see it? And" — she rested her head on her shoulder, looking sideways at him, almost shy — "my favorite: *Str8 Edge.*"

She was so sincere. Her green eyes were wide and fixed on him, long legs caught by the knee in the crooks of her elbows. He felt a heat in his face and worried he was blushing.

"Thank you" was all he could manage.

"No, thank *you* for making it."

He needed to change the subject; this was making him too uncomfortable. "What do you think of Toby's work? Honestly?"

"I love it," she said, and sighed. "He's a genius."

Darren sighed.

Marina continued. "I'm so fortunate to be at a place in my career where I can do the projects I believe in. I voice Pixar movies and shoot a Disney every so often, and endorse Aerotonics, so I can do projects like *Equus* the rest of the time. I passed up a Lars von Trier project to be here. It was a tough call, but *Equus* is particularly close to my heart."

"Shit, you passed on von Trier? He's one of my very favorites." *And my wife's all-time least favorite*, Darren thought uncomfortably, feeling a glimmer of guilt over this small alignment with Marina. "How come?"

"Subject matter. Horses are a passion of mine. I founded a charity a few years ago to help Thoroughbreds live peacefully after they've retired from racing. It's called Saving Steeds."

"And you really think Toby's a genius?"

"Well . . ." She paused and bit her bottom lip thoughtfully. "Let's say I find his work deeply felt, and therefore inspiring. I just wish he weren't so pompous. It holds him back."

"You think?"

"Absolutely!" she said. "He expends his energy in all the wrong places. His own self-importance. His own anger. Into running a fear-based production. The whole don't-let-me-catch-you-with-your-cell-phone-or-you're-fired thing! I understand we're all making art together here, and distractions are bad, but he doesn't need to infantilize us the way he does. Especially you."

"That's nice to hear. Sometimes I feel like it's all in my head, how Toby is with me."

"Oh, no, it's very real. You threaten him, because you're as talented as he is, if not more. You need to honor yourself by pushing back harder."

If not more. He'd heard Robin make these claims about him so many times, how talented he was, but it always felt like a lead-in to her real topic: *Please do something with your talent*. Coming from Marina, it felt . . . different. More legitimate, somehow.

"You're right, Marina. I need to see my own stamp on *Equus*."

She nodded. "Of course you do." She leaned back on her palms and tilted her face up to the trees. "Florida's so beautiful, isn't it? I love it here. It's so lush and full of life. I don't miss dried-out L.A. at all."

"Me neither," he said reflexively, then instantly felt awful for having said it. He hadn't meant it in a macro sense, he told himself. He missed Robin. He was just enjoying this particular moment.

Marina shot straight up from her reclined position, as if she'd been stung by a bee. "Hey! We should totally work together!"

"Like we are right now?"

"No, I mean on our own project. I have a production company, just a little one, but still. I could get money together, easy. You could direct, and I could produce and whatever else."

"Okay, Langley," he said, "let's make a movie."

"Come on, I'm serious! We could make something amazing. We should start as soon as we get back to L.A."

"After *Equus* I have to take some time off."

"How come? Come on, Darren, we *need* to collaborate! You *need* to keep making films. I can tell it's in your blood, like it's in mine."

His neck tightened. His stomach turned. He shifted and moved away from her; their knees had almost been touching. He suddenly felt terrible that he'd only spoken of Robin vaguely in passing, that he hadn't made it clear to her how important his marriage was. Marina was only twenty; marriage was a faraway abstraction to her. The burden was on him.

He played over what he knew he should say to Marina, right then and there, pulling a handful of sharp grass from the ground as he considered how to phrase it: *Robin and I have been trying to have a baby, an actual baby, not a film, for more than a year now, and . . .*

255

But Marina spoke first. "Delay is the enemy of inspiration, you."

"Is that a Toby-ism?"

"Maybe! Who cares? Can you at least tell me you'll think about working together?"

A light breeze had kicked up; he watched a strand of hair work its way from a braid and blow along her cheek. Backlit by the afternoon sun, her cheeks high with color, Marina was the most beautiful he'd ever seen her.

He knew it would never happen, working together. After *Equus,* his focus would have to be on being a husband, and hopefully a father, for a long time. That was what he wanted, in the big picture. But in the small one, he wanted to prolong this moment, the easy happiness and sense of possibility. He heard the staggered punch of a helicopter overhead, and vaguely wondered why. Maybe Toby was being airlifted to a dentist.

"Okay, Marina," he said. "Let's work together."

"Really?" she said, her eyebrows jumping. "Are you just saying that?" She gripped his upper arms with both hands and searched his eyes.

"No."

"I'm so excited," she said.

She leaned her face so close to his, their noses brushed.

"Marina," he said, trying to summon the will to pull back. He touched his lips to hers.

She didn't respond, but for a few beats, didn't move, either. Then she pulled away. "I have a boyfriend," she murmured. "And you have a wife."

"I was about to say that," Darren said. He pushed off the ground and onto his feet.

"Sorry," said Marina, standing up.

"Don't be," Darren said. He didn't hear the *click-click-click* of the paparazzi's camera shutter from the helicopter. He hadn't heard it that morning, either, when it was much closer, snapping from behind a dense thicket of dewberry while he was shooting Heather's scene at the barn. There were too many other sounds in his head.

34

SOMEONE FROM REALITY was on Lorelei's trail. There was no way Joel, the puppy-faced guy who'd approached her at Relapse last night, when she and Don had celebrated the $58 he'd won at Circus Circus, and his sidekick, Tamara, a chipper blond with a swingy ponytail, were actually part of a documentary film team working on a movie about the real lives of young people in Reno.

No way did this guy want to capture the insights of a couple of insiders like he claimed. Would they mind saying a few words for the camera? Ha! From the moment Joel approached her at the bar, with his clunky opening line — *Excuse me, are you a local?* — Lorelei had a gut feeling he was working for some awful, sad reality show like *Intervention* and *Runaway*. His interest in her was too sudden; no way would a *real* filmmaker making a documentary about Reno ask her for camera time out of the blue, as he had.

"I am *so* local," she'd answered, tweaked and punchy from a fat rail. "Born and raised here. Never left. Never plan to. Ask me any question about Reno."

"Um . . ." Joel fumbled with his wallet. "What . . . year was it founded?"

Anyone *actually* making a documentary about the city would

have come up with a better question. He was definitely bullshitting her.

"Eighteen-fifty-two," said Lorelei.

"Do you mind if I sit down?"

"Sure." She'd had nothing better to do. It was Tuesday night and the club was dead. Don had stepped outside to make a phone call and had yet to reappear. She'd done some Mote back at the motel and was feeling quite chatty. Chatty enough to spin long and elaborate fake answers to each of Joel's prompts: *Tell me about your high school experience. Describe a typical Saturday. When did you first go to a casino?* And then, *Do you ever use any drugs? Which ones?*, which were the most enjoyable to answer.

"That would be yes." She was pretty sure Joel had no idea she was currently high as a kite. "Coke, heroin, ecstasy, and a little meth." She ticked each one off on her fingers, then added, "But never pot. I *hate* pot."

It was great fun, lying to Joel this way. Heroin, ha! She could go on all night, and Joel was lapping it up, nodding continuously, eyes wide.

After an hour, he cut her off. "I have to get going. But Lorelei, thank you so much for your time and your openness. I think you'd be a great asset to our film. Can we talk again soon?"

He handed her a card.

Joel Picard
Independent Producer
800-555-8080
joel@filmreal.com

Anyone could have fake business cards made. Joel's was so generic he might have made it himself: white background, plain black font. Lorelei's hunch was stronger than ever. She stuck the card in the back pocket of her jeans.

"Definitely, Joel."

She knew the junkies and homeless runaways featured on "redemption" reality shows were basically tricked into participating. But she'd assumed producers must have an elaborate and compelling way of convincing their subjects to cooperate. Who would actually fall for the old "We're making a documentary!" line of shit Joel had fed her? Maybe the subjects they reeled in were idiots: full-blown junkies, fame-hounds from the Midwest, down-and-out homeless kids coveting the food the "filmmakers" would buy them when on camera interviews took place at mealtimes.

Whoever was behind Joel's advances certainly didn't think much of her intelligence. She suspected Robin. Lorelei had made a huge mistake by sending Darren texts asking for money. In the throes of being very broke and very spun, she'd swapped the reality of her new half brother — the spineless, smitten-with-Robin one — for the memory of her old one: the doting big sibling who called her Baby Chipmunk and filmed home movies of her when she was little, infinitely patient behind his heavy VHS camcorder as she delivered a "weather forecast" or sang a Madonna song, wearing a pantsuit or lingerie pilfered from her mother and adjusted to fit her with safety pins.

No doubt Darren had mainlined news of her plight straight to Robin, who'd never forgiven Lorelei or Colleen for creating five minutes of bad press for No Princess Talent. And then maybe Robin tapped some sleazy reality show producer to find Lorelei and humiliate her all over again.

But why would Robin bother? Lorelei wondered the next morning at the Bastard, as she squatted to Top Sheen the base of the salad bar. She'd always treated Lorelei like a charity case. Like her last-priority client. That she'd go to the trouble of hunting down Lorelei to expose her on some C-network reality show seemed unlikely.

Who knew, though, Lorelei thought, as she moved her rag in tight circles over the stainless steel salad bar, maybe No Princess had taken a nosedive since Lorelei had left. Maybe DeeDee Sims and Jonice White had come to their senses and joined a *real* agency. Maybe Robin was desperate.

Or could her mother be connected to Joel? Also unlikely. Her mother wouldn't do such a thing to her, would she? After the mess she'd already made with *Flo's Studio?* Also, her mom wasn't someone who made stuff happen. She was great at carrying out the details of an assigned plan, but she wasn't an instigator. She wasn't a leader. Take Lorelei's boobs. Prime example. Lorelei was still incredulous that she'd talked her mom into the surgery, still a little sick from having won that argument. It was the last thought that had occurred to her before counting backward to the anesthesia's brownout: *I can't believe my mother let me do this.*

Lorelei finished polishing the buffet, then popped into the bathroom for a tiny fingernail bump of Mote before doing the napkins. As she blazed through Chad's tedious five-step folding process, she realized that the sudden appearance of Joel the producer could be a stroke of luck for her. A golden opportunity for her own video project. How better to expose the phony evils of reality TV other than to show its phoniness in action? She began to think it through, as her napkin stack piled higher. First, she'd have to fill Don in. She hadn't seen him since last night. After his phone call, he hadn't returned to Relapse, but then she'd left the club shortly after Joel did for a party downtown the bartender told her about, where she stayed until it was time to come to work. Don was due at work himself in a few hours, and then she'd tell him about Joel, about her idea to let him believe they were agreeing to his so-called documentary when, in fact, they'd be setting him up to get the most awesome, ironic footage for *The LAND Project*. Lorelei would string Joel and his crew along until they were about to "surprise" her with the intervention — or whatever "gotcha" scene they were plotting — and then turn the tables on *them*. Let them know what lowbrow, phony pigs they were. She'd come up with one of her kickass speeches. Their jaws would be on the floor. And Don, if he could manage to have his act together, would capture the whole thing on video.

The more she envisioned it, the more excited she got. If they could pull this off, it could be huge. Bigger than the so-called Exotic Rant. Bigger than fucking *Flo's Studio,* even. Lorelei's napkin tower grew taller and taller. She chomped harder on her Juicy Fruit that had lost its flavor ages ago. She danced around a little to "Smokin' in the Boys Room," one of Chad's morning staples. He was still hiding back in his office, but he liked to control the sound system in the front of the house.

Ah, yes. If she was right about Joel's true intentions — and her sixth sense told her she was — then she could become a star on her own terms. Without Robin, without Flo Flanders. Without her mother.

Everything was looking up. Her future was teeming with possibility. First she'd gotten her and Don's old jobs back, here at the Bastard, just as she'd planned, thanks to a five-minute favor to Chad. A quick blow job was all it took for Lorelei to resume both gainful employment and her Mote supply. Not only had Chad hired her back; he'd agreed to a payday advance in exchange for a gram.

From the slots in the back of the Lucky, she heard the triple-digital ding of a winner, and an old guy who'd been playing for days yelled out, "Oh yeah!"

"Oh yeah!" Lorelei called back to him. It was going to be a good day. She sent him over some complimentary fries and a beer.

35

WHEN ROBIN COULDN'T sit in her clean house a second longer, she grabbed a stack of magazines and a floppy hat and got in her car. She would drive up to Jupiter's in Malibu, and sit where she'd sat with Darren so many times, on the splintery picnic benches of the fish shack's concrete patio. She would go and order a red basket of the hush puppies, watch the ocean, and wait for the answer to come.

On the winding drive up PCH, the Santa Monica Mountains bulged like broccoli heads. The April day was summer warm, a day the Beach Boys had built their entire catalog upon, and she rolled the windows down and let her hair loose. After five minutes she hit standstill traffic. She tried to stay patient, focusing on the frothy blue-gray water reaching onto the broad sweep of rust-colored sand, the beach volleyball players bouncing up to spike. But as the car heated up and her legs stuck to the faux leather upholstery, the scenery was no match for the exhaust-tinged air and the weight of her impossible secret.

Just the word *abortion* made her feel sick.

So did the thought of telling Darren what she'd done.

So did the thought of keeping the baby and not telling him.

It was a lose-lose-lose.

One thing she knew: she would never tell Ben Hessler.

Somewhere up ahead, a siren began to wail.

"Goddammit," Robin said, closing the windows and blasting the A/C. A traffic light rotated red-green-yellow-red-green-yellow while she didn't budge an inch. From the white convertible in front of her, a lithe girl in a striped bikini top, giant sunglasses, and short cutoffs hopped out of the backseat and crossed through traffic over to the beach. She broke into a run as she hit the sand, turning to wave and grin at her friends still in the car.

Robin watched the girl run all the way to the water. Then she picked the top magazine, *Posse,* from the pile on the passenger seat. Only in L.A. could you actually read while driving on a major state highway. It was the newest and best-selling celebrity rag on the market, popular because it had successfully branded itself as a "reality tabloid." Its "pledge to readers" claimed to "absolutely never" fabricate stories, thanks to having "the most intrepid reporters and readers on the planet." *Posse* also solicited photos and videos from readers who'd captured celebrities with their own cameras, offering cash rewards for those they chose to print or post to their website.

Robin thumbed through the latest issue, which featured a "tell-all" about a young actress who'd recently had ten plastic surgery procedures in a single day. Once a fresh-faced midwestern girl, the actress had morphed into a grotesque amalgam of every "desirable" feature: a tapered nose, eyebrows arched to a permanent startle, lips plumped like water balloons, cantaloupe breasts, her tight skin the color of a new penny.

Robin groaned, but also felt proud for the work she'd done at No Princess; she'd truly done everything in her power to steer her clients away from the entrance to that black tunnel.

And, with the exception of Lorelei, she'd succeeded.

Traffic remained immobile. Robin closed the sunroof cover to block the sun's glare, and flipped to the magazine's most popular feature, a several-page photo spread under the heading "You Decide!," which showcased candid photos of celebrities, in ambiguous or compromising situation, accompanied by a caption that asked an implicating question. Nobody wanted to appear in "You Decide!" This issue's first victim was a drunk-looking Cooper Manning, a chiseled, talentless actor who played a psychic pediatrician on the prime-time drama *Healed*. The photo showed him holding what appeared to be a joint while an appallingly young, waifish beauty took a hit. The caption read:

Is Cooper Manning "treating" his underage patients off-camera? YOU DECIDE!

Robin smiled. Cooper deserved it.

She flipped to a double-page spread of unclear photos of two people, a gorgeous teenager and a scruffy guy in his thirties: her hands on his back under a giant tree. High-fiving amid a group of people standing in an outdoor shed. Walking on a dirt path with their arms linked at the elbow. Sitting in the grass with their noses touching. The girl in skintight riding jodhpurs and tall boots.

Robin held the magazine closer to her face.

A clanging alarm bell reverberated through her.

Darren.

The man was Darren.

Unmistakably.

The caption: Cozying Up to the Crew

Darren and Marina Langley. Dallying in the grass. When he'd

sworn to Robin that he had barely one free second, and that when he did, he used it to call home.

If they were touching noses, were they sleeping together?

"No," she said to her empty car.

The car behind her honked long and loud. The accident had cleared; traffic was moving again. She clicked on her left-hand blinker and waited for a break in the oncoming, southbound traffic, ignoring the assault of horns behind her. When a gap in the other lane opened, she flipped a U-turn and drove back toward central Santa Monica.

Her breath came in shallow pants. All the self-soothing techniques she'd mastered in yoga were useless. The tears ran fast and hot down her cheeks; she swiped them with the back of her hand.

What was happening? How had her life unraveled so hideously in just a few weeks? Were the *Posse* photos some sort of cosmic comeuppance for her mistake with Bundy? Could Darren possibly know what she'd done?

Impossible, she told herself. Nobody knew.

Robin considered darker explanations: that she'd simply been trumped by a shinier, prettier, younger woman — the oldest story in the book. Who also happened to be a celebrity. Could Darren possibly be such a cliché? Or had Robin driven him away with her insistence on starting a family? Had he fallen into deeper, easier, better love with a twenty-year-old actress who wouldn't bother with babies for many years still?

No. Not Darren.

She passed Hotchkiss Park, a block from home. She was terrified at the thought of being alone in her quiet, sparkling clean house. She would swing by only to pack a bag and check flights to Miami. Then she'd be on her way to the only place she could stand to be when she felt unsafe: with her husband.

36

LORELEI HAD BEEN steeling herself for a busy double at the Bastard, noon to midnight on a Friday, but by six she'd had only a handful of tables, and the restaurant was deserted.

"Go home," Chad said with a wave of his hand, appearing from the back of the restaurant as she cleared an army of beer steins from her last party. She was excited to see they'd left her a twenty on a fifty-dollar tab.

"Yeah?" Lorelei transferred the glasses to a tray and swiped her rag over the tabletop. She didn't look up. Since her single back-office encounter with Chad, which she'd tried without success to erase from her mind, she looked at him as little as possible.

"I'm not paying you to stand around. Jorie'll be back from his break in ten. He's got dibs on the rest of the night and I don't need both of you." Jorie had been working for Chad for three years, a depressing duration, Lorelei thought, and Chad always gave him the best shifts.

"Cool with me." Lorelei moved her rag in vigorous circles, waiting for Chad to remove himself, but he didn't budge.

"What're you up to later?"

"Me?" Lorelei looked up. Chad was wearing black jeans, a size too small, and a long-sleeved powder-blue polo, tucked in. His moon-shaped face was stubbled and his layered hair — short on the sides, long in the back — looked puffy, as if he'd blow-dried it. Obviously, he'd spent some time on his "look," Lorelei thought, cringing. Abruptly, the memory of his upper legs, clammy and hairy pressed against her face, surfaced in her mind. She blinked her eyes hard to clear it away and suppressed a shudder.

"No, the other waitress with the hot legs wiping down my tables."

Lorelei's stomach tensed. She ignored him and began to re-set the table with clean napkins and silverware.

"There's a party happening downtown tonight," he said. "My friend Gene just moved into this sick condo. River views and a pool deck and shit. Thought you might be into it."

"I've got plans, thanks."

"Well, here, just in case," Chad said, sidling over to her and tucking a piece of paper into the pocket of her apron, pushing his fingers against her hip more than he needed to. "Here's the address. You can bring your little sidekick if he wants to come. Starts early. Goes late."

"Have fun," Lorelei said, repulsed that he'd touched her, even through the layers of her apron and clothes. She tucked the last fork and knife into the pocket of a green napkin. "I'm out of here."

"Don't miss me too much," Chad said, raising one brow and grinning at her. "I'll be at Gene's around eleven."

"Don't hold your breath," Lorelei said, turning away from him and hurrying to the bathroom for a quick pinch of Mote to improve her walk home.

"No drugs in my establishment, baby," he called to her back, a jokey leer in his voice.

She'd felt she might vomit from the effect of him when she stepped into the bathroom. But after she'd done a fingernail bump and exited into the fresh evening, having crushed her aw-ful Lucky apron patterned with gold dollar signs into her purse, her nausea subsided. The spring night was just beginning to descend, coloring the air with rose and lavender, and the high desert heat had mellowed to the brink of coolness. Up ahead, the Reno skyline flexed its colors: the lizard green of the Silver Legacy Casino, the bloodshot red of the Virginian. A near-full moon glowed over the mountains. Lorelei began to relax. Chad was behind her, a wide-open Friday night ahead. The Mote had banished the wave of self-loathing that had hit her in the restaurant, replaced it with confident optimism. She had fifty-five bucks and an eight ball in her purse. Overall, things were good. She stopped by a liquor store for a bottle of red wine, thinking she'd share it with Don, if he was around. Her mood had turned expansive.

"Oh, Donovan!" Lorelei sang as she opened the door to room 14.

"Lor!" said Don, sitting on the dresser, his praying mantis legs folded Indian-style. "We thought you were working a double. Whuddup?!" His eyes were wild; he was obviously jolted out of his mind. So was Ally, standing beside him in a skintight blue dress, tapping her hooker boots to some imaginary beat.

Across the room were Joel and Tamara, fiddling with gear. Joel had a camera on his shoulder, and Tamara, his assistant, was adjusting some lights—*Lorelei's* lights, the ones she'd bought at Home Depot for *The LAND Project*.

"What's going on?" said Lorelei.

"Sorry to surprise you, Lorelei," Joel answered. "Don and Allison are contributing to our documentary, like you. We're just here to get a little footage of you guys on a typical Friday night."

"Don suggested we use these," Tamara said, tapping the aluminum top of a bulb.

"Don, what the fuck?" said Lorelei.

"It's all good, it's all good," Don said. "The documentarians are documenting us. They're cool, bro."

"Don't call me bro, you asshole," she said.

"The documentarians won't smoke with us!" said Ally. "Even though we've got the sweetest shit." She picked a glass pipe off the top of the TV and pointed it toward Lorelei. "Want some? Lights, camera, action!"

"They're not 'documentarians,' you moron!" Rage surged in Lorelei and she threw the bottle of wine she'd just bought at the wall. It bounced off without breaking, and landed on the rug with a thud, intact. Tamara gasped. Ally covered her face with her forearms.

Lorelei whirled to Tamara. "Put my lights away!"

"Please, Lorelei," said Joel in a gentle voice. "Pretend we're not here. Your identities will be strictly confidential if we use this footage for our project."

"Liar!" Lorelei screamed. It was one thing for Don to be sleeping with a skeeve like Ally. But the two of them setting up camp in the room *she* was paying for, helping themselves to *her* lights, complying with the so-called documentarians who were clearly conspiring against her — it was all too much. After all she'd done for Don. "Get out of my room! All of you! Now!"

"Hey, hey, girlie," Ally said. "Let's turn that frown upside down." She stuck the pipe out to Lorelei again, grinning, eyes glossed and dopey. "Can someone put on some music? I need to listen to the Lollipop Skanks *right now.*"

Don had moved over to the sink and was brushing his teeth vigorously, but stopped long enough to say, "Lorelei doesn't smoke, Allz. Only snorts."

Allz. Lorelei wanted to kill him. She walked over to Ally and grabbed the pipe, the glass flimsy and hot in her fingers.

Ally laughed gaily. "Looks like Miss Snorty-pants is changing her tune." She proffered a lighter to Lorelei. "You'll want this too, babe." Lorelei snatched it.

"Careful, Lor," Don called from the sink. "Pipe can be kind of intense."

Lorelei shoved the pipe and lighter into her purse.

"Hey!" Ally protested.

Lorelei pushed past her and out the door, slamming it hard behind her. Then she turned and kicked it, stubbing her toe, and strode back into the neon-pulsed night.

37

AT RELAPSE, LORELEI snagged the last open barstool. The lounge was beginning to fill up, the speakers pumping bass-heavy house music. She hated the song, but was glad for the noise; she needed to lose herself in something. Walking in on Don and Ally together in front of a camera had shaken her up. Clearly, he'd replaced Lorelei with that third-rate stripper, and was perfectly comfortable letting Lorelei—and anyone else— know. It wasn't so much the jealousy that was burning Lorelei up, but the flagrant disrespect. That he'd bring Ally to *their* room, get high with her. *On camera.* Lorelei wondered if Joel and Tamara would film them having sex later. She wouldn't put it past them.

She ordered a vodka soda and contemplated her options for the night ahead. She refused to let Don and Ally ruin it for her. She downed her drink and felt a reckless mood coming on. And she was barely high yet.

"Another?" the bartender, a square-faced guy with shaved head and a soul patch, half-yelled to her over the music.

"A double this time," she yelled back, throwing a twenty on the bar.

"You look familiar." He streamed well vodka into a highball

glass and topped it with soda from a hose. Then he pushed it over to her with a wink.

"You don't," she said. He was cute, despite the soul patch and the wink. "Be right back." She headed to the bathroom for Mote and a makeup freshening.

"No, seriously," the bartender said when she returned to her seat, spirit refreshed and thoughts of Don and Ally pushed to the far back of her mind. "I recognize you. Are you an actress?"

Lorelei took a sip of her drink; the vodka burned into her chest. She smiled at him. "No. But I was on TV, for a short while." It was the first time anyone in Reno had recognized her. She went there wanting to hide, but suddenly, it felt good to be noticed. "I'm Lorelei."

"Peter," he said, extending his hand.

"When does your shift end, Peter?" she asked. "Because I know a party." She thought of the paper Chad had given her, in the pocket of the apron she'd stashed in her purse.

"At eight." Peter checked his watch. "Twenty minutes."

"Cheers." Lorelei lifted her glass toward him. "You're coming with me."

"Done and done," said Peter, winking again.

She drained her drink and pointed to the glass for another.

38

FROM THE MOMENT they left Relapse together, Peter's grip on her hand felt too tight. Her palm sweated profusely into his, but he didn't let go.

"It's downtown," she kept saying. "The party's downtown. I showed you the address." She'd showed Peter the paper with Chad's handwriting and he'd glanced at it, shoved it in his pocket, and grabbed her hand. Now, she wasn't sure where he was going, only that he was steering her *away* from downtown: the casino lights were missing from her eyeline, only the dotted lights of the suburbs were visible in the foothills ahead. The large amount of vodka she'd consumed at Relapse had blunted the small line of Mote she'd done in the bathroom. She swayed on her feet. Peter steadied her while continuing to walk quickly, practically pulling her, making abrupt turns down side streets and alleys.

"Peter, where're we going?"

"I just need to swing by my place. To change and grab my wallet. Two minutes." He chatted in a stream as they walked, something about his *cunt of a manager* and how he planned to quit Relapse as soon as he had enough cash, but Lorelei barely listened. She was too preoccupied with why they weren't walking straight to Chad's party.

The evening had given way to full darkness now, the moon high and faraway in the sky.

Abruptly, Peter stopped beside a red door, outside a sort of squat warehouse, and began fumbling with a key while keeping his other hand firmly around Lorelei's.

"Two minutes," he said again, and the words sounded threatening to Lorelei now. The unease coursing through her shifted to real panic, and she yanked her hand from his and stepped back, but he caught her with a fluid sweep of his arm around her waist.

"You're so petite," he said. "Chill out."

And then he was pulling her through the red door, into a broad, barely lit space with stale air smelling of sawdust and paint, the ceiling high and crossed with exposed beams. The door thwacked shut, sealing them in near darkness, but Peter did not turn on another light. Lorelei's heel pocked against the concrete floors covered with what appeared to be building materials, two-by-fours, paint cans, a workbench, plastic tarps. Her father popped into her mind. And then the sickening thought that she might not see him again. Or her mother. *Her mother.* Tears blurred Lorelei's eyes. This dusty, garage-like space couldn't be where Peter lived. He had not taken her here to change and pick up his wallet. How could she have been so naive?

She wanted to scream, but her voice had dried up in her throat. She could summon nothing but a moan. It was too late. She should have screamed blocks ago, out on the street.

"No," she managed, as she felt Peter's mouth on her neck. Licking her. Then small bites. His hands up and down her body, tugging at her clothes, at the tight skirt of her Bastard uniform and the buttons of her white shirt. He lifted her up and moved her over to a wall, pressing her against it.

"You are *so* hot, you little slut," he murmured.

"Get off me," Lorelei croaked.

He jerked the bottom of her skirt up along her torso so that it clenched her like a tube top. Pushed her harder against the wall, her purse still on her shoulder, the metal accents on its strap digging into her back. She heard the clink of his belt unbuckling and her mind snapped into temporary focus. Her voice unlocked.

"Hang on," she said, loudly. "Peter."

"Talk to me later, bitch," he breathed. "This was your idea." He shoved his hand into her underpants, groping her roughly. She struggled away from him, but it was no use. Then she remembered the contents of her purse, still securely on her shoulder.

She summoned a flirtatious tone and spoke into Peter's ear. "Hey, wait! Do you like to get high? Like really fucking high?"

She felt his body relent. He didn't release her, but his grip softened. His belt was unbuckled, but he did not pull it off.

"What did you have in mind?" he asked.

"Let me get something from my purse."

He continued to hold her wrist as she rummaged in her bag for Ally's pipe and lighter.

"Here," she said, offering both to him. "Best crystal in Reno. You first."

He released her wrist, took the pipe and BIC from her, and lit up.

"Oh my god," he said, moaning, as sharp, bitter smoke filled the air. He let her go and took a staggering step.

"May I?" Lorelei asked.

"Oh my god," he said again, in a loud, hard voice. Then he hopped up and down in place. "This *is* some serious shit."

"Can you share?"

Peter handed her the pipe and said, "Goddamn. I am the master of the universe." Then he dropped to the floor and began doing pushups.

Lorelei snapped the BIC and sucked hard on the glass tube. The smoke scalded her throat and lungs. It was like smoking bleach.

"Ouch," she coughed, and dropped the pipe to the concrete floor, where it shattered.

"Careful!" yelled Peter, without stopping his push-ups. *Now,* she thought, as a hot tingling sprouted in her chest and shot down her legs, up into her skull. Her body leapt into motion, seemingly at its own will. She kicked Peter, still in plank position, as hard as she could, planting the sharp toe of her high heel into his side.

"Ouch!" He folded on the ground. "You little skank!"

Lorelei hopped over the broken pipe glass, bolted to the red door, and snapped its lock open. Then she pulled it open, and ran out into the night.

The hours that came next were smeared and vague. She remembered plowing through a group of girls walking on the sidewalk, some sort of sports team. She remembered falling hard and skinning her knees. Taking off her shoes and tossing them into the street. She'd intended to run all the way to the Truckee River and jump in, navigating toward it on pure instinct, to try to cleanse herself of what had almost happened, and quell the intensity of the Mote she'd smoked. But when she finally reached the water, she was too scared to jump in. The water looked brackish and oily, the sky furry and low. She could only burrow herself near the base of a sprawling bush a few feet from the water, hoping the leaves concealed her completely, and pray that Peter — or something worse — would not find her. The rocky earth dug into her raw knees and she shivered violently against the cold desert night, curling into fetal position for warmth and squeezing her eyes shut.

"I'm sorry, Mommy," she whispered into the dirt. Over and over, until it sounded like a mantra, and soothed her.

Eventually, she rolled onto her side, pulling her knees up into her chest. She opened her eyes and reached up to part the close canopy of dense leaves, revealing a black sky pierced with hard stars. She heard voices on the riverbank. Laughter, bottles clinking, music playing from the speaker of a phone. Cigarette smoke wafted over her, and she tried not to choke on it. Her mind raced and veered erratically, landing on seemingly arbitrary images and memories: a photo of her mother in a red-and-white cheerleading uniform, a big H sewn across her chest. The sun-faded gray exterior of her childhood house in Fresno, with its patch of '70s-style rock siding her mother always hated. The crow's-feet around her father's eyes. The scrawniness of Don's shoulders. Jenna Conrad's condescending way of saying *That's really interesting*. And on and on.

Eventually, the sky grayed and brightened with dawn. She rose from her spot under the bush, shaky on her legs, wincing at the cracking sting around her knees. Her mouth was parched and her heart was still beating too fast, but she was okay. She was alive. Birds sang with the sunrise. The river sparked and silvered in the morning light. The world around her was no longer a terrifying menace.

She was shoeless, but she still had her purse. Not bad, she thought. It should only take her twenty minutes to get back to the Sleep Inn, even barefoot. She brushed dirt and grass from her filthy Lucky Bastard shirt and straightened out her skirt. She found sunglasses in her purse and put them on. And then she began to walk.

One decision was clear: She was done with Mote. Immediately, and forever.

She was too good for the life she was living.

Room 14 was a vacant wreck when she returned there from the riverbank, its air rank and stale. Beer bottles all over the floor, red wine soaked into the carpet. Overflowing ashtrays and a new constellation of cigarette burns on one of the comforters. Wrappers of vending-machine food on the bathroom counter, the remains of takeout on the faux wood table by the window, greasy sandwich wrappers reeking of onion. No sign of Don. Lorelei didn't touch the mess. She only went to the sink, avoiding looking at herself, drank palmfuls of water from the faucet and splashed it over her face. Then she hung the DO NOT DISTURB placard outside the door, unplugged the clock and the phone, climbed atop one of the beds, and shut her eyes.

Time passed—threads of light between the motel room's blinds appeared and receded—but she had no idea how much. Her exhaustion was like nothing she'd experienced before. It radiated from the cellular level, but failed to pull her to sleep because anxiety crackled through her body like electricity between phone lines. When Lorelei did manage to nod off, her sleep was trippy and shallow, studded with nightmares: her mother's head on the body of a scarecrow, strung up in a cornfield along I-5. Flo Flanders galloping on the back of a donkey, then becoming the donkey and braying with a wide-open mouth full of long teeth, frantic, relentless honks. Darren loping toward her with his arms stretched out for a hug, calling "Baby Chipmunk!", his shoulder hamburger-y with an open gunshot wound. And the most terrifying: the scene of walking downstairs into the den of her parents' house and seeing her mother on the couch facing away from Lorelei and toward the TV, which wasn't on. "What're you doing, Ma?" Lorelei asked, and when Colleen turned around, her mouth was sewn shut with a line of stitches stark as railroad track.

She dreamed repeatedly of getting high, yellow powder singeing her nostrils or poison-harsh smoke filling her lungs. Of returning to the warehouse the bartender had taken her to. Sometimes, Peter was the figure who forced her through the red door; other times it was Chad or men she didn't recognize.

More than once, Lorelei had woken up screaming.

Several times she thought she heard a key card clicking in the door of room 14 and bolted up, expecting to see Don walk through, but no one entered. Don stayed away. The parking lot remained empty of his green Honda. Housekeeping obeyed her DO NOT DISTURB placard.

Eventually, hunger forced her out of bed. Shaky on her feet, she pulled on yoga pants and a hoodie and slowly made her way to the door, stepping around the debris strewn about the carpet. Her purse was on the floor, somehow having made it back from the river, and she found cash still inside it. Then she gripped the door handle and took a deep breath, summoning the courage to open it. She felt like an utter stranger to the world on the other side. She wasn't sure what it would look like, or if it would have her.

Lorelei pulled the handle, and sunlight immediately assaulted her eyes. The desert air bore the coolness of morning. Its freshness made Lorelei want to cry. Barefoot, she went to the vending machine, squinting in the glare of the outdoor walkway, and bought orange juice, Combos, and a cinnamon roll. She made it back to the room without seeing anyone and sat at the filthy table to eat. She thought of her mother as she pulled the cinnamon roll from its package, its ample grease leaving a cloudy trail on the cellophane, and smiled despite the pang to her heart. Her mother would rather die than eat such a product. The pastry was soggy and painfully sweet, crusted with gluey icing. Objectively revolting, but delicious to Lorelei just then. The more she ate, the more she missed her mother. She stared at the boxy old phone on the nightstand and considered just picking up and dialing Colleen's cell. It was time to stop shutting her out. But what would she say? How would she explain the place she'd landed: alone in a trashed motel room, eating for the first time maybe in days, broke and lost, having narrowly escaped the grim fate of an almost methhead? Her mother could never know. Colleen, after all, had always sort of worshipped her. And her father might never forgive her. Lorelei couldn't bring herself to expose to her parents just how far she'd sunk in the last two months. She'd have to redeem herself a little first. But how? She'd never go back to the Lucky Bastard. Don and his car were gone, at least for now. She didn't even have enough money for bus fare back to Fresno.

She finished the cinnamon roll and then ate the Combos, washing them down with artificial-tasting orange juice and then tap water. Then she went into the bathroom for a shower, meeting her reflection on the way in. Black chars of makeup surrounded her eyes, dirt from the riverbank caked into one cheek, her hair stuck up in every direction, and she was too bony, her spandex pants hanging loosely off her frame. But she wasn't alarmed because, on a deeper level, she looked more like herself than she had in a long time. Her eyes were bright and rested. Her heart beat at a normal rate, no longer addled from Mote.

In the shower, Lorelei turned the water as hot as she could stand it and soaped every part of her body, including her hair — since the Sleep Inn didn't offer little bottles of shampoo and conditioner, she attempted to force a lather from the cheap soap. She closed her eyes and breathed in, taking air to the bottom of her lungs, noticing how different inhaling felt after some time without cigarettes.

And then an idea came to her.

She was a pretty good actress, she thought. A not-bad actress who enjoyed acting, until Robin had convinced her she was only good enough for reality.

What could be easier than playing the Lorelei Branch she'd just finished with? Lorelei the speed freak?

Yes, she thought, as she dried off with thin, bleach-scented towels. She would play the part of a tweaker on camera for Joel, until his real project was revealed to her. Then she could let them know that they hadn't tricked her at all. That she'd simply been *pretending* to be a drugged-out mess the whole time.

It was the sort of stunt that could make her famous in a good way, she thought, as she stepped back into jeans and a T-shirt reeking of smoke — she'd have to hit a Laundromat right away. It would eclipse her association with *Flo's Studio*. It would get her career on track. It might make her a minor hero.

It would certainly make her mother proud.

First, she'd need to rejoin the world. Her phone charger was where she'd left it, next to the Bible in the drawer of her nightstand. She plugged in her cell and reconnected the motel room's landline. Then she opened the door of room 14 and propped it by stuffing a dirty sock underneath it. Clean air streamed in, smelling faintly of laundry detergent, a smell she'd always liked. She felt her natural optimism returning on the spot, chemical-free. She would get herself out of this. She was smart and talented; Reno had just been a big detour. A mistake. She flipped the DO NOT DISTURB placard over to PLEASE SERVICE ROOM and smiled into the sunlight.

Joel and his assistant, Tamara, fell for her act, hook, line, and sinker. She calibrated the deterioration of her character carefully, interview by interview, over the course of two days — they preferred shooting her in short segments, ten or fifteen minutes, having her answer stupid questions for the camera — progressing from manic and aggressive to downright out of her mind, and, finally, faking a beautiful seizure. She'd never even witnessed a seizure before, hadn't even bothered to view one online! She acted on pure inspiration, starting with rapid blinks of one eye, spreading to a repetition of twitches in her cheek, a sharp hitch of her neck, and, finally, on the floor, bucking. Joel had yelled, "Oh my God," and Tamara had fully screamed, and they called 911. Lorelei was a tiny bit nervous when the paramedics examined her. She was dazed and limp, and said, "Um, no," in the tone of a liar when they asked her if she'd taken any drugs. They couldn't find anything wrong with her, so she refused their request to take her to the hospital for observation, and they let her go.

While she was being poked and prodded on a gurney by two muscular male EMTs, pretending to be in a post-seizure haze, she stole glimpses of Joel and Tamara. They'd stayed nearby — she'd done the interview in some back room of Circus Circus that Joel had booked — but were too quiet, talking into each other's ears and working their phones urgently.

When the EMTs finally left, Joel asked her if she was *really* okay, and Tamara hugged her.

Then Tamara said, "If you're up for it, I mean really only if you feel well enough, maybe we can try again tomorrow?"

"Sure," Lorelei said, her voice good and weak.

"We're going to put you in a cab back to your motel," Joel said. "On us. Get some rest, and meet us Friday, okay? We'll send a cab to the Sleep Inn at six-forty. I've also texted the info to you. Okay?"

Lorelei rubbed the side of her face gingerly. "My face still tingles a little," she said. One of the EMTs had told her she might expect this.

Tamara nodded. "You poor thing."

Joel handed her a blue-lined index card where he'd written in a black Sharpie: *Cielo Hotel, Friday 4/8, 7:00 P.M., Floor 37, Room 3742.*

"See you there," Lorelei said.

Bingo. Her dramatic climax had just been written.

39

ON THE MORNING of her big day in L.A., after one cleanse shake and two cups of black coffee, Colleen headed out of Fresno, with her favorite Double Negatives album, *Courage for the Snow White Clouds of a Sallow Sky,* turned up on the stereo. The day was astonishingly clear.

She'd hardly even had to lie to Carl. The Sequoia job was off to a great start: he liked the architect, the head builder, even the thirty-two-year-old technology mogul who owned the four-teen-hundred-acre ranch.

"It's so pristine up here," he'd said on the phone last night. "I miss you, Coll." But his voice wasn't needy; she could tell he felt good, working a big job on a prestigious property, being away from the bad yellowish air that often hung over Fresno like a nicotine stain.

"I miss you too, baby," she said. "In fact, I'm going a little stir-crazy. So Marilyn and I are headed down to L.A. to visit her niece, a little overnight girls' trip." It was true: Marilyn's niece went to Occidental College, near Pasadena. True that Marilyn would be visiting her that week. Not true that Colleen would be going along.

Carl didn't hesitate. "Have fun and be safe."

Lying to him was always easiest when they were getting along.

Colleen swung the Camry down the on-ramp to the I-5, al-most empty after the rush of morning commuters, and pushed up to eighty, stereo blaring. *"The mantra of the morning is / Again, again, again,"* sang Bundy on the chorus of one of her fa-vorite songs. It made her buoyant, every time. She was excited for the day ahead — first the meeting with Sashi, then Bundy's show — and all the unknowns, all the possibilities that accompanied it. She felt optimistic in a way that reminded her of being young, of getting ready to go out on a Friday evening in Hemet, with the night stretched in front of her, wide open with possibility. Lorelei used to make her feel like that. She was going to get her daughter back, she promised herself as she steered the car down the steep, winding grade of the Grapevine into the Valley. This trip was a step in the right direction.

She stopped only once to pee and get more coffee, near Magic Mountain, and made it to Burbank in plenty of time for her three o'clock meeting with Sashi. The exterior of the R&D headquarters was generic, with black glass, like any office building from the nineties. She stepped off the elevator to a wall of framed posters of R&D's hit shows. Smack in her face was the *Flo's Studio* display, a giant, heavily worked-over image of the four stars staring out with serious, smoldering gazes. Each wore a different style of jeans — low-slung boyfriends on Flo, capris on Zo, high-waisted on Hill, skinnies on Nia — and fabulous tops ranging from a flowing aqua trapeze on Hill to a fitted black leather tank on Nia, giving her the look of a jungle cat. Behind them were city lights and, dimly, the Hollywood sign. At the bottom edge of the poster, a caption read: Faux Friends. Faux Real.

Colleen's chest tightened in a familiar way: half rage, half regret. Lorelei belonged up there. She took a few deep gulps of air and looked away. She must move forward with what she was about to do: she had to find Lorelei and get their lives back on track. These people could help.

She checked in with a dapper gay male receptionist named Parker, refused his offers of water and espresso, and sat down on a hot pink couch to wait for Sashi.

A promo for *Soft Hogs* skated past on a mounted flat screen and melted into another for *Masticators: Miami*. Her stomach butterflied. Just hours from now, she would see Bundy.

"Col-*leen!*"

Sashi Sabaratnam looked younger and prettier than Colleen remembered. Her skin was perfect and her hair was caught up in a simple ponytail. Eyes like a doe's, petite frame, expensive, structured, mannish clothes — slim pants tapered to her ankles and a fitted blazer — that only made her look more feminine. She was probably thirty. Colleen could probably pass for thirty-five in her black pencil pants and floral silk top, her face practically lineless from the peel she'd done, worth every penny of the $235. But she knew she was missing Sashi's youthful glow. That, you couldn't buy.

She followed Sashi through a hallway and into an open space with very high ceilings, long tables with oversized monitors, and attractive people typing or talking into headsets. The room looked like an atrium: no walls, the only private offices along the periphery transparent glass boxes.

"This way, this way." She waved Colleen into one of the offices.

"I'm loving all the open concept," said Colleen.

"Have a seat," Sashi said, pointing to two white chairs behind a desk with nothing on it but a large Apple monitor, a slim keyboard, and a miniature remote control. Colleen sat, her nerves beginning, wishing she could pinch some Zenzo from her bag without Sashi noticing. But their elbows were practically touching, side by side in their white Aeron chairs.

Sashi picked up the remote from the desk and clicked a button, and taupe shades descended over the glass walls of the office.

"For privacy." She pronounced it in the British manner. "While we view some footage."

"Footage of what?" In the shaded room, Colleen felt a tug of claustrophobia.

Sashi smiled. "I told you, my team is good. Lorelei's already done some interviews with Joel, my field producer in Reno. I just got clips a half hour ago; otherwise I would've prepared you. If you're up for it, we can watch, and then move to the in-house studio and tape an interview with you. Are you keen to have a look?"

Colleen's heart began to hammer. "Yes."

Sashi patted the center of Colleen's back. "It might be difficult, to see her on camera when you haven't seen her for a long time."

"Go ahead." Colleen leaned forward and pressed her forearms into her stomach. With nothing in her stomach but black coffee and the cleanse shake, plus the promise of seeing Lorelei, her whole system felt clenched and unwell.

Sashi clicked the remote again, and the lights in the room dimmed. She tapped the keyboard and the monitor blazed to life, and there was Lorelei, standing against a dingy beige wall.

"Oh my God." Colleen hitched forward in her chair, causing it to roll backward, and covered her mouth with both hands.

Lorelei was scrawny skinny, sick-cat skinny. From under her short black-and-green skirt, with some sort of gold pattern — or was it an apron? — her legs poked out like straws. Her head was too big for her body; her cheekbones jutted out. Her hair was a monochromatic chocolate brown, the work of boxed drugstore dye, and hacked to just an inch-and-a-half from her scalp. She'd cut it herself and done a surprisingly decent job. Her eyes were huge in her face, heavy eyeliner around their whole peripheries.

"It's okay, Colleen." Sashi's hand was on her back. "Don't hold anything in. Just react."

Colleen nodded.

"Actually," Lorelei was saying, in a pointed, emphatic tone. "I feel very at home here in Reno. Much more so than I did in L.A. L.A.'s so phony, you know?"

"Say more about that," said a voice off camera.

"Sure, sure. Let's take lighting, for example, *por ejemplo*" — she talked fast — "so the major type of lighting in Reno is neon, which some might consider tacky, whereas in L.A., you've got this fucking mood lighting everywhere you go, in restaurants and bars, this really kind lighting, like someone spilled tequila all over everything. Mind if I smoke?"

"I'm not sure I'm following your example?" said the voice behind the camera.

"Listen more closely!" Lorelei squatted down in her heels to rummage a cigarette from her purse on the floor — a pricey Miu Miu Colleen didn't recognize — and lit up with a match, keeping the handbag in the crook of her elbow.

"My metaphor, or is it a simile; you never hear anyone mention similes, do you? It's always metaphor, metaphor, metaphor. The way people talk in L.A. is another example of its fakeness. In L.A., it's love, love, love. I've never been told 'I love you' by more people than I was in L.A. Or called, let me see ..." She held up her closed fist and raised a finger with each example: "Honey, baby, sweetie, cutie, biffy, bestie, and these all from people I knew for like five seconds!"

Her words were flying. "Can I have some goddamn water? Am I allowed to move?" She pointed off-screen.

"Help yourself," said the voice.

"That's enough!" said Colleen, squeezing her fingers into her palms. Clearly Lorelei was high as the moon. Colleen felt high, too.

Sashi pushed a button on the monitor and the screen went dark. "I'm so sorry," she said. "I know that was very upsetting."

"Why don't we go to Reno right now?" Colleen demanded. "Why aren't you staging your intervention or convention or whatever it is today? Obviously, she needs help!"

"Trust us. Please," said Sashi. "I've done this dozens of times. We need to wait just a little longer. Maybe only a few days. Lorelei is still somewhat hostile on and off camera. Belligerent, Joel says. We need to soften her tone, or the whole thing could backfire enormously."

Colleen stood up from her chair. "So what am I supposed to do between then and now? Now that you've shown me my daughter looking like a rack of bones and ranting gibberish, out of her mind on drugs?"

"I can only imagine how that must have made you feel. But I'd feel unethical withholding it. Please, try to take the long view. *RHF* has truly helped people in Lorelei's situation. Joel and our crew in Reno will be with her as much as possible in the next few days and will summon us when the time is right."

"And then what?"

"Then, we hop on a plane for the Convergence. It takes just an hour and a half to fly to Reno. It's easier than getting to Orange County."

"Who's *we*?"

"We've been in conversation with others who care very much for Lorelei's well-being. For now, I can't share their names. But don't worry; we've respected your request that we not reach out to your husband."

Colleen looked past Sashi to the glass wall with its high-tech covering, blocking the room's transparency like a giant Band-Aid. Sashi had asked to speak with Carl about the Convergence, several times; Colleen had insisted on handling it herself.

Of course, she hadn't said a word to him about it. She couldn't possibly, until the very last minute, when Lorelei's need for her parents would trump Carl's anger at Colleen for delving back into the same world that had almost ruined them all.

Sashi said, "Is your husband prepared to join us in Reno on very short notice, if need be?"

Colleen swallowed. "Yes. He is." Feeling claustrophobic, she strode over to the wall and lifted up the edge of the shade. "Can you open these please?"

"Of course." Sashi clicked the remote and the shades peeled up.

"Are we done?"

"We could be. Or you could stay a bit longer for an interview. We have an in-house studio downstairs that's very comfortable and private. I'd completely understand if you just want to leave, but an interview could really help shape the emotional resonance of the show."

This was one of Sashi's great gifts: presenting two options as if they were actually your choices, and then making you feel there was only one right answer.

Colleen looked into Sashi's eyes. "Do you have protein bars or anything around here? I need to eat something."

"Of course," Sashi said. "Odwalla, Luna, and thinkThin. There's a kitchen on the way to the studio. Let's go."

"No," Colleen said, thinking of the points of light just ahead: the purple bullet of Zenzo in a Tic Tac container in her purse, a nap at the Olive Motel in Silver Lake, and seeing Bundy Hesse. "I'd prefer to skip the interview."

Sashi touched her very white top teeth to her maroon-stained bottom lip. "Fair enough," she said, opening the door with her slender hand. "Why don't we take a walk and get you some lunch, and then see how you feel? There's a fantastic Bulgarian food truck that might still be op—"

"I'll just take that protein bar, if you don't mind," Colleen said. "I have another appointment"

40

"CAN I SWITCH you to beer?" The bartender, a chipper brunette a little older than Lorelei, wore a T-shirt with a brown bear on the front, BEST BURGERS SOUTH OF THE REDWOODS written across its flank in yellow letters. "It's happy hour, you know. Everything on draft, three bucks."

"No thanks. I'll just take some more hot water." Carl had been nursing a mug of Lipton tea for the past half hour while he waited for Wendy at the bar of the lodge-style restaurant he'd hastily chosen as a meeting place. Waited, and stewed over his decision to invite her to dinner. The last thing she'd said after the meeting last Sunday was "Call if you need a friend — I mean it." She'd pressed a business card into his hand. He'd slipped it into his wallet, thinking, *I've got friends, thanks,* but driving home, he tried to think of whom he'd actually call to talk about his problems at home. Alan, his tennis buddy of fifteen years? They played on Wednesday nights to earn their oversized hamburgers and beers afterward, to talk Broncos versus Raiders if it was football season, or the Dodgers versus the Giants the rest of the year. They covered family in an obligatory way: "Any improvements with Lorelei?" Jerry would ask, and after Carl said, then, "Marnie and I are praying for her, man. Every night." And then a clap to Carl's shoulder, a quick update on his own teenage girls, both active in their church youth group, and then on to sports. No, he would not be calling Jerry to say, *You know what? I'm miserable. Everyone in my family is starting to feel like a character in a bad movie. My daughter's disappeared and my wife's more in love with her treadmill than with me, and my son's become a big shot filmmaker, so want to come keep me company while I build cabinets in the mountains and listen to me complain about it?* And if not Jerry, then certainly not Marshall, his single employee, a strapping Australian guy in his thirties, who was so happy-go-lucky, so unwavering in his good moods, that Carl sometimes wondered if he was actually human. Maybe it was the accent — who knew? Marshall was great for banter — his knowledge of blues was practically encyclopedic — and he was a gifted carpenter, but despite the endless hours Carl spent working with him, the hundreds of lunches they'd eaten in half-built houses, talking subfloors and joint lines and how they couldn't wait for people to get over granite, he was certainly not about to get personal with Marshall.

He hadn't expected the loneliness to hit him as hard as it did when got to the job site. For the first few nights, he chided himself: *It's only a week, for God's sake, and you're less than two hours from home.* But on the third morning he'd woken at dawn, and the day ahead stretched before him with such interminable solitude, despite the company of Marshall and a half dozen other contractors, that he'd fished Wendy's card from his wallet and asked her to drive up for dinner. She'd accepted without a single question.

Carl had only allowed himself to invite her to dinner because he wasn't attracted to her. He just felt comfortable with her, like he would any potential friend. She made him feel good about himself, something Colleen currently did not. Men and women could be friends, right? A friendly dinner was allowable even if you were married, wasn't it? Colleen would probably just make fun of him if he told her, anyway. *Did she drive up, or fly with the wings of her hair?*

Now, waiting for her to arrive at the Three Rivers Bar and Grill, he was uneasy with his decision. A beer might help. He considered the list, rife with outdoorsy-sounding mircrobrews, but decided against it. Alcohol was becoming repellant to him.

He'd been a moderate, casual drinker his whole life, rarely pushing past two beers, but since Colleen's behavior at the Justuses' party, and the failure of a bottle of champagne to induce any sort of festive air between them the night he'd attempted to celebrate the Sequoia job, he'd made a shift. The very sight of liquor bottles, lining the bar like rows of big colorful teeth, gave him a sinking feeling. So did the bartender pulling amber beer from the tap into a frosted pint glass, leaving a perfect inch-high head. The bleedy red wine in orbed goblets, passing by on round serving trays. All of it felt like a threat to his clarity. His wife and daughter had inspired a new desire in him to feel lucid at all times. In fact, at the invitation of his current boss — the multimillionaire tech entrepreneur, barely thirty-two years old — Carl had spent the past two nights camping on the kid's private mountain property, even though he'd also paid for Carl's room at a cozy inn nearby. Carl bought a warm sleeping bag at Costco and didn't even bother with a tent, wanting to sleep right under the stars. Clarity, cold and unobstructed. The opposite of how Colleen made him feel lately. He couldn't put his finger on what she was hiding, but secrecy emanated from her as distinctly as new perfume. Part of him wanted to pin her down and demand that she tell him everything, but a bigger part of him was afraid to know. The way he could never ask about Lorelei's breasts. For now, all he could bring himself to do was embrace the Al-Anon way, and hope that Colleen would come around, and that they could survive whatever secrets she was harboring.

Plus, the truth was, Carl hated being alone. This measly week alone in the Sierra was killing him. When he'd won the job, he immediately envisioned an escape to the mountains with Colleen as a panacea. He'd hoped that a complete change of scenery together, without her laptop or her treadmill or her makeup trove, might somehow trigger a breakthrough, create an environment in which she actually wanted to talk to him. They'd had that together once, though it was hard to remember.

But of course, here he was, by himself with enormous trees and ice-blue alpine skies, lonelier than ever. So lonely that he'd invited Wendy to drive an hour and a half to have dinner with him.

"Hello, Grizzly Adams!"

Carl looked up to see Wendy striding to the bar, dressed in a denim shirt and jeans, a sturdy brown purse over her shoulder, her hair in its usual stiff feathers to her shoulders. Carl knew her look wasn't fashionable or current, but he liked it. She was just herself, comfortable in her own skin. The way a middle-aged woman should be.

Carl touched his three-day beard. "I never shave on a job. Kind of a superstition."

"It becomes you!" she said brightly. "Can we get a table? I'm starving!"

Carl flagged a server, who showed them to a table by an uncovered window, dark mountain shapes and moonlight outside it. After they ordered — salmon and water for Carl, steak and Coke with a cherry for Wendy, she leaned toward him and asked, "So any word from Lorelei?"

"Nothing," Carl said. "Back to silence. Which is making Colleen crazy. She wants to jump in the car and comb the entire state of Nevada, just because that was the area code Lorelei called me from."

"Poor Colleen."

"I guess." The hardness of his tone surprised him.

"You guess?"

Carl took a bite of fish. There was no going back now. "She makes things harder for us than they already are."

Wendy leaned in, brown eyes wide with sympathy. "It's common for one parent to take the side of the child, you know."

"She obsesses about all the wrong things. How we might track Lorelei down and bring her home, like she's a wild animal we can tame if we just build the right trap. How we might be able to convince her to come home, should she decide to grace us with a phone call. And then, to distract herself until Lorelei decides to grace us with a phone call, she obsesses about exercise and her clothes and reversing her wrinkles or whatever."

"Classic avoidance," Wendy said gently, lifting a bite of steak.

Carl wanted to keep talking. "She acts like she can't wait for me to leave any room we happen to be in at the same time. Like it's me against her, just because I have a different approach toward Lorelei. Just because I don't want to hunt her down and send her money to bribe her to come home."

"Just because *you* happen to be taking the healthy, strong approach," Wendy said. "Just because you're being the more responsible parent, acting in the best interest of your daughter. Just because you're willing to admit that you can't force people to do anything they don't want to do, and your wife does not."

"Thank you for saying that." Even if Wendy was parroting Al-Anon philosophy, Carl felt reassured by it.

"Don't thank me." She pushed her plate aside and reached forward to cup her hand over his. He almost pulled back, reflexively, but her palm was warm and her fingers clasped tight over his fist, her nails short and unpainted but pretty in their own way, and he closed his eyes, let himself enjoy the clean, simple feeling of having someone on his side.

"Coffee or dessert menus?" A waitress in the bear T-shirt smiled down at them.

"Both," said Wendy, not letting go of his hand.

41

COLLEEN CHECKED INTO the Olive Motel, seven miles from Moonrock, where Bundy was playing at eleven. She could still remember how funny and sexy and smart he'd made her feel back at the Justuses' party. She needed to feel that way again, just for one night.

The motel bed was a welcome sight. She set the alarm to wake her in a few hours, pulled the stiff motel curtains shut, and collapsed in the center of the old mattress.

At nine, strengthened by a dreamless nap, Colleen showered and ate a protein bar and an apple, and drank two bottles of water. She wanted a real drink, but the Olive Motel didn't have a minibar. She dressed in a manner she hoped was appropriate, having raided the leftovers of Lorelei's closet: a white baby-doll tee with a small pink-and-black skull printed in the center, her own jeans — skinny-style, but not too tight — and some black canvas sneakers of Lorelei's. And since there was just a touch of coolness in the air, she added a black cardigan of her own, expensive and perfectly cut in a way that added a dose of adulthood to the youthful ensemble. Dressing as though you didn't care much took as much care — if not more — than dressing as if you did, she thought, pulling her hair into a ponytail, noticing amber roots invading the blond she touched up at the salon every six weeks. An appointment she was overdue for.

Colleen assessed her reflection. When had her daughter worn this shirt with the pink skull? Where had she gone in it?

Had Lorelei stolen anything in this shirt? She knew Lorelei occasionally shoplifted — little things, like earrings from Walgreens (Colleen had watched her from a distance putting them into her own ears), sunglasses (she removed the tags and put them right on her head). Had Lorelei kissed any boys in this shirt, drunk beer from a can, smoked pot, snorted or smoked whatever it was that had her so skinny and manic? The shirt smelled only of lavender-scented detergent, with a vague underlay of Lorelei — a scent Colleen couldn't really describe, except that it was a young smell, weightless and clean, like ... what was it? She tried to remember flowers, from back when she planted flowers, years ago. Rhododendron?

It was 9:45. She would leave the motel in fifteen minutes, plenty of time for the 11:00 show. She hoped Bundy would be hanging around in the audience before the show started.

She turned the television on, for company, the stressful courtroom vibe of some crime show filling the air, and began to transfer her essentials from her large handbag to the small, cross-body purse, also from Lorelei's closet: a red canvas pouch with DICKIES written on the side. She packed her ID, a credit card, some cash, Zenzos in the Tic Tac container and Performa in a cylindrical, travel-sized tube that once contained Advil.

She had a flash of Bundy crushing up her Performa back in the Justuses' den, and without pausing to think it over, she crushed one up herself, alternating between the edge and the flat side of a credit card until she'd made a fine powder.

She rolled up a one-dollar bill and snorted it. She'd forgotten to shape the stuff into a line, but it didn't seem to matter.

The sting subsided fast. She slung the strap of Lorelei's bag over her shoulder, arranged the purse part on her opposite hip, and walked out of the Olive Motel into the fragrant spring night. The smell of jasmine and the sound of traffic on the freeway filled her with hope.

42

"WHAT'S WRONG?" ASKED Marina.

Night has just set in, blanketing the farm in a velvety darkness full of croaking frogs and chirping crickets. She was hanging out in the cutting trailer while Darren worked, sitting on the floor barefoot, as usual, poring over some new changes to the shooting script an intern had dropped off a few hours earlier. The room was dim — good for editing, not reading — but she claimed not to mind.

"You're not acting like yourself with me," she said. "Are you still embarrassed about the other day?"

Rather than let their almost-kiss hover unspoken between them, Marina insisted on "confronting the discomfort." Darren admired her approach, in theory, but in practice, he had a shitload of work to do, and her determination to "normalize" their friendship was wearing on him. The incident in the pasture filled him with self-loathing. Of course Marina hadn't actually intended to kiss him. She was gorgeous, twenty years old, famous. What had he been thinking? She'd touched her nose to his because underneath the Angelina Jolie glamour of her exterior, she was an affectionate semi-hippie at heart. She'd been exhilarated about working with Darren, period, and he'd misinterpreted her.

He loathed himself for even thinking about Marina, when his own wife had started avoiding him to a worrisome degree.

"I'm working, Marina," Darren said, wincing at a frame of Ven's bare butt. "That's all."

"Oh, come on. It's not your action, it's your essence. You're emanating weirdness. I just want things to normalize between us."

"They're normal." He sighed, watching a clip of Marina canter across his screen on horseback. It was strange to have her there in the room while he looked at her digital image on a big monitor at the same time.

"Then what's up?" she said. "Tell me."

"Other stuff."

"Like what?"

"Like . . ." He twisted his neck to look over his shoulder at her. By now he knew how persistent she could be; it was better just to deal with questions directly. " . . . the fact that my wife won't answer my calls or return my texts." There. He'd said it.

"So go see her," said Marina, without hesitation. "Just take two days and go. Work it out."

Did he detect a tiny note of jealousy in her voice? he wondered. Or was he just hoping it was there?

"Oh, please," he said. "Toby'd flip out. I'd get fired on the spot."

He turned back to his computer. On the screen Heather was shoving Ven's chest.

Marina pulled her ponytail over one shoulder with both hands. "Maybe not. There's much more respect between the two of you now. It's palpable. You could at least ask him."

"Give me a break. Toby doesn't let people visit their kids in the hospital when they're on location for his movie."

Marina paused and tilted her face to the ceiling. "Well," she said slowly. "You're a special case."

"Special how?"

She set the script aside and threaded the fingers of her right hand through the toes of her left foot. "Can I be honest? Can we be totally gloves-off with each other?"

"Go ahead." He was getting impatient. The lighting in an indoor scene they'd shot yesterday was off, and Toby would undoubtedly come by and discover it in a few hours.

"I was just going to say that I think it's okay to use your leverage just this once to get what you need from Toby. If it's for the sake of your marriage."

"Leverage? What leverage?" He braced himself for one of Marina's abstract musings.

"It's usually my policy never mention the money involved in the films I work on. Because I hate thinking of art as commodity."

"Go on."

"Fine. By *leverage,* I meant that since your father-in-law is partially backing *Equus,* Toby might be sympathetic to your situation."

Darren swiveled his chair around to face her, not comprehending. "Whose father-in-law?"

"Yours. Mel Justus."

"How do you know Mel? And what's he got to do with *Equus*?"

She arched her eyebrows. "Well, nothing, beyond the funding."

"But we're backed by New Dawn Films," he said. A sick feeling rose in his stomach. He shouldn't have eaten the rainbow trout from craft services.

"We are backed by New Dawn," she said, unspooling her fingers from her toes. "That's my production company."

"You have a production company?"

She nodded. "Remember, I told you under the tree the other day, after Toby got slammed in the mouth . . ."

Now he remembered.

"Since I eventually want to get into directing," Marina said. "I thought starting New Dawn would be a step in the right direction. We put up the first round of funding for *Equus,* but at the last minute Toby decided he needed more capital. We pitched *Equus* all over L.A., and the best offer came back from Justus Ventures. I met Mel in a meeting." She cleared her throat. "Two meetings."

"You've got to be kidding me."

"Seriously? You had no idea?"

"Zero. And what about Andy Patchell? Toby's cinematographer?" Darren couldn't keep his voice from rising. "Did they really split over *creative differences?*"

Marina picked at a frayed fiber on the area rug.

"Marina!" He stood up from the editing bay, shoving the flimsy desk. The twin monitors wobbled.

"Mel wanted you on the film. It was a stipulation of the financing."

He slapped a monitor with the back of his hand. It wobbled precariously. "Ouch. Goddammit!"

"Darren, I'm so sorry." Her voice began to quaver.

"Marina, now it's my turn to be gloves-off. I'm going to ask you something, and I need you to answer honestly."

"Anything." She sounded on the brink of crying. "Dishonesty isn't a part of who I am. I believe — "

He held up his hand. "Spare me. Just tell me: Why have you been so nice this whole time? It was so out of the blue."

Her eyes glassed over with tears. "I — I just felt a connection, Darren. From the first time we met, I felt this — "

"I was unconscious when met! You couldn't have felt a 'connection' from stumbling over me asleep in the grass."

Two fat tears trailed down her sculpted cheeks. "But I feel it now! It doesn't matter why we became friends. What matters is that we *are*."

"What are you not telling me?"

She threw her hands up in the air. "Fine. I'll tell you. After Justus Ventures signed on to *Equus*, Mel and I had a long lunch meeting. He said you were depressed about your marriage and needed a friend. And that these issues would interfere with your work on the set. He asked me to keep tabs on you, to 'keep your spirits up.' Those were his exact words. I assumed he meant Robin was leaving you. And then you've been so vague about her . . ." she trailed off.

"My marriage is fine! I've been vague because it's none of your business!" *And because you've been flirting with me nonstop,* he wanted to add. "Mel is a manipulative asshole. I'm surprised you didn't sense that, Marina. With your intuition and all."

"Mel wasn't being an asshole. He was just concerned!"

"Marina, he wasn't concerned. He was trying to break up my marriage."

"What?" She grabbed his arm, alarm crossing her face. "No way. That's insane. Mel's fundamentally a good guy. I've spent hours with him. He just — "

"I've spent seven years with him, Marina!"

" — he just doesn't know how to express his goodness without the use of money. Which is unevolved, yes, but hardly evil. He even put a bunch of money into Saving Steeds. My charity."

"Jesus Christ." He needed to get out of the trailer. There was no way he could convince Marina that she'd been a pawn of Mel's too. What was the point? Her idealism was too steadfast. Time would erode it eventually, but perhaps not until her beauty began to ebb and fade. "Look, I'm going for a walk. Alone."

"Are you mad at me? Are you still upset about the other day?"

"You wanted to kiss me." The accusation flew from his mouth, flat and factual.

"I know. But I just knew it wouldn't be right."

"It wouldn't have been," he said. "I'm married, and despite any suggestions to the contrary, from Mel or from me, I love my wife totally and completely. But I'm human and you're—" He faltered. *"You."*

She wasn't fully listening. Her eyes were focused on the door behind him, her mind already on a different track.

"We're on again, off again, you know," she said softly. "Currently off. So that's where my head was, when we were under the tree . . ."

"What? Who's 'we'?"

"Toby and me."

Darren pushed past her to open the door, and jumped from the top step of the trailer's entry over the four stairs leading to the ground. Soft, damp earth cushioned his feet as he landed, and he broke into a run.

"Darren," Marina called after him. "One more thing. Please."

He whirled around. *"What?"*

"Since you're already mad, I might as well tell you that I got a few texts saying we got papped."

"Got what?"

"Photographed by the paparazzi. You and me. I'm sure it's nothing. We've got nothing to hide. But I wanted to make sure you knew, just in case those slimebags at the tabloids give it some ridiculous spin."

"How noble of you, Marina," Darren said. "You're truly above it all." And he loped away into the night.

43

HIS NAME WAS there on the marquee, in green all-caps. It was finally happening. And Colleen was ready.

The club was absurdly crowded: getting to the bar, pushing into stranger after stranger. But still, she didn't care; she deserved to be here.

By the time Colleen arrived at the bar, sweat was beginning to claim the makeup from her face. She ordered a Jameson's, straight up.

"Jameson's, neat," said the bartender, a stocky guy in a T-shirt with an airplane over the caption BOEING OR I'M NOT GOING!

"Whatever!" she yelled back. She was in the mood to get the last word. She was feeling very good.

She never drank whiskey, but Carl did on rare occasions, taking practically a year to get through the one bottle of Dewar's he kept in a high cupboard of the kitchen. Once, she'd found that bottle in the bottom of a bag of Lorelei's, with all but an inch missing. Colleen had dumped the remaining splash and shoved the bottle deep in the recycling bin. The next day, she bought a new bottle, poured out a quarter of it—guessing Carl might have consumed that much himself before Lorelei took it—and returned it to its shelf in the kitchen. She never mentioned it to Carl or Lorelei, and neither of them brought it up, either. Colleen wasn't proud of that parenting decision, but all teenagers took their parents' booze, and Carl would've been unduly hard on Lorelei if he'd found out.

"That'll be eight," the bartender said, sliding a plastic cup into her hand.

"No change, thanks," Colleen said, handing him a ten and

downing the cup of whiskey in one swig. It was too crowded to even carry a cup around.

"Nice!" the bartender said.

The whiskey seared the back of her throat and landed sourly in her stomach. It felt good.

"Another, please," she said, setting the empty cup on the bar.

The stage was lit but empty. The crowd yelled into one another's ears and sloshed their beer onto the floor. Colleen checked her watch. Ten-thirty. She asked a pixie-ish girl wearing a green barrette in her blond hair if she knew when the next band started, and the girl looked at her watchless wrist and yelled, "I just got here, I'm pretty sure the DNs are at midnight!"

The DNs. The Double Negatives. On the stage, three people now appeared: two skinny guys in snap-down Western shirts and a heavyset girl holding a violin. She had dyed red hair, lots of dark eyeliner, and some sort of hideous black skirt made of — crinoline?

"Hey, we're called Music for Graveyards," she said into the microphone.

Colleen found the music, a sort of slowed-down rock with strings rising over it, surprisingly beautiful, both sad and affirming, and she liked how the girl played her violin vigorously with her eyes squeezed shut. The crowd hushed.

Nobody danced exactly, but a collective shifting of body weight from one foot to the other had begun throughout the room. Colleen found it unsatisfying; she wanted to grab another person and move around. Had she and Carl ever danced to live music together? She could recall only a single time, to the Allman Brothers at the Fresno Fairgrounds, at least fifteen years ago. The crowd had been bearded and stoned, and she hadn't cared for the rambling, jangly music, but Carl had pulled her close and danced her around the grass, singing along with the band in her ear, and she'd felt giddy in his arms.

Colleen's whiskey cup was empty, ice sweating through the plastic. It was much easier to get to the bar this time since the crowd was transfixed by Music for Graveyards.

Time sped up, or did it slow down? One minute the singer, one of the skinny Western-shirt guys, was thanking the crowd in his monotone voice, and the next, Bundy was right there. He stood at center stage, guitar slung over his shoulder, in a black T-shirt and gray jeans over boots that looked like they were meant for motorcycle riding. He had a beer in his hand and sunglasses propped on his head, as if he'd just stepped inside from a sunny day. The crowd pressed forward, and Colleen had to move forcefully through it toward the stage. She pushed on and on—*excuse me, excuse me*—and people stepped aside, complying. She possessed a sort of power tonight, and the kids responded to it.

She reached the base of the stage, and Bundy was right there, above her, her chin level with his motorcycle boots. It hardly felt real to be near him again. He looked larger, more handsome, more solid than in her memory. There were two other guys about his age on the stage and a girl who looked like she'd been poured from a pitcher of water, impossibly thin with flowing ash-blond hair and a gauzy white dress. She was tipped up on her heels, speaking in the ear of one of the guys, the one with long sideburns in a grandpa cardigan. He wrinkled his brow in concentration, straining to hear her over the burble of the crowd. Then he leaned down to yell something back.

It was some sort of argument, and it was delaying the start

of the Double Negatives show. Bundy just stood there, drinking from a can of beer that said *Pork Juice Lager* on it.

She was close enough to read his beer can. Closer than she might ever be again. This was her chance to say hi.

The volume of the crowd had swelled.

"Bundy!" she yelled.

He couldn't hear her.

She yelled his name as loud as she could, but he didn't even look down.

She reached out and grabbed his ankle, gripping hard so he could feel it through the leather of his boot.

Surprised, he tried to step backward.

She let go one second too late. He stumbled, and landed in a seated position on the stage floor. A minor fall, but clumsy-looking.

A piercing whistle came from the crowd, soaring up over the general racket. A female voice screamed "Yeah, Bun-DEEEEE!" and then there were more whistles and affectionate-sounding catcalls.

Bundy stood up, and Colleen saw that he was not smiling. That he was, in fact, pissed. He walked to the edge of the stage and hooked his finger toward her, summoning her to come close.

Before he could say anything, she rose on her toes and shouted, "I'm so sorry! It's me, Colleen from that party in Bev — "

He leaned down, his face inches from hers. When he spoke, she could smell the Pork Juice Lager on his breath.

"Touch me again and I'll call security."

He hopped back toward his band, shouted something at them, and then said into the microphone, "This one's from our new album, coming out next month." Music crashed into the air.

Colleen felt like she had been punched in the stomach. She whirled around and tried to bolt away, but a wall of people had closed in behind her. The crowd began a collective up and down motion, a sort of group hop.

She was trapped.

Bundy's music felt like an attack: It was noisier, showier, more chaotic than it had ever sounded over all those sweet miles on the treadmill, in the car. Then, his voice had sounded vulnerable; now it was just whiny. Like suddenly seeing into the mechanics of a dream, the disappointment of how wild colors and transformations were just a by-product of synaptic firings and gray matter.

"Let me through!" she screamed into the ear of the girl behind her. "It's an emergency! Please!"

Somehow, the girl made room.

Colleen yelled the same thing to the next person, a guy in a gray fedora. He jerked away from her, freeing up another slice of space. She darted into it. And yelled again to the next person, shoving her way through the pulsing crowd toward an exit, any exit, and in minutes she was free, outside in the cooling desert night.

She found a patch of grass beside the parking lot and dropped to her knees, pitching forward until her nose touched the earth. She stayed that way for a long time, her eyes pinched shut, her body trembling. Trying to erase what had just happened. To wipe every trace of Bundy Hesse from her mind.

When she rose to her feet, she wanted nothing but to get out of Los Angeles. For good.

"I hate you," she said to the palm fronds overhead. Her throat was raw from all the screaming, her voice chalky.

Colleen would not stay in this city another minute. It had done nothing but humiliate and reject her. What had taken her so long to learn? Brushing the grass from her clothes, she crossed the parking lot to her Camry. She wouldn't wait for Sashi, for some television network, to tell her when she could see her daughter. She would drive to LAX right now and catch the next flight to Reno. She would find Lorelei and bring her home.

44

AFTER BOLTING FROM the cutting trailer, Darren jogged straight across the property toward the grassy square that served as the production's parking lot. It was a half mile away, up near the farm's main entrance. Near the main barn, crew members settling in to their nightly hangout crisscrossed him with the flashlights and called out, *Hey, Darren, want a beer?*

He wasn't sure what he was doing — he didn't have keys to a single one of the SUVs, pickup trucks, or jeeps scattered in the makeshift lot. The sky was clear and star-pocked, the moon clean and high. He pulled at the door of the first vehicle he passed, a monster-sized Lincoln Navigator, and it opened. He hopped up into the front seat and found the key in the ignition. He turned the engine and rolled the windows down. Where should he go? Miami? The ocean? He switched the engine off and laid his head against the steering wheel.

All along, he'd been working for Mel. Mel had bought him the job. Aspen Green had been lying, with the stuff about Toby falling in love with *Str8t Edge* at Telluride.

Had Robin known all along that Mel was backing *Equus*? If so, his perception of his marriage would be permanently rocked. Maybe irreparably so. If her discomfort with his taking the job, and her elusiveness since he'd been away, were related to Mel's influence, well, then Robin wasn't the wife he thought she was.

If Robin had concealed Mel's involvement in the movie, what else was she not telling Darren?

He pulled his phone from his pocket and speed-dialed her. Straight to voicemail. "Robin, goddammit, call me back," he said.

It was the rudest thing he'd ever said to her, but a fresh wave of anger, mingled with fear, had grabbed him and wouldn't let go. He had the impulse to do something even more childish, to behave the way he never did: vengefully, irrationally. If Toby was there, he would have yelled *I quit!* But Toby was off in the tropical night, obsessing over some *Equus Revisited* minutiae.

Darren used his phone to CashNow Lorelei five hundred bucks.

The second the transaction went through, his phone rang. He jumped. "Hello?"

"Darren, it's Sashi Sabaratnam. I'm calling about your sister, Lorelei."

His chest froze. "What? Who is this?"

"Sashi Sabaratnam. Executive producer of *Real Happy Family,* a television show that saves families in danger of collapse. Your sister has asked for our help. And to help her, we need your cooperation. We're assembling Lorelei's loved ones in Reno, Nevada, as soon as possible, to address her drug and alcohol problems, which have become very severe, and to help your entire family begin the healing process. Time is of the essence. Lorelei is not well."

Darren swallowed hard, opened the door of the SUV, and climbed out. "Sashi, you realize I'm Robin Justus's husband, right?"

"Excuse me?"

"Robin Justus is my wife. She's also Lorelei's agent. So I'm not sure why I haven't heard about this from her. If Lorelei was on a new show, Robin would be the first to know. And, seeing how Lorelei is my sister, she would've told me." Unease flooded through him; *would* Robin have told him? Was this why she'd been avoiding him? Because she'd been involved in some covert operation with a reality show?

His head was spinning. The past hour had delivered more bewildering information than he could process.

"Robin has nothing to do with this," said Sashi. "Whatsoever. This is about the Branch family. Of which, as I understand from Lorelei, you are a crucial part. You're extremely important to your sister, who has spun out of control. So I hope you'll come to support her . . ." She began to rattle off logistics about meeting in Reno.

When she was done, he repeated back to her, numbly, "So . . . the Cielo Hotel in Reno. Six, Friday?"

"Six Pacific, yes," Sashi said.

Darren kicked the side of the SUV as hard as he could. The side of the truck felt like concrete against his foot. He groaned and limped away toward the dark trees.

He was out of resources. Utterly bereft. And so entirely confused, so exhausted on every level, that there was only one person left in the world who could steady him.

He took a deep breath and called his father.

45

MUST TALK TO YOU re Lorelei Branch; please call me asap.

"Ugh," Robin had said to her empty bedroom. "No thanks."

She'd found a red-eye to Miami and was in the middle of

packing for her trip when Sashi Sabaratnam's text arrived. The sun had just set, the new night a lead blue through the trees outside her upstairs window. She'd known Sashi for years and had once thought her a cut above other reality people — intelligent and polished. But Robin's opinion had nosedived after Sashi had been happy to exploit Colleen's gaffe from the *Flo's Studio* shoot, causing even more damage to Lorelei's already-imploded career. Sashi looked for The Angle everywhere, for the character or storyline that would captivate the biggest audience. She was good at what she did.

So when Sashi texted out of the blue, Robin knew it was for the sake of whatever reality universe she was constructing at the time, maybe a *Flo's Studio* spinoff. Sashi was probably just hooking her with the question about Lorelei, assuming Robin would bite out of curiosity.

It worked. As Robin rolled a few T-shirts into tight cylinders to fit into a small carry-on, she wondered if Sashi knew something about what was going on with Lorelei. Robin's own desire to know was lukewarm; Lorelei's toxic behavior, in the months after the *Flo's Studio* disaster, had sapped what was left of Robin's investment in her sister-in-law. She'd signed Lorelei only as a favor to Darren anyway; Lorelei had a pretty face and a perfect, petite body, but her talents were vague and undeveloped, and while she possessed a high level of native intelligence, her native laziness routinely trumped it. Which drove Robin crazy. Lorelei wanted to be on TV, but didn't want to learn to act. Had natural singing ability, but no interest in voice training. Lorelei's beauty was workable enough, with her porcelain Irish skin and mass of reddish corkscrew curls, her nose that tapered to a delicate upturn, her cheekbones that revealed themselves despite the roundness of her face. She was easy to shoot from any angle.

But Lorelei's only real passion, as far as Robin could tell, was becoming famous. It didn't help that Colleen substantiated her daughter's attitude. The two of them — and they were inseparable — seemed to think success in Hollywood was a matter of getting dressed up and then waiting for Robin to make something happen.

Because she loved Darren, Robin had tried. Or at least, she'd gone through the motions enough to keep everyone reasonably happy, making the easy phone calls required to book Lorelei on commercial auditions. Sure, she could have done more, coached Lorelei harder, demanded she pick a talent and cultivate it, assigned her classic TV shows to study, actresses to emulate. But Lorelei's entitled attitude demotivated Robin. And there had been Colleen to contend with, glued to Lorelei's side, bringing her hummingbird energy to every meeting, every audition. Robin had taken Lorelei and Colleen aside separately on several occasions to ask, gently, whether each woman believed the "team" approach to Lorelei's career was beneficial.

"She needs me there," Colleen had snapped. "She'd be a nervous wreck otherwise. Ask her."

"She deserves to be there," Lorelei said. "She's done so much for me, my whole life."

"That's her choice," Robin said. "You're allowed to make your own choices, too."

"I don't mind having her around," Lorelei had said, unconvincingly. "It would be a lot worse to hurt her feelings."

Part of Robin was appalled by the unhealthy loyalty Colleen had instilled in Lorelei. But another part of her was envious. She couldn't imagine hurting her own mother by merely imposing distance. Linda wouldn't even notice. It hadn't helped that, shortly after signing Lorelei, Robin's priorities began to veer away from formulating the success of young women and toward getting herself pregnant.

Lorelei's *Flo's Studio* stint had fallen into Robin's lap; a casting agent from the show had called, asking if No Princess had any talent suited to becoming the next "Faux Girl." *Perfect,* Robin had thought. Fashion-focused reality TV would seem wildly glamorous to someone like Lorelei, but would be a low-stakes, low-effort endeavor for Robin.

Robin hadn't expected Lorelei to do as well as she had, but the candy-eyed solipsism of *Flo's Studio* awakened Lorelei's spirit, and in just a half dozen episodes, she'd become a darling among the show's sizable fan base. Robin had already begun getting calls from event promoters and low-list media outlets, asking whether Lorelei was available to promote a new vodka in Vegas or answer ten questions about her fashion habits.

Robin had even begun to get a little bit excited. Lorelei got mentions on popular websites like StarGazer and RealiTea. A photo of high school girls wearing *Team Lorelei* T-shirts appeared in *Us Weekly*. Perez Hilton named her one of Ten Hot Reality TV Faces to Watch.

And then, during the show's climactic episode — the reveal of the new Faux Girl selection — Colleen got wasted and belligerently racist on countless cameras, which was then broadcast to every corner of the Internet, destroying Lorelei's every future possibility. Nobody wanted to touch fledgling reality talent with a ranting, hateful lunatic of a stage mother.

For the first time, Robin felt real compassion for Lorelei. She was vacuous, but she hadn't deserved what Colleen had put her through.

So Robin had done everything a good agent should have: assembled a list of options for Lorelei, all of which were in her best interest, and tried to help her select the choice that resonated with her most. She could have done any number of interviews to share her side of the story: *Tosh.0, TMZ,* People

.com, the *Posse* website. She could have taken the high road and done a little theater somewhere, until the hype dissipated. Or she could have simply taken some time off. Robin had issued only one hard rule: Lorelei *had* to distance herself from her mother. Even if that meant temporarily living in Robin's carriage house, Robin had said, intending to illustrate how serious she was about separating Lorelei and Colleen, rather than to issue an actual invitation. But Lorelei had jumped on the chance to move to Santa Monica, and Darren had been so grateful for Robin's "generosity" that Robin kept her mouth shut, despite the hesitation flaring inside her, and handed the cottage keys over to Lorelei.

Had Lorelei simply laid low in Santa Monica for a few months, as was the plan, the *Flo's Studio* gaffe could have been nothing more than a small career stumble for her. But then she'd become such a Hollywood cliché, drinking and drugging at the clubs, pocketing any cash she found lying around the house, driving home from Hollywood at all hours, wasted, until Robin convinced Darren that they needed to kick her out. Lorelei had beaten them to it, though, moving first to a friend's place, and then to her current undisclosed location.

Robin had a gut feeling that Lorelei was fine, wherever she was, and that her abrupt departure from L.A. was a childish attempt at dramatic effect, specifically to rattle Colleen. But Robin's hunch was of no consolation to Darren. He was genuinely distraught over his sister's disappearance. If Sashi had real news, he deserved to know. Robin was angry with him, but not enough to deny him such important information.

She zipped her suitcase shut, pulled on a sweatshirt, and went downstairs into the backyard to call Sashi back. The evening air was always cool in Santa Monica, and tonight was unusually quiet and still; she could hear the *shush* of the waves

313

three blocks away. She plunked into an Adirondack chair beneath the avocado tree, the one Darren had worked so hard to transplant and keep healthy. It was producing more fruit than ever right now, but Robin had been too distracted to keep up with picking the avocados, so they'd fallen to the ground and begun to rot, turning from dark green to wormy brown.

"Thank goodness!" Sashi said, after a half ring. "I was so much hoping you'd call."

"Let's hear it, Sashi," Robin said.

"Do you know I'm at *RHF* these days?"

"I didn't," Robin said. "I'd've pegged you as too highbrow for *RHF*. I thought you were at *Startup*." *Startup* was expensively produced eye-candy chronicling the interoffice drama of an Internet company on Silicon Beach, L.A.'s slower, less-brilliant version of Silicon Valley. Like *Flo's Studio,* the show basically documented the gossip of winners. *Real Happy Family,* in contrast, was one of the R&D's lowest-grade shows, the kind that relied heavily on the willingness of pathetic people to expose themselves on camera.

"Well, I stand behind *RHF* more than any show I've ever worked on. It's about repairing families."

"Sashi! Come on! You're not that naive."

"We're doing good work for our subjects. Which brings me to your client, Lorelei Branch."

"Former client."

"Former client. And sister-in-law, if I'm not mistaken."

"Yes."

"Lorelei's been working with us."

"I don't believe it."

"A family member nominated her for a Convergence, and it looks like we're going to move forward."

Colleen. Of course. Stooping to the bottom tier of potential fame after she'd made such a fool of herself riding her daughter's coattails on *Flo's Studio*.

Robin reached down and hurled a soft avocado into the trees. "Don't talk to me like that, Sashi," she snapped. "Don't say shit like *nominated* and *moved forward*. Just tell me in plain language what's going on."

"Lorelei is in serious distress. We've conducted voluntary interviews. And captured disturbing behavior on camera. We're concerned enough to schedule the Convergence as soon as possible."

"'Disturbing behavior'? What does that mean?"

"Well," Sashi paused. "Lorelei is pretty strung out on something. This morning she had a seizure during her interview."

"What? A seizure? Did she go to the hospital? Sashi, what the fuck?"

"We called 911, but by the time the paramedics arrived, she'd recovered. They pronounced her out of danger and tried to convince her to go to the hospital for observation. She refused."

"Sashi, I need you to tell me everything. My husband adores his sister. Do not hold anything back for the sake of your fucking show. How bad is it?"

Sashi sighed. "I'm saddened by your low opinion of me, frankly, but that's another conversation. I don't know what's wrong with Lorelei. She's addled and manic during her interviews, and also extremely thin. Addicts aren't exactly the most forthcoming, you know. That's why it's so important that we pull off the Convergence. It could be Lorelei's only chance."

Robin almost laughed at the absurdity of the statement, but nothing seemed funny. "There's no way you'll pull it off. Lorelei's too smart to tolerate an intervention. No one will show up but her mother, who's highly unstable, and you'll just end up with a huge mess like *Flo's Studio,* except you won't be able to capitalize on it this time, because no one in America cares."

"Again, I'll choose to ignore your insult," Sashi said. "But to your point that no one but Lorelei's mother would show up for the Convergence: You're wrong. Quite a few people have already committed to participating. Your husband, for one."

"You talked to him?"

"I did."

Is this what Darren had been trying to tell her, in the message — *Goddammit, Robin . . .* — he'd left for her a few days ago? The one she'd ignored first because of her mistake, and then because of the *Posse* photos?

"You'd better not be lying, Sashi."

"I promise you, I'm not. I'm simply inviting you to join us in a therapeutic event that could transform the life of your sister-in-law for the better."

"It's a television stunt, Sashi."

"Given your history with Lorelei, I'm surprised at your resistance," Sashi said coldly. "After all, you're the one who steered Lorelei into *Flo's Studio,* which was not a positive experience for her, neither professionally nor personally."

"Don't 'neither-nor' me, Sashi!" Robin picked up another avocado and threw it at the fence, where it made a soft *thwock.* "*You* made *Flo's Studio* miserable for Lorelei. Don't you dare pin it on me. I know you're just trying to bully me into showing up in Reno for your bottom-feeder show."

But as she was declaring — practically screaming — her opposition to attending the Convergence, her mind was moving in a different direction: If Darren was going to be in Reno on Friday, wouldn't it be her easiest, quickest opportunity to see him? To look him in the eye and straighten everything out? To ask him if he'd fallen in love with Marina Langley?

If Darren could convince her that their marriage was still alive — that there was some explanation behind the *Posse* photos — then they could spend the night together, and Robin's baby would become Darren's baby.

And if Darren confirmed her worst fear — that Marina Langley was in fact the new love of his life — she'd just leave him, have her baby alone, and let Darren wonder for the rest of his life who the child's father was. Which probably wouldn't bother him that much, since he'd be in the sculpted arms of Marina Langley.

The second possibility would destroy Robin's faith in everything she'd built her life upon in the last seven years.

"Robin? Are you still there?"

"I'm here."

"I'll respect whatever decision you make. But I do encourage you to come to Reno. Lorelei's in a bad way."

"Has Darren already booked a flight?"

"I've got his flight information right here. He arrives in Reno at four P.M. tomorrow."

Robin wasn't at all spiritual, but she had to admit: There seemed to be larger forces at work here. The universe, as the Vanity Buddhist girls emerging from hot yoga would say, wanted her to go to Reno, to decide her own fate and that of the speck of a human inside her.

Sashi's voice resumed its confident cheer. "I'll email you the logistics and a call sheet. Robin at No Princess, right? The Convergence is at six P.M. on Friday at the Cielo Hotel, right on the main strip, but we want you in town for interviews tomorrow and in case anything unforeseen happens. My field producer, Joel, will be in touch. The network can comp your ticket and two nights at the hotel."

"All right," Robin said and stood, touching her hand to her

belly, a gesture she'd envied in pregnant women so many times. "I'll see you Friday."

A desire to be at the beach overtook her like sudden hunger. She wanted to touch the water. It was only three blocks away, but too often she forgot it was there. First, though, she picked up all the avocados and put them in the green compost bin on the side of the garage. Every last one. Then she walked to the beach and watched the Ferris wheel on the pier flash its colored lights against the night sky, beautiful despite its stars being blotted out by neon and fog.

46

AT ONE A.M., traffic was sparse. The airport was less than thirty miles away, but Colleen needed to take four different freeways. She saw signs for the 101 and followed them, stopping at the drive-thru of a Jack in the Box for a cup of weak, bitter coffee.

She drove in silence. For months, she'd been listening to Bundy Hesse and the Double Negatives every time she got in the car, but those days were over. She couldn't figure out something else to listen to that wouldn't remind her of Lorelei. Lorelei had introduced Colleen to almost everything currently on Colleen's iPod: the Tyson Twins, Minny Danvers, the Lollipop Skanks.

Any of those would hurt too much. She rolled down the windows. The wind whipped through the car. Colleen angled onto the 10 going west. Her fists clenched around the steering wheel, and she leaned forward in her seat as she drove, unable to relax.

Driving alone on the near-empty freeway made her feel exposed, as if someone could see her from overhead. Like God, or Carl. What had he been thinking, as he dropped off to sleep in his motel room up in Sequoia country, many hours ago, *American Builder* probably still tented on his chest? Was he missing her? Or was it a relief, her absence, being left alone to work with his hands in the clean mountain air? Had he pictured Colleen and Marilyn on the trip they never took, heads propped to elbows as they faced each other, chatting from identical hotel beds? Was Carl still awake right now?

She'd been so young when they met. Colleen knew Carl fallen in love with her as a *project*. He was a builder, after all; he loved improving on something, then standing back to admire his work. When he'd spotted her in Hemet, in her bleached-white cheerleading sneakers, and heard her optimistic plot to escape to Disneyland, he'd told her, *You deserve better than dressing up as a cartoon character.* He'd set out to build her into a better adult.

She had believed that he would.

Except that their definitions of "better" turned out to be so different. An unremarkable house in Fresno, a backyard with a grill, two children, dinners together: That was all Carl wanted. It wasn't his fault he wasn't ambitious. When Colleen had met him, all of eighteen and drunk at Sizzler, she hadn't been ambitious either. But she'd grown up. She'd outgrown him. Raising Lorelei had showed her there was so much possibility in the world, beyond family dinners, beyond Fresno.

If she could just make it to Reno, Colleen thought as she drove toward LAX, they could get back on track together, she and Lorelei. Maybe she'd find the courage to leave Carl. She deserved someone different, and so did he. Someone like the sad woman with feathered hair they'd met at Al-Anon, who'd nodded her head through the whole meeting as if all the answers were right there in the room.

Carl had felt the same way at Al-Anon, but Colleen had rolled her eyes. Maybe she even sneered.

Now she wished she hadn't been so unkind. "I'm sorry," she said to the sky, to Carl. She wasn't sure if she loved him anymore, but she owed him an apology.

Many apologies.

Maybe she and Lorelei could still get a place together somewhere in the Valley, close to auditions. They'd find Lorelei a new agent, someone who appreciated her.

The 10 West merged with the 405 South, ten lanes across. Five more miles. Please, she thought, let me make it to Reno before something truly awful happens to Lorelei. Her mind replayed Sashi's video, Lorelei so skinny and manic, and Colleen stepped harder on the gas, overwhelmed with the desire to talk her daughter.

"Hi, honey," she said to the highway. "It's me, Mommy. What are you doing right now?" It felt like Lorelei might hear her somehow. "Please tell me you're not doing drugs. Please tell me you're not pregnant. I'm sorry to bring these things up but I'm just speaking my mind. I hate not being able to picture where you're living, where you're working — are you working? — what you do all day. I know which CVS you shop in because of the MasterCard, but that's okay, we don't need to talk about that. I just want to bring you home, okay? You'll have so much opportunity, so much more than whatever you're doing in Reno. If you come back, we can start over, because no one cares about *Flo's Studio* anymore."

Colleen talked on, the night air swirling around her, the whiskey and sedatives finally lifting, her reflexes improving, her hope increasing as she exited onto La Tijera.

She felt downright sober, approaching exuberant, when the flashing CHP lights tossed a red glow into her car and she heard the choppy pulses of a siren.

"I clocked you at eighty-five," said the cop, a woman of about forty with a body shaped like a block. "But that's not really why I flagged you. You're weaving like a loom. How much you had to drink tonight?"

"Barely anything," said Colleen. "I'm just tired."

"Gotta breathalyze you."

"No," said Colleen.

"License and registration, please."

Colleen breathalyzed at .11 percent.

"You, Ms. Branch," said the cop, "are wasted. You'll be coming with me. I'll have to cuff you now."

"You can't be serious."

After she'd cuffed Colleen's hands behind her back, the cop guided her from the Camry into the backseat of her cruiser, her short dull nails digging into Colleen's upper arm.

Colleen began to cry, jagged sounds from deep inside her. She felt the prospect of Reno evaporate. She'd never get to Lorelei now.

"Take it easy," said the cop. "This happens to all of you people."

"Wh — what people?"

"All you TV people. I recognize you from some show. Can't place it, but I know your face. So don't worry. A DUI only makes you more famous."

The cop chuckled to herself and shut the door to the cruiser's backseat, trapping Colleen inside.

47

IT WAS NEARLY midnight, but Darren saw a strip of light beneath the door of Toby's trailer. He took a deep breath and knocked.

Toby was at his desk in an undershirt and boxers, his bald head exposed, laptop open to *Equus* footage beside a tub of cashews and several bottles of dark red Vitaminwater.

"Branch! Branchy-Branch-Branch. Come in." He twisted around in his chair and beckoned heartily. His upper lip was still puffy, from the incident with Fargo, and a small strip of white adhesive concealed the three stitches he'd needed. "To what do I owe the pleasure of this booty call? Please tell me it's something to do with shooting Ven so he doesn't look so tall in every fucking frame. I mean, I know Willie's supposed to be oversized for a jockey, that it's crucial to his leitmotif, but—"

"Toby, I have to leave for forty-eight hours. I have a serious family emergency. I wouldn't ask if I didn't absolutely have to. I can be back Saturday morning."

"Saturday morning?"

"Yes. Back on set by nine."

"You've got to be kidding me." Toby stood up and reached for his hat.

"I'm not. My sister's in serious trouble."

"Branch." Toby looked hard at Darren, tugging at his beard, which had grown considerably bushier over the past few weeks. "We're shooting part of a fucking horse race tomorrow! I have six horse trailers showing up in the morning. I have four animal handlers, twelve professional riders, three dozen extras, a bunch of grooms, and a fucking vet booked."

"I know," Darren said, summoning all his calm. "Joey and Sy can handle it."

"Are you high? Joey's your assistant. Sy's a fucking intern."

"They're smart kids who know what they're doing, Toby. My family needs me. I hope you can understand."

Toby grabbed the Vitaminwater. He twisted the cap open,

322

drained half the bottle, and dropped it on the floor. "Branch, I think we've both been looking for a reason for this."

"A reason for what?" Darren said.

"You've got my permission to leave tomorrow. Because you're fired."

48

COLLEEN'S BOOKING AT the precinct in Westchester was a blur. She couldn't stop crying, and a cruel headache had set in. The cop who'd pulled her over turned her over to another cop, a young guy with a mustache and sideburns who couldn't be more than thirty.

"Take it easy, Miss Branch," he kept saying. She couldn't stop crying to answer the intake questions, or for the mug shot and fingerprinting. Gently, he extended a plastic bin toward her and pointed to the Dickies bag she hadn't removed from its cross-body position over her T-shirt since leaving Moonrock.

"What?" she said.

"Your purse. In the bin, please."

She unzipped it to remove her phone.

"Leave it closed. All personal items must be turned over. You'll get them back upon release." He scratched at his mustache.

"What?" She thought of her pills, stashed in the bag's inner pockets. "What about my phone? When will I be released?"

"Bag, ma'am. Now." He pushed the bin closer, and she dropped it inside. "When you get released is a matter of when somebody comes and posts your bail. You got someone in mind?"

Without a single question, Sashi had come for her, just after dawn. Colleen hadn't known who else to call. Darren was across the country. Marilyn would be too shocked. Carl was out of the question. So Colleen left Sashi a message, delivering the basic facts, fighting to suppress the shakiness in her voice, and asking that she come to the precinct, whispering "I may need to borrow some cash for bail" at the very end of her explanation, squeezing her eyes shut with embarrassment.

Then Colleen spent a few hours waiting in a holding area that resembled a bus stop: plastic orange chairs bolted to the floor, fluorescent lighting, ancient TV droning late-night info-mercials from an upper corner of the room. The guard who'd shown her to the room had handed her a small cup of water, which she'd gulped down, but her head continued to throb. The only other person in the holding area appeared to be a homeless man in a filthy coat who was stretched out across three chairs, braying snores. Colleen alternated between pacing the room and sitting with her legs drawn up in a hard chair, head resting between her knees. She'd just begun to doze when she felt a rough shake to her shoulder.

"Colleen Branch," said a khaki-clad guard with a grizzled face. "You've got company. Come with me." He escorted Colleen to the front of the building, where she saw Sashi standing in the gray-floored, gray-walled reception area, looking fresh from a shower in leggings and a fitted white sweatshirt, her hair damp.

"Sashi!"

"Oh, you poor darling," Sashi said, pulling Colleen into a hug. She smelled of rosewater and minty toothpaste, exactly the opposite of the precinct's dank air.

"Thank you for coming," Colleen whispered, fighting tears.

"That's enough, ladies," said the guard. "Over here, please." He pointed to the Plexiglas-enclosed counter.

A mousy woman seated at a computer on the other side peered up at Colleen through glasses on a chain around her neck. "We're returning your purse and its contents, minus three unmarked white tablets and two capsules labeled as Performa, twenty milligrams each. Are these pills necessary to your immediate health?"

"No," said Colleen quietly, her face hot. What was Sashi thinking, overhearing this?

"Can you provide the name of your prescribing physician?"

"I . . . not at this time."

"We'll be keeping them, then. But you can have this." She opened a slot in the Plexiglas and pushed through a large Ziploc containing Colleen's Dickies bag. "And I'll need" — she paused, tapping at her keyboard — "eleven-hundred-twenty-two dollars from you."

"I —" Colleen began, but Sashi cut in. "Here," Sashi said, pushing a silver credit card through the slot.

As they stepped outside the precinct, Sashi was upbeat as ever, as though she were simply meeting Colleen for breakfast. She linked her arm through Colleen's, as if they were high school girlfriends. The sun was just beginning to brighten the commercial stretch of car washes, taco joints, and 99-cent stores. There were only two cars in the lot — Colleen's Camry and Sashi's brand-new white BMW. The 328i was Colleen's dream car, and she knew it retailed at around forty grand. Why couldn't she be more like Sashi? She remembered Bundy's angry whisper in her ear. The pulse of the siren. Her DUI. The laughing cop who recognized her from *Flo's Studio*.

"Oh, Colleen, what you've been through!" said Sashi. "But it's going to be all right. You're coming to my house to rest up. I'm ten minutes from here, in Marina del Rey."

"Thank you for everything, but I need to get home," Colleen said. "You've already done too much, Sashi."

"Actually, we're due in Reno tonight," Sashi said. "Joel called late last night. It's time for the Convergence. Lorelei needs us."

"Oh my God."

"I know, it's a lot to handle after what you went through last night. But we have no choice. We need to contact your husband and book his flight right now. If you're not up for calling him, I'm happy to do it. Then we'll rest up at my house for a few hours and fly out this afternoon."

"Carl and I, um . . . " Colleen said. "We're not in the best of touch right now. He doesn't know the latest on Lorelei's situation. Or anything about last night . . . " She trailed off.

"Colleen, I hope this isn't overstepping my boundaries, but I'm going to suggest we not hit him with too much information at once. Let's keep our eye on the ball: Lorelei. It might be too overwhelming to hear urgent news of his daughter along with news of your, uh, minor legal snafu. Which, of course, I will keep *totally and one hundred percent* mum. I'm not encouraging you to lie, but to delay the delivery of item number two. We need to get him to Reno."

"Okay," Colleen said, weakly. "I'll call him."

"I'll take care of him," Sashi said. "Don't worry a thing about it." Sashi opened the passenger door of her gleaming car. "Let me drive you. I'll make arrangements for your car." Unable to protest, Colleen limped into Sashi's Beemer, which smelled of new leather. She fastened her seat belt.

Sashi pressed a silver button on the dashboard and the console lit up silently.

"Is this a hybrid?" Colleen asked.

Sashi nodded. "BMW finally caught up with every other car company." She handed her phone to Colleen. "You can use this to call Carl, if yours is low on juice. We should get in touch with him right away. Shall we do it together on speaker?"

"No," Colleen said, too forcefully.

"No problem." Sashi steered her soundless car to the exit of the parking lot. "Even better to do it yourself." She didn't have to add *right now*.

"I'll do it." Colleen pulled her own phone out of the plastic bag and attempted to power it on. It was dead. "My phone's fine."

"He'll need to be at the Cielo Hotel by six," said Sashi, her eyes on the road as she entered the ramp to the 405 and accelerated to merge onto the freeway, traffic already considerable despite the early hour. "We can send a car to pick him up from the airport. We'll be checked in under the name Joel Rapp. He should come straight up to the room."

Colleen held her phone up to her right ear, by the car window, where Sashi couldn't see it. She closed her eyes and breathed deeply, summoning Lorelei.

Help me do this.

She waited a few beats, and then said, into her dead phone. "Carl. Baby, it's me. I just heard from the network, and it's time. Lorelei needs us in Reno now . . ."

49

ON SASHI'S LIVING room sofa, Colleen dreamed of driving with Lorelei on the freeway: they were in some sort of oversized military SUV, and wind whipped loudly through the car, smelling faintly acrid, as if something toxic was burning nearby. Lorelei was driving too fast, and Colleen was afraid. They were driving to an appointment to have Lorelei's breasts enlarged again. Lorelei was chatting excitedly, but the wind and the music were so loud that Colleen couldn't make out anything she was saying.

"What, honey?" Colleen yelled. "I can't hear you." She reached to turn down the music, but the giant car's stereo looked like a hybrid of an iPhone interface and a jumbo jet's control panel, impossible to figure out. She stabbed at random buttons, but the music just got louder and louder, until it shook the car.

"Turn it off!" she screamed at Lorelei, but Lorelei kept smiling, talking, her ponytail dipping and diving in the air.

Colleen woke drenched in sweat. Somehow she'd changed into a gray UCLA T-shirt and plaid blue-and-gray pajama pants. Sashi's. The living room was fresh and airy, a sharp contrast to the way Colleen felt: parched mouth, headachy, puffy eyed. Sashi had thought to leave a tall bottle of water beside the couch, along with a couple of Advil, and Colleen downed it all. A soft breeze stirred a translucent white curtain away from an open window. Sashi's living room walls were painted pale yellow and decorated with framed, old-fashioned movie posters, and some arty black-and-white photographs of Sashi and a handsome white man with smiling eyes.

Colleen rose from the couch — creaky and stiff and sore all over, as if she'd aged decades overnight — and moved as fast as she could past Sashi's silent bedroom to a bathroom down the hall. A fashionably retro claw-foot tub was flush to a tile-topped ledge arranged with expensive bath products. There was a glass bowl full of pebbles and a slim vase with purple petunias.

She looked in the mirror over the sink and quickly looked away. Her face was blotchy and haggard; she looked fifty. She soaked a washcloth with cold water and rubbed it around her eyes to remove the mascara burrowed into her newly visible crow's feet. She found some moisturizer in the medicine cabinet, smeared it all over her face and neck, and went back to the couch, where she pulled Sashi's afghan up over her.

The next thing she heard was "Rise and shine!" and opened her eyes to Sashi dressed in a loose, short yellow dress, her hair caught in a girlish ponytail. Colleen shielded her eyes. The room was too bright, Sashi too fresh and pretty in her dandelion frock.

"Hi," said Colleen.

"Aha!" Sashi said. She pulled a small rolling suitcase from the closet and shut the door. "I've been going nuts trying to find this thing." She turned to Colleen and smiled. "Can I bring you coffee? OJ? Water?"

"Yes."

"All three?" Sashi crossed the living room into the kitchen.

"Just coffee and water, please," Colleen said.

Sashi set a tray with a steaming mug and tall glass of ice water on the ottoman.

"Thank you."

"So," Sashi said. "We're on a two o'clock flight out of LAX. That'll get us to Reno in plenty of time to prep for the Convergence tomorrow, shoot a few preliminary interviews. When does Carl's flight get in?"

Her fake phone call came crashing back and she stifled a moan. She took a slow sip of coffee, picturing him sanding wood in the hull of a half-built mansion, with giant Sequoia trees and clean blue sky above him. She owed him a real phone call. When she got to Reno, she promised herself, and calmed down a little. Right now, her palms wouldn't stop sweating, and she couldn't get her heart rate down to normal. No matter how much slow yoga breathing she did, it felt rabbity in her chest. She longed for a Zenzo.

"I'm not sure. He was going to book something and text me.

But he promised to be at the Cielo by six. He'll take a cab from the airport."

"Brilliant," said Sashi. "We need to leave in an hour, and I want to touch you up and pick some wardrobe items before we go."

"I'm a mess," Colleen said.

"You're going to look fantastic. Lucky for you, in a former life, I was a makeup artist. I've done a lot of hair, too."

"A former life?" Colleen asked, feeling an iota better from the caffeine and water. "What are you, like twenty-seven?"

"Twenty-nine next month. I'll have you gorgeous in a half hour . . ."

"The show's really happening tomorrow night?" The prospect of seeing Lorelei in just twenty-four hours was almost too much. A helpless urgency took hold, like being trapped in traffic en route to somewhere you wanted desperately to be.

"Absolutely. My team from R&D is there getting all set up. Lorelei's committed to arriving at seven P.M. at the hotel where we're all scheduled to assemble."

"Wow."

"I know! So we've got to get a move on. I've already set up in the bathroom for your mini-makeover. Are you ready?"

"Okay." Colleen stood.

"May I ask a favor?"

"Yes. God, look at all you've done for me. You're like an angel."

"Could we get some footage of this? You getting ready?"
Colleen groaned.

"I'm just thinking, it might be useful B-roll, if this *RHF* segment ends up airing."

Well. She'd already made a colossal fool of herself to a national audience. She'd already alienated her daughter, and was close to losing her husband. She'd thrown herself at a musician who thought she was psychotic. She'd gotten a DUI. "Sure," she said, and followed Sashi to the bathroom.

50

ROBIN STEPPED OUT onto the thirty-second floor of the Cielo Hotel. The hushed, empty hallway was carpeted in mottled green, like flattened treetops. On the white wall opposite the elevator hung a large blue-tinted glass frame, with nothing inside it. To the left a glass cube table with a hole in the center held the stem of a single sunflower, its yellow face open toward the ceiling.

There was no one in sight, but she had the sense of being watched. She walked to her right. The room numbers, etched on white placards, ascended: 3232, 3234, 3236, around the corner . . . and she arrived: 3242. Darren. He'd be waiting for her on the other side.

Robin knocked.

51

CARL IMAGINED HOME, and the whir of the treadmill and the skinless chicken breasts defrosting in the sink, and Colleen seeming sorry that he was there, as if his mere presence interfered with a plan to which he was not privy. On his last night in the Sequoia, the sky was velvety black and wild with stars. Lying beneath it, the nylon and down of his sleeping bag pulled to his chin and a wool sock hat to the bridge of his nose, Carl tried to imagine leaving Colleen. His dinner with Wendy, followed by four days with too much time to think, while he and Marshall finished and installed cherrywood cabinets in the tech entrepreneur's vast kitchen, had led him to a single conclusion: he was not happy in his marriage. He tried to think through the mechanics of ending it: breaking the news, packing up, moving out. Colleen would have the house, and her fair share of everything. He wouldn't want it to be ugly. He'd get out of the state altogether, maybe move somewhere cold and outdoorsy, without the bad air and population glut of California. Montana or Colorado.

Colleen made him feel like a permanent nuisance. When he'd confessed this to Wendy, her eyes had actually filled up with tears.

"What's the matter?" he'd asked, confused.

"It's just upsetting that someone could make a man like you feel that way," she'd said. "We all deserve to be loved as we love."

In the parking lot of the restaurant, she'd pulled him into a lingering hug before driving off into the night, and they held each other a beat too long, acknowledging the possibility of something between them. And then they both let go. Wendy was right. He deserved to be loved better.

The baleful wail of a coyote echoed through the canyon. The night was windless and still, the moon a clean white crescent. Carl stared at it and tried to envision going straight up to Colleen and saying, *We need to talk,* and telling her: it was over. He tried to imagine the next steps: consulting with a divorce attorney, finding an apartment and contract work down in Orange County, where rich people were always building. He'd leave Colleen with the house. She could have Fresno.

But in his gut, he knew he wouldn't go through with it. He

wasn't ready to leave her, not quite yet. She deserved one last chance. After all, she'd endured plenty of her own misery in the past year. Even if she'd brought it on herself, encouraging Lorelei's absurd career path. Maybe he hadn't been compassionate enough. Maybe if he took a different, kinder, less judgmental approach, his wife would open up to him again. Maybe she'd agree to counseling. Maybe she'd realize she needed to stop drinking completely.

One more chance. He owed her that.

Carl groped for his phone to check the time: almost midnight. He was exhausted, but sleep felt far away. For the first time all week, the ground beneath him felt too hard and cold, the night too quiet and filled with the eyes of invisible animals. He stood up from his sleeping bag, a little shaky on his legs. He didn't want to be outside anymore. He still had his motel key. The room was paid for through checkout tomorrow, so he would go sleep in a real bed for a few hours. As he pulled on his coat and boots and bunched his sleeping bag into its stuff sack, he thought suddenly of Wendy, her wavy hairstyle and denim shirts, and smiled to himself. He was grateful to her. For now, he had all the clarity he needed.

52

AFTERWARD, ROBIN AND Darren lay back, side by side, hands clamped. The room's broad windows faced the airport and occasional planes climbed up an invisible hypotenuse to the top of the sky. The A/C hummed. The sunlight changed from the bright flatness of midmorning to the richer hues of afternoon. Beyond the airport rose the Sierra mountains.

"It's almost like watching a film of planes taking off," Robin said, kicking one leg outside the thick white comforter. "Can't you see it, projected on the wall of some hipster restaurant, playing on loop?"

"I think we've been there," Darren said. "I think I had tuna carpaccio and a beet and goat cheese salad."

She laughed. "With arugula."

"With arugula grown in their roof garden." He rolled on his side to face her.

On the floor next to the bed was a closed copy of *Posse*. All it took for Robin was watching Darren's face as he saw the photos of Marina and him for the first time. He explained the whole situation, how she was a dippy Vanity Buddhist who maybe had a crush on him, that they'd struck up an unlikely but utterly platonic friendship. Robin knew he was telling the truth. She hoped he believed her with the same certainty when she'd promised him she'd known nothing about Mel bribing Toby King to hire him. When Darren asked her if she'd been involved, she felt she'd been slapped, the notion was so repulsive.

Now, facing each other in the center of the huge hotel bed, the length of their bodies an inch apart, she leaned in to kiss his lips, and as he responded, she felt a physical lightening, an absolution in progress.

Now that Darren's lips were pressed to hers, Ben Hessler had never knocked on the door of her childhood bedroom at her parents' party. He hadn't settled in that room with her, the one redecorated to erase the person Robin had once been, sitting first on the floor with his knees drawn up, then moving to sit beside her on the bed. He hadn't spent an hour talking to her about the past. Hadn't resurrected, in his languid way of speaking, the Robin she'd once been, the smart girl who would be a brilliant shrink. The person she'd been before No Princess. The person who would have met her husband and started a family before her ovaries began to calcify.

No, Ben had never knocked on her door.

He hadn't offered her absinthe, and she hadn't accepted an inch of it, and then another, in a thimble-sized espresso cup her mother's decorator had placed in her renovated bedroom, next to a tiny Italian machine in the new "daydream nook" — by the window that looked over the backyard.

She hadn't looked at Ben next to her on the bed, and been reminded, by his long frame and light blue eyes and olive skin, of some iteration of Darren. She hadn't thought, in that moment, padded and bleary from the absinthe, that Ben seemed a looser, funnier, more successful version of her husband. One who had followed his passion from the time it had first stirred inside him, who wasn't crippled by some notion of artistic purity, or self-doubt, or laziness. She hadn't looked at Ben and, for a few crucial minutes, hated her husband for not being there, in her childhood bedroom, when she'd given herself shots all week and endured the artificially induced surges of hormone and emotion. She hadn't let Ben into her bed.

No, she hadn't thought or done any of those things. Between the crisp-soft sheets of the Cielo Hotel's king-sized bed, Darren warm and completely present beside her, the scent of his skin musky but underpinned with soap, she couldn't imagine ever having thought such awful things about her sweet husband.

Some reality was realer than others. Her love for Darren — and his for her — trumped the mistake she had made. The baby really would be their baby. It would be true.

"Robin? Are you okay? Are you crying?"

She burrowed against him, fitted her body as closely with his as she could, breathed in his smell.

"I don't care about Marina Langley," she whispered. "Everything is perfect."

And it was.

53

THE FIRST PERSON Colleen saw when she and Sashi entered room 3742 of the Cielo Hotel was Darren, and seeing him felt like a little jolt of heaven. It had been so long. She had almost forgotten the air of comfort he exuded: his solid frame and clear blue eyes, his clean jawline that suggested honesty somehow.

"Darren!" Colleen said. "Baby!"

Darren was seated alone in one chair of eight arranged in a semicircle in the middle of the room. Against one wall there was a long desk and a chair. He stood to hug her, and his embrace felt warm and complete. She held on a little too long, wanting to pull him somewhere private and ask him all the questions Robin had refused to answer: What, exactly, had Lorelei said in her texts over the past few weeks? What did he think she'd been doing? How worried was he? Gently, he moved out of her embrace.

"Welcome, Colleen," said a middle-aged, pantsuited Latina woman at the desk, now covered with papers. "I'm Dr. Vanessa Morales." She shook Colleen's hand. Of course — Colleen recognized her from television. She was *Real Happy Family*'s "consulting clinical psychologist" who moderated the Convergences on-screen. Her voice was a low octave, soothing.

"We were just about to get started with a little preparation," Dr. Morales said to Colleen. "To help us receive Lorelei in the warmest, most constructive manner possible. We're just waiting for a few others, and then we'll get going."

The bathroom door opened and Robin stepped out in a black sweater and jeans.

"Hey, Colleen," she said casually. Robin looked smaller, better than Colleen remembered. She met Colleen's eyes and smiled with her mouth closed. Colleen took a breath, reminding herself that the cameras were there, and smiled back. They paused, both considering a hug, but Robin took a seat on the other side of Darren, and reached across him to grasp Colleen's hand.

"Is this everyone, Sashi?" Dr. Morales asked.

"Colleen?" Sashi said. "Still no call back from Carl?"

"No," Colleen lied. "I tried him again a little while ago."

"Let's proceed, then," Sashi said.

Dr. Morales nodded, panning her gentle smile around the room. "Everyone please get out your Dedication. As you might imagine, when Lorelei arrives, she'll be startled. She may express anger and fear. She may speak in an outraged or accusatory way. Please don't be alarmed. We must allow her to simply react."

From her purse, Colleen pulled out the folded paper she'd placed there three days ago, her Dedication, the words she'd say during the Convergence, if everything went according to plan.

And so she'd written: *Lorelei, I'm so sorry. I made mistakes that caused your mistakes. All of this is my fault, but I believe in my heart it's not even close to too late to start over. You are still beautiful and perfect and can still have everything you deserve.*

"What if she just bolts right back out of the room?" Darren asked.

"We take measures to prevent that," Dr. Morales said. "Two

members of the R&D team will be stationed by the door, to ensure Lorelei's well-being."

"Like bouncers?" Robin asked, sounding skeptical.

Dr. Morales laughed. "In a manner of speaking. But gentle bouncers. Now, the most important thing to remember is to stay calm — not to match Lorelei's emotional pitch. I am not saying you shouldn't welcome whatever emotions come to you, or that you should suppress any feelings. Because the Convergence is all about those feelings. I just don't want anyone to be frightened by how they feel, or by how they see Lorelei responding. It can be very raw. Even if you've watched many episodes of *RHF*, you can't fully prepare for what it feels like to participate. I'd like to lead everyone through a breathing exercise before Lorelei arrives. It's the best tool I can give you to prepare. I don't want to orchestrate anything beyond breath; everything else should just unfold naturally. Everyone ready to breathe?"

Colleen bobbed her head in unison with everyone else.

A cricket sound filled the room. Somebody's ring tone. Joel looked down at his phone, and hurried to the center of the chair arc and handed it to Dr. Morales. When she looked up, she was frowning.

"It seems," she said, "that Lorelei is delayed."

"Where?" asked Colleen.

"Let me call her," said Joel. "Just give me a minute." He stepped into the bathroom and shut the door.

"Oh my God," said Colleen. "She's not going to show. After all this, she's not going to come."

"They'll figure out how to get her here," Robin said.

Joel stuck his head out of the bathroom. "Sashi? Could I speak to you for a minute?"

Sashi disappeared into the bathroom.

Colleen gripped the metal ridges along the seat of her chair with both hands.

Darren put his hand on hers.

The bathroom door opened, and Sashi walked to the center of the circle.

She cleared her throat. "We're going to relocate," she said. "Lorelei is not feeling well and says she is unable to leave her motel room. So we'll go to her. Let's go."

Someone rapped on the hotel room door, even and steady.

"She's here!" said Colleen, bolting up from her seat, but Dr. Morales held her hand up.

"No, Colleen. Let me." Calmly, she crossed the room and opened the door.

"Dad," Darren said, standing. "I didn't think you'd make it."

Standing in the doorway in his beige work coveralls, his face windburned and expressionless, was Carl.

54

LORELEI COULD TELL from the way Joel had sounded on the phone — nervous, let down — that this Cielo Hotel appointment was more than a regular interview. She'd texted him from CVS, where she'd stopped after being out all day, applying for jobs, to pick up extra-pale face powder and Vaseline. Her skin was naturally pale, but just one sober week of sleep and sunshine had restored too healthy a color to pass for a tweaker's complexion. She needed powder to achieve the appropriate wanness, and the Vaseline to make her hair good and unwashed looking. She was proud of the drugged-out disorientation she'd conveyed in her text to Joel: *Sory, ac-*

cidntally took sleeping pill I thot was advil, too tired to come to hotel, call me.

He'd called her right away. "Look, it's okay. Just stay where you are."

Lorelei spoke slowly, repeating herself, slurring a little: "I . . . can . . . can . . . still taaaaalk. I just need to keep . . . to keep . . . lying down."

"Drink some water," he said. "Tamara and I will be there in under twenty."

Smiling, she'd paid for her things and hurried across the street to the Sleep Inn to prepare for her big scene.

But when she arrived back at room 14, the door opened only a few inches before bouncing back toward her. The chain was on. Someone was inside. The housekeeper? She knocked hard; no one answered. The heavy blackout shades were closed. She could see nothing inside but dim light.

"Keisha?" she called into the slice of open space between the door and its frame. Maybe she was in there, rummaging for Mote, despite having declared it "nasty"? Lorelei's heart galloped. Joel and Tamara and God knew who else would be here any minute.

She remembered the window, how she and Don could never get it to fully close, and she knew who was in the room. Dropping her CVS bag, she ran her fingers along the bottom of the sill, feeling for the little gap of space that had caused so much paranoia. She found it and yanked up. The window lifted and Lorelei pushed through the cardboardy curtains and stepped inside.

Don lay faceup on the bed, eyes open and unseeing, skin the color of a fish's belly. On the nightstand was an ashtray full of butts and a lone syringe.

55

COLLEEN HAD IMPULSIVELY rushed to hug Carl when he'd appeared in the doorway of the hotel room, but he'd kept his hands at his sides. During the rushed relocation of the Convergence — a dozen people scrambling downstairs into taxis, Sashi trying to maintain some semblance of order — he'd barely looked at her. He'd stayed glued to Darren's side — Robin glued to his other — leaving Colleen to trail behind the three of them as they walked through the hotel lobby to the taxis waiting outside. Sashi had been too busy directing the group to notice Colleen walking alone. It had been Robin, of all people, who'd suddenly turned to look back at Colleen and stopped in her tracks to wait for her to catch up, letting Carl and Darren go on ahead.

She touched Colleen's arm, and that was all it took.

"I'm afraid we're too late," Colleen sobbed. "I'm afraid Lorelei's — "

"No," Robin cut in, firmly, putting her arm around Colleen's waist. Her touch was soft and comforting. Robin quickened her pace, pulling Colleen with her, her canvas sneakers matching Colleen's shiny ballet flats stride for stride. "She's not. Don't even think it."

At the motel — the neon *p* of the Sleep Inn sign was burned out, a menacing detail — Dr. Morales wanted Colleen and Carl to go first. To be the ones to knock on Lorelei's door, to lead the way for the cameras to capture her in whatever state of distress she was in.

"You're her parents," Dr. Morales said. "You have every right to be the first ones to walk through that door. If you want to."

"They do," Sashi answered.

Colleen reached for Carl's hand, but he pulled it away. "You go," he said.

56

LORELEI HAD JUST hung up with 911 when the knock came on the door of room 14. Could the EMTs already be here? She hadn't heard sirens, but maybe. They'd told her to wait, but she couldn't stand being in view of Don's body. She bounded to the door and flung it open.

Her mother had grown disturbingly skinny and her clothes — red jeans and a clingy white top — looked like someone else's. But she was really, truly there: her mom, somehow in Reno, at the Sleep Inn, on a welcome mat with its fuzz worn off.

"Mom, oh, Mom!" Lorelei yelled, wild with relief, and pitched herself into Colleen's arms. She squeezed her eyes shut and stayed there, breathing in the scent of her mother, the faint gardenias of her perfume, only dimly aware of other voices around her, bodies shuffling, shadows crossing the pooled light of the outdoor walkway.

"Baby," Colleen was saying. Running her hands through Lorelei's hair and over her face. "You're here. You're here." Over and over.

A siren screamed into the parking lot, and Lorelei finally let go of her mother and opened her eyes. In front of them was a small, hushed crowd. Her father, in dirty work coveralls, looking like he hadn't slept in a week. Darren and Robin, entwined. A familiar-looking Indian woman, young and pretty, and an older woman in a pantsuit.

And, of course, Joel. Camera hoisted to his shoulder. Tamara holding a boom mike.

The pantsuited woman spoke. "Lorelei, you are surrounded tonight by people who love you. Can you tell us how you're feeling in this very moment?"

Lorelei clutched her mother's hand. "I feel like the luckiest person alive," she said, her voice cracking with tears as the EMTs in navy button-downs with yellow badges pushed up to the door of room 14.

She was telling the truth.

THE R&D NETWORK / REAL HAPPY FAMILY

Voice Call Transcript

Date: 4/20/2013

Outbound Caller: Sashi Baratnam, Executive Producer

Call Recipient: Lorelei Branch, RHF Subject

Automated voice: This call may be recorded for the accuracy and integrity of Real Happy Family's story documentation. Any content may be reproduced within any stage of production, including televised broadcast, of Real Happy Family. By engaging in this call, both parties consent to the possibility that its content will be utilized at the discretion of the Real & Documented Network.

Sashi: Lorelei, sweetheart, it's Sashi.

Lorelei: So I'm being recorded, and you can just use what I say any way you like?

Sashi [laughs]: That's just a legal disclaimer, darling. I'm here at the office, on a landline. The system records all calls. It's just a formality. Network protocol.

Lorelei: Can you call me from your cell?

Sashi: Unnecessary. I just have a few quick questions. Nothing that should make you uncomfortable.

Lorelei [pause]: Okay.

Sashi: We think our footage from the night of your scheduled Convergence is very usable.

Lorelei: How? The Convergence never happened. In case you forgot, my . . . [voice breaks] my friend OD'd instead. How can you even care about the show now?

Sashi: Because it could be deeply powerful. It could honor Don and help save other people from similar tragedy. It could be reality TV that actu-

344

ally matters. That's why I'm calling. To ask you to consider allowing us to move forward with the episode. With utmost discretion and sensitivity to Don's family, of course.

Lorelei [pause]: I don't know, it seems . . . gross. Or exploitat — [stumbles on the word, trails off]

Sashi [interrupts]: Exploitative? To the contrary. It will be dignified and respectful. Let me ask you something, Lorelei. What's next for you?

Lorelei: I'm not sure yet. I just got back to Fresno a few days ago. I'm regrouping.

Sashi: Remind me. Did you go to college?

Lorelei: No.

Sashi: And what's on your reel besides a Preventus ad and a few Flo's Studio's *episodes?*

Lorelei [pause]: Nothing.

Sashi: Then I think you should consider continuing to work with us.

Lorelei: Continuing? You've already got all your footage. What else would I need to do?

Sashi: We certainly do have footage, Lorelei. Hours and hours. A good deal of which captures you exhibiting troubling behavior, clearly under the influence of methamphetamine and whatever else you were consuming in Reno.

Lorelei: What's your point?

Sashi: I don't know if Don's death scared you sober or if you're just on hiatus from using, but I hope I'm not the first to suggest that you need to spend some time rehabilitating.

Lorelei: That's what I'm doing now. I'm at home with my parents.

Sashi: That's not enough. At least, not enough by the ethical standards of RHF. *If we are going to portray you on the show, we can only do it if we're absolutely certain of your remorse over your time in Reno and your commitment to change. Any expert will testify that someone who was behaving the way you were in Nevada is not likely to transform in a matter of days because of one traumatic event.*

Lorelei: So what are you saying?

Sashi: It's simple. You spend thirty days in rehab, and get to be part of groundbreaking television. You also move your life forward with integrity. And maybe, in the process, you become recognizable to the American public again. Your career regains a glimmer of possibility.

Lorelei: Being known as a tweaker who went to rehab? That's going to put my career back on track?

Sashi: It certainly could. All that matters is that people know your face. And that they're rooting for you. Robin Justus is your agent. She's smart; she'll figure out how to make this a big win for you.

Lorelei: And what if I don't go to rehab?

Sashi: Then the show is off. RHF will move on. There are hundreds of other stories.

Lorelei: Why am I getting this threatening vibe from you?

Sashi [laughs]: Threatening? I have no idea what you're talking about, my dear. I am simply asking you to do the right thing. To take care of yourself and your family by getting help. To publicly show that you have been impacted by your experience with addiction and by the death of your friend. RHF is a show with a message. People can change. Families can be repaired. If you can't demonstrate your transformation, our message is a lie.

Lorelei [crying sounds]: I — I —

Sashi: Would you like some time to think on it? Perhaps discuss with your mother? I know how close the two of you are.

Lorelei [muffled]: Yes.

Sashi: Excellent. I'll call you tomorrow evening.

EP #84: LORELEI BRANCH CONVERGENCE
AUTH: Sabaratnam/Meloy
May 2, 2013

SHOT	KEY VISUALS	KEY AUDIO
Int. Cielo Hotel.	LONG SHOT circle of convergence PARTICIPANTS. CLOSEUP COLLEEN & DARREN's clasped hands. C.U. of COLLEEN's face (anxious expression).	CUT TO COLLEEN Interview: I hadn't realized how much I missed Darren until I saw him in that room. Knowing he'd made such an effort to be in Reno for Lorelei was overwhelming.
Int. Cielo Hotel.	P.O.V. COLLEEN, Moving Shot ROBIN exiting bathroom	CUT TO COLLEEN Interview: Robin and I may have had our differences, but she'd been an incredible mentor to Lorelei. This was no time for grudges.
Int. Cielo Hotel.	Various CLOSEUPS of PARTICIPANTS as someone KNOCKS on hotel door	COLLEEN: She's here!
Int. Cielo Hotel.	P.O.V. COLLEEN: Door opens to reveal CARL on other side. CUT TO C.U. of COLLEEN'S face Insert TITLE: CARL BRANCH declined to provide commentary.	CUT TO COLLEEN Interview: My heart literally froze in my chest when I saw my husband standing there, instead of my daughter. My whole world started to spin

Ext. Reno Street.	LONG SHOTS of entire group walking. Create atmo via neon/building lights. MED. SHOTS of COLLEEN and CARL, to emphasize their distance from one another	CUT TO COLLEEN Interview: To have Carl push me away at a time like that, when we were about to discover the truth about our daughter, was dev- astating. My mind went to all sorts of dark places. I kept picturing him with Wendy, the woman he'd flirted with at our Al-Anon meet- ings. I wanted to throw up. But I had to stay strong, for Lorelei.
	Include BEATS: her voice-catches, she sniffs, wipes eyes, etc.	
	Include GESTURES: she places face in hands	
Ext. Sleep Inn	PAN UP from PARTICI- PANTS to neon motel sign with final letter burned out, then down to reveal COPS and AM- BULANCE in parking lot	V.O. COLLEEN: I couldn't believe this seedy place was where they'd found my baby. And there were cops and an ambu- lance outside the motel. I was sure Lorelei was dead behind the door. My heart was liter- ally slamming in my chest. I knew I was possibly about to face the worst mo- ment of my life.

https://www.realityroundup.com/
REALITY ROUNDUP
The Deepest Scoop on your Favorite Shows

MUST-WATCH OF THE WEEK: REAL HAPPY FAMILY, SEASON 6 PREMIERE

By Brooke Baker

The much-rumored controversy behind *RHF*'s startling season opener finally comes to light in this riveting episode. The show was mired in legal controversy and risked cancellation after a heroin overdose of one of its subjects, Don Massey, 22, was inadvertently captured on camera last March. The producers insisted on including the tragedy in the storyline or threatened to scrap the episode, which R&D had expected to spike last season's flaccid ratings because of its focus on Lorelei Branch. Branch flickered briefly on R&D's smash hit *Flo's Studio* before her stage-mother-from-hell made fast enemies with star Flo Flanders, landing her daughter off the show and in tabloid hell. Branch had fled L.A. for Reno with then boyfriend Don Massey, and descended into meth addiction before the ever-intrepid *RHF* crew found her.

Despite the cloudy ethics surrounding Thursday's episode — Massey's lawyers fought hard to eliminate their client's appearance and lost — the result is both harrowing and mesmerizing to watch. Veteran reality producer Sashi Sabaratnam scores again with a raw and moving portrait of bad choices, transformation, and the destruction in between. Don't miss it.

FEBRUARY 2014

Epilogue

COLLEEN WRAPPED MILO in a receiving blanket and settled in a chair beneath the avocado tree, careful to keep his face in the shade. Two months old, he slept most of the time, and she loved to watch, his perfect little mouth curling into a smile, or pursing into a suckling motion, perhaps dreaming of milk, or his earlier life in Robin's belly.

Midmorning was her favorite time of day, when Robin, Darren, and Lorelei were on the set of *Family Documentary* in Burbank and she got to be alone with her grandson. That she was a grandmother at only forty-one didn't matter. What mattered was her connection to Milo, the surge of love she'd felt for him the moment he'd arrived home from the hospital, and how readily Darren and Robin had invited her to be a significant part of his life. It didn't matter that she and Lorelei were living in a cottage in their backyard, sleeping in twin beds at opposite sides of a single bedroom. They stayed up late giggling like best friends, and Lorelei told her everything that had happened during filming that day, the unintentionally hilarious things Heather di Notia had said, how real her fake kisses with her costar Max Riggs seemed, how talented a director Darren was proving to be.

It didn't matter to Colleen that she had very little money, aside from the modest check Carl sent her each month, and no credit card, or that all of her clothes these days were Robin's hand-me-downs from before getting pregnant. It mattered to her a little that she had gained enough weight to almost fit into some of them, but she could live with it. Without Performa, disciplined dieting was hard, and while she enjoyed jogging with Lorelei along the beach, she hadn't gone to a Pilates class or the gym since they'd moved to Santa Monica. She no longer wanted to. She preferred to sit in the sun, holding Milo.

That Robin trusted her to babysit every morning was a surprise, but then, they'd had seven months of living together before Milo was born to transform their relationship. When Carl had refused to let Colleen move back in, after she'd confessed to everything — her MasterCard, her ridiculous and fleeting crush on Bundy Hesse, plotting the Convergence with Sashi, her DUI (Darren had sent a note that gave her the courage: *If he wants to punish you for the truth, then he'll have to live with it, but your mind and your heart will be clean*) — Robin had insisted she and Lorelei move into the carriage house. She'd been generous and kind throughout her pregnancy, stocking their fridge from the farmers' market and Trader Joe's, buying them bicycles, and giving them a set of keys to her car. Colleen was initially suspicious of the new, nice Robin, but had come to believe that this was the real Robin, that she'd just been incomplete and unhappy before she had Milo.

After Robin settled in to being pregnant, she no longer saw No Princess as contrary to family life, and found herself missing the work. Expanding the business had been Darren's idea. Now, her old partner Gregory ran No Princess Talent and Robin was in charge of No Princess Pictures. In her second trimester, she and Darren had developed a script for a movie they planned to make themselves, huddling for hours in their office upstairs, and talking with contagious excitement about it when Colleen and Lorelei joined them in the main house for dinner made by Robin, who was an excellent cook. Lorelei had come up with the title — *Family Documentary* — funny because it was not a documentary at all, but a feature film with a considerable budget. It was a satiric drama about a family whose lives become impossibly tangled up in reality television, the twist being that the daughter ends up shooting a rogue reality show of her own, which documents her life on the streets of Reno. Darren was directing it and they'd cast DeeDee Sims in the lead role. Lorelei had a small but significant part, as a bulldog producer on the fictional reality show. She came home from the set bright-eyed and brimming with chatter. She had her dark moments, of course, like when Don's mother had finally e-mailed back, and Lorelei had gone to his family's house in Glendale for an awful, tear-soaked visit, but Carl paid for her to visit a weekly therapist, and overall, she was happier and more sure of herself than Colleen had ever seen her. As for Carl, well, he was gradually beginning to forgive them. She talked to him on the phone once a week or so, mostly about Lorelei, but she sensed the ice field around him thawing. Maybe one day they would get back together. And if they did, maybe things between them could be different, could be better. And if not, well, she was only forty-one. Men still gave her second looks, even here in L.A.

Milo mewled and opened his eyes, blinking up at Colleen as he wiggled awake in the crook of her arm.

"Hello, Baby Chipmunk," she said, nuzzling down to kiss him. She reached to the ground to unzip a bottle of milk Robin had pumped earlier. As Milo sucked, he sighed through his nose, a little goat-like sound of perfect contentment that radiated through the whole of his twelve-pound body and into hers. She could already see resemblances to Darren in the taper of his chin and the glass blue of his eyes.

Robin wouldn't be home for another two hours, so she decided to walk Milo down to the beach in the SUV-like stroller, a surprise from Darren. (Colleen had googled the cost: $1,400.) She'd come to love the bustle of the urban seascape: the muscle-legged cyclists; hippies with skin like old leather; girls with toned brown legs in short-shorts, running on crazy bouncing boots, big O-shaped springs attached to the bottom of their sneakers; moms with babies bound to their chests; surfers and paddleboarders like upright seals on top of the water. She loved the sight of the Santa Monica Pier as she ambled north: the Ferris wheel dipping down over the water, the screams from the roller coaster, the I ♥ L.A. T-shirts hanging off the tchotchke stands, the strange stretch of sand next to the pier with giant sets of rings to swing on, as if a men's gymnastics team had designed a playground.

She reached the footpath and swung the stroller onto it, Milo asleep again and the sunshine gentle on her face. She'd forgotten sunscreen, but oh well. The ocean was at low tide, the waves tame and sparkling with light. The green mountains cut the sky over Malibu, near the cliffs of the Palisades where Lorelei Goldenmoor once lived, the place her mother went in her mind to escape the punishing heat of the Hemet desert and the body that kept her on the couch, while Colleen cheered and flew up, up, up.

Colleen walked north toward the mountains, pulling the stroller's canopy down to shield Milo from the sun, sand on the walking trail making gritty sounds under her sneakers. Just ahead, a teenager stood on a bench beside the footpath, barefoot and playing the guitar, its case open at her feet for contributions. Her straight blond hair spilled almost to her waist, her face obscured by huge sunglasses and a floppy white hat.

Nobody was stopped to listen to her, but as Colleen and Milo approached, the girl spoke. "Okay, so here's my version of one of my favorite songs from the past few years."

In a clear, sweet voice, she sang: *"I got stuck in the Midwest / Of the West Coast / Burned by the sun / When I needed it most."*

Colleen rummaged in a pocket on the back of the stroller where Robin often left a little cash. There was a twenty-dollar bill, crunched down in the corner of the nylon fabric. She smoothed it flat and laid it in the girl's guitar case.

Acknowledgments

ENDLESS GRATITUDE TO my agent and brilliant reader, Jenni Ferrari-Adler, for believing in this book, and for making everything happen.

Julia Fierro, forever my mentor and literary kindred spirit: my life as a fiction writer would never have awakened without her.

I'm permanently indebted to Liz Egan, for seeing a spark in this manuscript and knowing exactly how to make it much brighter. Thanks also to my excellent editor, Katie Salisbury, for her wise and attentive guidance.

Without the unwavering support of my writerly friends on both coasts, I might have shriveled into an artless corporateer: thank you, thank you, Katherine Satorious, Amy Bourne, Catherine Meng, Jackie Delamatre, Brooke Watkins, Lauren Belski, Ben Greenberg, Linda Davis, and Naomi Eagleson.

The sisterly love and support of Stacey Wolfson, Jill Braunstein, and Linda Harris never fails to buoy me. Their early enthusiasm for this book was crucial to my motivation, and I'm so thankful for it.

Stratospheric thanks to my parents, Gary Wolfson, the true

King of Storyland, and Cathy Wolfson, my staunchest defender, for always assuming my success and loving me ferociously. Equal gratitude to my brothers, Gregory, Jonathan, and Justin Wolfson, for their sharp insights, inspiring feedback, and general hilariousness when I needed it most.

I'm not sure how I got so lucky as to have a mother-in-law like Ruth Wimsatt, who read an unreasonable number of drafts of this book and championed it from the beginning. She makes me feel much mightier than I am.

Thanks to my three darlings: Townes and Kirby, who were ever-patient with Mama when she missed breakfast after breakfast to write, and Cassidy, who set my ultimate deadline.

And finally, deepest thanks of all to my husband and greatest ally, Kris, for his boundless patience and friendship, and for taking me more seriously than I could ever take myself.

CAELI WOLFSON WIDGER lives with her family in Santa Monica, California. Her work has appeared in such publications as the *New York Times Magazine, Another Chicago Magazine,* and the *Madison Review,* as well as on NPR and CBS Radio. She earned her MFA from the University of Montana and has taught creative writing at the Sackett Street Writers' Workshop, University College London, and Johns Hopkins University. *Real Happy Family* is her first novel.